I0655065

THE STAR CHILD

THE CAST IRON FARM SERIES
BOOK 2

ALI SPOONER

ALSO BY ALI SPOONER

SINGLE STORIES

The Mountain Whispers
Heart Strings Attached
Free to Love
Single Stories:
The Trophy Wives Club
The Bee Charmer
Ruined
Back in the Saddle
Open Your Heart
South of Heaven
Shotgun Rider
The Settlement
Love's Playlist
Cowgirl Up
Twisted Lives
The Epitaph
Terminal Event
Bailey's Run

SERIES

The Island Series
Neptune's Ring
Venus Rising

The Star Child

The Hunter Series
The Devil's Tree
Bound

Sasha Thibodaux Series
Sugarland
Bayou Justice
Line of Sight

Strong Southern Women Series
Diamond Dreams
Gator Girlz
True North

THE STAR CHILD

THE CAST IRON FARM SERIES
BOOK 2

ALI SPOONER

Affinity
Rainbow Publications

2020

The Star Child
© 2020 by Ali Spooner

Affinity E-Book Press NZ LTD
Canterbury, New Zealand

1st Edition

978-1-98-858889-6

Editor: Angie Koenig
Proof Editor: Alexis Smith
Cover Design: Irish Dragon Design
Production Design: Affinity Publication Services

ACKNOWLEDGMENTS

I would like to thank my fans for following my stories, providing great feedback, and encouragement. Writing wouldn't be so much fun without you. Thanks to Affinity, Irish Dragon for the cover art and the team of editors, readers, and publishers who continue to help me grow as a writer.

DEDICATION

In memory of my mother Laura, who enjoyed the mountains of North Carolina as much as I do. Thanks for all the great memories we shared. Miss you and love you…MOST!

Ali Spooner

TABLE OF CONTENTS

The Star Child

PROLOGUE

Y'all ain't gonna believe this...

CHAPTER ONE

Eli Fortner sat on the front porch, quietly cursing the directions that accompanied the two firewood racks.

"Screw this," she growled to Cruz, who cocked her head as she smiled. Eli balled the paper in a wad. "That stuff is only good for the compost bin. I don't know why in God's name they have to make something so simple as using six bolts so confusing."

"Do I hear cursing coming from out here, Aunt Eli?" Mitch asked. He sat down on the step beside the aunt he adored and casually tossed a tennis ball for Cruz to chase.

Eli smiled at her seventeen-year-old nephew. "I don't know why I bother reading the directions to these damned things. It's six bolts for goodness sake."

"Do you want me to finish putting them together for you?"

"Naw, I got this. I just needed to fuss about the confusing directions. How is your schoolwork coming?"

Mitch ran his hand through his thick mop of dark hair. "Not bad, I've got maybe another thirty minutes to finish for the day."

"Your job is going to be helping me fill these things up when I finally get them together."

"Not today." He grinned. "Whit and I are starting on the solar panels today. Evan is coming out after lunch to help. Where is the cute little Love Muffin anyway?" he teased.

"You'd better not let her catch you calling her that or she'll skin your hide," Eli warned. "She worked in the lab last night, so she's sleeping in over at her place. I'm sure she'll be along soon if ya'll have plans today." Eli grinned at the nickname Mitch had given Whit. It fit her so well and Eli knew that Mitch thought the world of Whit. It was also an unspoken gesture from Mitch that he approved of their relationship. He would have never dreamed of giving Sara, her ex, a nickname, unless it was "the bitch" or something more derogatory.

"I can't wait to get started," he said and rubbed his hands together. Cruz had returned with the ball, and he tossed it again.

"Go finish your schoolwork and you can make us some sandwiches for lunch. By the time you finish, it should be okay to call and wake the cute little Love Muffin." Eli grinned. "I'm going to finish here and load the chainsaw in the Gator, and after lunch, I'll start cutting the downed trees into sections."

"Don't even worry about stacking them. I'll load the logs onto the Gator and bring them down when we have finished for the day. I'll get Evan to help, and we can catch up to you quickly."

"Done," she said and sat the smaller of the two racks on the ground. "This one we will use for the smaller logs in the fire pit. I should be able to cut a bunch of the small stuff to fit so we won't have to do any splitting. The fireplace is a whole other story."

"Let me carry that out for you, and I'll get back to work," Mitch said, and placed the small rack close to the fire pit.

"Thanks, Mitch," she said when he walked back onto the porch.

"No problem. Turkey sandwiches good for you?"

"Perfect," Eli answered.

He nodded and disappeared into the cabin.

Eli pulled out the contents of the second box and opened the package with the hardware. "No need for these," she said and tossed them back in the box. Eli used the ratchet and quickly had the second rack assembled and placed on the southern end of the front porch.

"All set," she said as she picked up the cardboard boxes and carried them to the compost pile. Eli tore them into smaller strips and tossed them inside. She returned the tools and loaded the chainsaw and supplies into the rear of the Gator.

Eli had parked the Gator by the front steps and was walking toward the cabin when she heard the sound of helicopter rotors. "What the hell?" she said as the sound grew louder. A large black helicopter flew over the cabin and hovered over her open field for several seconds before touching the ground. The side door flew open, and two soldiers approached the cabin.

Mitch stood in the doorway of the cabin; his mouth hung open as he saw the two soldiers approaching. "What the hell?" he said, repeating Eli's question.

"I don't have a clue, Mitch, but it looks like we are about to find out." Cruz began stalking toward the approaching men, her hackles standing along her spine. Eli saw one of the men reach for his sidearm. "Easy, Cruz, come," she shouted over the dying noise of the rotors.

Mitch walked down the steps and stood beside her.

"You can stop right there, and take your hand off your weapon," Eli growled.

The soldiers stopped a few feet away from them and stood at attention. The man that had reached for his weapon was red-faced.

"I'm sorry to disturb you, ma'am, but we have orders to collect Dr. Brewer this morning."

"Collect her for whom?" Eli asked.

"That's classified information, ma'am, but her presence in Washington is necessary," he answered. "Her country needs her."

"You realize she does not live here, correct?" Eli answered. "Her home is next door," Eli pointed across the stream.

"Yes, ma'am, we apologize for the inconvenience, but we have used this landing spot before. We had no knowledge anyone was living here."

Eli's phone was vibrating on her hip. She reached down for it and saw Whit was calling. She took a step away from the men and answered the call. She listened for several minutes as Whit brought her up to speed on what was going on. While she was sleeping, she had missed an urgent call from the Pentagon, requesting her assistance. She would need to leave and would be away for several days.

"Pack your bag, and I'll drive over for you. Mitch has made lunch. I'll get him to pack a sandwich for you." She listened for several more seconds. "Yes, I understand. Be there in a minute." Eli ended the call and holstered her phone. "I'll drive over and get her," she told the men.

"I will accompany you," the officer said.

"No, you won't. You will stay right here," Eli told him firmly and didn't wait for a reply. "Mitch, pack a couple of sandwiches for Whit and see if these gentlemen would like

14

one as well. I'll be back in a few minutes." She climbed into the Gator and tore off down the drive.

†

Whit had showered and was drying her hair when she heard the approach of helicopter rotors. She rushed to her computer to find an urgent message flashing. Whit grabbed her cell phone to call Eli as she dressed.

"I am so sorry for this intrusion. I did not see the message that a team was coming for me until I heard the helicopter approaching. I need to go to the Pentagon for a few days." Whit waited several seconds for Eli to digest the information. "Will you come to get me? Maybe I can explain this better?" She waited for Eli's answer. "I love you, Eli." She heard Eli end the call.

"Shit."

Whit was worried about the tone in Eli's voice. She hurried to collect her ready bag and hygiene products as she waited for Eli. Whit never received details other than a team was on the way to retrieve her. She knew that once airborne she would receive a portfolio with information regarding the mission. Whit quickly fed her two cats, Oscar and Walter.

"You guys will have to stay with Eli for a few days."

She heard Eli's boots on the front porch and ran to meet her at the door. "I'm so sorry this happened so suddenly. It must be something very urgent." Whit took Eli in her arms and kissed her. "I won't be gone a minute more than necessary."

"That sonofabitch was going to draw his gun on Cruz," Eli growled.

15

"I am so sorry, Eli. I would never dream of scaring you or Cruz in any way. I didn't have time to alert you they were coming."

"Damned good thing I don't have chickens yet. They'd be so traumatized they wouldn't lay for weeks." Eli grinned. "In fairness, you did warn me that this could happen. I just didn't expect this."

"I know, and I'm so sorry. I will talk with whoever threatened Cruz."

"I don't think that's necessary. I think the soldier received my message loud and clear."

"I know I don't have to ask, but will you keep an eye on Oscar and Walter?"

"You know I will. Mitch will be disappointed he can't start the project with you, but he'll understand the country needs you, and you'll be back soon."

"As fast as I can. I'll call you whenever I can, but at least once a day. I have no idea what kind of hornet's nest I'm walking into in Washington."

"I'll hold the fort down here while you go save the world," Eli said. "Just come home as soon as you can."

"You can bet I will." Whit reached for Eli, and they kissed before walking out the front door.

†

Mitch, being the gregarious young man that he was, was getting the grand tour of the Blackhawk helicopter when Eli returned with Whit. Mitch was sitting next to the pilot when they pulled up beside the machine.

"Hello again, Dr. Brewer."

"Welcome back, Roger. We need to discuss your landing protocols on this trip."

"Yes, Ma'am, but we had strict orders to get back as soon as possible. I truly am sorry for any inconvenience we caused, ma'am," he tipped his hat to Eli.

"I'll know better what to expect next time," Eli said and offered him her hand.

"Yes, ma'am," he said and shook her hand. "We do need to get going, though."

"Mitch, I think that means you need to get back out here," Eli called into her nephew.

"This is so cool, Aunt Eli. I put your lunch on the seat," he told Whit and pointed at the paper plate loaded with sandwiches and chips. "The water is in the cup holder."

"Thanks, Mitch," Whit replied as he stepped onto the ground. "We'll get started on the solar panels when I get back." She stepped forward and hugged him. "Take care of everybody while I'm gone."

"I will," he answered and reluctantly let go. "Hurry home. Hey, maybe I can get a ride when you come back."

Roger chuckled. "We'll see. Maybe we could sneak a quick one in. It will have to be top secret, so we don't get in trouble."

"Awesome," Mitch answered.

"Grab Cruz, and let's get out of the way." Eli hugged Whit. "Call when you can."

The pilot waited for them to move away from the chopper before engaging the rotors. Eli could see Whit strapped into her seat as the door slid closed. The whirring of the blades blew the grass around them and suddenly lifted from the ground and took flight.

Eli looked at Mitch with tears in her eyes.

"Don't worry. Whit will be back soon." They watched the helicopter until it was out of sight, and when the sounds disappeared, Mitch asked, "You ready to cut some wood? It looks like I'm all yours for a few days."

"You better give Evan a call to tell him the solar panel project is on hold. Maybe the two of you can try out some of those fishing spots he's been teasing you about."

"Maybe, but I don't want to leave you here alone."

"I'll be fine for a day if you want to go fishing. I promised you'd be having some fun, too, remember."

"Any time spent with you is fun, Aunt Eli."

"Come on, you big goof. Let's eat and get to cutting some wood. Are there sandwiches left?"

"Yes, ma'am, the soldiers declined my offer. That Blackhawk sure is a sweet piece of machinery."

"Hop in. Have you ever considered going into the military? There's lots of machinery to learn to work on there."

"I thought about it, but that thought didn't last long. I think I'll stick to the private sector. Better pay, fewer hazards. I do have to register for the draft next year though, when I turn eighteen."

"Man, where has the time gone? I can't believe you're almost eighteen already. It just seems like yesterday I was changing your stinky diapers."

"You did not," Mitch cried out.

Eli nodded. "Many times, until your dad finally got the hang of things." She grinned. "I saw your little pieces parts before you even realized you had them."

"Okay, time for a subject change. I'm going to call Evan while you start eating. I'll be inside in a few."

"See you, Cupcake," she teased, and walked into the cabin. Eli froze when she heard Whit's voice. *I'll be home soon.* "Not soon enough for me," she spoke to the empty room.

†

Whit saw the tears in Eli's eyes as they stepped away from the hug. *She does love me. I'll be home soon.*

When they settled into their flight pattern, she turned to Roger, a soldier sitting across from her.

"Where to today?"

"The Pentagon, ma'am. You need to review this file before we reach there."

Whit took the file he offered and broke the *Top Secret* seal on the record. "I hope this doesn't mean I have to kill you when we arrive."

Roger smirked. "No, ma'am, I think we're safe."

Whit returned his smile and immersed herself in the contents of the file. She studied the names and photos included in the portfolio and read each of the bios carefully. She remembered one of the faces from a previous terror attack. He was a ruthless mastermind of a particularly brutal attack in the Mideast who was able to slip through detection and disappear, at least until now. The mere fact he had resurfaced sent a shiver down her spine.

She reopened the record and moved forward to her mission at hand. Whit's challenge was to answer a series of questions regarding the probability of a future act of terrorism potentially aimed at the United States. She was surprised to read that the allegation of a potential threat was from a secret outer space satellite. Whit couldn't help but wonder if her recent discovery of the dark area, which she had sent data on to NASA, could be related. She doubted a terrorist, even one with a rich vein of financial backing, would have the technology to develop such a plan. She couldn't ignore the possibility even if it was farfetched. Whit took out the pen provided and started making notes. When the helicopter touched down, Whit closed the file she had been making notes on and stretched her legs as they waited to depart the chopper.

Whit had lost track of time and was amazed at how quickly they arrived at the airport at Langley. The sunlight was bright as she pulled on some shades.

She glanced out the window at a pair of black SUVs waiting for them to arrive. *I wonder if they get a massive discount on all the big black SUVs?* She couldn't help but grin at the thought.

"I'll get your bag, ma'am." The young soldier reached above her to collect her bag. "There's a car waiting for us," he said as he led her to the chopper door.

A door opened on the black vehicle, and Whit climbed inside. She knew a short drive would deliver her to a small operations building where she would meet with a group to discuss the project.

A female agent she recognized as Anita met her at the door and led her to the briefing room. "Can I get you something to eat or drink?"

"I'll take some water. I had a sandwich on the flight in."

"Yes, ma'am, I'll be right back."

CHAPTER TWO

Mitch strolled into the cabin and picked up his drink. "Evan and I will go fishing in the morning. If we aren't successful, we'll come home to work on more firewood."

"That's a good plan. I think I'll do some exploring while you're gone." Eli took a bite from her sandwich.

Mitch frowned. "Now you've got me curious. Where do you plan to explore?"

Eli chuckled. "I haven't seen what is at the top of the mountain or what's on the other side."

"Trees and a lot of them," Mitch stated. "At least promise me, you'll be carrying your gun."

"I will. I know critters are starting to crawl around a bit more."

"It's the two-legged critters I'm worried about, but do watch where you're stepping. Wear your mid-calf boots, too, please."

Eli raised her hands in a gesture of submission. "I promise to be careful."

Mitch picked up a sandwich. "Evan will be out by one. I think we can get a great head start on cutting."

"Will you add the can of spray paint? There may be more trees we need to remove."

"I'm all over it. I'll grab the paint and meet you at the Gators."

"Thanks, Mitch." Eli ate the last of her meal and plucked two drinks from the refrigerator. When she walked outside, Mitch was sitting in one of the Gators watching Cruz and Molly play. For a brief second, Eli saw the boy in Mitch as he laughed at their antics, but as soon as he turned toward her, she saw the young man he had grown to be.

"Do I need to put these two up for safety?" he asked.

"No, I don't think we'll be felling trees today, so they should be good. If we decide differently, I'll send you down to secure them."

"I'll follow you then if you're ready," Mitch said.

Eli tossed him a bottle and climbed inside the Gator. She picked up the sunglasses and slipped them over her head. Ever since her concussion, Eli wore them when outside for protection, and to keep the sun from triggering a headache. Eli had planned to start at the top of the trail and work her way back down. Dozens of small trees were down that she would cut to lengths to use for firewood and at the fire pit.

Eli climbed out of the four-wheeler. "If you want, put your gloves on and use the hatchet to start removing the smaller limbs. I'll check the fluids in the saw and start cutting sections."

Eli was preparing to start the saw when she felt a vibration in her pocket. She pulled out her phone to find a text from Whit. *Made it safely. I'll call tonight. Love you.* Eli smiled as she wrote back. *Love you too.* She looked up to see Mitch grinning at her. "Love Muffin made it safely."

"That's good to know," he answered and resumed trimming limbs.

Eli pulled the rope to start the saw and began cutting trees. She cut the smaller logs into foot-long sections that would work in the fire pit, but as the trunk grew in diameter, she cut them into longer lengths for the fireplace. She noticed several of the branches were too thin for the fire pit but were the right size to make into walking sticks. That would be the perfect hobby for her to enjoy at night. She could sit around the fire pit or on the porch, carving and sanding the limbs. Eli remembered the visit from the hiker, Margret, and wondered if a walking stick would have made hiking easier for her. She could make some and offer them to hikers that came through on their journey.

When Eli had sectioned six trees, she turned off the saw. "I had an idea," she said to Mitch, who was offering her a drink.

"Should I be worried?" He smirked.

"That's always a possibility, smart ass," she said and punched him in the shoulder. "Some of the larger branches you're trimming would make great walking sticks. I could skin the bark off them, sand them down, and stain or seal them naturally to leave at the overnight shelter for hikers."

"That's a great idea. What lengths do you want them cut?" Mitch asked.

"Start with sixty inches, and we can trim down from there."

"I'll measure and cut one to use as a pattern."

"They don't need to be straight either. Some contours would add some character," Eli instructed.

"Curves, got it." Mitch chuckled, and measured out the length Eli had requested.

"You can use the small chainsaw for that. Please be careful."

"Yes, Mama," he teased.

She watched as he checked the fluid levels and then started the small saw. He treated the saw with respect just as his dad had taught him. Mitch cut several of the small branches to length and then stopped the saw. He looked up at her.

"Great job," she praised.

"Thanks. I'll put these behind your seat, so we don't get them confused."

Eli nodded and continued refilling her saw. "Use the small saw to buck the limbs off. It will go faster, but don't get in a rush."

"Yes, ma'am," Mitch said and carried the cut limbs to the Gator.

Eli resumed cutting the downed trees into sections, pausing to check on Mitch. He had created a small pile of cut limbs and a more massive pile of brush. *We may need to consider purchasing a small wood chipper. We could use the wood chips in Molly's stall.* The thought of Molly reminded her to search for Molly and Cruz. They had been playing for hours and had curled up in the sunshine to nap. She shut down her saw, and Cruz's head whipped up. Mitch was still happily trimming when he realized Eli's saw had stopped.

"Everything okay?" he shouted over the drone of his saw.

Eli nodded and gave him a sign to shut down the saw. "We've made a good dent here this afternoon. Why don't we take a couple of loads down to the cabin?"

"I can manage that if you want to keep cutting. We only have three trees left in this area."

Eli's arms were beginning to ache, but Mitch was correct. If she could section three more logs, they would finish in this area. "Let me get a drink and refuel. Have you given any consideration to dinner tonight?"

"I thought I'd treat you to dinner if you're up to a ride into town. We could hit the diner or the steak place."

"If you are planning to buy, you decide. I'm good with either."

"Steak it is then." Mitch grinned and placed his saw on the floorboard. "I'll get busy loading while you finish off the last of the logs."

Eli picked up her saw. "That works for me," she answered and started the engine.

Mitch had made two trips down to the cabin by the time she finished the third log. Eli placed her saw in the Gator and took a drink of water. She picked up her phone, but there was no message or missed call from Whit, so she pulled her glove back on and began carrying the bigger logs to stack in the back of her vehicle.

Molly and Cruz had followed Mitch down the mountain, and she looked up to see them running toward her as Mitch drove up the trail. They skidded to a halt in front of her. Eli stored the log in the bed and knelt to pet them.

"Are you two having fun today?" Molly took off running, kicking her back feet high into the air as Cruz chased after her. Eli laughed. "I guess the answer is yes."

Mitch pulled closer to the cut wood, and they resumed loading. "The small rack at the fire pit is nearly full," he said as he picked up a large section. "Will some of these need to be split?"

"Probably so. I've been considering buying a small chipper for the brush piles. Maybe a log splitter wouldn't be a bad idea, either."

"Do you want to make a stop at John Deere on our way to dinner?"

"Yeah, we could do that." Eli placed a final log in the back of her vehicle. "Do you want to take this load down while I finish loading yours?"

"Sure, I think one or two more loads should have us finished here," Mitch said.

"Hurry back then," Eli grinned at him and started adding logs to his vehicle.

Eli had his bed loaded by the time Mitch returned and pulled between the last of the cut logs. "We should be able to get the rest in your bed and call it a night. I'll clean up the saws if you want to go ahead and shower."

"That sounds good. I want to check on the garden, too, to see if we have stuff growing yet. I know it's only been a few days, but I'm anxious about our first garden attempt."

"That garden is going to grow more food than you can imagine," Mitch replied. "I can use the small tiller on it later this week if you think it's necessary."

"We shouldn't need to do that yet, but we'll see. Let's go unload, and we can check it together."

Eli followed Mitch down the trail, and they stacked the remaining logs in the bigger rack.

"That was a good day's work," Mitch told her as they surveyed the stacks.

"Yes, it is. We've got an excellent start on the firewood. I wonder if we should build another rack out by the barn."

"That's not a bad idea, and that way we can cut everything you might need for this winter and let it begin to season. I don't imagine you cherish the thought of going out for firewood in the dead of winter."

"No, I don't, and I'm glad we have central heat and air, but there's nothing like a warm fire in the fireplace on a cold morning." She handed Mitch a log to stack.

"I can just imagine you and the Love Muffin, snuggled in front of the fire, sipping coffee and watching snowflakes fall," Mitch told her.

"That does sound rather romantic, doesn't it?" Eli grinned at him.

"Yeah, it does. Have you heard any more from Whit yet?"

"Not yet. I imagine Whit will call later tonight."

Tomboy jumped up on the stack of logs and meowed.

"I know, we haven't filled the cat feeders up today," Eli said as she stroked down his back. "You sure are growing fast. Almost as big as Cajun." She scratched under his chin and listened to him purr.

"I think he loves you just a little bit, too," Mitch said as he hefted the last log into place. "Let's go check the garden. I'll clean the saws and feed the tribe while you get ready."

"Sounds good. I'm getting hungry," Eli said. "You driving us over? My legs are tired."

"I think everything on me is tired," Mitch said. "I bet we will both be sore tomorrow."

"We got a lot done today, so a day of fun is what we both need tomorrow. Do you have everything you need to fish?"

"I should be in great shape. If not, I can stop on our way tomorrow." Mitch climbed behind the wheel and drove them to the garden plot.

"You two have to stay outside," Eli told Cruz and Molly when they reached the gate. She was excited to see green sprouts on many of the rows of seeds they had planted. "That looks promising." She pointed out the new growth to Mitch. "The tomato plants are growing well too."

"We'll be eating homegrown vegetables before long," he answered.

"Yes, we will," Eli answered and walked down several of the rows. "It looks like everything is coming up on schedule."

Mitch tapped her on her shoulder and pointed to the berry bushes. "It looks like some of them have blooms."

They moved closer to the bushes and found several blooms.

"We may not have many this year, but everything looks healthy. I spotted some wild blackberry bushes up near the top of the property. We can pick those, and I'm sure Whit's will produce well."

"I miss her," Mitch said. "It's way too quiet around here."

"I miss her, too," Eli said. "I hope she won't be away for long." She looked up at Mitch. "C'mon, let's get rolling. I'm hungry."

"Yes, ma'am," he said, and walked over to hold the gate open for her.

†

Mitch watched Eli enter the cabin and went to work. He took the limbs he had cut for her and stacked them on the end of the porch. He planned to find her a sturdy knife at John Deere for her to use. Molly trotted into her stall and patiently waited for her food and water while the cats made their hunger known through a chorus of meows. Mitch looked up in time to see Cajun sliding down the slide to make his wishes known as well.

"You guys are rotten," he said as he filled the feeders. When he walked out of the barn, he noticed Oscar and Walter on the front porch. "I'll get to you two in just a minute."

He parked both Gators in the barn and cleaned the sawdust from the chainsaws, then added more fuel and oil before storing them. "All set here," he told Cruz, who followed him step for step. "I bet you're hungry too. You played hard today."

Mitch fed Oscar, Walter, and Cruz, then walked into his room to shower and dress for dinner.

†

Eli stripped out of her clothes and was surprised by how tired her arms and legs were. She felt like she was in decent shape, but a day on the mountain cutting firewood taught her differently. The hot shower felt good as the water pulsed down on her tired body. *A good meal and a little bit of shopping and I'll be ready for bed.* She dressed in jeans and a Polo shirt before going down to check on Mitch.

Eli heard the shower running in his room and started toward the porch. Her phone rang, and she saw it was Whit calling. She answered and took a seat on the couch.

"Hey, sweetie." She listened for several minutes as Whit updated her as much as she could. Eli could hear the strain of tension in Whit's voice, and she knew she shouldn't pry into a sensitive conversation. "Yes, Mitch and I were busy today. We brought in a bunch of firewood and checked on the progress of the garden. We have lots of growth on several of the rows." She paused for a few seconds. "We're going to town to stop by John Deere, and then Mitch is treating me to dinner on the town. He says he misses you, and it's too quiet with you gone. I reckon I'm not working him hard enough." Eli chuckled. "Yes, I know. We are taking the day off for fun tomorrow. He and Evan are going fishing, and I'm going to do some exploring on the mountain. I wish you were here too."

Eli listened for several more minutes until she could hear someone calling Whit's name. "Okay, call when you can. We love and miss you, too. Yes, Oscar and Walter are good. I'll talk to you soon."

Mitch walked out and noticed the frown on her face. "Is everything okay?"

Eli's head snapped up. She hadn't heard him enter the room. "Yes, just missing her, and there's not a lot of information she can share about the reason for her trip. I enjoy a good mystery, but not when it involves someone I love."

"You have to trust that Whit is telling you all that she can. It has to be something important for the government to take such action."

"She's at the Pentagon, that much she told me."

"That's about as Top Secret of a location as you can get. I think the fact she still has access to a cell phone while inside tells you the amount of trust they have in her, so you should, too. That woman adores you."

Eli stood and hugged him. "Are you sure you're only seventeen? Sometimes you think so much older than your age."

"I'll take that as a compliment, I think."

"It's very much intended to be a compliment. I love you, Mitch, don't ever forget that."

"More," he grinned. "C'mon, I'm about to faint from hunger."

"I guess that means we eat first and then go to John Deere."

"I am hungry, Aunt Eli, but we can go there first."

"No, let's go eat. I'm hungry too."

She tossed the keys to him and put Cruz in her crate. "We'll be back soon," she promised, and turned to Mitch. "We need to check the mail on the way out."

"Your wish is my command." Mitch bowed as he held the door open for her.

"Lock it behind you, silly goof."

They stopped at the mailbox, and Mitch jumped out to close the gate and grab the mail. He grinned as he walked back to the truck and handed a letter to Eli. "Looks like you got something from Carol."

Eli opened the envelope and read the card inside. Carol had been her friend forever, and even though the betrayal of their friendship had occurred, Eli forgave her and, in an odd way, had Carol to thank for her present life. Her actions started the ball rolling that allowed Eli to start living her dreams and get out of the rut she was stuck in with her ex, Sara.

"She's checking on us and wants to know if she can visit the first week of June when the school year is out."

"How do you feel about that?"

"I welcomed her to visit anytime. Remind me to give her a call later tonight to confirm."

"Will do," Mitch said, and drove into town. "How hungry are you? Do you want to drop by John Deere now or after we eat?"

Eli looked at her watch. "Let's reconsider eating first. Go ahead and stop, and then we can take our time at dinner."

"You got it," Mitch replied, and turned his blinker on to enter the parking lot.

†

Mitch left Eli with Alan Morris, the owner of the John Deere dealership, discussing the chipper and wood splitter and walked over to the outdoor gear section. Mitch stopped at a knife display and was looking over the selection when a young woman approached him.

"Is there something I can help you with?" she asked.

Mitch looked up into beautiful blue eyes. He felt the rush of heat to his cheeks. "I uh, I'm looking for a whittling knife for my aunt," he spewed out in one breath."

"Is that your aunt?" the young woman asked, nodding toward Eli.

"Yes, it is. Eli's ordering more equipment."

"I would recommend this one," she said. "It's a little pricey, but it's the best." She reached into the display and pulled out a lockback Case knife with *John Deere* engraved in the blade and on a leather carrying case. "It also comes with the moonstone for sharpening, but it holds an edge for a long time."

Mitch examined the blade, and it was sharp enough to shave the hair from his arm. "This will be perfect."

"My name is Jessie. Is there anything I can get you?"

Your phone number, and say yes to a date for this weekend. "I think that will do for now. I'm Mitch Fortner. It's a pleasure to meet you, Jessie."

"Likewise, Mr. Fortner. Are you new here? I don't remember seeing you at school."

"My Aunt Eli moved to the area a few weeks ago, and I'll be living with her through the summer to help her get settled in. Then I'll return home to Alabama for my senior year."

She removed the price tag and rang up his purchase. "Would you like this in a box?"

"Yes, that would be great. Thank you," Mitch said as he gave her the cash.

Jessie handed him the change and box. "Would you like the box and receipt in a bag?"

"Thanks, but the box will do fine." He took the receipt and saw her number written on the paper. He smiled and tucked it into his pocket.

"You're very welcome." She smiled. "I hope to see you again soon."

"Thanks, Jessie. You probably will. It is our favorite place to shop."

"See you soon then," she answered, and Mitch turned away to walk back over to Eli.

Alan smiled when he approached. "I see you met my daughter, Jessie," he said as he reached out to shake Mitch's hand.

"Yes, I did. Jessie helped me with a selection."

Eli noted the box in his hand but did not comment.

"Thank you for your continued business. When would you like the equipment delivered?" Alan asked.

"We are having a fun day tomorrow, so how about Friday?" Eli suggested.

"Friday would be perfect. I'll bring it out myself. Have you had much opportunity to fish yet?" he asked Mitch.

"Evan Merrill and I are going fishing tomorrow," Mitch answered.

"Fantastic news. Evan is a fine young man and has a reputation as an excellent fisherman. He'll know what spots for you to try out. Good luck, and don't be a stranger this summer."

"Thanks," Mitch said. He looked at Eli. "Ready to roll?"

"Sure am. It was good to see you again, Alan. We'll be looking forward to your delivery Friday."

"Wonderful. Have a great evening," Alan said as he walked them to the door.

When they were back inside the car, Mitch handed Eli the box. "I wanted you to have this."

Eli opened the box and pulled the knife from the sheath. "This is a great knife. Case knives are one of the oldest and best brands. Thank you, but you didn't need to spend your money on this."

"It was my pleasure. It will be great for making your walking sticks and using around the farm. It's sharp enough to shave hair, so be careful."

"I will, and thank you." Eli slipped the knife back into the carrying sheath and fastened it to her belt. "Perfect," she said and looked up to see him smiling.

"Thanks for all that you've done for me. Now enough of the mushy stuff, let's eat."

"You're driving, so let's go," she teased.

CHAPTER THREE

Whit was exhausted. The briefing and introductions of the team seemed endless to her. When the session ended, Whit was taken to the hotel they had reserved for her stay. She dropped her bag on the bed and placed a room service order for dinner. While she waited, Whit called home.

"Hey, sweetie," she replied when a sleepy sounding Eli answered. "Did I wake you? I know it's late, but I'm just now getting into my hotel room." She listened to Eli as she told her about the day she and Mitch had spent on the trail and their trip to town.

"It sounds like the two of you got a lot accomplished today. I wish I were there to help." She listened to the soft chuckle. "The garden is progressing fine. Mother nature needs some time to let things grow. I can imagine you going out and measuring the sprouts every day." The sound of Eli's laughter warmed her heart. "Yeah, I know, I probably shouldn't have given you that idea, but it is quite the visual. Yes, it was an incredibly long day, and I don't know how long I will be away. I'm hoping no longer than the weekend. I only brought five outfits," she chuckled. "Yes, I know they have laundry services, but I'd prefer to come home. I'm glad you're taking a day off to explore and fish. You both deserve some fun. Are my boys behaving themselves?"

Whit exchanged conversation with Eli for several more minutes. "Yes, we both should try to get some rest. I'll try to call you tomorrow before things get heated up again. Love you too. Sweet dreams."

Whit ended the call and felt a sense of comfort, listening to Eli's rich voice. Their relationship was still young and fresh, but some days it seemed they'd known each other longer. It was clear Eli understood her boundaries when it came to discussing the mission, and she did not pry for information. Whit was unpacking her bag when the room service was delivered. Whit signed the check as the server set out her meal. She lifted the cover and took in the aroma. *It won't be Eli's cooking, but I can at least dine well while I'm here.* Whit hadn't realized how hungry she was until she sat down to the meal. The sandwiches Mitch had sent with her seemed days ago. She devoured the dinner and started drawing a hot bath while she prepared her clothes for the next day.

†

Eli could get a good night's rest now that she'd heard from Whit. She was beginning to worry about her when the phone rang. *I wonder if her gift reaches this far, and she knew I was thinking about her?*

"Hello. I'm glad you called. I was beginning to get worried. No, I wasn't asleep yet. Just tired from all of our firewood activities today. Yeah, I wish you were here too. Mitch and I got a lot done. Are they working you to death yet?" Eli got lost in the sound of Whit's voice and didn't realize Whit had asked her a question. "No, I'm not asleep. I was just listening to your voice. Yes, we had a fantastic meal, and Mitch bought me a beautiful knife from John Deere. I thought I'd try my hand at making walking sticks to give the hikers coming through on the Appalachian Trail." She listened to Whit's reply. "I thought it would be a wind-down activity I could do on the porch or around the fire pit after working around the farm." She heard Whit's soft laughter. "Yes, I'm now calling it a farm, since we are finally growing things," Eli replied. Whit responded, saying she could see her out measuring the growth of the plants, which brought laughter to her. "I hadn't thought of that idea," she teased back. Eli could hear the weariness in Whit's voice. "I think you should eat a hearty meal and take a soaking bath before calling it a night. I'll look forward to your call tomorrow. Love you."

Eli put her phone on charge and moved Tomboy on the bed. "You sure have become a bed hog," she said as she gave herself room to crawl under the sheets.

He waited until she got settled then crept over to lay beside her, his head resting against her hip. Eli reached down to stroke the young cat's head. "Bed hog, but a loveable one. Goodnight, sweet boy."

†

Cruz went flying down the stairs when she woke and heard Mitch in the kitchen. The noise startled Tomboy, who got tangled in the bed covers and pulled half of them off the bed as he followed Cruz down the steps.

"What the hell?" Eli said to a now empty bedroom. She climbed from the bed and walked to the top of the stairs. "What on earth are you doing down there to get everyone stirred up?" she called down to Mitch.

"Sorry, Aunt Eli. I was trying to be quiet, but you know how that goes. I'm sorry I woke everyone up. Go back to bed, and I promise to be quiet."

"I'm wide awake now. Start me a cup of coffee, please, and I'll be down in a minute."

"Yes, ma'am," he answered as Eli walked back into her room.

"Feed those monsters, too, since they're up."

"On it," he called to her.

Eli pulled on her robe and ran her fingers through her hair before walking downstairs. "What's got you up so early?"

"I told Evan I'd be ready by six, so we can hit the hot spots before anyone else. I thought I'd make some sausage and biscuits to take with us."

Eli entered the kitchen. "Hand me the sausage, and I'll start cooking those while you feed the animals."

Mitch handed her a box of sausage patties, and Eli turned the oven to preheat for the biscuits. "How many biscuits do you want?"

"I was thinking maybe four each," Mitch answered as he filled Cruz and Tomboy's bowls.

Eli pulled out a bag of frozen biscuits and placed a dozen in a baking pan. "I think I'll have some, too. Since I'm up," she winked at Mitch.

"I really was trying to be quiet," he answered. "The harder I tried, the louder I got."

"No problem. I don't need to sleep the day away. I can fill a small pack with biscuits and water and leave when you boys do." The glorious sound of the coffee maker finishing her cup was music to her ears. "Thank goodness for coffee." Eli prepared her drink and sipped on it as the sausage cooked. "Do you have your fishing gear ready?"

"It won't take me long."

"Get it together while I cook breakfast. That way, you will be all set when Evan arrives."

"Yes, ma'am," he answered and slipped outside.

Eli had placed the pan in the oven when Mitch returned. "All set?"

"I've got all my gear on the porch."

"Cooler and filet knife?"

"Dang, I knew I forgot something. Is the cooler out in the workshop?"

"Yes, it is. Your filet knife is right beside it. Do you want me to whip up some hushpuppy mix and a salad to go with the fish?"

"You're pretty confident we'll catch some?" he asked.

"Of course. I expect the two great white fishermen to come back with enough to feed both families," Eli replied.

"No pressure there," he smirked.

"When have you failed to catch fish since you arrived?"

"Well, I haven't, but I don't want to jinx myself either."

"You won't let me down. Besides, if you strike out, you can come home and fish here. You always catch here."

"That's true." Mitch nodded as he filled a small cooler with bottled water and ice. "What time do you want me home?"

"Whenever you're ready to come home. I'll probably spend the morning on the mountain and be back after lunch if

I don't find something interesting." Eli turned the sausage on the grill. "Is this going to be enough to hold you until lunch?"

"If not, I'm sure we can stop and get something. You know I won't starve in a few hours," Mitch grinned.

"I don't want your mama accusing me of starving her baby," Eli teased.

Mitch patted his stomach. "No chance of that."

"You have slimmed down since you got here," Eli replied.

"I've lost ten pounds, but I feel great."

"You keep up all the physical activity, and you'll keep trimming down and pack on some more muscle."

"I wouldn't mind that at all," Mitch said, and started displaying his bodybuilder poses, making Eli laugh at his antics.

"Careful, you don't blow out gas bubbles with all that straining. I don't want you funking up my kitchen air."

"My farts don't stink, Aunt Eli," he laughed.

"You're right, that's beyond stink," she waved her hand in front of her face. "Go now," she hollered and pointed at the door.

"C'mon, Cruz. I can tell when I'm not wanted," Mitch said, and she raced to the front door.

"Leave it open to get some fresh air in here," Eli called after them.

After finishing the sausage, Eli sipped her coffee while she waited for the biscuits to bake. She could hear Mitch and Cruz playing outside and walked to the door and watched them until the timer sounded. Mitch had placed his cooler on the porch and was playing fetch with Cruz. "Come get washed up. The biscuits are ready."

Mitch tossed the tennis ball as far as he could and started jogging toward the porch. Cruz raced after the ball and nearly beat him back to the steps. "Damn, she's fast."

"Do you want me to put these in a storage container or wrap them in aluminum foil to keep them warm?"

"All but this one," he said as he grabbed a hot biscuit and placed a sausage patty on it. "Hot, hot, hot," he said as he placed the food on the counter.

"It did just come out of the oven," Eli reminded him.

"I'll get the foil while that cools," Mitch replied as he walked past her.

Eli placed the sausage patties in a container while Mitch wrapped the biscuits in foil. She walked to the refrigerator and pulled out a jar of Whit's blackberry jelly and placed a small spoonful and a patty on a biscuit.

"Yum," she said after she bit into the bread. "You want to take this jelly with you?"

"Naw, we'll rough it," Mitch answered.

"Suit yourself," Eli replied, made a second biscuit, and wrapped the remaining two in foil. "That will make a good snack on the trail."

"Don't forget your gun," Mitch reminded her.

"I won't," she promised.

Mitch turned at the sound of Evan's truck coming up the drive. "Right on time."

"You two have fun today."

"We will. You be careful. I've got my phone if you need me for anything," Mitch said and patted his hip.

Eli followed him out to the porch and saw Evan walking toward them.

"We've got sausage biscuits," Mitch said, holding up his stash.

"Mom baked cookies for us last night. At least we won't be hungry. Hey, Eli."

"Hey, Evan. Y'all have fun and be careful today."

"Yes, ma'am," Evan said, and picked up Mitch's tackle box and cooler. "I hope we can fill this up today. Mom's expecting fish for dinner."

"I am, too, so good luck to you both."

Mitch trotted back to grab his fly rod. "See ya later, Aunt Eli."

"Bye. Have fun."

Mitch was wearing a broad smile as he waved while Evan drove away. She waved back and turned toward the barn to tend to the animals. Eli checked the feed in the bins and made sure Molly had fresh water. "Sorry, you can't go with us today," she said. "We'll be back after lunch, so you'll have plenty of time to play."

Cruz trotted along after her as she walked back into the cabin and climbed the stairs. After dressing and brushing her teeth, Eli clipped her holster on her hip and slipped into her hiking boots. She grabbed a small daypack and placed her biscuits and bottles of water inside.

"All set?" she asked Cruz, who was dancing around the kitchen.

Eli plucked her John Deere cap off the wall and placed the pack on her shoulders before leaving the cabin. The air was still crisp, but she knew she would warm up quickly once she started up the trail. As she placed the last bite of the second biscuit in her mouth, the explosion of sweetness from the jelly hit her taste buds, and she immediately thought of Whit. *Maybe I should take a small basket. I might find wild berries.* Eli stopped in the barn to pick up a small wicker basket.

"This will do nicely," she said and started up the trail.

Eli set a leisurely pace as she started up the mountain. She stopped in the meadow and was delighted to find evidence that deer had found the salt and mineral blocks she had left for them. She and Mitch could set up a feeder for the fall when the foliage they fed on started to become scarce. Cruz trotted around the area with her nose to the ground taking in the different animal scents.

Eli felt the first trickle of sweat roll down her temple as she climbed the trail. She had taken for granted the ease of movement using the Gator, and the walk was becoming more difficult with every step of elevation. The sunglasses cut the glare from the rays of sunlight bursting through the leaves, and a welcome breeze brought a variety of scents. Clover was blooming, and wildflowers along the trail, too numerous to miss, filled the morning air. Freshness was too simple of a description, but that was what came to her mind. Everything seemed fresh and renewed after a night's slumber. When she reached the head of the trail leading to the Appalachian Trail, she decided to turn left and walk west. She had explored east for a short distance, but never west. With each step, Eli journeyed on a new adventure. When the survey marker for her upper boundary came into view, Eli took a right-hand turn onto a small game trail leading farther up the mountain. She followed it for several minutes before a clearing appeared with a small outcropping of boulders. Eli walked over to one of the rocks and sat, staring out at the valley below, still cloaked in the late morning mist. She twisted the top from a bottle of water and took a long drink. Cruz sat at her feet and drank from a pool of water she collected in her hand. A hawk shrieked in the distance, and Eli looked up to watch him dive toward his prey. He became lost in the shroud of mist, and Eli watched to see if he would return. After several minutes, with no further sight of the majestic bird, Eli chose to continue her hike.

Cruz trotted ahead, nose to the ground, until she reached a smaller trail headed deeper into the forest. She stopped and looked back at Eli. Eli peered into the dense forest at what appeared to be a game trail. She knelt next to Cruz and stroked her head.

"Why not? We've got all morning. Let's go."

†

Evan drove to the first spot they would try, and they got geared up to fish. "We've got a beautiful morning," Evan said as he checked the fly on the end of his line.

"Yeah, we do. Couldn't ask for better," Mitch answered. "Speaking of beautiful, I met Jessie Morris at the John Deere place."

"She's a real sweetheart," Evan said. "She works with her dad every chance she gets."

"Sounds like someone else I know." Mitch grinned.

"I've been working with dad ever since elementary school," Evan said. "There's no place else I'd rather work."

"Y'all have a fantastic business. A little bit of everything a person could want." Mitch grinned. "Does she have a boyfriend?"

"I'm not sure," Evan answered. "You interested? I can get Erin to find out. Maybe we could do a double date."

"Well, she did give me her number when we were at the store earlier."

"Maybe you should give her a call. See if she wants to go to dinner and a movie Saturday night."

"I'd like that. Maybe I'll give Jessie a call tonight," Mitch said, and he could feel a blush creep up his neck.

"C'mon, Romeo. There's fish to catch," Evan teased.

Mitch picked up his rod and followed Evan to the river.

44

The rock formations along the trail seem to grow with every step higher on the mountain. Eli recognized that once she crossed over from her property, she was on National Forest Land. The path was growing thinner, and she had lost sight of Cruz. "Cruz," Eli called out. She listened until she heard Cruz whine, and then continued up the path at a faster pace. When Eli reached her, Eli looked up and saw what had caught Cruz's attention. She was sitting, staring into the mouth of a cave.

"What have you found?"

Cruz whined and wiggled her butt in excitement. Eli pulled her daypack off her shoulders and pulled out a small flashlight. After shouldering the bag, Eli looked at the area surrounding the cave and noted it was inside a rather large rock formation, so there was no way she could gauge how big or deep the cave was. Eli was fairly sure any bear that had chosen this as a den for hibernation would have already vacated the premises, but to be safe, she pulled out her pistol and shifted the flashlight to her left hand. As they approached, Cruz stopped and sneezed. Eli felt a draft of musty-smelling air coming from the mouth of the cave, and she had an odd thought that the mountain was taking a breath.

"You could use a breath mint," she spoke aloud, and Cruz looked at her and cocked her head. "Not you. I just thought that the mountain was breathing, and it could use a breath mint." Cruz just stared at her. "I know your Mama's thinking crazy. Just ignore me."

Cruz chuffed, and then took another few steps inside.

The mouth was big enough for Eli to bend slightly and enter standing up, and it opened into a large area, with a ceiling of twelve feet or higher. The sun's rays were coming through the opening, casting an eerie glow on the rock walls. Eli was glad for the light from the flashlight as she turned in a circle inside the cave. There were scorched spots on the cave floor that gave evidence of human visitation, but nothing that looked remotely fresh. Her flashlight beam shone on one of the sections of the back wall, and she was surprised to see a blue glow light up the area. Her immediate thought went to Whit's story about her mom, and the alien she had sworn was Whit's father. Eli walked closer and learned that blue flecks of crystal or maybe quartz in the rock were giving off the bluish glow. The color was mesmerizing, and with a stronger light, Eli could see how the cave would appear to glow. Eli felt the hairs on her arms raise in gooseflesh. There were three darkened areas that, as she approached, Eli discovered were passages that led from the main cavern. Her heart pounded with excitement and trepidation. As much as she would love to explore farther into the cave, she knew it was not a wise choice. No one had a clue where she was, and if an accident were to happen, she would be in dire circumstances. She would have to wait for Mitch or even Whit to return home before she ventured any farther.

"This is as far as we will go, for now, Cruz," she said and turned back toward the mouth of the cave.

The fresh air tasted good when she emerged from the cave. She turned back to look at the immense rock formation. "It's not safe to wander inside, but it won't hurt to climb and look around a bit. We still need to be careful," she said as she holstered her gun and returned the flashlight to the pack. She examined the rocks and visually planned a route that would take her to what she believed was the top of the cave. Eli took a drink of water and cupped her hand for Cruz to drink.

"Are you ready?" she asked as she wiped her hands on her shorts.

Eli began climbing the rock formation, being careful of where she was placing her hands and feet. The bears were gone, but that didn't mean snakes or other reptiles wouldn't be out sunning themselves. That reminded Eli to get a snakebite kit or several to place in her daypack and around the farm. It wouldn't save anyone from a bite, but it may provide enough time for emergency care. Eli felt a burn in her leg muscles and trickles of sweat roll down her face as she climbed. The elevation hadn't appeared that steep from the ground, but Eli found it challenging. After several minutes, Eli felt the ground even out, allowing the final climb to the top to be much more comfortable. Eli was surprised to find a small pyramid of rocks piled together. That was definitely not natural and had to be a human-made structure, maybe some sort of marker. Not a grave marker as the stone would have prevented that from being possible.

"Things just keep getting more curious by the minute, Cruz." She pulled out her phone and snapped a photo.

Slightly winded by the climb, Eli leaned against a large boulder and took a sip of water.

"You hungry?" Cruz wiggled her entire rear end. "I know, that was a silly question." Eli opened the pack and pulled out the two biscuits, tearing one into smaller sections for Cruz. "Chew this, don't gobble them," she warned as she laid the pieces on the rock beside her and handed one to Cruz. She held the bit in her hand for a few seconds so Cruz would have to nibble, as she took a bite of her treat. Once more, the explosion of sweetness from the jelly reminded her of Whit.

"I bet she's not having as much fun as we are," she said to Cruz. "I bet Whit is tucked away in some secret room, away from all this glorious weather."

Her eyes scanned the top of the rock formation as she finished her snack. She noticed a small area that didn't have any of the hardy moss growing around it, and it struck her as odd. "Let's go check this out."

Eli brushed the crumbs from her shorts and shouldered her pack. When they arrived at the area, Eli noticed an opening that was faded gray by what she presumed was soot stains from the past. Eli knew that this area of North Carolina had been home to Cherokee Indians, and she wondered if she had stumbled upon a location they had used on hunting expeditions. Or maybe a band of warriors had used the place for shelter during tribal wars. Her mind was reeling with possibilities. The mist had finally burned off, and the view from the top of the formation was terrific. The valley filled with green squares of growing crops, and to her right was a sea of green from the dense forest. Birds sang, and a cool breeze welcomed her as she reached the pinnacle of the formation. Eli remembered Whit telling the boys about caves in the area, which left her wondering if she knew of this particular cave. She would ask her about it when Whit returned.

"I think it's time we start heading for home."

Eli and Cruz followed the ridge of the rock formation for several hundred feet until it began gently sloping. It was easier than climbing, but Eli felt the weariness in her muscles as they reached what she hoped was the section of trail that would lead them home. They hadn't found any berries, but the cave they stumbled across was much more exciting. Eli let out a sigh of relief when she spotted the boundary marker for her property. They continued to walk until they found the path that would lead them home.

When the top of the barn came into view, Cruz raced ahead and emerged from the barn with Molly hot in her tracks. "You two feel free to play all you want. I'm going to fix a sandwich and kick back on the porch."

Molly and Cruz raced across the open field as Eli walked inside. She was surprised to see that it was nearly two in the afternoon. "No wonder I'm hungry." She made a sandwich and poured a glass of tea before returning to the porch. Her eyes landed on the pile of limbs that Mitch had stacked on the end of the porch.

"One of those would have been handy today. I think I'll start working on one while I rest."

CHAPTER FOUR

"Dang, that's the biggest one yet," Evan said as Mitch held up his latest catch. "You are a beast of a fisherman," he teased.

"This is a great spot. A few more like this one, and we'll have a nice dinner for everyone," Mitch replied as he placed the fish in the cooler.

"Amen to that. I don't know about you, but I'm starting to get hungry," Evan said as he cast his line.

"It is almost two. Let's catch a couple more, and I'll treat us to some burgers."

"Man, that sounds good. My biscuits and cookies are long gone. Got one," he hollered as he set his hook.

Mitch picked up his rod, and after twenty minutes, they had four more fish in the cooler. "I think this should do, don't you?" he asked Evan.

"I think this will be plenty. Will you and Eli eat more than six?"

"No, we only need two each. You can take the rest of the fish for your family. We can clean them at our place, and you can take the filets home."

"Sounds like a great plan. We can dress the fish here if you want?"

"Heck, no, I'm ready for a burger or two," Mitch grinned.

"I hear ya. Let's get a move on then." Evan grabbed the chest while Mitch picked up the rods and tackle boxes.

They loaded the truck and headed for the closest burger place. "I've got to wash my hands," Mitch said.

"Me too, I smell pretty fishy," Evan agreed.

"I think I want two of everything," Mitch said once they emerged from the restroom and walked to the counter. "We worked up an appetite out there." They placed their orders and waited for the food.

"It's all the fresh air," Evan said. "Gives you an appetite even when you're having fun."

"That was fun. Thanks for taking me fishing today."

"We all needed a break. Eli's been working us hard." Evan chuckled.

"She's only got two speeds, full speed and off," Mitch replied. "You know I was thinking of something today."

"Should I be worried?" Evan asked cautiously.

"Very funny, smart guy. You know how Whit crosses over the stream on that old log. What if we made a bridge wide enough you could drive a Gator over?"

"There's plenty of trees we can use for support. A few two-by-twelves cut into widths and bolted down wouldn't be hard at all to do. We could throw that together in half a day. I'm sure Dad has the wood in stock."

"How long would it take if we cut our own boards?" Mitch asked. "We don't have the equipment, but I know it's on Aunt Eli's and Dad's bucket list to set up a small wood mill."

"We can look at ordering the equipment, but you're talking weeks to months to dry the boards naturally if you don't take them to a kiln to be dried." Evan scratched his head in thought. "Even then, you're talking considerable time."

"Buying from your dad, it is then. I can't wait that long."

"I'll ask him to get together some pricing on a chain saw system if that's what you're thinking of using."

"Yeah, that would be great. Dad will be here for some long weekends, and I'd like to have it set up before he arrives. Maybe we could build a covered addition to the workshop to set it up in."

"That would be easy. Eli has the auger for digging holes, so we just need to cut some trees for corner poles, and we can build trusses and put on a tin roof."

"I'm not sure I can handle all that," Mitch admitted as they took the trays of food to a table.

"Good thing you have me for a friend. There's not much this ole' country boy can't build. You got the muscle, I got the know-how." Evan grinned and bit into a burger. "Damn, this is great."

"Give me a price on the supplies we'll need for the bridge and covered area, and I'll give you the money."

"You can handle the cost of the covering and sawmill supplies, and I'll get the bridge. What your aunt has been paying me is insane, and Whit has done a lot for me over the years. It would be nice to do this to pay them back."

"I won't argue with that. Both women are fantastic. I can't wait for Whit to come back."

"Is she off on one of her government assignments?" Evan asked.

"Yeah, but of course she can't tell us anything. That Blackhawk landing in our fields was exciting. Scared the heck out of the animals, though."

"It's a good thing y'all don't have any laying hens. They wouldn't produce for weeks after that kind of trauma."

"That's for sure. I don't know if Eli is ready for chickens yet. But you never know, she may decide to start building coops tomorrow."

"She could make some portable ones out near the garden, and that will help to keep the insects down, add fertilizer for the garden. You can move them around to keep from wearing out a single area."

"Dad's already got a few plans for coops he wants to try. He's been dreaming of butt nuggets for months."

"Butt nuggets? Now that's a new one," Evan chuckled.

"Dad's got a colorful vocabulary," Mitch replied. "Sometimes, I never know what's going to come out of his mouth."

"I understand that. My Dad gets on a roll too sometimes."

"And then they wonder where we got it from." Mitch chuckled.

"Ain't that the truth." Evan opened up a second burger and took a bite. "These sure hit the spot."

"True dat," Mitch replied and kept on eating.

†

Whit keyed up her laptop and connected it remotely to her telescope in the lab. She had trained the viewfinder on the area she had been watching for weeks. The shadowed area was more pronounced in size, but one thing was for sure, it wasn't a satellite the terrorist had proclaimed he would use for his next attack. There were hundreds, possibly a thousand, satellites orbiting the earth at any given time. Her task was to evaluate them and determine if the mastermind was controlling any of them. The consultants from NASA had new software they had developed that would allow Whit and several others to sort through the data collected and transmitted by the targeted satellites. The task would take days to complete, even with four people scouring cyberspace. If they could locate the satellite, then they could pinpoint the location from where he was transmitting.

Whit plugged a thumb drive into her system and waited for the program to download. She glanced at her watch. It was only five, and she didn't want to risk waking Eli, so she walked over to the coffee pot and poured a cup. She'd intended to give Eli a few more hours of sleep before she called. Whit sipped on the coffee and sat at her workstation to open the newly-installed program.

For three hours, she pored over the mapped locations of the satellites and checked off one after another. Her coffee had long gone cold when she raised it to her lips, and she decided to take a short break. She walked into the break room to pour a cup of fresh coffee. Someone had brought in fresh bagels and flavored cream cheese. She slathered one of them with strawberry and sat at a table to eat and try to give Eli a call. She dialed Eli's number, and it rang until it transferred to voicemail. Whit looked at her watch again and found it odd that Eli did not answer. She dialed back this time and left a voice mail, followed by a text message. Whit was disappointed she didn't get to speak with Eli but would try again later. She took her coffee and bagel then returned to her workstation. A glance at the satellite maps showed how few they had been able to disqualify and the massive number yet to evaluate. Whit momentarily felt overwhelmed with the task. She knew that they were limited on time and buckled down to resume her search.

†

Eli picked out a branch and pulled the knife Mitch had given her and sat in one of the porch chairs. She began removing the bark from the limb and studied the grain of the wood underneath. Eli focused on the project, unaware of the passage of time until she heard the mailman, Mr. Henry, bounding up the driveway. She stopped whittling and walked out to meet him.

"Good afternoon, Mr. Henry. How are you this fine day?"

"I'm doing well, Ms. Fortner. How are you?"

"Fine as frog hair," Eli answered with a wink. "Hey, Mr. Henry, may I ask you a question?"

"You just did, but I'll allow you one more," he teased.

"I went exploring earlier today, and I found a cave over on the National Forest side of the mountain. I know you spent time here. Have you ever been there?"

He lifted his hat and scratched his head, pondering her question. "Does it have a pyramid of rocks on top of the outcropping?"

Eli became excited. "Yes, in fact, it does. So, you've been there?"

"A few times, yes. I did some research into the cave as a young man, and I found out it had a tragic past. During the Trail of Tears, the Cherokee lost this land to the white man. Forced to travel to a reservation in Oklahoma, many did not survive the trip. A small band of warriors escaped and waged hit and run attacks on the soldiers who were supervising the forced march." Mr. Henry paused and took a sip of water from his bottle. "During their passage through this area, the warriors sought refuge in that cave. The soldiers eventually hunted them down, and all but one, a young man barely more than a child, perished. The survivor was shackled and forced to march with the rest of his tribe."

"That's horrible," Eli said.

"Yes, it was a very tragic time for the Native Americans. The young man eventually escaped the confinement of the reservation and made his way back here. He built the pyramid of stone as a tribute to the fallen warriors. Then he took his life to join his brothers in the afterlife. The report said the rocks were stained red from the flow of his blood for many years." He looked at Eli.

She could see the sparkle of excitement in his eyes as he continued his story.

"The young warrior was supposedly named Pisgah, and the Pisgah National Forest named to honor him. I've never been able to corroborate that, but it does put a romantic spin on such a short and tragic life."

Eli nodded. "That it does. Thank you for sharing that with me. Is the cave safe to enter? I only explored the initial cavern."

"Honey, that rock formation has stood for thousands of years. It would take a bomb or significant earthquake to shake its foundation. I wouldn't recommend exploring it alone, though. Might be some ferocious critters up in there. Would make a mighty fine den for bears in the winter."

"I will assuredly keep that in mind."

"Where's Mitch today?"

"He and Evan decided to do some fishing. I expect he'll be home shortly with a cooler full of fish."

They both looked up at the sound of Evan's truck. "What did I tell ya," she grinned.

"Oh, before I forget, I got a package too big for the box, so I brought it up to ya," Mr. Henry stated and handed her the box and her mail.

"Thanks, Mr. Henry. You want to stick around and see what the boys caught?"

"Might as well. I'm near done with my route today." He climbed out of the mail truck and walked with Eli over to where Evan parked.

"Hey, Mr. Henry," Mitch said as he climbed out. "Man, did we catch some beauties, Aunt Eli."

"Open the cooler and let's see," Eli said.

Evan dragged the cooler to the tailgate and swung open the lid. "You boys got quite a mess of fish today," Mr. Henry said, letting out a low whistle.

"Probably more than we can eat," Evan admitted. "Mitch and I are going to clean and filet them. Would you and Mrs. Henry like a couple for dinner? I can drop them off on my way back to town."

"That would be fantastic. I can't remember the last time we had freshly caught trout. Two will be plenty for us. Thank you, boys. I'd better be on my way and call the missus to tell her we have fish for dinner." He smiled. "I'll see you next week, Ms. Fortner."

"Thanks again, Mr. Henry. Enjoy the fish."

"Oh, we will," he said and limped back to the truck.

"I guess I'd better whip up some hushpuppy mix and toss a salad," Eli said. "Do you two need anything?"

"No, ma'am, I think we're good. Wait, on second thought, can you bring out that box of zip lock bags for us to put the filets in?"

"You betcha," Eli said and walked inside.

†

Eli felt her phone vibrate and looked to find she had a voicemail and text message from Whit. *Sorry, I missed you. I'll call again later today or tonight. Love you.* Eli smiled and returned the text. *Love and miss you too. Must have been out of range when you called.* She hit send and listened to the voicemail. She noticed the time and reckoned that would have been around the time she was in or near the cave. *She doubted she had any coverage that far up the mountain— another reason to not explore the cave alone.* Eli smiled and grabbed the box of storage bags to take out to the boys.

"Holy cow, that's a lot of fish," she said when she saw the fish laid out on a makeshift table the boys had set up near the compost bin.

"Lots of good eating for all of us tonight," Evan remarked.

"That was very kind of you to share your catch with Mr. Henry. I'm sure he will appreciate fresh fish," she told the boys.

"There's plenty to go around. I thought we could send Mr. Henry six filets and still leave plenty for us," Evan said.

"By the looks of that pile of fish, I'd have to agree," Eli said. "Would you like me to whip up a bigger batch of hushpuppy mix for you to take home and give some to Mr. Henry?"

"You will love Aunt Eli's hushpuppies," Mitch said.

"I'd like that," Evan said. "Don't tell Mom, but hers are kinda bland."

"My lips are sealed. I'll mix up an extra-large batch. Let me know if y'all need anything."

"Yes, ma'am," Mitch said as he began cutting filets.

Eli returned to the kitchen and began mixing the ingredients for her special hushpuppies, and filled a large container for Evan and a smaller one for Mr. Henry. She was tossing the salad when the boys brought in a bag of filets. "Those look magnificent."

"Cajun thought so, too. We had to shoo him away several times. I'm still not sure he's not going to raid the compost bin tonight."

"I wouldn't be surprised either. Y'all had a great catch today."

"Thanks. We're going to wash up in the laundry room, and I'll be in once Evan is on his way home."

"Are you starving or want to wait a bit to eat?" she asked Mitch.

"We raided a burger place and gorged on burgers. I can hold off a while unless you're starving."

"Naw, I'm good. So, take your time with Evan. I think I'm going to whittle a little more."

"Did you start on a walking stick?"

"I did. Come and take a look once Evan leaves. I'll be on the porch."

"Yes, ma'am. See you in a few."

†

Mitch walked back outside to join Evan, who was rinsing the cooler. "Are you working with your Dad tomorrow, or do you want to come and help us break in our new log splitter and chipper?"

"How can I resist such an offer?" Evan teased. "You going to give Jessie a call tonight?"

"I was thinking about it," Mitch replied. "You think Erin would like to double date? Maybe dinner and a movie?"

"I'm sure that could happen," Evan grinned. "Say five on Saturday?"

"I'll let you know tomorrow, hopefully."

"I bet she says yes," Evan replied.

"I hope so," Mitch grinned, and his braces flashed.

"What time should I plan on being here in the morning?"

"I think the delivery is at eight. Come whatever time you're ready. We can always find something to do."

"I think I'll drop by the store and see about picking up the two-by-twelves for the bridge and see what other materials we need. What size shelter were you thinking?"

"A twelve by twelve would match the dimensions of the shop walls and should give plenty of room for milling."

Evan nodded. "That's what I was thinking, too. Maybe Dad and I can draw something up tonight, and it'll give us a better idea of materials."

"Good deal, thanks," Mitch answered. "Thanks again for a great day of fishing."

"I enjoyed it, too. Hopefully, we can have more days like today. Maybe that could be a date idea as well," Evan suggested. "Erin loves to fish, and I bet Jessie might too."

"Maybe if dinner and a movie go well, we can shoot for fishing," Mitch replied.

"Have faith. I better get moving," Evan said as he climbed into his truck."

"Wait, let me run in and get the hushpuppy mix," Mitch said and jogged into the house.

"Thanks. I forgot all about it," Evan said and placed it on the seat. "See you tomorrow."

†

Eli waved as Evan drove away. Mitch walked over to her and sat on the railing.

"That's looking good," he said, gesturing to the stick. "Will you sand it down or leave it rough?"

"I thought I'd sand it and put a light stain on it or just some polyurethane. I'm kind of digging the grain."

"It is pretty. I'd go natural or at the most a very light-colored stain." He shifted on the rail. "Would you mind if I ask Jessie out on a date Saturday night?"

"I think that would be great," Eli replied.

"Evan and I discussed a double date for dinner and a movie."

"Go for it," she encouraged.

"I will," Mitch said and stepped down from the railing as he walked toward the front of the cabin.

Eli smiled as she heard Mitch talking. She was very proud of the young man he had become. Several minutes later, she heard him yell.

"Yes!" he cried out, startling Cruz from her nap.

As he turned the corner around the house and came into view, Eli looked up. "I take it she said yes."

"She did indeed." He smiled. "I'll need to figure out what to wear now." He frowned.

"You have some relatively new jeans and some new Dri-fit shirts you haven't worn yet. If you select an outfit, I'll iron it for you."

"Deal," he said. "Do you want me to fry the fish and hushpuppies?"

"If you'd like. I'm pretty relaxed right here," Eli said.

"I'll call you in for supper then," Mitch grinned and walked inside.

"This is the life, Cruz," she chuckled. "Let me finish here, and we'll put Molly up for the night and get everyone fed."

Eli raked the bits of bark into a bucket and stored them for kindling at the fire pit. Cruz trotted along beside her to the barn, and Molly raced ahead to enter her stall for dinnertime. Eli freshened her hay and poured feed into her bin, petting the sweet animal for several minutes before the chorus of hungry cats reached a crescendo.

"You guys are not going to starve to death in one day," she told Cajun as she filled the feeders. "I heard you munched on some fresh fish," she said as she stroked the playful cat's head. Oscar and Walter had taken up residence in the barn and walked over for attention. "Hopefully, Whit will be home soon. I know you miss her too."

Oscar looked up at her with his deep-green eyes and began weaving between her legs. "You are more than welcome to come inside tonight if you wish," she told him as she scratched under his chin, and he began purring.

"Supper is ready," Mitch called from the front porch.

"On my way," Eli answered.

When she walked into the kitchen, Mitch looked up from pouring tea. "I put food down for Cruz and Tomboy so that we can eat in peace," he chuckled.

"Smart move," Eli replied and looked at the food Mitch had placed on the table. "This looks delicious. Good job, Mitch."

"Thanks, I hope everything tastes okay. I'm still learning my way in the kitchen."

"You're doing great." Eli sat across from Mitch. "Did you have a fun day with Evan?"

"I did. We had a great day to fish. He showed me some great spots. While I was relaxing, I did some thinking about a couple of projects."

"Really? Do tell."

"I will pay for them on my own, and Evan has agreed to help me out with the labor."

"You know I'll pay for anything you need. Just tell me how much."

"I know, but I'd like to do these two on my own."

"I can respect that. What are the projects?"

"I want to build a bridge wide enough to drive the Gator over, so going between the two properties is safer. We have enough trees for the poles, and Evan is going to spring for the two-by-twelves and hardware."

"That's a great idea, and it does make a lot of sense, too. What's the second project?"

"You know how Dad is always talking about a portable sawmill? I'd like permission to build a twelve-by-twelve covered area off the workshop to use for his mill."

"I'll make you a deal. You cover the materials and labor, and I'll buy the mill. They can get pricey."

Mitch swallowed the bite of food he was chewing. "I can handle that. I'd like to have the covering built by the time he gets here in a few weeks."

"I don't see a problem with that. Your dad will be impressed, and Whit will be happy she doesn't have to cross that log anymore. If you need help with the supplies, just let me know, okay?"

"Yes, ma'am, I will. What did you do today?"

"I went for a hike and found a mysterious cave on the National Park side of the mountain. Mr. Henry said it has Native American history surrounding it, and he and Whit's grandfather went inside it many times as kids."

"Did you explore it?"

"Just the very opening. I didn't want to risk something happening, and no one knowing where I was."

"That was a smart decision. So, when are we going back?"

"I think we'd better wait until Whit comes back so we can have someone outside if needed for help. It looks sound and has been there for probably thousands of years, but it's better to be safe."

"Speaking of Love Muffin, have you talked to her today?"

"Not yet, she called when I was out of cell range. She left a voicemail and sent me a text that I answered."

"I'll be glad when she gets back."

Eli was surprised by his comment. "Why is that?"

"Because you seem happier when she's around. Not that you've moped around or anything, but you always smile when she's near."

"That is a very astute observation, Dr. Fortner."

"I'm glad you agree. I'll send you my bill tomorrow." He chuckled.

"What's the plan for tomorrow? Do you want to start on some of your new projects? After the equipment is delivered, I can start splitting firewood and chipping those limbs."

"Evan is coming out in the morning. I think he'll probably bring a load of two-by-twelves, so maybe we can knock out the bridge."

"If we have enough light left, do you want to pick out a location and measure?"

Mitch wiped his mouth. "Sure, we can do that. Let's go. I'll clean the kitchen when we get back. There's not much left to do."

"I'll rinse the dishes and put them in the dishwasher if you want to go out for a measuring tape and the can of bright orange paint."

"On my way," Mitch said, and drank the last of his tea. "C'mon Cruz," he called as he walked to the door, and she bolted out ahead of him.

Eli quickly rinsed the dishes and stored the leftover salad. She was closing the dishwasher as Mitch returned. "That was good timing. Better grab a flashlight just in case."

Mitch opened a cabinet and took out a flashlight. "Ready to roll?"

"Right behind you."

"That could be a dangerous position to be in after me just eating," he warned.

"That's true. I'll go first," Eli teased back.

†

They walked the trail until they reached a spot just below the fallen tree.

"What do you think about this area?" Eli asked Mitch.

"Looks pretty good. Nice and level and not too wide," Mitch answered. "Let's measure to see how wide it is." He took one end of the tape measure and started walking toward the water.

Eli was about to stop him when she realized Mitch had put on his rubber boots. The water wasn't deep enough to overrun the top of his boots, so she needn't worry. When he reached the far bank, he stopped.

"Fourteen feet from bank to bank. A twenty-four-foot log would reach and give five or so feet extra support on both banks. Two other ideas just hit me, too," Mitch said. "I think we need some sort of railing on the bottom to keep from running off the edge, and some of those solar-powered lights would be great, too."

"That does make good sense. Could we use some of the smaller downed trees for the railing and attach them to the boards?"

"I don't see why not. We'd only need the fourteen-foot length for the rail. I bet we could bore right through the poles, and use a long spike to nail them to the bridge."

Eli popped the lid off the spray paint and marked the ground for the bridge. "I'll drive into town tomorrow and buy some of the solar lights and short shepherd hooks for the lighting. What do you think? Three on each side?"

"I like this project already," Mitch grinned.

The night was falling quickly, but Eli looked at Mitch. "You want to find your trees?"

"Sure. I think I know the perfect two for the bridge," he said. "Follow me."

"No way, you've already warned me about walking behind you."

"No worries, I got rid of the gas crossing the creek." He chuckled.

"Well, thank God for that," she said and punched him in the shoulder.

Mitch led her to the two trees he was considering.

"You know what?" Eli said. "I bet we could use the tops of these trees for your railing. They look tall enough."

"I think you're right about that. Should we mark these two?"

"Yeah, I think they will be perfect."

Mitch took the can of paint from her and sprayed a small dot at the base of each tree.

"What you don't use, I can make into firewood," she said. "We can use some of the wood chips I'll make with the chipper to build a little ramp up to the bridge."

"There will be enough scraps leftover from the planks to help support the ramps." He patted her shoulder as they turned to walk back home. "Whit is going to love this."

"Yes, she will," Eli said.

"What are you going to do tonight?" Mitch asked.

"I don't know. I thought I might pull out some sandpaper and keep working on a walking stick down by the fire pit. You game for a fire and a beer?"

"I'll start the fire if you'll grab us a beer. You want me to grab some sandpaper?"

"I've already got it. Meet you at the pit in a minute."

She watched Mitch disappear around the end of the cabin and went inside to get two beers. Darkness had fallen, and there was a slight chill in the air, but she felt sure the fire and some activity would keep her warm. She picked up her walking stick and a sheet of sandpaper before joining Mitch at the fire pit.

"With those shavings, this should take off quickly. That was a good idea," Mitch said as Eli took a seat.

"I bet we could use some of the chipped wood for that, too," she answered.

"Let it dry out a bit, and it would work well. I thought we could use the auger attachment to bore some holes to add a short post on either side of the bridge logs with some concrete to keep it from shifting. I think we've got a few bags left."

"You're getting good with project planning," Eli praised Mitch.

He shrugged. "Just makes sense to me."

"I like it," Eli said. She handed him a beer as he came to sit beside her. "I think you've earned this today. That was a great dinner."

"I am learning to cook better here. Thanks for teaching me."

"Not much teaching going on. You're doing things on your own. I don't even have to coach you. You figure it out on your own and have cooked some great meals. Your dad would be proud."

Mitch grinned at her. "He doesn't allow me the opportunities you do."

"Your dad is used to doing most of the cooking and probably doesn't have the patience he needs to teach you and

Brad. He just wants to get home from work and get something cooked." She took a sip of her beer. "I bet he will notice a huge difference in you when he comes for a visit. Maybe I'm biased, but I think you've grown since you've been here, and I don't mean physically, even though you are putting on some muscle."

"You allow me to make mistakes. I don't always have to be perfect."

"I've always found that's how I learn things. If I make a mistake, I try something different until I get it right. There's no such thing as perfect."

"I love you, Aunt Eli," he said and touched his bottle to hers.

"More," Eli answered with a grin.

"No way, man." He took a long drink. "This beer tastes good."

"Yes, it does. I'd say we had a good day. Fun, good food, a toasty fire, and a relaxing night."

"I'd have to agree, and I'm excited about getting to work tomorrow."

"Is Evan's dad getting some prices together for the sawmill?"

"Yes, he said he'd let me know."

"I'll go there for the solar lights and shepherd hooks, and see what he has available. Do we want a chainsaw mill or go for the band saw?"

Mitch laughed. "He's been drooling over a portable chainsaw mill for years. The Norwood or Alaska system would work. The Norwood is more expensive, but I think it would give him more options."

"Chainsaw mill it is then. We'll need to build some drying racks for that. Maybe in the barn? What do you think?"

68

"I thought Dad and I could do that when he comes up. I'd like to have some logs cut for him. I bet we could section out some of the downed trees or even some of the standing dead trees. If it's not wormy, he can get some great boards and the rest we can use for firewood or kindling."

"We'll have both options available to him. He'll be here in a few weeks. That should give us plenty of time to bring some down."

"I can't wait for Whit to come home so we can get the solar system up," Mitch said. "That's going to be such a fun project."

"I think she's as excited about it as you are. She was afraid of letting you down when she left."

"She was needed elsewhere, and I don't plan on leaving anytime soon. This country's security is more important."

"I hope they can work out whatever they needed her for and get it resolved quickly."

"Me, too!" Mitch grinned. "Hey, that's looking good," he said, pointing to the stick.

"It's getting there. I can't believe how relaxing this is for me."

"You can use that when you go hiking. May come in handy if you run into a snake or other critter."

"That's true. The stick would scare anything off before I took a step. I'm digging the grains in this wood. I think a layer of clear coat will be all I need."

"I saw a show once. I think it was about building off the grid or something like that, and the builders scorched the logs with a blowtorch to give them a different look. It was beautiful."

"That's an idea I could play with," Eli replied. "I think I'm about toast for tonight. That hike was more strenuous than I anticipated. I've gotten spoiled using the Gator."

"Time to shower and hit the bed? We both have busy days planned for tomorrow."

"You going to come in, too?"

"I think I'll call Dad and then shut the lid on the fire, but I won't be out long. See you in the morning."

"Goodnight. Love ya."

"More," he replied.

"Tell your parents, and Brad, I said hello, and I love them."

"Will do. How about some French Toast in the morning with bacon?" he asked.

"Sounds great. The first one up starts cooking."

"Deal."

"Come on, Cruz, let's go."

†

Whit's team had spent ten hours poring over the satellite coordinates, and they still hadn't located the correct one. She felt frustrated and exhausted. "I don't know about you all, but my eyes are starting to cross. Let's get some sleep and start again in the morning."

There were no complaints to her suggestion, and the team rode back to the hotel in silence. Whit was so tired she didn't bother with room service. All she wanted was a hot shower and to talk to Eli. Afterward, if she was hungry, she could order something. Once in her room, she started her shower and stripped out of her clothes.

The shower further relaxed her, and then she crawled onto the bed and picked up her phone. She dialed Eli and prayed she would answer. On the third ring, she smiled when she heard Eli's sexy voice. "Hey, Babe, I was hoping it wasn't too late." Her smile grew. "Yeah, I just got out of a shower, too. I'm beyond exhausted. No, I haven't decided if I want anything to eat. I know I'll sleep better with something on my stomach. I wonder if they can bring me a peanut butter and jelly sandwich and a glass of milk?"

She listened to Eli as she shared the day she and Mitch had. "The fish dinner sounds fantastic. Did he cook it all himself? He's blossoming with you. You should be proud of him. I'm glad you both had a fun day."

Eli told her about the cave and her conversation with Mr. Henry.

"I'm not sure I've ever been to that cave. We'll have to check it out when I get home. No, I don't have a clue when I can come back home. I feel like we're getting closer, but we're not there yet. Yeah, I know we'll get it done. Okay, I'll get some rest. I'll try to call in the morning. It may be early. Love you, too. Goodnight, Eli. Hello to Mitch for me."

†

Eli stepped out of the shower when she heard her phone ringing. She grabbed a towel and rushed to the bedroom. She answered and put the phone on speaker so she could dry off.

"Hey, hang on a sec, I'm dripping wet. I just got out of the shower. Yes, I bet. You sound tired. Did you get something to eat?" Her smile grew as she listened to Whit. *Damn, I miss her.* "Yes, we had a fun day today. Mitch and Evan went fishing and came home with a cooler full of fish, enough to drop some by for Mr. Henry and his wife. I sent them some hushpuppy mix, too." She listened to Whit. "Yes, he cooked everything and did an excellent job. He's becoming a good cook." When Whit asked her what she had done, she hesitated about telling her about the cave but decided to go ahead. "On my hike today, I found a cave over on the Park side of the mountain. Mr. Henry says he and your grandfather used to play in it as kids. He said it had some Native American history behind it. We will check it out when you get home. No, I didn't feel comfortable going too deep since Mitch had no idea where I was." She could hear the weariness in Whit's voice. "Please get something to eat so you'll sleep well tonight. Call anytime you want in the morning. I'll be up early, so call whenever you get a chance. Love you, too. Mitch sends his love. He's ready for you to come home also. Goodnight, Whit."

Eli slipped into her sleep pants and a T-shirt and took the towel back to the bathroom. She had heard Mitch come inside while she was on the phone with Whit and could now hear his shower running. Tomboy came rushing up the stairs and jumped on the bed.

"You always arrive in time to snuggle," she teased and scratched under his chin. "Goodnight, Cruz," she said and crawled into bed. "Move over you bed hog," she told Tomboy, who relented and moved over in the bed to allow her to lie down. She turned off her lamp and listened to the breeze whispering through her window.

CHAPTER FIVE

Whit and her team had gone in early, long before the rest of the staff were on duty. They had managed to clear one hundred other satellite locations before it was time for a coffee break. "I don't usually drink much coffee, but this stuff is a high-octane fuel," Whit told one of the team as she poured a fresh cup.

Raymond had been on research teams with her before and nodded at her comment. "Jet fuel is more like it. I was beginning to worry that I wouldn't fall asleep last night, but as soon as I hit the bed, I was out."

"Me, too. I convinced room service to deliver two peanut butter and jelly sandwiches and several cartons of milk. After that, I was history until about four. Then I woke with a start."

"Did you have a bad dream?" he asked.

"No, I don't think so. I woke up with the thought that today we would find our prey."

Raymond picked up his coffee. "I hope you are correct. It's always fun working with you, but I'm worried about this terrorist."

"I am, too. This man is enough of a loose cannon to rain all kinds of hell down on us. There's no telling what kind of financial backing he has to bring this plan to life. Too many factions in the Middle East hate America."

"That's unfortunate but true. I can remember the time when we had many allies there, but no more." Raymond let out a deep sigh. "Let's find him today."

"I've got a new idea, and I want to see if it will help narrow our search a bit. I'll let you know if it works."

Instead of locating the satellite, Whit focused on the areas of transmission from locations in the Middle East. While there were still many locations, it did narrow down the search range. She compared the sites to the ones already searched and marked off another dozen as legitimate communication systems.

She finished off her bagel and coffee as she searched the grid. Whit stood, preparing for a bathroom break when her computer pinged with the coordinates for a location. She zoomed in on the GPS coordinates to an area known as the Kurd Mountain in Northwest Syria. In the middle of an orchard, she found a small building with a retractable roof that looked entirely out of place. There was a rough-looking truck sitting beside the building, which had an armed guard at the entrance.

"That seems odd," she spoke aloud.

"Did you find anything?" Raymond asked.

"Maybe, come take a look at this," Whit said, and motioned him to her workstation. She zoomed in closer on

Google Maps, and they could make out an armed guard outside the building.

"Why would anyone need armed protection in the middle of an orchard?" Raymond asked.

"Exactly. Someone is transmitting to a satellite in sector four," Whit said as she traced the transmission destination. She pulled up the data they had on the associated satellite. "It's an older Russian model, from the mid-eighties, registered to the Demron group in Syria. Will you locate the general while I see what I can find out about Demron?"

"Absolutely," Raymond said, and left the room.

Several of the other team members looked up at Whit. "Okay, people, let's see what we can find out about the Demron Group." Heads dropped back down, and their keyboards came to life.

Minutes later, when Raymond returned with the general and staff in tow, Whit handed him a printout of the transmitter location. "We are trying to uncover information on the Demron Group now," she reported.

"We've heard that name before," the general responded. "We'll get the CIA on this, too. Good work, team." He turned to leave, then stopped. "Just in case this information doesn't pan out, keep searching for other potentials."

"Yes, sir, we will," Whit answered. Her adrenalin was pumping through her veins as she turned back to the team. "We were looking at this the wrong way. I reversed our search pattern to come up with this hit. Instead of focusing on the satellites, focus on the transmissions coming from the region."

Whit walked to the restroom to relieve her bladder. She leaned against the wall after washing her hands. The adrenalin had given her a rush of energy, but now she needed to regain her focus. She looked into the mirror and saw the weariness in her face. "It's time to finish this up and go home."

†

Mitch was already cooking when Eli came down the stairs. "You got it smelling good in here," she commented.

"Nothing like waking to the smell of bacon in the morning." He grinned as he turned to watch her enter the kitchen. "I've got the bacon done if you would like to start on the French toast." He reached over to start the coffee brewing. "After you fix your coffee, of course."

"Did you sleep well last night?" she asked.

"Like a rock. That's for sure one thing I don't have any problem with up here. All the fresh air and exercise puts me right out at night."

"Me, too, with an occasional dream tossed in for good measure." Eli removed a carton of eggs, milk, and the butter dish from the fridge. "Are you starving this morning?"

"Four pieces should be fine for me," he replied as he placed the last strips of bacon on a plate to cool. "Do you think we'll have time to cut down the trees before our delivery arrives?"

"I think we'll have ample time to do that, get them bucked, and hauled down to the bridge site."

"I'd love to finish that project today. I think with Evan and me working together; we can knock it out."

"I don't see why not. I can work on the chipping of the brush, and bring down a load when I have one ready. Did you check to make sure the batteries for the drills were charged last night?"

"All set with extras for spares."

76

"You want to load the Gator with chainsaws and supplies while I finish cooking?"

"Sure thing."

"Don't forget the tape measure and a length of rope so we can drag them down."

"I'm all over it, Aunt Eli," he answered and, snuck a piece of bacon from the plate.

"Take Cruz with you. Check the feed for the cats and Molly, please."

"Yes, ma'am. Come on, Cruz," he called, and they disappeared through the front door.

†

Mitch was pulling the tractor from the barn when she called him in for breakfast. *At least he's thinking this morning. I didn't think about pulling the logs with the tractor.* She watched him jump down from the tractor. "That's smart. Let the big equipment do the work."

"Made good sense to me," Mitch said as he jogged up the cabin steps.

"Let's eat and get to work," Eli said and followed him inside.

†

Whit stared at her computer screen. She had continued her search and located another site, five miles away, that was transmitting to the satellite. "We have a secondary site," she announced.

77

All heads in the room turned to look at Whit. "Five miles away is another transmission site, using the same satellite."

"We have ground forces moving toward the first site. I will have the team divide and send a group to the other location. What are the GPS coordinates?"

Whit moved her mouse across the screen, and Raymond recorded the coordinates.

The general looked at Whit. "Great work. Please continue your search, and I'll direct the teams on the ground. Let me know if you find another transmission site."

"Thanks. We will continue to search for others." Whit turned to her team. "Let's get back to it. We're on the home stretch now."

†

"Timber," Eli called out and stepped away from the falling tree. She and Mitch watched it fall ten feet from the first. "Let's get these bucked and cut into the lengths you need."

Mitch started the smaller saw, and they worked together to remove the branches from the fallen trees. Eli pulled out the tape measure and marked the lengths on the logs. "Do you want to do the cutting?"

"You go ahead, and I'll move these branches into a pile for you."

"Deal," Eli said and started the saw. A few minutes later, sections in the lengths they needed for the base and the railings were ready to be hauled down to the stream. "Tie the rope around the two big logs, and attach the line to the tractor hitch. I'm going to section the rest of these logs for splitting."

Eli cut a dozen sections while Mitch connected the line to the logs. She turned off the saw as he finished tying the rope. Do you want to drag them down to the stream?"

Mitch grinned down at her. "I'll be back in a few minutes." He climbed into the cab of the tractor.

"Go slow and careful. Try to get the logs as close to the bank as you can. Be cautious, and I'll get the others ready to move. They are small enough for me to move easily."

"Don't strain. I'll get the logs when I return." He waved and started the tractor.

Eli looked around the site, and she located several flat areas. She would propose they bring the log splitter and chipper up to the site. It would be easier to transport the finished products to the cabin once prepared. Eli went to work, cutting the remaining logs into sections while she waited for Mitch to return. She could feel a trickle of sweat slide down her spine as she cut the last length. She cut the power on the saw and turned to find Mitch walking toward her with a bottle of water.

She took the bottle and downed a long drink. "Thanks. That hit the spot."

"Let's drag these last two down, and by then, it should be time for the delivery," he suggested.

"That sounds good. What do you think about bringing the splitter and chipper up here?"

Mitch took his cap off and scratched his head. "The chipper, yes, but I think you should have the splitter down near the cabin. It would make one less lift if you just took the logs down, split, and stacked them there."

"That does make good sense. I'll haul the chipper up here while you and Evan start on the bridge."

"We can pull it up here for you. I'll put the bucket on the tractor, and you can aim the shredder shoot right into it."

Eli smiled at him. "When did you get so smart?"

"Must be the company I've been keeping." Mitch grinned.

"Remind me to thank Evan when he gets here then," she teased.

"I meant you, silly. You would have come up with the idea soon enough. I just beat you to the punch." His braces flashed in the morning sun as he laughed.

"C'mon, Cruz. Let's head down the mountain," she told Mitch. "You can drive, and I'll meet you there."

Mitch nodded and carefully pulled the remaining logs down the mountain. Evan was pulling into the yard as Eli arrived.

"Whoa, you're loaded down," she said.

"Good morning. Yeah, I think I hit the jackpot," Evan answered.

"I'd say so. Mitch just pulled the last two logs to the site and is taking the tractor back up the mountain. Do you want to drive up to the bridge site, so there's not much distance to carry things?"

"That would be a great idea."

Eli turned her head at the sound of a large truck pulling onto the property. The chipper and log splitter rested on the flatbed. She smiled when she saw another of her dreams coming true.

"Good morning," she called out when the man stepped out of the truck.

"Good morning to you, Ms. Fortner. How are you today?"

"I'm doing great, Mr. Morris, and yourself?"

"Finer than frog's hair." He grinned. "Where would you like this equipment?"

"I'd like the splitter close to the barn, and I'm going to pull the chipper up the trail a bit. You can drop it over there," Eli pointed to the mouth of the trail.

Evan and Mitch walked up. "Morning, Mr. Morris," Mitch grinned.

"Morning, boys. You two want to give me a hand here?"

"Sure thing. Do you want to back the truck closer to the barn? We can drop the equipment there."

Thirty minutes later, Eli and Mitch were confident of the operation of both new pieces of equipment. "Be sure to wear safety gear, especially when using the chipper."

"Will do, Mr. Morris," Mitch replied.

"I reckon I'll see you tomorrow night then. Jessie is very excited about your date," Mr. Morris replied.

"I am, too, sir. Does she like to fish? Evan and I thought we could take the girls fishing on Sunday if that's alright."

"You'll have to drag her out of the water. She loves to fish," Mr. Morris chuckled. "Y'all have a great day and be careful. I'll see you soon."

"Thanks, Mr. Morris," Eli said as she walked him to his truck.

"No, ma'am, thank you for all your business. I appreciate hearing from you," he said. "I'm so excited to see this place come to life again. By the way, where's Whit?"

"She got pulled away on business for a few days," Eli answered.

"Another secret mission for the government," he said.

"Something like that."

"Well, tell her hello for me when you talk to her."

"Will do, Mr. Morris. Thanks again."

Eli waved and watched him drive away and then went in search of the boys. They were already attaching the chipper to the Gator, preparing to pull it up the mountain.

"If you two can handle setting that up, I'll go to town for my other supplies. Call me if you can think of anything else you need. How do steaks and all the fixings sound for dinner? Evan, can you stay?"

"We will have to bust it to get everything we planned done today. I'd love one of your steaks," Evan answered.

"I'll make it happen then. Any special requests?"

"Will you sauté onions and mushrooms like you did last time?" Mitch asked.

"Sure, that's no problem. I'll be back in a bit."

"Be careful, Aunt Eli."

Eli looked at Cruz. "You too. Do you want me to put Cruz up before I go?"

"No, ma'am, I'll let Molly out, and that will keep her busy for a while."

"I'll be back soon, then." Eli walked into the cabin for her keys and wallet before driving to town.

CHAPTER SIX

"I believe those are the only two, general," Whit told him after the team pored through the remaining data.

"That was great work," he praised. "Our teams on the ground should be reporting in soon." He looked back at Whit. "Thank you for all that you and the team have done. I think it's safe to say you can return to your homes tomorrow after a well-deserved night's rest and a hot meal." He chuckled. "I hope you will take full advantage of the hotel's restaurant and order the biggest steaks they have on the menu."

A soldier rushed into the room and handed a note to the general. He read the message and looked up at Whit. "The mission was a complete success, two significant targets captured, and their equipment and capabilities destroyed."

The group applauded. "That's great news," Whit replied.

"You can rest well tonight, knowing there is one less group targeting the United States now." He smiled. "Thanks again for all your hard work."

"You heard the man, let's pack it in, folks. It's time for us to head home." Whit was excited to be going home and was contacted by the general's staff to arrange for an early morning flight. "The sooner, the better," she told them and carried her case of files down to the waiting van.

†

Eli stopped by the hardware store and made the purchases for the solar lanterns and chainsaw mill.

"I've got everything in stock for the mill in an off-site warehouse. I'll have one of the boys load the lanterns and shepherd hooks in the back of your truck. Is there anything else I can get for you?" Evan's dad asked.

"Do you have a small, hand-held blow torch?" Eli asked.

"I do, and I'll get a case of gas canisters for it as well. Those are handy little devices."

"Yes, they are."

Eli paid for her purchases and drove to the grocery store. When she returned to the cabin, she put the groceries away, marinated the steaks, and loaded the supplies in the Gator's back. She could hear the drone of power tools as she approached. Evan looked up from sawing boards and smiled. Mitch was busy fastening boards to the logs, and also looked up to see her approach.

"Welcome back," he called out as she parked and took six shepherd hooks from the Gator's back and laid them on the ground.

"Hang on, and I'll help you," Mitch said.

84

"Y'all have made great progress," she said as she handed him the first two lanterns. "There's a plastic tab that needs removing, so they will start to charge."

"I'm all over it," Mitch replied as he sat them next to the hooks and pulled out the tabs. "These are going to work great."

"I bought some fresh deli meat. Whenever you two are ready we can take a lunch break," Eli told them. "Give me a shout when you get hungry. I'm going to start chipping."

"Be careful, and keep your phone handy," Mitch told her.

"I will," she replied. Eli drove the Gator to the worksite. The boys had positioned the bucket on the tractor to receive the wood chips straight from the chipper. "This will do."

Eli took a drink of water, then placed a pair of goggles over her eyes, and leather work gloves on her hands. She pushed the button to start the motor, and the chipper roared to life. Eli picked up the first limb from the brush pile and fed it through the chipper. The machine hungrily devoured the tree limb, and Eli continued to feed it until the bucket was full of chips. She turned off the motor and climbed into the tractor cab. Eli reached the bridge and was impressed to see the boys had installed the planks nearly halfway across the stream. She watched how easily they worked together, and it brought a smile to her face.

"Where do you want these?" she shouted above the noise of the tractor.

"Dump them over there." Mitch pointed to a small cleared spot.

Eli emptied the bucket and turned off the tractor. "It's looking good," she said as she stepped out onto the first of the planks. Solid too."

They heard a loud splash and turned to watch Molly chase Cruz down the creek. "Don't scare my fish off," Mitch hollered to them, then broke out laughing. They were both drenched but appeared to be having great fun.

"You two starting to get hungry yet?" Eli asked.

"I could eat a few sandwiches," Evan answered.

"Me, too, Aunt Eli. Do you want me to make some?"

"Nope, I've got this. You two have a bridge to build. I'll be back shortly."

Eli drove down to the cabin and began building sandwiches. She pulled out a bag of chips, paper plates, napkins, and filled a cooler with soft drinks and water. Eli grabbed a bag of chocolate chip cookies for dessert. She packed the food into a box and was about to leave the cabin when her phone rang.

She was excited to see it was Whit calling. She pressed the speaker button to answer. "Hey, baby!"

"Hey, sweetie. I've got great news. I'll be home tomorrow."

"That is fantastic news. I am so excited to see you. So are Mitch and the fur babies."

"Are they all behaving themselves?" Whit asked with a chuckle.

"Oscar thinks he owns the place. He and Walter have enjoyed spending the last few nights curled up on the rug in front of the fireplace. Everyone is doing well, though."

"How about you? You doing okay?"

"I'm trying to stay busy to keep from worrying about you. We had a chipper and a log splitter delivered today, so I've been chipping some brush."

"That will be very useful around the place. What's Mitch up to?"

"He and Evan are working on some projects. He wants to build a small wood mill for his dad, so they are working on that." She didn't want to reveal the surprise the boys were building for her.

"That sounds wonderful. How is the garden doing?"

"Everything is growing well. The creek keeps everything watered, and I check it regularly for weeds."

"It sounds like you've got everything in hand."

"I just need you to be home. I take it your mission was successful."

"Yes, it was. We got the results just a little while ago and were released to return home. It was too late to schedule a flight today, but I'll be on my way in the morning."

"Do I need to pick you up somewhere?"

"Nope, I'm getting a ride back in the Blackhawk that brought me, so prepare for some noise."

"Mitch will be ecstatic. By the way, he has a date tomorrow night, so we have the cabin all to ourselves for a while."

"A date? With who?"

"Jessie Morris. They are going to double date for dinner and a movie with Evan and Erin."

"I'm so happy for him. Jessie is a good kid. It sounds like he and Evan have grown to be good friends, too."

"They work so well together it makes me smile to watch them. I think Mark will be very impressed by his growth and the projects we've been able to complete. I can't wait for them to get here."

"Me, too. I'll call you later tonight. I want to get my stuff packed and eat a fantastic steak dinner courtesy of Uncle Sam."

"Ha! I bet it won't be near as good as the ones I'm cooking for the boys and me tonight."

"I doubt it even comes close, but I'll be one step closer to home, and you can cook one for me next week."

"You have a deal, my love. I love and miss you."

"Ditto. I'll be home soon. Talk to you later. Tell the boys hello for me."

"I will. Goodbye for now."

"Goodbye, Eli."

Eli ended the call and pumped her fist in the air. "Yes!" she cried out. Walter, who had been sleeping in front of the fireplace, lifted his head to look at her. "Mama's coming home, Walter." He yawned and snuggled back in for his nap.

†

Eli took the platter of sandwiches, and bags of chips out to a Gator before returning for the cooler. As she pulled up to the building site, she was impressed to see the boys had finished planking the bridge. "Wow, this is looking great," she said as she turned the engine off. "Ready for a break?"

"I don't know whose stomach is growling the loudest," Mitch told her.

"Wait until you see the steaks I've got marinating. They are huge."

"You've got my mouth watering already," Evan said as he bit into a sandwich.

"These should hold you over for a little while. Whit said to tell you both 'hello.' She'll be home tomorrow." She grinned at Mitch. "You'll be pleased to hear she's coming back on the Blackhawk."

"That is such a sweet ride," he answered. "Maybe I can get a quick ride this time."

"We'll see," Eli answered. "Do you think you'll have this finished today?"

"Heck yeah, and possibly a start on the wood mill," Mitch replied.

"The rails and support posts should go up rather quickly, and we can hang the lights," Evan stated. "The concrete is setting up on the ramps, and it won't take long to add the wood chips and some river rock to stabilize them."

"How's it coming with the chipper?" Mitch asked.

"I've got a lot of the brush piles chipped already, so let me know if y'all need another bucket load brought down." She took a drink and placed the bottle in the cup holder. "I'm anxious to try out that log splitter. I may section out one or two of the logs to bring down to try it out."

"Just be careful with that saw," Mitch told her.

"We could go knock it out for you quickly," Evan offered.

"No, but thanks. You've got a bridge to complete before Whit gets home. I'll be careful."

Eli climbed out of the Gator and walked over to the tractor. "I'll see you guys in a while."

Eli drove the tractor back up the mountain trail and lowered the bucket even with the ground. She intended to cut the larger trunk sections of the trees to experiment using the splitter. Once she had them cut, she could roll them into the bucket.

Eli put on her protective equipment and started the saw. She measured out three-foot sections and cut the log three-quarters of the way through. When Eli reached the end and began rolling the tree over to finish the cuts, she was surprised to find the first tree left her with twenty sections. Eli maneuvered half of them into the bucket on the tractor and drove toward the barn. She waved at the boys as she passed the bridge and pulled up next to the splitter. Eli carefully placed the first log onto the equipment and started the engine. Eli watched as the hydraulic wedge dug into the wood with the ease of pushing a button, splitting the log in half. She repositioned the wood and cut it into a quarter.

"So much easier and faster than doing this by hand." Eli split a small pile and then began stacking them on a wood rack next to the barn. Cruz and Molly raced to her once the splitter was shut down and followed her every step as she stored the cut wood. When she had finished the first load, she paused for a drink. Molly rushed up beside her for some attention.

"I think you will love the smell of fresh wood chips," she told the small goat as she stroked down her neck. "One more load to split, and then I'll go harvest some veggies for dinner."

Eli split the second load of wood and was surprised to find one rack was nearly full with split logs. "Not bad for a morning's work," she said as she clapped her gloved hands together to knock off debris, then placed them on the tractor seat. Eli walked onto the porch for a large wicker basket Whit used to harvest vegetables and started toward the bridge. What she found was astonishing. Mitch and Evan had finished the railing on the bridge and were drilling holes into large blocks to support the shepherd hooks and solar lights.

"You guys are amazing," she said as she stepped onto the bridge deck.

Mitch looked at her with a broad smile on his face. "I think we did pretty danged good myself."

"I'd agree. This bridge is impressive work." She tried bouncing on her heels, but the bridge remained strong. "Very sturdy."

"Where are you off to?" Mitch asked.

"I'm going to raid Whit's garden. Anything in particular you'd like for dinner?"

"Some grilled corn and some sautéed squash and onions. Maybe some peppers to go on the steaks, too," Mitch added.

"Some of her pole beans if she has some ready," Evan said. "Whit grows some of the best ones around."

"All that sounds doable with a nice salad," Eli answered. "I'll be back."

Oscar, who had sprawled out in the sun watching the boy's work, jumped to his feet and followed Eli across the bridge. He sprinted ahead of her and leapt onto the front porch. "No, Oscar, not today, but she will be home tomorrow. I'm here to raid the garden."

Eli continued to the garden plot and was picking pole beans when she noticed Oscar weaving in between the corn stalks. "I know. I miss her too. Hopefully, she won't get called away anytime soon." Eli knelt and scratched beneath Oscar's chin. Eli plucked several ears of corn from their stalks and shucked the protective layers from around them, dropping them to the ground to return to nourish the soil. Eli worked her way through the garden, harvesting the items she planned to use for dinner, then latched the gate behind her once Oscar had rushed past.

"You know, I bet I could convince the boys to take a break from building to catch a few fish. I think everyone deserves a nice treat tonight." Oscar licked his lips and ran ahead of her over the bridge. "I bet he's going to tell the others to ruin the surprise." She laughed to herself.

Mitch and Evan had finished packing their tools into the Gator and were admiring their handiwork when Eli returned across the bridge.

"Y'all did a wonderful job," she praised as Mitch stepped forward to take the basket of vegetables from her.

"I agree," Mitch replied. "We think we did a pretty dang good job."

"I was wondering if I could ask you two for something," Eli said.

"Sure. What's up?" Evan replied.

"I'm not sure what you have planned next, but do you think you two could catch a couple of fish so I can treat all the cats tonight?"

Mitch smiled at Evan. "Just give us time to set the posts at the wood mill site, and we will more than gladly catch a mess of fish for our feline fur babies."

"Good deal. Everyone will eat well tonight," Eli said as they walked toward the Gator.

"Hop in. We'll give you a ride, and I'll carry the basket inside for you," Mitch told her.

When they arrived at the barn, Mitch took a look at the stacked wood. "You did a great job on that split wood. I guess we'll have to make some additional racks."

"That splitter worked like a dream," she told them. "I can't imagine how many hours of labor that thing will save me."

"More than enough to pay for itself," Evan said. "Do you want me to put the auger bit on the tractor while you carry that in for Eli?"

"Sure. I'll be back in a jiff. Then we can fish while the posts are setting. I've already moved the concrete over to the site."

"Good job. Let's get moving."

After Mitch carried the vegetables inside, Eli placed them near the sink, washing them and preparing them for their dinner. She periodically looked out the window to watch Mitch and Evan working. Evan had become a good friend in a short time, and Eli was glad Mitch had someone close to his age to bond with in his new surroundings. They worked well together and shared a love of fishing. She finished tossing a salad and placed it in the refrigerator to chill. Eli put the beans on to cook while she chopped the mushrooms, squash, and onions.

The boys had finished the last post when Eli placed the bowls of veggies in the fridge before cooking. She reached inside and spooned out a dollop of bacon grease to season the beans. Eli heard the tractor and Gator motors starting, and watched as the boys returned them to the barn for the evening. They both carried a fishing rod as they emerged from the barn.

She stepped out on the porch. "You sure you two aren't too tired to fish?"

"Nevah," Mitch declared. "There no such thing as being too tired when the fish are biting. How many do you want?"

"I think four decent sized ones will do. If you'll filet them, I can sauté them in some butter, and those cats won't know what hit them," Eli chuckled. "Have you seen Cruz and Molly lately?"

"We put Molly up and fed her for the evening. Cruz has been asleep on the porch for the last half hour," Mitch answered. "I think they finally played themselves out."

Eli turned to find Cruz curled up in one of the porch chairs.

"Why don't you grab a cold one and relax on the deck while we fish?"

"That's not a bad idea at all, Mitch. I think I just might."

Eli returned inside and dropped some kibble in Cruz's bowl and added a container of fresh drinking water. Tomboy was lazing on the arm of the couch. He lifted his head to check what she was doing then resumed his nap. She checked the beans and grabbed a cold beer from the refrigerator. As she slid the sliding glass door open, Cruz came rushing through the house. She took the chair next to Eli that was close enough for Eli to pet her as she relaxed.

†

After dinner, everyone was content. The cats sang a chorus of meows as Mitch and Evan approached with the pans of cooked fish. Tomboy, Oscar, and Walter ate their treat inside while Cruz settled for her kibble and some leftover steak.

Mitch rinsed the pans and stuck them in the dishwasher. "I don't think any of us will have a hard time sleeping tonight," he said. "Hard work and our bellies full of good food."

"All we need now is a hot shower and our comfy beds," Evan agreed. "That was a fantastic dinner."

"Thanks for all your hard work today. Whit is going to be so surprised when she gets home."

"It was pretty fun," Evan said. "I'll check with dad on the chainsaw mill when I get home. If it came in today, I'd bring it with me."

"No rush, you guys need to finish up early tomorrow so you can ready for your night out."

"We should be able to finish up by midday," Evan said. "The supports and roof should go up relatively easy. Maybe if we have time, we can assemble some drying racks for him in the barn with some of the leftover lumber."

"He is going to be so stoked." Mitch grinned.

"I reckon I'd better hit the road so that I can get this funk off me. Thanks again for a wonderful dinner."

"Thanks for all your hard work," Eli said.

"Leave the rest of the dishes, and I'll take care of them in a few minutes," Mitch said.

Eli was about to argue with him when her phone started ringing.

"See, you need to talk to the Love Muffin." He grinned, and followed Evan out the door as Eli answered and sat on the couch.

Whit was excited about coming home and promised to arrive before lunch. She and Eli shared a short conversation before Mitch returned, and Whit told her she was going to turn in early.

"I can't wait to see you," Eli said before signing off.

"Me too," Mitch hollered from the kitchen.

"Love you, too. Goodnight."

"It will be great having her back at home," Mitch told Eli as she walked into the kitchen.

"Yes, it will. Do you need help?"

"No, ma'am, I've got this. I'm going to take a long, hot shower and hit the sack."

"I'm going to sit down by the water for a little bit. I'll shower when you get done. Get a good night's sleep."

"Yes, ma'am, you too. Tomorrow's a big day."

"Yes, it is."

Eli took a beer from the refrigerator and walked out to the porch. Cruz followed beside her as she walked to the fire ring and took a seat. Cruz laid her head in her lap as Eli stared into the night sky. Her hand instinctively stroked Cruz's head as she enjoyed the night breeze. "Very peaceful, isn't it?" she asked Cruz.

Cruz let out a soft woof, and Eli could feel the dog wiggling under her hand.

Eli finished her beer and felt her eyes growing heavy. "It's time to call it a night, baby girl. Let's go."

Cruz trotted beside her as she entered the cabin and placed her bottle in the garbage. There was no sound coming from Mitch's room. Cruz ran ahead as she climbed the stairs for a shower and some sleep.

CHAPTER SEVEN

Eli woke early and carefully extracted Tomboy from his comfortable spot draped across her belly. After dressing, she crept down the stairs. Eli made a cup of coffee and walked out to the garden plot. The sun was barely beginning to light the horizon when she opened the gate and stepped inside. Eli walked between rows, stopping to inspect the growth and look for signs of insects or weeds. She was pleased with the progress of her vegetables and thought they could have crops to harvest by next month's end. The soil was moist, hydrated by the irrigation system Eli and Whit had installed using the western creek. She planned to finish the firewood today, and she would till the soil when Whit and Mitch started work on the solar system. It wasn't easy to tell which of them was more excited about the project.

Mark, Laura, and Brad would arrive at the end of next week. Eli knew it was essential to Mitch to have the sawmill set up for his dad's inspection. Eli planned to offer her assistance if Mitch and Evan needed her help. If not, she would continue chipping and bring logs down to split. Eli had developed a working rhythm and was pleased with her accomplishments the previous day. She would work until Whit came home, then spend the rest of the day with her. The thought of Whit coming home brought a smile to her face. She continued to walk the rows until her mug was empty, then walked to the cabin for a refill.

Mitch was making a cup for her when she entered the kitchen. "I figured you were ready for a second cup." He handed her the steaming mug.

"Did I wake you?"

"No, ma'am. I smelled the coffee so I knew you were up. Where'd you go?"

"I was checking the garden. The crops are growing well. We may have some veggies ready by the end of next month."

"It's going to be so cool to eat what you've grown. I know we can get whatever we need from Whit's garden, but it's not the same."

"I know what you mean. Hopefully, in a few years, the garden will produce as well as Whit's."

"I'm sure it will. I was going to have some cereal this morning. Do you want some?"

"I'll have a bowl with you," Eli answered.

"Coming right up," Mitch said and took bowls from the cupboard. He joined Eli at the table, and they chatted as they ate.

"What are you planning for today," Mitch asked?

"If you and Evan don't need me, I'll work on cutting more logs to split and chipping the rest of the brush."

"I think we can handle building the rest of the sawmill. I hope the mill has arrived from the warehouse, and he brings it out, so we can set it up and try it out."

"Do you want me to bring a few logs down to use for practice?"

"A couple of eight-foot ones would be great. We can cut some boards to build the drying racks."

"That won't be a problem. I plan on taking the afternoon off when Whit arrives."

"We won't work late either, so we can get cleaned up for date night. Are you planning to cook, or are you going to take Whit to the diner?"

"The diner does sound good. That's a great idea. Where are you guys going?"

"To a pizza joint Evan likes. He says it's the best in the area."

"Sounds encouraging. If it's a tasty spot, we may try it out sometime."

"Evan knows everywhere to go. Pays to be a local, I guess."

"You guys have turned into good friends."

"Yeah, he's a cool dude." Mitch grinned as he heard a vehicle approach.

"Sounds like cool dude just arrived." Eli stood and rinsed her empty bowl. "Hand me your bowl, and I'll stick it in the dishwasher."

Mitch hastily handed her his bowl and rushed to the door. "He has it," he hollered back to her when he opened the door.

"Great news," she answered, but Mitch had already rushed out the door. She chuckled as she rinsed the bowl and placed it in the dishwasher. It felt great to see Mitch excited about working hard. He'd probably still be in bed if he were at home, and he would waste the day playing video games with Brad. He had blossomed so much since their first trip.

Evan was a positive influence on him and was teaching him a lot about building.

When Eli walked outside, both young men were busy unloading Evan's truck. Cruz was following them step for step, but as soon as she saw Eli, she rushed to her.

"Let's go feed the crew."

Swarmed by cats as she filled the cat feeder, Eli then checked the supply of fresh drinking water. Cruz had opened the gate to Molly's stall and was licking her friend's face. Eli deposited a scoop of food in Molly's trough and walked through the barn to open the back door. Then she climbed in to start the tractor to warm up while she loaded the chainsaw, wedges, and ax in the bucket. She looked at Cruz. "You want to stay down here and play with the boys and Molly?"

Cruz cocked her head and rushed to her. Eli knelt and hugged the squirming dog. "Okay, I'll put Molly up for now, and you can ride on the tractor."

Cruz didn't need a second invitation, and as soon as Eli stood, she jumped into the tractor seat. Eli closed Molly in her stall as the playful goat looked up at her. "Don't worry. I'll send Cruz back for you soon."

Eli wanted to drop a few more trees for the sawmill project and firewood. She knew Cruz would remain seated in the tractor, but she couldn't rely on Molly staying out of danger from falling trees. Once she had them on the ground, she'd send Cruz back for her playmate, and they could run themselves silly.

A glance toward the sawmill site revealed Evan and Mitch assembling joists for the tin roof they would install to finish the covering. Mitch looked up and waved as she started the tractor toward the trail. Eli grinned at the sight of her John Deere hat on the gear shift and pulled it onto her head. "Now I'm all set," she told Cruz as they drove up the mountainside. Eli passed the area they had worked on the day before and pressed on to the edge of the clearing Eli had picked out for Mark's build site. There were six trees she wanted to fell to open up a pathway into the clearing. They were the perfect size for the logs she would take to Mitch and Evan. She pulled the tractor to a stop, and after servicing the chainsaw, put her sunglasses on.

"Back into the tractor for you, baby girl," she told Cruz, who jumped back into the tractor. "Stay," Eli commanded, and Cruz laid down in the seat. "Good girl."

Eli made quick work of felling the trees and trimming the branches. She measured out eight-foot sections and cut them to length. The rest she would use for firewood. Eli positioned the tractor and carefully loaded the logs into the bucket. She was rapidly working up a sweat even though the morning breeze was crisp, and the area was well shaded. After loading eight logs, Eli climbed back into the tractor.

"Okay, you can go get Molly." Cruz raced ahead of her and disappeared into the barn. When Eli passed the barn, Molly and Cruz rushed out and ran across the field. Evan and Mitch were working on the last joist when she pulled up to the mill. "Where would you like these?"

"You can drop them over there." Mitch pointed to the front of the compost bin. "You've been busy," he said after she lowered the bucket and dropped the logs.

"You're getting good with a chainsaw," Evan said. He and Mitch walked over to her.

"I'm getting some good practice with it," Eli replied.

Evan opened the cooler on his tailgate and handed her a Gatorade. "You look like you need this."

"Thanks." Eli took a long drink. "That hits the spot."

Mitch lifted one end of a log. "Those are heavy. I would have come up and loaded them."

"I needed a good workout." Eli laughed and flexed her arms. "I'm getting some guns."

"Quite impressive." Mitch flexed his muscles. "Now, these are guns."

"I'd bet pound for pound on Eli, my friend," Evan chimed in. "You may be bigger, younger, and stronger, but she's a force to be reckoned with."

Eli took a bow. "Well spoken, Master Evan." She chuckled. "It looks like you guys are ready to hang some tin."

Evan nodded. "Yes, ma'am. That shouldn't take long, and then we can set up the mill and give it a workout."

"We need to get some pictures of that to show your dad, but only after he sees the mill for himself. I'd hate to spoil the surprise. Do you have experience with one of these, Evan?"

"I've set up several for customers. This model is a jewel, and is easy to operate."

"I'm going to finish my chores, but call me when you're ready to cut so I can learn too."

"Yes, ma'am," Evan replied. "You heard the lady, let's get back to work," he teased Mitch.

"See ya in a bit." Eli climbed onto the tractor and started back up the trail. Cruz and Molly darted ahead of her at full speed. When she returned to the cutting site, she loaded the small branches for chipping into the bucket and deposited them at the chipper. Eli then returned to haul the remainder of the log sections down for firewood. She trimmed them in one to three-foot length and tossed them in the bucket. The shorter logs she would use at the fire pit and the longer rounds for the cabin. By the time cooler weather arrived, the wood would be seasoned and ready for the fireplace. Eli drove the tractor to the fire pit to unload the small logs, placing them in the small rack before stacking the longer sections next to the barn.

A glance at the mill revealed the backside of the tin was in place, and Mitch and Evan were beginning on the front half. Eli had a small pile of brush to chip, and she'd have her chores finished. After storing the tractor in the barn, Eli walked back to the chipper and started the motor. The hungry blades chewed into the branches, and she was almost done with the pile when the trees started swaying. Eli looked up to see a large Blackhawk helicopter passing low overhead. Whit was home, and her heart raced in her chest as she shut down the chipper and started down the mountain.

When she passed the barn, the chopper had landed, and Eli could hear Cruz barking at the strange machine. Whit had emerged and knelt to call Cruz to her. Eli locked eyes with her when Whit looked up in search of her, and smiles grew on their faces.

"Good morning, ma'am," a soldier greeted Eli as she approached.

"Good morning, sir. Welcome back, and thank you for returning Dr. Brewer safely."

"Our pleasure, ma'am. With your permission, we agreed to take Mitch and his friend for a spin around the mountain. Is that okay with you?"

Eli looked at Mitch, who was about to burst at the seams. "I'd probably be shot if I declined your offer. Thank you for giving them a ride."

"Yes." Mitch cried out and pumped his fist in the air. "Let's go, Evan."

"Thanks, Lieutenant." Whit took her bag from him. "Just don't let them drive."

The man chuckled. "I don't think Uncle Sam would approve. We'll be back shortly. Thanks again, ma'am, for your service."

"Thank you for everything you do for our country," Whit answered.

Whit and Eli backed away from the chopper as Mitch and Evan climbed into a harness. They waved as the helicopter lifted slowly from the ground and started toward town.

Eli leaned down to kiss Whit. "Welcome home." She took the bag from Whit and slipped her arm around Whit's shoulder as they walked toward the cabin.

"You all have been busy," Whit said as they walked. "Look at all that firewood. You should be all set for the winter." She chuckled. "How did you get all that split so perfectly?"

"I bought a log splitter and a chipper while you were gone. I figured the equipment would be useful to have around here. Split those logs like they were carving through butter."

"Impressive. Is that the sawmill the boys were working on?"

"Yes, it looks like they have all the tin on the roof and are in the process of setting up the mill. I brought some logs down that they will cut boards from to build some drying racks for the barn." She kissed Whit again. "They've been working hard."

"It looks like you all have."

Oscar must have heard Whit's voice, and he came running out of the barn. "Hey, there, old man." Whit leaned down to scoop him in her arms, kissing the top of his head. "Have you been behaving yourself?"

"Everyone has been doing well. Oscar and Walter have decided to join Tomboy and the rest of us in the house. They all got a treat of fresh-caught fish last night."

"Spoiling them rotten." Whit stroked the top of the cat's head. "It's so good to be home and to see you."

"We've all been anxious for your return. The boys are double dating tonight, so I thought we might go to the diner, if that's good for you."

"That sounds perfect. I need a sandwich to hold me over, though. I'm starving."

They climbed the steps to the cabin. "If you want to take your bag upstairs, I'll start on some sandwiches. I know the boys will be ready to eat when they return. It was nice of the pilots to offer the boys a ride."

"They wanted to before, but we were so pressed for time. I think the crew was eager to see more of the area today before returning to the city."

"It's so different than the concrete jungle." Eli watched her start climbing the stairs before walking to the kitchen. Eli had made several sandwiches when she heard the rumble of the rotors in the distance. "Do you think they would have time for a sandwich?"

"I think we should make them a plate of sandwiches with chips and drinks. They probably can't stay, but they could eat on the return flight."

"Grab a bag of chips and three drinks while I load the sandwiches," Eli said.

Whit and Eli emerged from the cabin as the chopper touched down. Cruz and Molly decided to stay on the porch as they delivered the sandwiches to the crew.

"Thanks again for a wonderful ride," Mitch said as he stepped off the platform. "That was awesome."

"Our pleasure," the soldier answered. He smiled at the stack of sandwiches Eli was handing to him. "Those look delicious. Thank you."

"Have a safe trip back, and I hope it will be a while before I see you again," Whit said.

"No way," Mitch answered. "He's going to come back to go fishing when he gets some leave."

"Vacation is fine, and you're always welcome here." Whit handed him the chips and drinks.

"Thanks again," he said. They watched as he stepped inside the helicopter, and the pilot took flight once they were a safe distance away.

"That was freaking awesome," Mitch told them.

"It was pretty amazing," Evan added. "A different view from the air."

"Yes, it is," Whit agreed. "Are you two hungry?"

"I could eat," Evan replied.

"Always." Mitch grinned. "Can we eat some lunch and then take a ride in the Gators?"

"I think that sounds perfect. Then y'all can get that mill set up, and Evan can teach us all how to use it."

"It shouldn't take much longer. We should get the boards cut, and Mitch has the plans for building the racks. I think my dad is missing me at the store."

"We appreciate all your help. Your dad probably misses spending time with you." Eli smiled at him. "You're welcome to come out at any time, and I hope we see a lot of you this summer."

"You can bet on that, if for nothing else, some good fishing."

"I promise not to work you too hard when you do show up. I do want to try to cut the hayfield this summer, though."

Evan looked at Eli. "Are you planning on buying some livestock, or do you want to sell the hay?"

"I haven't decided yet, but it probably won't happen until next year. There's so much else that I'd like to accomplish first."

"I'll keep my ears open for a customer to buy the hay. That shouldn't be a problem."

"Thanks, Evan. How many sandwiches do y'all want?"

Mitch looked at Evan. "I think two apiece will hold us over until we go out to eat."

Evan nodded. "Yeah, that should do."

They had reached the cabin. Whit opened the door for the group. "Go wash up, and we'll build some sandwiches."

Eli followed them inside and refilled the water bowl for the animals. Whit had spread out a dozen slices of bread and was adding condiments and meat.

"Will you eat more than one?" Whit asked.

"Nope, I want to save room for some dessert tonight." Eli made a rubbing motion across her stomach.

"That works for me. Maybe we can make a shopping list and pick up a few things after we eat. Your supplies are running low."

"We've been working pretty hard this week. Shopping would be a good idea, though, and help us walk off dessert."

"That's the spirit." Eli walked behind Whit to take paper plates and a bag of chips from the pantry.

The boys settled around the table and made quick work of the sandwiches and chips. "Why don't y'all bring the Gators around while we tidy up here," Eli suggested.

"Yes, ma'am," Mitch said, and Evan followed him out the door.

"They seem pretty excited. I'm wondering if it's the mill or the date night that has them fired up?" Whit chuckled.

"Maybe a bit of both. Let's get moving. I could use a shower before we head out for our date night, too."

"I can tell you've been working hard. Even your cap has a salt stain." Whit used the bill of Eli's cap to pull her lips down for a kiss."

"It feels so good to see how much gets accomplished. Let's go meet the boys."

As they stepped onto the ground, Mitch climbed in with Evan. "You can drive," Eli said.

Evan started up the mountain path with Whit right behind him. When they came in sight of the bridge, Mitch turned in his seat to look at Whit."

Whit pressed the brake on the Gator. "What on earth?"

"They wanted to build a more secure way to cross over to your property than that old log."

"Oh my gosh. You two did this?" Whit stepped out of the Gator and walked to the bridge.

"Most of it. Eli helped with the logs, braces, and some chippings," Mitch said.

"They did all the hard work," Eli chimed in.

"This is amazing. Solar lights too?"

"That was Eli's idea and contribution. We wanted to build this for you for all you have done for all of us," Evan stated.

Eli saw tears welling in Whit's eyes as she surveyed the bridge. "Go ahead and try it out," she suggested, giving Whit a chance to compose herself.

Whit walked back and climbed into the Gator. "Hop in," she said when she drove to the edge of the bridge.

Eli and the boys piled in, and Whit drove the Gator across the bridge. "Wow, this feels solid," she said as they drove onto her property.

"The lights illuminate it well at night, too, so when you come home from working in the lab, you won't run off into the water." Mitch grinned when Whit smacked him on the leg.

"I don't drive that bad."

"How do you know I was talking about you?" He winked at Eli.

"Point taken," Whit said with a chuckle. "This is great."

"Hey, while we're over here, drive down and check your mail. I haven't checked it in a few days," Eli suggested.

The drive was much smoother since Eli had graded it out with the tractor. "This ride doesn't jar your teeth out anymore," she told Eli.

Mitch hopped out and jogged to the mailbox. He pulled out several mail flyers. "You haven't been working Mr. Henry too hard," he huffed as he handed Eli the small stack of paper.

"More fodder for the compost bin," Whit said and spun the Gator back toward the house. She drove across the bridge and stopped at the empty Gator. "I can't begin to thank you two enough for this."

"It was a pleasure to be able to build this for you. I've wanted to build a bridge since I was little," Evan said.

"Y'all did a fantastic job, and it will survive for years. Thank you both."

"Are you ready to mill some wood?" Mitch asked.

"Let's put the Gators away, and we can help set it up."

"We got this, Aunt Eli. Why don't y'all relax down by the water until we're ready?"

Whit was smiling at Eli. "I've got no problem with that. Just give us a holler when you're ready."

Molly and Cruz met them at the barn. They walked through the herd of cats as they made their way through the barn. "It looks like everyone has settled in well," Whit said. Cajun let out a meow from the hayloft. "Yes, I see you lording over your kingdom."

Cajun stretched, pleased that Whit had addressed him and curled into a ball for a nap.

Eli reached for Whit's hand, and they walked down to the fire pit. Whit spotted the full wood rack. "You brought in all this wood?"

"Yes, ma'am, I did."

"I'm very impressed with the amount of work you all have done since I've been away. The place is shaping up well." She sat next to Eli. "Do you think Mitch is ready to take on the solar project?"

"I would think so. Mitch and Evan unloaded the last of the supplies you ordered earlier in the week. I believe they have plans to take the girls fishing tomorrow, so maybe plan to start Monday."

"That works for me. What other plans do you have for next week?"

"I thought I'd till the garden while you all are working on the solar system. After that, I plan to open up the trails a bit and cut the fallen trees into useable sections. If nothing else, we can use them for kindling or fire pit wood." Eli smiled at Whit. "I also need to get some tomato cages. They are starting to grow."

"Count how many you need. I think I have a few that aren't in use. We can take a drive over to the barn in the morning and get those and make a run to town for the rest."

"Are you pleased with the bridge?"

"Oh, my goodness, yes. That will make life much easier, not to mention safer crossing between the properties."

"They are very proud of themselves. Mitch can't wait for his dad to come up."

"Mark and the rest of the family will be here soon, right?"

"I expect them any time after Thursday. I think they are going to call in sick to work."

"I don't blame them. I know Mark is itching to get here. I wouldn't be surprised if they drive up Thursday night. We can check in with him this weekend."

Whit reached over to hold Eli's hand. "I guess we'd better make a good shopping list."

Eli ran her fingers over Whit's knuckles. "Naw, we can get some basics and then shop mid-week. I don't want to spend your first night home, buying and storing groceries."

"What did you have in mind, Miss Fortner?"

"Something that has nothing to do with groceries." Eli chuckled until her laughter was interrupted by Mitch.

"We're all set to start milling," he called.

"Be right there," Eli hollered. "Our presence in the wood mill has been requested." She held out her hand to help Whit to her feet. "This is going to be fun."

They walked over to the mill and watched Evan and Mitch place a log in the carriage. Evan gave them a short lecture on the safe operation of the mill and how to shift the gauges to cut a variety of widths of boards. When he finished talking, he handed them safety glasses. "All set?"

"Oh, yeah," Mitch answered.

"I'll make the first few cuts, and then you can take over." Evan grinned at Mitch's excitement. "You'll need to show your dad how to run this, so pay attention."

"I'm all over it."

Within an hour, the boys had cut the logs Eli had brought them. The stack of two-by-four and two-by-six boards was impressive.

"Now that's a stack of boards," Eli said.

Evan pulled off his glasses. "Not finished wood, but it'll do for building the drying racks. We would need a planer to make it finished enough for real construction."

"Not to worry, dad has a planer and is good at using it. He started teaching Brad and me to use one a few years ago. You can bet that will be one of the first tools set up in the workshop."

"Should I go ahead and cut some logs for Mark? Do they need to dry a few days?"

"I think I'd wait until Wednesday or Thursday to cut some. That way, they aren't on the ground long," Evan recommended. "I don't think we have rain coming, so a few days should be okay. Especially since he will plane them into finished boards eventually." Evan looked at Mitch. "Do you want to carry these over to the barn, so they will be ready when you build the drying racks?"

Mitch nodded. "Yeah, that would be great. Then we need to call it a day and get ready for our dates."

"We can help, and then you two can get spiffed up," Eli teased.

After stacking the boards in the barn, Mitch, Eli, and Whit walked into the cabin while Evan headed home.

"Are you all set for clothes for your date? Do you need any help?"

"Thanks, Aunt Eli, but I've got this covered. I still had a new pair of jeans that you had ironed. I'm going to dust off my good boots and hit the shower."

"Okay, just checking." She couldn't help but grin at him. "Do you feel like helping me feed the animals?"

"Yeah, you've got me curious about the garden. Can we take a peek at it first?"

"Absolutely. Hey, Mitch, we're going shopping after dinner. Is there anything you need?"

"I could use some hygiene stuff. Can we have some spaghetti next week?"

"Sure can. Just make a list of what you need when you get dressed. Is Evan coming to pick you up?"

"Yes, he'll be here at six."

"You better get a move on then. You shaving?"

"Yes, ma'am," he answered.

"Okay, we'll see you in a bit. Love ya!"

"Love you, more."

"No way, man. Come on, Whit." Eli opened the door. Cruz and Molly met them on the porch. "Do you two want to go visit the garden?"

Whit stopped. "You'd better keep Molly out. She could eat up all your plants."

"Okay, they stay outside of the fence."

"Have you had any problems with rabbits or anything munching on the plants?"

"So far, no, but there are birds already nesting in the fruit trees."

Whit reached for Eli's hand. "That's not a problem. They will help keep the insects down."

"Look," Eli said, pointing to the creek bank. A doe and her twin fawns were taking a drink. "Cruz, stay," she commanded.

They watched for several minutes until the family crossed the creek and disappeared into the woods. "I can never get enough of that," Eli said.

"Keep your feeders full, salt licks out, and you will see them year-round."

Eli opened the gate to the garden. "You two have to stay out here," she told Cruz, who whined to follow her. "Go play with Molly before it gets dark."

Eli watched as Cruz caught the scent of the deer and trotted to the water's edge.

"You weren't kidding when you said things were growing well. You've already got blooms on the squash and cucumbers. Baby tomatoes, too."

Eli watched with pride as Whit inspected the growth in the garden. "Between the two gardens, I don't think we will starve."

"Very unlikely," Whit replied. "I counted twenty tomato plants. I think I may have ten cages we can use. Do you want to work on that tomorrow while the boys are gone fishing?"

"That would be great. I'd also like to ride up the mountain and mark some trees to cut for the mill, and you can help me decide if we should widen the trails or not."

"That will be a fun and relaxing day. I think we both need that." She reached for Eli's hand. "Let's go feed the critters, and check on Mitch."

After filling the feeders and putting Molly away for the night, Eli and Whit returned to the cabin. Mitch was busily making a shopping list. "Is there anything else, in particular, you would like to eat next week? Give some thought to what we want when the family is here too. I'll go back shopping mid-week for that."

"If you'll get the fixings, I'll grill us some bacon cheeseburgers tomorrow night. We also need some fresh bread and deli meats for sandwiches."

"Homemade burgers do sound nice. I think I'll grill some chicken and fresh veggies too."

"It looks like I have plenty to harvest," Whit said.

"I know Mark is looking forward to some homegrown veggies. He swears the food grown up here is so much better."

Whit nodded. "It is, the soil is much sweeter here than most places."

"Brad and I can catch up some fish while they're here, and we can do a fish fry one night."

"That's always a big hit. I think I'll get a Boston butt or two that your dad can use to break in the Big Green Egg grill."

"Now, we are talking. Do you think I could invite Evan and the girls out for the butt?"

"I would like that very much. Say Saturday night?" Eli suggested.

"That sounds great."

"You look rather handsome, by the way. You clean up pretty well."

Eli watched a blush rise to his face.

"I hope Jessie thinks so."

"Are you still planning to take them fishing tomorrow?"

"Yes, ma'am, Evan's already got a spot picked out. We're going to cook whatever we catch for our picnic. Hey, that reminds me, could you whip up a batch of hushpuppy mix for us to take?"

Eli returned his smile. "Yes, I'll put it together in the morning so it will still be fresh."

"Thanks, Aunt Eli. You're the best." Mitch bent down and kissed her cheek.

They heard Evan pull up in the drive. "You two have fun tonight. I promise to be quiet when I come in."

"You guys have a good time and stay safe. Tell Evan he's more than welcome to stay the night if it's late when y'all return."

"Will do. Love y'all," Mitch said.

Before Eli could answer, Whit chimed in. "Most," she said.

Eli and Mitch broke out laughing. "Yep, she's part of the family now. See ya!" Mitch left the cabin, and Eli watched him trot out to Evan's truck.

"You love that kid just a little bit, don't ya?" Whit teased.

"As if I birthed him myself. We've always had a good relationship."

"You would make a good mom. Have you ever considered it?"

"Being a mom? No, not really. Have you?"

"Sometimes. I see how the two of you interact, and I wonder what it would be like to have a little one of our own."

"I'd have no problem helping to raise a little one," Eli answered. "It's something we need to think about."

"I'd like that. I'm getting hungry. Are you ready to get showered and dressed to go to town?"

"Would you care to join me?" Eli held out her hand to Whit.

"I thought you'd never ask." Whit took her hand, and they walked upstairs.

CHAPTER EIGHT

The meal at the diner was spectacular, and Eli went overboard at the grocery store, filling two carts with food and supplies. By the time they returned home and stored their purchases, it was nearly ten.

"Why did you let me buy so much?" Eli teased as she closed the pantry door.

"We weren't even hungry after that meal." Whit shrugged. "I don't know what got into us." She giggled.

Cruz trotted back inside after emptying her bladder. "I know we were gone a lot longer than we expected." Eli took out a dog treat and gave it to Cruz.

Whit looked at Eli. "I don't know about you, but I'm exhausted. That fabulous shower was a lovely welcome home surprise. Would you be disappointed if we just crashed tonight?"

"Heaven's no, as long as you are in my arms, I could never be disappointed."

"Let's get naked then," Whit said as she started toward the stairs.

Tomboy was already stretched out across the bed when they entered the room. "He's gotten spoiled sleeping in your spot."

Whit reached down to scratch under his chin. "Well, Mama's home now, so you're going to have to give up that spot."

His purring filled the room. "Somehow, I don't think he's buying it." Eli picked up her toothbrush and grinned at her lover.

"Enjoy your last few moments of leisure," Whit said and joined Eli in the bathroom. "You know, I think I'll call and order a coconut cream pie from the diner for this weekend."

"Uh, uh," Eli mumbled with a mouth full of toothbrush and paste. She lifted her hand and raised two fingers.

Whit laughed. "Okay, two it is."

Whit snuggled into Eli's warm body. "I missed you so much." Whit allowed her fingertips to caress Eli's skin.

"I missed you too. I hope it's a long time before the government calls you away again. I know what you do is important, but that doesn't make me miss you any less."

"It was so much harder for me this time, knowing I had you and Mitch waiting for me. I still can't get over how much you have accomplished here. That bridge is just amazing."

"Evan and Mitch are very proud of their work. I'm glad they have formed a friendship."

"Evan is a fine young man, and he appears to be a great influence on Mitch."

"He is. There have been several mornings when he's been up and about before I have started to stir. He's excited about the projects around here."

"I can't wait until we can get the solar panels functional. I love doing stuff like that." Whit snuggled in closer.

Eli stroked softly down Whit's arm. "What do you think of building some chicken coops? I know we go through a bunch of eggs."

"That's a great idea. Maybe that could be a project for Mark and the boys to try out his new sawmill."

Eli chuckled. "That's what I had in mind. Get several rolls of chicken wire, a heavy-duty staple gun, and several sets of wheels so we could make them portable."

"I like that. Not completely free-range, but the hens could help keep the insect population down around the gardens. I wouldn't mind having one around my place."

"Let's go to town and pick up some supplies and check on laying hens tomorrow while the boys are on their fishing date." Eli could feel the smile growing on her face as she daydreamed of chickens.

Whit fell silent, and Eli looked down to find her sleeping. She kissed the top of her head and turned out the light. Eli felt a movement on the bed and reached down to run her fingers through Tomboy's soft fur. "Goodnight, little boy," she whispered.

†

Eli was jarred awake by the shrilling ring of her cell phone on the bedside table. Whit had rolled away from her, so she reached over to pick up the phone. "One o'clock in the morning," she said and then saw the call was from Mitch. "Mitch, are you okay?" She had hit the speakerphone function, and Whit sat up when she heard his voice.

"Yes, everyone is okay. I just wanted to let you know I won't be in until late. We were coming back from dropping Jessie off when a buck decided to land on Evan's windshield. His windshield is trash, and he's got a few dents in the hood, but we are all safe. We were lucky he could pull off the road when we came to a halt."

"Oh my gosh," Eli cried out. "Nobody is hurt?"

"No, ma'am, not even the buck. He stood, shook his head a few times, and ran into the woods." Mitch chuckled. "Damn good-sized buck too."

"At least everyone is safe. Do I need to come and get you?"

"No ma'am, Evan's dad is on his way, and we're waiting on the tow truck. I'll be home after we've dropped Erin home. I didn't want you to worry."

"Thanks, Mitch. I'll see you when you get home."

"Okay, Aunt Eli. Love you."

"Most," Eli said and ended the call.

Eli sat on the edge of the bed, and Whit moved over to be beside her. She placed a comforting arm around Eli's shoulder. "You're trembling, Eli. Relax, Mitch, and the others are safe."

"I know, but my heart started beating crazy when I saw it was Mitch calling. I know he said everyone was fine, but my stomach still churned."

Whit reached over to turn on the light. She could see tears welling in Eli's eyes. "It's okay. Would you like me to start some coffee? I don't think either of us will sleep until he's home."

"Yes, please. I'll get dressed and be down in a minute." Eli could feel her body shivering from the inside as Whit stood and took the warmth of her body away. She pulled on a robe, then smiled as Whit left the room. Cruz stretched and looked at Eli. "I know it's early, but go on, and Whit can let you out."

Eli pulled on a pair of cargo shorts and a T-shirt, then slipped her feet into her comfortable boat shoes. She washed her face and ran a brush through her hair before going downstairs. She could smell the aroma of coffee as she descended.

Whit had already brewed a cup and handed it to Eli as she entered the kitchen. "Are you okay?"

Eli could see Whit's face full of concern. "Yes, just a bit of a shock to get a call like that. I'm okay, though. This coffee is great."

"Go sit on the couch, and I'll join you in just a minute."

Eli flipped the switch in the living room, and Walter and Oscar looked up at her, eyes blinking at the bright light. "Sorry, boys, I know it's early." She sat beside Walter curled up at the end of the sofa. Her hand stroked down his side, and Eli's reward was a loud purr. She smiled up at Whit when she sat down beside her.

"You know if we decide to have a child, there may be many nights we sit up like this, waiting for them to come home." She smiled at Eli. "Of course, that will be many years after we're up all night for two-hour feedings, diaper changes, and bouts of colic."

"I still think it would be worth it, even if it makes my heart pound out of my chest."

Whit placed her hand in Eli's. "I do too."

"Do you think I should call Mark and let him know what happened?"

"No, I'd let Mitch break that news to him. Everyone is safe, so I'd let Mark get his beauty sleep."

Eli started to chuckle. "I hope he sleeps for a while then."

"Aw c'mon now, Mark's a handsome guy."

"I know, but he'll always be my bratty baby brother."

"That you adore almost as much as his kids."

"True, but I'd never admit that to any of them."

Whit smirked. "I don't think that's necessary. They already know how much you love them."

"Yeah, I reckon they do. So, what should we do while we wait?" Eli grinned at Whit. "I'm kind of hungry."

"I'll make some biscuits if you'll cook us some meat. There is blackberry jelly in the fridge, and if you want eggs, I'll cook you some."

"Damn, that does sound good." Eli sipped her coffee. "Let's finish this cup, and we can start cooking. I bet Mitch will want something once he comes inside and smells your biscuits."

"You'd better cook sausage then so I can make Mitch gravy. You know how he loves it."

"Mitch. What about me? I love your gravy and biscuits."

Whit leaned over and kissed Eli. "For you, I will cook it anytime."

"I do love you. Your cooking, too."

Whit reached out and traced the small scar on Eli's head from her fall. "How are you feeling? I haven't remembered to ask you since I got home."

"I'm okay. I'm still a bit sensitive to bright sun, but the headaches are few and far between."

"Good. You gave me a huge scare with your fall from grace."

"You did such a fine job of doctoring me, I couldn't help but get better."

Cruz trotted back inside. She sprawled out with her head resting on Eli's foot. "Don't get comfortable. We're going to cook some breakfast in a few minutes."

Cruz let out an audible sigh but remained firmly in place.

"Maybe after Mitch gets home and we get some food in our bellies, we can go back to bed," Eli suggested.

"That's a great plan. Maybe sleep past the sunrise for a change. You stay here and finish your coffee, and I'll start on biscuits."

"I'll start the sausage in a few minutes. You can turn the flat top on to get it warm for me, please."

"You got it." Whit walked to the kitchen, and Eli could hear her in the pantry.

Eli looked at the clock on the mantle to find an hour had passed since Mitch called. Hopefully, he would be on his way home soon. She reached down to pet Cruz's head. "Time for this Mama to get busy too."

Cruz lifted her head and yawned before stretching back out on the rug. Eli chuckled. "You guys enjoy your nap." Walter blinked his green eyes at her.

When she walked into the kitchen, Whit was preparing the dough. She had swiped her hand across her cheek and left a trail of flour behind. Eli wet a paper towel and wiped it from her face. "You looked like you had war paint on," she teased.

Eli was removing the last sausage patty from the flat top when Cruz let out a soft woof. Eli looked out the kitchen window to see a truck approaching. She walked out the front door just as Mitch was climbing out of the truck. Evan had his window down. "I'm glad you're all okay. Thank you for bringing Mitch home."

"You're welcome," Evan's dad said. "That deer did a number on his windshield, but it all turned out. Glass can be replaced, but these kids can't."

"Amen to that. We're cooking up some breakfast if you'd like to join us."

"Thanks, Eli, but I'm ready for bed," Evan answered.

She could see the frown on his face, and she put a comforting hand on his arm. "Don't worry. Your truck will be good as new soon."

"I know. I've just never been so scared," Evan answered.

"It is scary, but your quick thinking kept everyone safe. For that, I am grateful. I don't know what I'd do without all the help you and Mitch have been around here."

"Thanks, Eli. That means a lot."

"Y'all still going fishing tomorrow?" Eli asked.

"I'm going to call him after we've both had some sleep. I can always use my truck to haul us around," Mitch said. "She ain't as pretty as yours, but she'll get us around."

Evan laughed and finally smiled. "Call me."

"Be safe driving home," Eli told them. "Lots more deer out and about."

"See ya," Evan replied, and they turned around.

Eli wrapped Mitch in a big bear hug. "Damn, you scared me."

"I know the feeling. I'm not sure this underwear will ever be the same." Mitch chuckled. When Mitch arrived at the door, he stopped. "Is Whit making biscuits and gravy?"

Eli grinned up at him. "Yes, she is."

"Awesome," Mitch said, and held the door for Eli.

A pan full of biscuits was cooling on the counter as Whit stirred the skillet of gravy she was making. "Did you ask him if he wanted eggs?"

"Nope. Do you want eggs, Mitch?" Eli asked.

"Could you whip up some scrambled with cheese?"

"I will if you bring down some plates and get biscuits buttered for all of us." Eli stepped around Whit and opened the refrigerator. "Hey, what do you think about helping your dad build chicken coops next weekend? As many eggs, as we eat, it would be helpful to have a good supply."

"I think it's a fantastic idea." Mitch pulled three plates from the cabinet.

"Great. Whit and I will go to town later today and pick up the chicken wire and some supplies. Do you think you will still go fishing?"

"I'd like too. Maybe just me and Evan, though. Hitting that deer got him pretty shaken up."

"If he still wants to go, why don't you bring him out here? He's always welcome. I hope he knows that."

"He does. He loves it out here. He said he might need to come work for you to help pay for the truck's repairs. I think he was joking, though."

"We can always find something for him to do," Eli replied.

"You know, my cabin and the lab could use a fresh coat of stain. I've been putting it off for a few years," Whit said. "If he's interested, I'd pay him for that."

Mitch leaned against the counter. "I think he'd jump all over that. Evan loves being out here. He hopes one day he'll own a place like this."

"I have no doubt he will." Eli mixed up the half dozen eggs in the bowl and added shredded cheese. "Scrambled eggs are coming up."

†

"I could get used to breakfast in the middle of the night," Mitch claimed as he finished his meal.

"That was pretty awesome, but don't think you need to give us a scare. We can cook it anytime. We cooked, so you can clean," Eli teased.

"Not a problem. I know you ladies need your rest." He chuckled. "Thank you for a great meal. I'll see you later."

"Get some rest." Eli reached for Whit's hand. "Let's see if we can get back to sleep."

123

Eli stripped out of her clothes while Whit hung her robe. "No more excitement for tonight," Eli said as she climbed into bed and took Whit in her arms.

"Spoon me," Whit requested.

"With pleasure." Eli wrapped her body around Whit and snuggled under the covers. "Heaven," she whispered in Whit's ear. "Love you."

"More," Whit responded and pulled Eli closer.

†

The sunlight coming through the window woke Eli. It was seven, and Whit softly snored next to her. She climbed from the bed, dressed, and walked downstairs for coffee. The clicking of Cruz's claws on the wooden floors echoed through the cabin. "Shhh," she whispered to Cruz, who trotted outside once the door opened. Eli made a coffee and walked down to the fire pit. The morning air was crisp against her skin as the rays of sunlight played through the overhang of leaves. The gentle ripple of the water sang to her as she relaxed and enjoyed the coffee. *I would have never imagined a year ago that I would be living out my dreams and be lucky enough to find Whit. In hindsight, Sara was wrong on so many levels. Her betrayal started everything in motion, and I've never been happier.*

Eli finished her coffee and walked down to the water's edge. She was watching fish as they swam, resting for several minutes in one of the pools before continuing the journey. She was concentrating and didn't hear the footsteps approaching.

"What ya looking for?" Mitch watched Eli jump and started to laugh. "I didn't mean to scare you." He handed her a fresh coffee and grinned. "Accept a peace offering?"

124

"You're lucky you were bearing coffee. You scared the bejesus out of me, twice in less than twelve hours."

"Sorry, Aunt Eli. I didn't mean to scare you at all. Is Love Muffin still in bed?"

"Yeah, she was sleeping soundly, so I decided to let her sleep in a bit."

Mitch kneeled beside her. "It's so beautiful here. I wish I could stay forever."

"You will always have a home here. When you finish school, you're welcome to move up permanently."

"I would like that. This place feels like home."

"I know what you mean. Hey, how did your date go?"

"It was going well until the deer incident. I like Jessie a lot. She enjoys fishing, and unlike the girls in Montgomery, she isn't afraid to get her hands dirty."

"What does she want to do after high school?"

"She plans on going to Western to become a school teacher. She loves kids and wants to be an elementary school teacher."

"There's nothing wrong with that. Does Jessie want to come back and teach here?"

"Yes, she does. She can always work with her dad and brothers at the dealership if she can't find a teaching job."

"What about you? Have you given more thought to what you want?"

Mitch scratched his head. "I'm still leaning toward mechanic school. Maybe her Dad can hire me to work on John Deere equipment."

"That's a good possibility. Are you going to ask Evan if he wants to come out to fish?"

"I thought I'd let him sleep in for a while."

"Whit was serious when she had a proposition for the two of you. She wants to see if y'all would be interested in staining her cabin and the lab."

"Oh, heck yeah. I know Evan's dad will pay for the repairs, but Evan would prefer to pay for it himself. That would be an excellent way for him to make some money. I'm not worried about money if she wants to pay him for the job."

"You know Whit won't do that. She'll pay you both for doing the work together." Eli stood and walked back to her chair. "I know Evan mentioned working for his dad next week, but maybe he can start the staining during the weekend."

"I'll call him and let him know Whit wants to talk to him."

"She is very impressed with the bridge y'all built. She's remarked about it several times already."

Mitch smiled. "It was a fun project."

"You should be proud of all that you've accomplished. I am proud of you. I still want to know what happened to the little boy who used to bounce on my knee."

"He grew so big he'd break your knee. I always hated to see you go home. You're like a second Mom, only cooler."

"You better not let your mom hear you say that. She'll skin us both."

"You know what I mean. Don't ya?"

"Yeah, I think I do. If I had a son, I'd wish him to be just like you."

Cruz trotted down to the water, followed by Molly. Cruz had let the goat out of her stall. When Eli looked up, she saw Whit headed toward them. "Good morning."

"Good morning, you two," Whit said as she took a seat. "I didn't know how long you've been awake, so I didn't bring you a refill."

Eli lifted her cup. "That's okay. I'm going to need to go get rid of some soon."

Whit settled back in the chair. "It's a beautiful morning, isn't it?"

"Yes, it's quickly becoming my favorite time of day. The air is still crisp and fresh." Eli cocked her head. "I just realized today is Sunday. The hardware store will be closed today, so we'll have to wait until tomorrow to get the wire and supplies."

"That's no problem. We still have time before the crew arrives."

"I can run to town while you two start the solar panel installation," Eli told Mitch.

"Oh, heck yeah. I can't wait," Mitch replied.

"So, what do you want to do today?" Whit asked.

"If the boys go fishing, we can mark some trees for culling, and spend the day on the mountain. Maybe check out the cave?"

Whit's head snapped up. "I had forgotten about that."

Mitch groaned. "Aw, man. I want to explore that cave."

"You can fish for a while and then join us at the cave. Do you remember how to get there?"

"Yeah, finding it again isn't going to be a problem."

"Then, that's the plan." Eli looked at Whit. "I'll fill a backpack with some sandwiches and snacks if you'll get the headlamps and a flashlight from the workshop." She then turned to Mitch. "If you get hungry, make a sandwich. Whenever you two want to join us, come on up."

Mitch nodded. "Just remember to take a cell phone, please. You may not have service, but at least we can try if needed."

"That's true, and it will double for a camera." Whit looked at her watch. "It's just a little past eight. Are you going to call your dad this morning?"

"Yes, but I don't want to tell him about last night. I'm okay, and I don't want him to worry unnecessarily."

Eli shrugged. "That's your call to make, but I'd recommend being honest with him. It won't be pretty if he finds out another way."

"That's a good point, Aunt Eli. Let me grab my phone, and we can call before they head to Mass."

They watched him disappear into the house. "I think that was good advice. I don't think Mark would take too kindly to finding out by accident."

Eli shook her head. "No, he wouldn't, and I don't want him to think he can't trust Mitch, or us for that matter. We've always had an open and honest rapport."

"I think I could go for another coffee. Care to join me?" Whit stood and reached for Eli's cup.

"Maybe one more." She smiled and gave Whit the empty cup.

"Make sure Mitch asks his dad what they want foodwise while they are here, so we know if we need to go shopping again. I'll be back in a few."

"I miss you already," Eli smiled.

Mitch passed Whit as he returned. "She reminded me to ask Dad about food. You think she's afraid we'll starve?"

"Nope, she just wants to be prepared."

Mitch called Mark and explained the excitement from the previous night. While concerned for his safety, Mark told Mitch he was glad he was honest with him. Mitch looked up to see Whit returning with coffee. "Aunt Eli wants to know what you want to cook while you all are here. She and Whit have already tried to buy out the store."

They could all hear Mark laughing at Mitch's comment. Mitch gave him the rundown of the major meals planned. "Yeah, I think we can plan to go to the diner for at least one meal," Mitch replied with a wink to Eli. Mitch's smile grew as he continued to talk with his dad. "Yeah, we love y'all,

128

too. Can't wait to see you." When he ended the call, Mitch said, "They'll be here late Thursday. Probably around ten."

"That's excellent news. I'm excited to see the crew," Eli answered.

"Me too. So, does it sound like we need more groceries?" Whit chuckled.

"No, I think you two have us well covered. Dad does want a return trip to the diner."

"That's easy. Maybe we can do that Friday night. I have a feeling he will want to mill some boards and maybe start building chicken coops. He's going to be so excited." Eli took a sip of her coffee. "I'm proud of you for being honest with your Dad."

"Like you, he was just glad that nobody was hurt. He understands the perils of driving in the country at night."

"He should. He hadn't had his driver's license for more than two months when he hit a wild hog. It tore the front of his truck up bad."

"Oh, snap. Dad's never shared that story with us."

"Maybe he will tell you about it after the run-in with the deer. You know we're so old, he may have forgotten." Eli chuckled.

Mitch grinned. "Yeah, maybe so. You didn't forget, though."

"You forget, I'm exceptional," Eli teased.

"That's true," Mitch agreed. "I'm going to text sleeping beauty and see if he's up yet."

"Okay." Eli looked at Whit. "Are you ready to get our gear together?"

Whit nodded. "Spray paint, flashlight, and headlamps. Correct?"

"Yes, ma'am. I'll pack a cell phone, snacks, and drinks," Eli replied.

Whit headed to the workshop as Eli and Mitch walked inside while he awaited a text from Evan.

"Send me a text if you can, before entering the cave. At least that way I'll know how long you've been inside."

"That's a good idea." Eli opened the pantry and pulled out some snacks and fruit, placing them inside a small backpack.

Mitch chuckled. "You're going on a short trip, not a three-day adventure."

"I know, but I have a nephew who will probably get hungry before we return." Eli punched him in the arm.

"Good point. No need for me to lug stuff up the mountain if you've already taken care of it." He chuckled.

"Exactly." Eli turned when she heard Whit approach. "Will you put Molly up? Cruz will be fine on the trail, but I don't want Molly wandering off."

"You got it. Come on, Cruz, let's go put your buddy up for now."

"Check the feeders if you will, please."

"Yes, ma'am."

Eli smiled at Whit. "I've got to get rid of that coffee, and then I'll be ready to go."

"That's not a bad idea," Whit agreed.

Mitch was emerging from the barn when Eli and Whit left the cabin. "I'm going to pick Evan up. I think he's more excited about the cave than fishing if you can believe that."

"Oh, I can believe that," Whit answered. "Good fun, exploring a cave."

Mitch put his hands on his hips. "Humph. Are you implying it's not fun to fish?"

"Not at all, but you can walk out of your house to fish. You have to hike up to the cave to explore," she explained.

"Okay, I'll let you off the hook. This time," Mitch warned with a grin. "Please be safe, and we'll see you in a few hours if not before."

"Will do. You drive safe." Eli smiled and reached for Whit's hand.

"Love you," Mitch hollered.

Whit looked at Eli and nodded. "More," they yelled back in unison and then disappeared onto the trail. They could hear Mitch laughing for several seconds.

CHAPTER NINE

The fresh breeze carried the scent of mountain laurel and spruce as Eli and Whit walked up the trail. They stopped at the former worksite, and Eli showed Whit the chipper and the massive mound of chippings she had made from the small limbs from the trees and brush.

"That will help the compost bin, and you can use it in Molly's stall, too, as extra bedding. The more fragrant chips you can use around the fire pit."

Eli looked at Whit. "There's a use for almost everything here, isn't there?"

"Pretty much. There's an abundance of plants that you can transform for medicinal purposes as salves and anti-inflammatory treatments. In addition to the wild berries, there are herbs and mushrooms we can gather to supplement our cooking."

Eli shrugged. "I'll have to rely on your expertise for that. I'd hate to poison us with the wrong mushroom."

"I've got some handbooks you can read that help you to identify plants that grow native here."

"I'd like that," Eli replied. Cruz was tracking a scent near the pile of chips, and she trotted ahead of them after her prey. "Don't wander off too far," Eli called after her.

They continued to walk until they reached the orchard. The nut trees were growing well. The irrigation system was doing a great job of keeping the soil moist around them. "I love how things proliferate here."

"It's the fertile soil, moderate temperatures, and rainfall that the region receives. It also helps to choose good stock grown from this area."

Cruz came back when they returned to the path. Eli pointed out a few small trees. "I'd like to take these out to make the trail just a bit wider up to the building site I've picked out for Mark."

Whit used the paint can to mark a bright orange spot on the trunks of the trees Eli had selected. "When do you think Mark would like to begin building?"

"Probably a year or so down the road. I have a plan I'd like to discuss with you. Maybe it will help to sweeten the pot for Mark."

"That sounds devious. Do tell."

As they walked farther into the field, Eli pointed toward the western creek. "Just across the water, there is a decent drive that goes down to the highway. When Mitch returns home to finish school, I'd like to begin work on the cabin." She pointed to a narrow portion of the creek. "I'd like to have a full load-bearing bridge constructed for the contractor to use. I don't want all that heavy equipment passing our home every day."

"That makes good sense. So, you're going to keep it a secret if you're planning to wait for Mitch to leave?"

"I love him dearly, but I don't think Mitch could keep that secret until Christmas. That's when I'd like to gift them the keys to their new home. If it's here waiting for them, that might influence their decision."

"You are sneaky, but I love it. Mark already has the plans drawn up, doesn't he?"

"Yes, I gave them to one of the builders you suggested. He doesn't foresee any issue with having it ready by Christmas if he can start in early August."

"What about the drive and bridge?"

"We can start on that anytime. I'll tell Mitch we are putting in a second means of egress for when they do start building. It's the truth."

"Yes, it is. I think it's a wonderful plan." Whit kissed Eli. "You are so thoughtful. That makes me love you even more."

"I love you, too." They continued to walk toward the creek. "Where do you think the bridge would work best?"

Whit helped her pick out the location for the bridge, marking the trees that needed removing. "More firewood to cut and split," Whit said.

"I don't reckon we can have too much firewood. Can we?"

Whit chuckled. "Not unless you go Chainsaw Massacre crazy with your saw."

Eli broke out laughing. "No chance of that. With the trees we've marked for culling and the ones already on the ground, we will have more than ample firewood."

Whit pointed out a tree. "There are several standing dead trees Mark will probably want to use for lumber. They make excellent boards."

"Are you ready for some spelunking?" Eli asked.

"So, ready," Whit answered.

Eli shouldered her backpack, and they started up the ridge. "I love how it always stays cool on the trail. The canopy blocks the sun and heat from bearing down on us."

"There will be plenty of heat and sun for you as the summer arrives, but nothing like you're used to in Florida."

"I sure won't miss the humidity," Eli added.

"I bet it can get overwhelming down there. Do you plan on going back anytime soon?"

"Maybe at the end of the summer after the tourists have returned home. The traffic can get horrible, especially at the beach during the summer. Would you like to go?"

"I've never seen the Gulf of Mexico," Whit replied. "I've been to the Outer Banks, but that's it for beaches."

"I will show you the beautiful sugar white sands of the Gulf beaches if you'll show me the Outer Banks."

"You, my love, have yourself a deal."

They reached the trailhead and turned left. The sun was nearly overhead when they reached the clearing in front of the cave. "Would you like a snack and something to drink before we go in?"

"That's a good idea." Whit grinned when Eli pulled two sausage biscuits out of her pack. "Where did those come from?"

Eli smirked. "I hid them behind the milk jug so Mitch wouldn't see them. They are left over from our early breakfast."

"You are so sneaky, but I love it." Whit unwrapped a biscuit and took a bite, then smiled. "You added jelly, too."

"Yes, ma'am, I did. Isn't it about time to start hunting for more wild blackberries?"

"It most certainly is. Maybe this week. I should have some bushes around the garden that may also be ripe. Are you implying we need to make some jelly?"

"Jelly, pies, pancakes. Whatever works for you," Eli said. She opened a bottle of water and took a long drink, then offered the bottle to Whit.

"It will take Mitch and me several days with the solar panels. Maybe after you've finished the tilling, you can harvest some berries. I think I have plenty of recycled jars, but I'll need you to pick up some fruit pectin, sugar, and lids."

"If you'll make a list, I'll get them tomorrow when I go into town for chicken wire and hardware. Do you want me to pick up some stain samples while I'm there?"

"That would be fantastic." Whit popped the last bite into her mouth. "That was tasty."

Eli sent a text to Mitch. *Going in.*

She bent to place her phone back in the backpack and was surprised when her phone pinged with a text. *See you in a bit.*

"Well, we at least have text capabilities from up here," she told Whit.

"Probably high enough to hit the towers with little interference." Whit placed the empty bottle in the backpack, slung over Eli's shoulder.

Eli handed her a headlamp, then pulled one over the brim of her cap. "All set?"

"Waiting on you." Whit grinned.

As they approached the mouth of the cave, Cruz trotted over to them. Eli looked at Whit. "What do you think? Should she go or stay?"

Cruz looked from Eli to Whit. Whit laughed softly. "I can't resist that look. Let her come with us."

"You heard the lady, Cruz, let's go."

As they entered the cave, Whit looked around. "I wouldn't have thought it would have been this big."

"You know it won't hurt to mark our turns, just in case we get disoriented," Eli said. "It appears to go pretty deep into the mountain."

Once they moved from the entrance, the sunlight disappeared, and they both turned on their headlamps. "This feels a little spooky," Whit admitted.

"You don't have to go if you feel creeped out."

"No, I'm okay, just keep your gun handy."

Eli reached down, releasing the catch on the holster that would allow for a quick draw if needed. "All set."

Cruz walked in front of them but did not move out of the light's reach. When she got close to the edge, she would slow to wait for them to catch up. As they approached the first split, Eli asked, "Which way do you want to go? I've been into the right wing, and it splits again about one hundred feet in."

"Left then?" Whit asked.

"Sure." They turned left, and Whit made a small arrow on the wall to mark their direction.

"I'm glad you remembered."

A few minutes later, they reached the end of the tunnel. They had seen evidence of charcoal left from an extinguished fire. There was no way to determine the age of the activity. Nothing was remaining to give them any further clues of who had used the tunnel for shelter.

"Dead end," Eli said. "Let's head back to the right wing."

As they entered the tunnel leading into the right wing, Eli noticed markings on the walls. She wasn't able to illuminate the space before, so she had turned around and exited from this point. With two powerful headlamps, the walls came to life. Quartz crystal in the walls reflected the light into the room.

"Wow," Whit whispered in response to the images. "This is Cherokee artwork. That's an Eagle Dancer," she explained as she pointed to a solitary figure with an eagle's head and feathers adorning both arms.

"Mr. Henry said some Cherokee warriors had taken refuge here while they were making attacks on the soldiers who were marching their people on the Trail of Tears. Severely outnumbered, they killed many soldiers before the army tracked them down, and many died here."

"Their struggles are captured here," Whit said as she pointed to a colorful area. "Soldiers in blue coats rode horses while native women, children, and elders were herded like cattle. Clan members forced to march quickly regardless of the weather. It didn't matter their age or sex; if they couldn't keep up, the soldiers shot them."

Eli frowned. "It's horrible they experienced such cruel treatment. The lands, their homes, dignity, and many lives stripped from them due to the white man's greed and ignorance."

"It wasn't the best decision made by a new nation. The tribes still struggle to survive on reservations that do not support their way of life. If the government finds a way to profit, they make no qualms about taking more of their lands." Whit brushed a tear from her cheek.

Eli stepped forward and wrapped her lover in a warm embrace. She held her for several long seconds until Whit said, "What is that?"

Eli turned to look at what Whit was indicating. The entrance to another cavern had begun to pulse with blue light. "That's odd. It wasn't like that before."

"No, it wasn't," Whit agreed and began walking forward.

Eli rushed to catch up to her, and they walked toward the brilliant light.

Whit gasped as they stepped into the room. Hundreds of blue crystals buried in the rock walls glowed brightly. She turned in a circle to take in the scope of the room. She stopped suddenly and said, "On no," then proceeded to faint.

Eli, who had been watching Whit closely, moved quickly to catch her falling body and eased her to the ground.

"Whit," she called out and tried to arouse her lover. Eli was startled by the rapid sideways movement of Whit's closed eyes, indicative of REM sleep. *There's no way she could be in REM mode so quickly, but it appears she is dreaming.*

The light in the area began to dim as one by one, the crystals faded out. Disturbed by the growing darkness, Eli picked Whit's body off the ground and rushed back to the cave entrance. Relief flooded through her when she saw daylight, and Eli rushed to the boulder where they had sat earlier and placed Whit on the warmed rock. She dropped the backpack to the ground and pulled her shirt over her head. Eli poured fresh water on her shirt and began to pat Whit's face while calling her name. Eli could feel the hot rush of tears as they burned down her cheeks.

"Whit, darling, please wake up."

Cruz, who had rushed ahead of them, started barking.

†

"Is that Cruz?" Evan asked as he and Mitch hiked up the trail.

"Yes, something's going on," Mitch said as he took off in a full sprint.

Evan caught up with him quickly, and they came to a sliding halt when they reached Cruz and saw Whit lying on the boulder.

Eli looked up at the sound of their approach, and Mitch could see the tears running down her face and the look of worry in her eyes.

"What happened?"

"We were inside the cave, and something peculiar happened, and Whit passed out."

"What can we do?" Evan asked.

"I'm trying to rouse her," Eli answered.

†

They were all standing over her when she gasped a deep breath. Whit's eyes began to flutter, and finally opened. She stared up at them.

"What's going on?" she croaked out in a whisper.

"You passed out on me," Eli said. She handed her a bottle of water. "Take a sip."

Whit took a drink. Her throat felt parched. She looked at Eli and saw that she'd been crying and she was very pale. Whit reached up and brushed back a tear.

"I'm okay. Will you let me sit up?"

Eli and Mitch took a hand and raised her to a seated position. "Thanks, that's much better. What the hell happened?"

"That's what we'd like to know," Mitch said. "I can't leave you two unattended without something going on," he teased, but Whit could see the worry in his face.

"We were exploring the cave. We had stopped in the right wing to admire the artwork painted on the walls. All of a sudden, the rear of the cave we were in started to pulse with blue light, indicating another opening deeper in the mountain."

"Artwork?" Mitch asked.

"Cherokee. Marking the Trail of Tears, we think," Eli explained.

"So, what made you pass out?" Evan asked.

"I'm not entirely sure, but I felt compelled to approach the light. Suddenly, I felt a wave of emotion pulse through me, and I was looking up into three worried faces the next thing I knew." She forced a smile.

Mitch looked at Eli.

Eli shrugged. "When she passed out, the crystals in the walls began to fade and go out. The sudden darkness was spooking me, so I grabbed Whit and rushed out here."

"Are you feeling okay?" Mitch asked Whit.

She nodded. "Yes, I am."

"Are you okay if Evan and I go take a look?"

"Yes, take these." Eli handed them the headlamps. "Be careful." She also took her pistol and offered it to him. "Just in case."

Eli sat down next to Whit, and they watched Mitch and Evan disappear inside the cave. Cruz trotted along behind them.

"What happened?" she asked Whit.

"I'm still trying to wrap my head around it. Can we talk later? I don't want to freak the boys out. I'm okay, so you don't need to worry."

"I'll trust you on that. You scared the crap out of me."

"I'm sorry, but you'll understand later. I promise."

†

"This place is awesome," Mitch said as his headlamp illuminated the artwork on the walls.

"Yeah, it is," Evan replied as his fingers traced the wall. "I don't see any glowing lights in here, do you?"

"No, but Eli said it was a separate opening at the back of this one."

"Let's go then," Evan replied. He started walking to the rear of the cave.

Mitch followed him through a short passage into a new cavern. It was completely dark when they entered. He could see Cruz sniffing something on the ground.

Evan walked forward, and his foot landed on something. "What the heck?" He bent down and picked up a light blue crystal.

"It's warm." He handed the object to Mitch.

"The air is chilly in here, but you're right, this does feel warm." Mitch looked down. "There are more," he said. He aimed his headlamp at the base of the wall.

"There must be a hundred or more," Evan said. He bent down and picked up several crystals. "These are warm too."

Mitch retrieved several of the crystals, filling the pocket of his shorts. "Do you recognize these?"

Evan shook his head. "I've never seen anything like these before. They are such a unique color."

Mitch walked to the back wall and found another opening. "There's more," he said as he turned back to Evan. "You up for exploring?"

"Heck yeah," he answered.

"Are you coming, Cruz?" Mitch called. Cruz raced ahead of them into the next room.

†

Eli brushed back Whit's hair. "Are you sure you're okay?"

"Yes, I am, sweetie. Will you please relax?"

"I'll relax when the boys come out of that cave, and I get you home safe."

Whit chuckled.

"What are you laughing at?"

"Now you know how I felt when you busted your head open. At least I didn't lose any blood."

"Point made."

"I promise you that I'm okay, babe."

"You looked like you were dreaming. Your eyes were moving back and forth like you were in REM sleep. I know that's impossible, though."

†

"Evan, come look at this," Mitch called out as he knelt on the floor of the cave.

"Wow, that's an arrowhead made of flint. There's no telling how old that is. I've found an old fire pit, but that's about it. There's a smaller tunnel, but I don't think we should search that today."

"Eli is probably already pacing, wondering where we are. Let's head back and show them what we found."

As they walked back through the large area, Mitch scooped up a few more of the dislodged crystals.

†

"It was similar to dreaming, but I knew I wasn't asleep," Whit was saying when she saw Mitch and Evan return. "Hey, there you are."

Eli looked up to see them approach. Both were wearing grins. "What did you find?"

"These," Evan said. He reached into his pocket and pulled out a handful of the light blue crystals. "They weren't glowing, but they were still warm." He handed one to Eli and one to Whit.

The crystal in Whit's palm began to pulse as soon as it touched her skin.

"Damn," Mitch said. He looked at the crystal Eli held, and it had not changed. "What is going on here?" He took the crystal from Eli's hand and placed it in Whit's, and it began to glow.

Cruz began whining as she watched the crystal glow. "It's okay, girl."

Whit handed it back to Eli, and it stopped glowing. "That's peculiar," Eli said. She returned it to Whit's palm, and it began pulsing. "I'll be damned."

"I can't explain it either. How many did you get?"

"We picked up a dozen or so, but there are many more," Evan said. "Show them what else you found."

Mitch pulled the arrowhead from his pocket and held it out. "Flint, according to Evan."

"Yes, I'd agree. It's beautiful," Whit said.

"There was a large opening at the back of the cavern you all were in and a smaller tunnel. We didn't figure this was the time to explore that."

"I'm glad you didn't. I was beginning to get worried." Eli smiled. "There will be plenty of time to explore that later. Did everything look stable to you?"

"Yeah, it did," Evan answered. "The tunnel is on the smaller side, but I think it's passable."

"We'll come back some other time," Eli told the boys. "Maybe after our family visits. Your dad may get a kick out of it, though."

"I know Brad would, but we can play it by ear. I know Dad may want to work on the chicken coops."

"Yeah, but I don't want him to work the entire time he is here. He needs a break, too," Eli told him.

"That is a therapy for Dad. Besides, he's got all of his gophers to run for this or carry that. His best job is the supervisor. He'll let us build the coops."

"If y'all do it this weekend, I can help," Evan said.

"Which reminds me," Whit said. "I've got a proposition for you. I'd like you and Mitch to stain my cabin and the lab when you're not working at the store."

"You know you don't have to pay me for doing stuff for y'all," Evan replied.

"Trucks don't pay to fix themselves, and I'm not good at staining," Whit grinned. "I end up wearing most of it."

"You do have a point. I won't start this weekend while the family is visiting, but I can work a few hours each night until it gets dark and then finish it off the next weekend if that works for you."

Whit nodded. "That sounds perfect. I'm a few years behind on that project."

"Maybe if you have some stain leftover, you can do the coops," Eli said.

"Those hens will be living in style," Whit chuckled.

"Nothing but the best for our ladies," Eli said.

"Have you looked into purchasing hens yet?" Evan asked. "My cousin, Riley, raises some of the top layers in the state. I'm sure he could work you up a deal for a couple of dozen."

"That sounds good to me. We can work on a list of what we'll need to build the portable coops and supplies for the hens." Eli looked at Whit. "I don't know about y'all, but I'm hungry. Are y'all up for a trip to the diner?"

"Oh, heck yeah," Mitch said.

Evan nodded, and Whit answered, "That's too hard to pass up."

"Did y'all catch any fish?" Eli asked Mitch.

"Naw, we didn't even wet a line. We decided to come and explore with y'all."

"If you want, you can fish when we get back, or just chill. It's up to you," Eli said.

Whit nodded. "Sounds like a deal to me. If the guys want to fish, you and I can work on our lists."

"Let's do this then." Eli stood and offered her hand to Whit. She noticed that Whit slipped several crystals in her pocket.

"I'll take your backpack." Mitch picked up the bag and tossed it over his shoulder. "Man, I sure hope they have country fried steak today."

"Stop it. You'll get my mouth watering," Eli complained.

"Too late," Whit chimed in. "I'm going to be so disappointed if they don't, Mitch."

"Well, let's go find out. C'mon, Cruz," Eli called, and the dog raced ahead.

†

The diner did have country-fried steak, and all four were stuffed after the meal and a slice of pie. Whit also put in an order for two pies for Friday. Eli paid for the meals and the pies.

"I can pick them up Friday after work and bring them out," Evan offered.

"We have plans to have dinner here Friday night," Mitch reminded Eli.

"That's right, but you can still join us," Eli told Evan.

"I never pass up a chance to eat here," he grinned.

†

The boys decided to fish for a while when they returned home. Whit grabbed a notepad and followed Eli down to the fire pit. They could make their list and watch the guys fish.

They made quick work of the list, and when Whit laid the pad down, she looked up at Eli. "I guess I need to try to explain what happened today, although I'm not sure myself."

"Yes, you have me curious."

"Do you remember when I told you about my mom?"

"Yes, I do," Eli answered.

"She said that she had met the star man on the top of the mountain, and they made love in a cave filled with blue crystal light," Whit said.

Eli's brows shot upward. "Do you think that's where we were today?"

"Yes. I know it was. A sudden wave of emotion hit me when we entered, and I believe that cave was where I was conceived." Whit paused for a moment. "I was dreaming; however, it wasn't REM sleep. It was like I was there with them, and I swear her lover, my father looked up, and called me a star child. His green eyes were shining with emotion as they gazed at me."

Eli was speechless. She didn't know what to say to Whit.

"It would appear my mom wasn't as crazy as people believed she was. She was telling the truth, at least as far as

147

that goes. I don't doubt her grief drove her over the edge, but she was right on some circumstances."

Eli felt completely confused. "What do you think all this means? The crystals glowing in your presence and all that?"

"I'm not sure. I'm as confused about some things as you are." Whit removed a crystal from her pocket. They were both surprised when it didn't begin to pulse.

"I wonder if you have to be near the cave for them to pulse?" Eli asked.

Whit stared at the crystal in her palm. "I don't know, but I don't have the energy to find out right now. I want to send one of these off to see if it can be certified to determine what it is."

Eli scratched her head. "This may sound weird, but do you think it was some sort of psychic message left for you to one day find?" She looked into Whit's green eyes, sparkling with tears.

Whit smiled at her. "I think that is precisely what it was. Something to let me know my mom was telling the truth about my father and who I am." She dropped her head. "It does sound crazy, though, that I am a star child, a hybrid human being."

Eli used her fingertips to lift Whit's chin. "Much stranger things have happened, and I'd bet they are still happening, but we just don't know it. The thought doesn't scare me one bit. I'd love you regardless."

A shout from the creek interrupted their tender moment. Mitch had hooked into a monster trout and was reeling him toward the bank. They looked up together at the commotion. "We'd better go see what he's hooked," Whit suggested.

Eli nodded and followed her to the creek. When Mitch finally lifted it from the water, Whit cried out. "Holy cow, that is one huge fish."

"By far, the biggest I've ever seen," Evan agreed. "I think you should mount that bad boy."

"Really?" Mitch asked. He held the fish up for all to see.

"Oh, your dad has to see this." Eli pulled out her phone and snapped a photo. "He's going to love it." She sent the picture to Mark.

Mitch looked at Evan. "What do I need to do to have him mounted?"

"First, you need to freeze him lying flat until you can get him to a taxidermist." Evan looked at Whit. "Do you have any small garbage bags we can put him in?"

"Yeah, I don't think he's gonna make it into a gallon Ziplock." She grinned at Mitch. "Man, what a fish."

Eli broke out laughing. "Your dad says *OMG*," she told Mitch. Two seconds later, her phone rang, and she put him on speaker.

"Damn, that's a nice fish, son."

"Thanks, Dad, it was a blast landing this beast."

"I bet. The fish looks huge in the picture. Eli's not messing with Photoshop, is she?" Mark laughed.

"Nope. He's probably a good ten pounds. I've never seen one this big," Evan told him.

"You, I trust, Evan. The others, so, so," Mark teased. "Probably too tough to eat, so what are you going to do with him?"

Mitch grinned at Eli. "I think there's a perfect spot next to the fireplace here. I'll let Aunt Eli keep him until we have a cabin of our own."

"You may not get him back then," Eli teased. "I will consider visitation rights, though."

"That sounds like a good deal, son. Wait until your brother sees this. He is going to go nuts."

"Where is the brat?"

"He and his mom ran to the grocery store. They should be back soon. I'll be sure to rub it in for you a little bit. That's one damn big fish. I don't think we can beat that."

"I don't think so, either."

"Oh, hey, your mom and I have decided to take half a day on Thursday off so we can come up sooner. We decided we needed to use vacation instead of calling in."

"That's great news. I can't wait to see all of you." Mitch winked at Eli. "I think you're going to be impressed with all the changes."

"I'm sure I will be. Hang on, your mom and Brad just got home. Brad, you've got to come and see this."

"Dang, Bro, that fish is huge," Brad squealed over the phone. "I can't wait to go fishing with you and Dad."

"It will be awesome," Mitch promised. "We can catch a mess of fish for dinner if you get here in time to fish. Aunt Eli can show the old folks around, and we'll catch dinner."

"Sounds cool, Bro."

"I think he's just afraid I'll out fish you two," Mark told them.

"You got that right, Dad," Mitch said. "I think you might be busy on this trip, though."

"I can't wait, son. I'll see you all soon. Love y'all."

"Most," Mitch answered.

Whit returned with a garbage bag and a long cardboard box. "This might work," she said. She handed Evan the bag, and they watched the fish disappear.

"This is perfect," Evan said as he laid the fish inside the box. "Stick him in the freezer until you call the taxidermist in town to get him mounted."

"You might want to consider putting him in my chest freezer," Whit said. "The one here is filled to the rim, right now."

"Thanks, Whit."

"You know where the keys are, right?"

"Yes, ma'am, under the butter churn," Mitch grinned back at her. "We'll drive over, and I'll take Evan home afterward."

"Sounds like a plan. I'll see you tomorrow, Evan. Hey, let me give you our supply list, and you can get them ready for me to pick up. We'd also like some stain samples."

"Any preferences?" Evan asked Whit.

Whit nodded. "Not too light, but not too dark."

"Hickory or pecan range?"

"Those should do fine. Thanks."

"I'll see you later," Mitch said. He picked up the box, holding his prize as Evan replaced the rods on the front porch.

"Be safe," Eli called after them.

"Always," Mitch hollered back.

Eli reached for Whit's hand. "How about a cup of coffee?"

"That sounds good. I need to spend some time up at the lab tonight, if you'd care to join me," Whit offered.

"I think I'll stay here and do some things I've been putting off. Maybe if I'm not there to distract you, you'll come back sooner." Eli grinned. "I'll keep the bed warm."

"It'll be a lot faster now that I can drive a Gator up to the lab and have such a nice bridge for a shortcut."

"Yes, it will." Eli smiled as they walked inside.

CHAPTER TEN

"I'll see you in a few hours," Whit said as she bent down to kiss Eli.

"We'll be right here waiting." Eli stroked down Cruz's flank, then tossed the ball again. "Be careful."

Eli watched Whit enter the barn, and a few moments later, exit in one of the Gators and drive toward the bridge. Whit would be much safer driving across the bridge instead of crossing over the fallen tree. A smile came to her face as the memory of Evan and Mitch working on the bridge crossed her mind.

"One more toss and I've got to get busy," Eli told Cruz. The ball sailed across the yard, with Cruz in pursuit. When she returned carrying the ball, Eli placed it on the step. "Let's go get a drink."

Eli filled Cruz's bowl with ice water and grabbed a beer for herself. She reached into her pocket and pulled out one of the strange crystals. "Let's see if we can find out what you are." Sitting at the desk she used for office space, Eli powered up the laptop and took a long draw from her beer. For over an hour, she scoured the internet, looking for a match to the blue crystal.

"Close but no cigar," Eli spoke aloud. She picked up the gem and could feel its warmth in her hand as she studied it, but there was no pulse of light. "What are you?"

Eli dropped her bottle in the garbage, and walked outside and sat on the steps looking up at the sky. Mitch pulled into the yard.

"Welcome back," she said as he approached.

"Thanks. What are you doing out here?"

"Just enjoying this nice evening," she replied.

Mitch sat next to her and rubbed Cruz's head. "It is pleasant." He picked up the ball and tossed it across the yard. "Where's the Love Muffin?"

Eli grinned at his nickname for Whit. "She's working up at the lab for a few hours. Putting your bridge to good use."

"She gave us a good scare today. Is everything all right?"

"I think so. Those crystals triggered Whit's memory of her mom, and the intensity of it was more than she could bear."

"Does this have to do with the star child claim?"

Eli snapped her head around to look into his face. "Have you talked about this with Whit?"

"A little." He drew in a deep breath. "Do you think the crystals could be a beacon, left behind in hopes that one day Whit would find them and activate them?"

Eli hadn't given thought to that, and she felt her heart drop into her stomach. "I don't know, Mitch. It has me perplexed, especially since they lit up in her presence. They don't down here, which is odd."

"They don't pulse, you mean?"

"Yes, when we were sitting at the fire pit earlier today, she took one out, but nothing happened."

Mitch shrugged. "Maybe she has to be in a certain proximity to the cave."

"That's what Whit was thinking as well. We'll have to test that theory out soon."

"Let me know if I can help in any way. I don't want to see her pass out again anytime soon."

"Me either, once was scary enough." She reached over and draped an arm around his shoulders. "That fish, today, was just incredible."

"For sure, the biggest fish I've ever caught. I can't wait to see him mounted."

"Me too. It will look great hanging on my wall. I keep thinking about those singing wall fish. If he turns and looks at me singing, 'take me to the water,' I may pass out."

Mitch laughed. "Should I have a button added to the mounting board just for you?"

"Naw, I don't think that's necessary. That can be our inside joke."

"Are you going to sit out here for a while?"

"Maybe just a bit. Why?"

"I'm going to get showered and dressed for bed. Tomorrow is the big day. Do you think Whit will need to sleep in after working tonight?"

"Doubtful. Whit's excited to get the project started, too. I don't think she'll work too late."

"I'm so excited." Mitch couldn't wipe the grin off his face.

"Go hit the shower. What do you want for breakfast?"

"How about some dried beef on toast? We haven't had that in a while."

"Perfect. That will stick to your ribs while you're working hard. SOS it is. Love you, Mitch."

"More," he answered. Mitch leaned over and kissed her cheek. "See you in the morning."

"Goodnight." Cruz stretched out on the bottom step after Mitch left, and Tomboy came trotting out from the barn. "You always know when it's bedtime, don't you?" She scratched under his chin, and he began purring. "Let's go."

Eli stood and stretched. She looked up toward the lab and could faintly see lights on. Eli smiled. "Goodnight, Star Child," she whispered.

"See you soon. Love you," traveled to Eli's ears on the soft breeze.

"Not sure I'll ever get used to that. Let's go, Cruz."

†

Whit heard Eli's goodnight wish and answered her calling. She had searched the internet to attempt to identify the crystal, with no luck. Finally, she snapped a photo and emailed it to several colleagues, hoping for their assistance.

She zoomed in on the black mass she'd been following for months and recorded the new data on its size and location. She forwarded the information to one of her partners at NASA to review. Whit tried to concentrate on the project, but her thoughts kept drifting back to the crystal.

Eli had gone to bed more than an hour ago. Whit felt it was safe to drive the Gator across the bridge without fear of waking anyone in the cabin. Mitch had extinguished his lights long ago, and he would be sleeping soundly.

Whit shut down the lab after checking her email and left. Oscar and Walter had curled up in the Gator and were sleeping as Whit climbed behind the wheel. The full moon was bright, so she left the headlights off as she drove to the bridge and crossed slowly. She pulled up behind the barn and shooed the two cats from the Gator. "I'll be back soon. You can hang out in the barn until then."

Whit drove the Gator to the workshop to retrieve a headlamp and flashlight. Eli would probably go insane if she learned that Whit had returned to the cave alone, but she felt compelled to go. *I could go in and wake her, but I won't.* When she emerged from the workshop, she was startled.

†

Mitch woke up from a strange dream and walked into the kitchen for a drink. He glanced out of the window above the sink to find a Gator parked in front of the workshop. A sliver of light shone through the partially closed door. "What are you up to?" He placed his glass in the sink and rushed to his room for shoes. He cracked the door of the cabin and saw the Gator still sitting there. "I bet she's going back to the cave." *Not without me.* Mitch grabbed a flashlight beside the door and jogged across the yard. He sat in the passenger seat and waited for Whit to emerge.

†

Whit stepped out of the workshop and froze when she saw Mitch sitting in the Gator. She walked over to it and sat behind the wheel. "What are you doing up?"

"I got thirsty. When I saw you sneaking around out here, I decided to investigate. Since you have a headlamp and flashlight, I believe you plan to return to the cave." He paused for a few seconds. "You know, Aunt Eli would have a cow if you went by yourself, so you have two options."

"Which are?"

"Simple, take me, or go inside and wake her to go with you. I'd personally vote for option one, but that's entirely up to you."

"I swear you two are just alike," Whit answered.

"So, are you going with option one? If so, stop by the cabin so I can get some protection. There's no telling what may be lurking in the dark."

"Go get the pistol, and I'll go back in and get you a headlamp. If you insist on going, you need to wear one."

"Yes, ma'am," he answered and jogged back to the house.

Whit returned to the workshop for a second headlamp. Mitch was creeping out of the cabin when she returned to the Gator. She waited for Mitch to climb in.

"Okay, I have a feeling about where we are going, but I don't know why?" Mitch asked.

Whit turned to him. "I've got to know more about that cave and those crystals. They don't pulse down here. I want to know if it is a matter of proximity to the cave or a one-time thing." She frowned.

"I'm your Huckleberry then. Let's go."

"Thanks, Mitch."

Whit drove the Gator to the trail and turned on the headlights. The canopy of trees blocked the moonlight, and the path ahead was pitch black. It wouldn't lead them to the top, but it would be much less walking. When they arrive at the end of the path, Whit parked the Gator. "You can wait here if you want."

"No, I can't. I am your sworn protector. Aunt Eli will skin me alive if anything happens to you. I'm in it until the end."

"Let's do it then." Whit climbed from the Gator and switched on the headlamp. "It sure is dark," she whispered.

"Yeah, it is, and there's probably all kinds of critters out tonight, so don't freak out if you hear bushes rustling." Mitch walked beside her with his hand on the pistol.

The lamps lit the path several yards ahead of them, but it did little to penetrate the darkness surrounding them as they climbed the mountain. When they had cleared the trees and stepped onto the open trail, Mitch said, "Wow. Would you look at that view?"

Whit glanced over to see him pointing toward the sky. The night was cloudless, and the stars appeared close enough to get a beautiful view with the naked eye. "It's perfect, isn't it?"

"Yes, it is," he answered in a voice filled with awe. "This is better than any planetarium. Not quite your lab, but still great."

"A great view for sure. You'll have to bring Brad up here one night."

"The heck with Brad. I'm bringing Jessie," he chuckled.

"Yeah, I guess that works too. You like Jessie a lot?"

"She's pretty cool."

Even though it was dark, Whit could see the red creeping up to his face. "Enough to raise a blush. That's a good sign," she teased.

"Stop it already."

As they approached the boulder outside the cave, Whit felt the crystal in her pocket start to warm. She pulled it out of her pocket, and it began to pulse in her hand.

"What you reckon all this means?" Mitch asked.

"I don't know." Whit handed the crystal to Mitch, and they watched it fade.

Mitch handed it back, and it started to glow. "It would appear it only reacts to you."

When Mitch looked into her face, he could see tears sliding down her face. "What's wrong?"

Whit hadn't realized she was crying and wiped away her tears. "Let's sit for a minute," she said and pointed to the boulder. Whit waited until Mitch took a seat beside her. "I don't know how much Eli has told you about my family, specifically my mother."

"Not a whole lot. I know your grandparents raised you. You've lived here pretty much all your life, and you are a brilliant scientist."

"I probably shouldn't tell you the entire story, but you deserve the truth and can make your own decisions."

"That sounds pretty serious," Mitch said and leaned in and bumped her shoulder with his.

"What I'm about to share with you only a few people know. It tends to freak people out a bit. If it scares you, I apologize in advance, okay?"

She smiled, but Mitch could see it was a forced expression. "I trust you," he said and placed his arm around her.

"Thanks, Mitch."

Whit wiped back another tear. "When my mother was young, about your age, she became pregnant with me. Of course, her father was livid and wanted to know who the young man was that had knocked up his baby."

"I bet he was a hot mess."

Whit nodded. "I can imagine he was. My grandpa was not easily rattled by much. My mom insisted she was walking along the ridge of the mountain one day and met a man. She said he was the most beautiful man she had ever seen, with sparkling green eyes."

"Like yours?" he asked.

"Yes, my mom had brown eyes, so they must have come from my father. When pressed for a name, all she could say was that he was a star man who came down to give her a star child." She paused to let that sink in.

"So, you believe your dad was not from this world?"

"I didn't for a long time. My mom was obsessed with her story and grief. When her star man didn't return for her; she went over the edge. Ultimately, she was hospitalized for her safety. She had become a danger to herself and wasn't providing what I needed as a child."

"Did you get a chance to know her at all?"

Whit looked into Mitch's eyes and saw them glistening with tears. "The memories I have of her do not match the woman I see in pictures of her. The last time I saw her, she looked twenty years older than she should have, and she had a wild look in her eyes. I was so scared, and my grandpa never took me back. He continued to visit, but each time he came home, he looked more desperate." She took a deep breath. "His baby girl was struggling, and there was nothing he could do to make her better."

"That had to be difficult on all of you."

"By the time she committed suicide by storing her meds until she had enough, I honestly can't say I remembered much of her as a loving mom."

"I'm sure she loved you, even if it was in her strange way," Mitch said.

"I didn't even cry at her funeral. That much, I do remember."

"How old were you?"

"Six or seven. Grandpa brought her home for burial in the local Baptist church cemetery. He and Grandma were buried next to her."

"So, what's the importance of these crystals?"

"Mom said they made love in a cave filled with brilliant blue light. When I stepped inside that inner cave, a flood of emotion hit me, and it was like I was dreaming. I saw them together as I was conceived. He looked directly at me and called me his star child. I think that's when I fainted."

"That's an incredible story. It does make sense." He shrugged. "Maybe I've watched too much Sci-fi on TV. Do you think the crystals were left as a gift to you? Could your appearance in the cave have triggered a message he left for you?"

"Mitch, that's probably the most astute answer I could have come up for myself."

"That could explain why the crystals only react to you. They don't light up for anyone else, do they?"

"No, and only when I'm close."

"Well, that answers one of your questions. Do you have others?"

"A multitude. I want to go back inside and see the cave again, but I don't think I'm ready for that tonight. I got the answer I needed for now."

"Thank you for sharing that part of your life with me, and I'm honored that you trust me enough to share. Your secrets are safe with me. I promise."

"Pinky promise? She held up her right hand."

Mitch laughed. "Pinky promise," He hooked his little finger with Whit's. "I should be glad you didn't ask for a blood oath."

Whit smiled at him. "I believe in the power of a pinky promise. No blood needed."

"Thank God," he swiped at his brow in mock relief.

"Come on, silly. We need to get some sleep. We've got a busy day tomorrow."

"Yes, we do." Mitch lifted Whit from the boulder. "Come on, Star Child," he said and pulled her into a hug. He tossed an arm around her shoulders, and they walked to the Gator.

"Will you drive us home? I'm out of energy."

"Absolutely. I'll drop you off at the house, store the Gator and equipment."

"I can take the equipment back to the workshop while you park the Gator."

"Let's roll. If we're lucky, we can get a few hours before Aunt Eli wakes us with the smell of SOS."

"Oh, heck yeah. I love that stuff."

†

Mitch waited for her at the front door, and they entered together. "See you soon," he whispered as they stepped inside.

"Goodnight, Mitch. Thanks for being with me tonight."

"My pleasure. Thanks for sharing."

†

Whit climbed the stairs and stripped out of her clothes. She pulled back the covers and snuggled into Eli.

Eli moaned. "There you are. I was about to get worried."

"I'm here, my love," Whit answered and heard a soft snore from Eli

.

CHAPTER ELEVEN

Eli gently unwrapped her body from around Whit's and climbed from the bed. It was six o'clock, so she would dress and have some coffee before cooking breakfast. Hopefully, Whit and Mitch could get a bit more sleep. She was surprised when she walked downstairs that Cruz was nowhere in sight. Typically, she waited for Eli before coming down. Eli flipped the coffee pot on and brewed a coffee.

When she opened the cabin door, she could see Cruz chasing after her Frisbee. A glance toward the fire pit revealed Mitch was already awake and dressed for the day. He looked up when she approached.

"Good morning. You're up bright and early." Eli took a seat near the fire pit.

"I've only been up for a short while. Cruz heard me get up, so I thought I'd bring her outside before she woke you."

"That was very sweet of you. Are you all set for the big project today?"

"Yes, ma'am. Rip-roaring and ready to go."

She smiled at him. "Let me get this coffee down, and I'll go in and start breakfast."

"There's no rush. I know you need that caffeine rushing through your veins," Mitch teased.

"You'll learn to appreciate the quality of coffee in a few years. Gets you going in more ways than one." She grinned.

"That is way too much information this early," he groaned.

Eli took a sip of coffee. "It looks like you will have good weather today."

"Chance of rain showers but not until early evening," Mitch replied.

Eli sighed. "I love a gentle rainstorm. It can be very soothing, especially on a tin roof." She grinned at Mitch. "How do you feel about hanging a porch swing on the front porch?"

"It can only add to the enjoyment we have out here. Over near the grill?"

"Yes, that's what I was thinking, too. We can keep the cook company."

"If you get a raw wood one, I can use some of the leftovers from the stain from Whit's project to treat the swing."

"Perfect," Eli said. "I'll pick one up today when I go in for supplies."

Cruz trotted over and laid the Frisbee at Eli's feet. "Did Mitch wear you out?" Cruz looked up at her, wearing her best doggie smile. "I think she's happy here, don't you?"

"Oh, heck yeah. Cruz gets to be with you every day. She has plenty of space to run and playmates to keep her busy."

"Would you mind feeding the cats and Molly while I start breakfast?"

"Not at all. I'll help with the toast and set the table when I get done."

†

Eli walked into the kitchen to brew another coffee and start breakfast. She was chopping the dried beef when Mitch returned. "That was quick," she said. "Wash up, and let's get busy. How hungry are you?"

"I think it's a six-slice day. That should hold me until lunch."

"Grab a loaf of bread and get to cooking then," Eli said. She walked to the pantry for supplies. "Hand me the milk, please."

Mitch had just dropped the first four slices of bread in the toaster. "You got it," he replied. He handed her the gallon of milk to start her mixture.

"Have you heard anything to indicate Love Muffin is awake yet?"

Eli grinned at the nickname. "Nope, not yet. If the smell doesn't wake her, I'll go fetch her."

"Fetch who?" a sleepy voice asked from the top of the stairs.

"You. Love Muffin," Eli teased. "We're working on breakfast."

Whit yawned. "Let me brush my teeth and run a comb through my hair, and I'll be down. Get that coffee perking. I need a double dose this morning."

Mitch chuckled and pulled a large mug down for Whit. "Go ahead and fix two now?" he asked Eli.

"I would. It sounds like Whit needs a jump-start this morning. A week away from the mountain and look what happens. Pour her a big glass of apple juice too, please."

"That sounds good. You want one?"

"Heck yeah," Eli answered. She whisked the mixture and added flour.

The bread popped up in the toaster. "Four up," Eli called out.

Mitch rushed over to remove the toast and add four more slices. "And four more down," he chuckled. He spread butter on the toast and then cut them into bite-sized squares."

Eli shook her head. "Your dad has you so spoiled. We always had to cut our own."

"You never saw Brad try to stuff a whole slice in his mouth all at once, did you?"

"Ha! Your dad tried that once, and he got banished from the table."

"Another story he never shared with us. I'm getting such a good education from you, Aunt Eli," he joked.

"Good Lord, what kind of education?" Whit asked as she entered the kitchen and took the mug of coffee.

"On all the things my dad did growing up. I'm getting the scoop from Aunt Eli.'

"I'm sure that scoop goes both ways," Whit teased as she looked over Eli's shoulder. "That smells heavenly."

"Have a seat, and it will be ready in just a few minutes. Mitch, will you go ahead and set up a few plates with toast?"

"You bet," he answered. The next round of toast popped up, and he cut several slices onto a plate for Whit and another for Eli.

When the topping was ready, Eli scooped ladles onto the toast. "You and Whit get started. and I'll get the last toast."

"I can wait," he said.

"Nope, you've got six slices to eat, so you better get started."

"I'm all over it," he said and carried the plates to the table. "Madame, your breakfast is served." He placed a steaming plate of food in front of Whit.

"I have died and gone to heaven. An angel just served me breakfast."

Eli shook her head. "It's getting deep in this kitchen." When the toast popped up, she buttered the slices and left them on a plate. "Your next round is ready when you are, Mitch."

"I'll grab it in just a minute. What a great batch."

Eli picked up her plate and joined them at the table. "It's such an easy breakfast to make, and it stays with you for a while."

"I can remember my grandma making this when I was young," Whit said.

"I think we all grew up on it in the south. Cheap to make and can be stretched to feed a large family."

Mitch refilled his plate. "Will that be enough, or do you need more?" He returned to his seat. "If I eat more than this, I'll have to take a nap."

"No time for that," Whit said. "We've got a lot of work ahead of us."

"Do you believe it will be operational by the time Mark gets here?"

"Unless we have an unforeseen problem. I think it should all be smooth sailing. After we get the panels installed and adjusted, we can work on the battery bank. The generator is already in place, so that can serve as a back-up if needed." She wiped her mouth. "We do need to decide where you want to store the batteries, though."

"What options do we have?" Eli asked.

"The barn is a few feet closer to the house than the laundry room, but I'd suggest the latter for safety purposes. If something were to go wrong, Molly and the other animals would be safe."

"Is there a risk of fire?" Mitch asked.

"There's always a minimal risk when you deal with power and wiring. I don't foresee any problems, but nobody can guarantee complete safety. There are overload safeguards in the system that should handle anything except maybe a direct lightning strike."

"Do you have everything you need?" Eli asked.

Whit scratched her head. "The only thing we didn't plan for was trenching to bury the lines to the batteries and the cabin."

Mitch perked up. "I can dig them."

Eli nodded. "You could, but it would take you hours. If we rented a machine, we could trench it in less than an hour. I'll see if Evan's dad rents them."

"I'm sure they probably do," Whit said.

Eli drained her glass of juice after finishing her meal. "That was good. I'll straighten the kitchen and head to town while you two start on the system."

"Do you want me to move the tiller to the garden for you?" Mitch asked.

"That would be great. I can jump on that when I get back."

Whit stood and looked at Mitch. "You ready to roll?"

"Heck yeah. Thanks for breakfast."

"You're welcome. I'll be back soon. I think I'll see if Cruz wants to ride with me."

"She'd probably enjoy a ride," Whit said.

"Hey, remind Evan to give you the number to the taxidermist, please," Mitch said before heading outside.

Whit carried the rest of the plates to the counter. "That was a great breakfast. Be careful, and I'll see you when you return."

Eli was rinsing the dishes at the sink when she saw Mitch moving the tiller to the garden. Whit had disappeared inside the barn and minutes later, drove the tractor out with the auger attachment. *You gotta love a woman who can handle a tractor.* Eli felt the smile grow on her face.

She grabbed her wallet and keys before walking to the door. Cruz trotted over to her. "You want to go for a ride?" Her entire body shook with excitement, and when Eli opened the door, she ran straight to the truck. "I guess that's a yes."

Whit had retrieved a can of orange paint and marked the ground where they would bury the posts to mount the solar panels. She had already marked lines where they would trench to the laundry room and another route to the cabin's breaker box.

After attaching the harness to Cruz, Eli pulled onto the drive. She blew her horn and waved to Mitch and Whit.

†

The wind blew the fragrance of blooming trees and flowers into the truck as they drove to town. As they approached the humane society, Eli decided to drop in and make an appointment for Cruz and provide an update on the crew.

As soon as they walked in, Cruz rushed over to Erin.

"Hey, Cruz. How are you, baby girl?"

"She's doing great. The cats have all settled in well, too. I needed to make an appointment for Cruz to see the Doc for a checkup. She and Molly are doing great."

Dr. Loren walked out. "I thought I heard you. How are you, Cruz?" She knelt to give her some loving and was given a lick to her cheek. "What a charmer? Is everything going well? No issues?"

"None whatsoever. Everyone has settled in well, and Molly and Cruz are perfect together. I wanted to make an appointment for a checkup for Cruz."

"Are you headed into town?" Dr. Loren asked.

"I've got to pick up some supplies at the hardware store."

"You want to leave her and pick her up on your way back through?"

"I could do that. Can you stay with Doc and Erin?" she asked Cruz.

Cruz wiggled and licked Erin's hand.

"I guess so. I won't be gone long."

"Take your time. Cruz can hang out with me after Doc finishes with her."

"Tomboy will need to come in soon for a snip job."

"How's he doing?" Erin asked.

"He's taken over the bed, but he's a sweet cat. Cajun is the king of the barn, and Walter and Oscar have bonded well."

"That's great news." She turned to Erin. "Schedule Tomboy for another two weeks. He should be old enough by then."

"Will do."

Eli bent down to Cruz. "I'll be back for you in just a bit."

"You want us to bathe and trim her nails?" Erin asked.

"That would be wonderful."

"We'll see you later then. C'mon, Cruz, lets go get a bath," Erin called to her.

Cruz looked up at Eli. "Go ahead. I'll be back in a bit."

"Thanks for working her in, Doc."

"No problem. It's been slow today."

"See ya."

†

Whit and Mitch had their design marked and were ready to start drilling the postholes. "Do you want to do the honors?" Whit asked.

"Absolutely." He walked toward the tractor. "How deep?"

"Three feet should give us a good base with the concrete."

Mitch climbed onto the tractor. "You want to guide me to the right spots?"

Whit nodded. She used hand signals to get him set up over each of the targets. Within an hour, they had the four poles set for the base of the panels. "That's a good start. Let's give this concrete some time to set. We can uncrate the solar panels, and carry them here, build a platform to set up the batteries in the laundry room."

"How big of a platform do we need to build? We've got lumber leftover from making the sawmill and can use a few of the boards we cut."

Whit smiled at Mitch. "Let's move the battery packs to the laundry room, and then we can measure them properly. They aren't light, so it needs to be made sturdy."

"I'll drive the tractor to the barn and meet you there. Are we going to carry the panels by hand?"

Whit nodded. "They aren't too heavy if we take them one at a time. Nothing we can't handle." She walked into the barn and began surveying the supplies. She was frowning when Mitch arrived.

"What's wrong?"

"I underestimated the conduit length. We are going to need at least two more rolls."

"No problem. I'll give Aunt Eli a call and have her add four. It can't hurt to have extra."

"Good deal. I'll check to see if there's anything else."

Mitch called Eli to pass on the information. "Is there anything else we need?"

"Ask her to pick up six sets of heavy braces for our battery base legs."

"On it," Mitch said and relayed the information to Eli.

After carrying the panels to their build site, Whit turned to Mitch. "I saw several four-by-fours in the barn. Can you bring three over to the workshop?"

"Yes, ma'am."

Whit prepared the table saw, and then picked up a measuring tape and carpenter pencil. When Mitch carried the first post in, she had him lay it on the table. She measured to make sure the post was eight feet long, marking a spot four feet to give her two base legs. She measured, and scored the remaining two, then assisted Mitch in cutting them to length.

"We have legs. Now, we need a section of plywood six-feet long, by three-feet wide. Then we can rip a few of the boards for the walls of the platform."

Whit supervised as Mitch measured the plywood carefully and used a skill saw to cut the required board. "Good job. Now let's attach it to the legs. We can add the braces when Eli returns."

They set the small table on its legs, and Mitch beamed with pride.

"One final task to complete, and then we can begin attaching the panels."

"What's that?" he asked.

"We need to unroll and stretch this conduit line next to our marks to relax. When Eli returns with the trencher, you can get to work on digging our trenches."

After installing the mounting brackets and swivel controls, Whit decided they needed a break. "We've managed to get a lot done, and it's almost lunchtime. Why don't we take a break and toss a nice salad for lunch? By that time, maybe Eli will be back. I can't imagine what's taking so long."

"That sounds good to me." Mitch wiped the sweat from his face. "My breakfast is long gone."

✝

"Thanks, Evan," Eli said as he loaded the last of the supplies in the bed of her truck.

"If you give me your keys, I'll attach the trailer with the trencher to your hitch, and you'll be good to go. Oh, we can't forget these." He handed her the stain sample charts. We've got most of these in stock in five-gallon buckets. She's going to need several for both projects."

"Dang, I almost forgot. I also need a wooden porch swing to hang on the porch. I want it stained the same color as Whit's cabin."

"Pick one out, and I'll bring it out later. If Whit can choose her stain, Dad said I could take off early this week to get a few hours of staining completed."

"Whit's going to love that. How about that one?" Eli said. She pointed to an ornately carved swing."

"That's beautiful and will look great. We've got one still in the box in the warehouse. Mitch can help me hang it tonight after the stain dries."

174

"Perfect," Eli answered.

"I'll be right back with your truck."

She watched Evan drive her truck onto the lot.

"We sure appreciate the business and the extra work you're giving Evan," his dad said when she paid the bill.

"You've raised a fine young man and a hard worker. You should be proud of him."

"We are. Very much so. I'm glad Evan's doing the extra work to pay for his truck repairs. The insurance covers some, but not all of it."

Eli nodded. "I understand. You know how it is. We always have more projects than we have the time or energy to complete, so Evan's doing us a great favor."

Evan pulled her truck to the front of the store. "Thanks again, Ms. Fortner."

"Thank you," she replied. "I'm sure I'll see you soon."

✝

"That looks pretty dang cool," Mitch grinned at Whit. They had chosen to use some of the boards they had cut with the sawmill, which still had live edges, meaning bark, on the boards' sides.

Whit nodded. "I agree. I like the rustic look of the platform. Once we install the braces, we will be ready to add the battery banks."

Mitch looked at his watch. "It's almost eleven. Where could she be? I thought she'd be back an hour ago."

"There's no telling. Call Eli if you're worried."

"She's a Fortner. She'll show up right when lunch is ready. Just wait and see."

Whit chuckled. "Let's go whip up a salad and test your theory."

They worked together in the kitchen to build a large chef salad, and they were setting the table when they heard Eli's truck return.

"What did I tell you?" Mitch grinned at Whit.

"Why don't you go out and see if she needs help carrying anything while I pour some tea?"

"Yes, ma'am," he answered.

†

Cruz jumped out of the truck as Mitch stepped off the porch. A blue bandana gave him a hint that Cruz had been to a groomer.

"We were about to send out an all-points bulletin for you."

"I got a bit sidetracked. Help me carry some stuff inside, and I'll tell you all about it."

Mitch tucked a box under his arm and carried three bags inside while Eli lifted four more from the backseat. "Let's drop these in the kitchen."

When they stepped inside, Whit grinned at Eli. "Mitch was spot on. He said you would show up just as lunch was ready."

Eli glanced at the bowl of salad on the table. "That looks delicious."

"Wash up and come join me at the table."

"Oh, sweet," Mitch said. He sat the box he carried on the counter. "An ice cream churn. That is going to get some good use this summer."

"So, other than buying an ice cream maker, what else were you doing?"

"Well, I stopped by to see Doc Loren. She worked Cruz in for an exam, and then Erin bathed her and trimmed her nails. Tomboy has an appointment in two weeks to get his snip job done, too."

"Poor baby," Mitch said. He squirmed in his seat.

"I picked up the supplies and talked to Evan and his Dad for a bit. That reminds me, Evan's Dad is letting him off early this week to start your staining project. I've got to call him with your sample choice so Evan can bring it out and get started today." Eli pulled the samples from her pocket and handed them to Whit. "I'm going to have him stain the swing to match. I can't wait for you to see it after it's hung."

"Oh, these are nice," Whit cooed as she flipped through the samples.

Eli took a drink and then placed a salad on her plate. "So, what did y'all get done?"

"We sunk the posts and installed the hardware for the panels. We built a platform for the battery bank and laid out the conduit line we had. It's a good thing you brought more. We're going to need it."

"Wow, you two have been busy. Evan hooked a trailer with the trencher to my truck. If we finish the trenching, he offered to return it for us in the morning."

"That shouldn't be a problem. I'll show Mitch how to run it while you start tilling the garden," Whit said.

"I can hardly wait," Eli grinned.

"Don't forget a hat and your sunglasses. We don't need you getting a headache from the glare from the sun."

"Yes, Mama," Eli teased. "Thanks for the reminder."

Mitch frowned. "Are you still getting headaches from whacking your head? I thought you were all healed from that."

Eli nodded. "All healed, but my eyes are still sensitive to the sunlight. If I protect them, I do just fine."

Mitch took a bite of salad. "I can do the tilling if you want."

"I'm perfectly capable of tilling a garden," Eli answered. "You can keep us all hydrated though while we work. It's warming up quick out there."

"We should start getting in our afternoon shower cycle soon. It'll be a gentle rain for maybe an hour and cool things back down."

Mitch chuckled. "That would just make it steamier back home."

"Yeah, no kidding," Eli agreed. "I sure don't miss the humidity."

"Me either. If I were cutting yards right now, I'd be soaked."

"That reminds me. We should probably use the bush-hog attachment to trim the front yard and a path to the garden before your dad gets here."

"I'll do that in the morning, while you cook breakfast. It won't take me long at all," Mitch offered.

Eli smiled. "You have a deal. How about pancakes?"

"Sounds good to me. Did you get chocolate chips to go in the ice cream?" Mitch asked.

"They are in the bag I carried in. Do you want chocolate chip pancakes?"

"Yeah, they are the bomb." He grinned.

"We can probably harvest some blackberries or blueberries to use in the ice cream," Whit suggested.

"I can remember making ice cream when we were kids. We had the old-fashioned kind you had to crank forever, and someone had to sit on the lid while you cranked."

"Aunt Eli, some modernization is a good thing. Just fill it up and plug that baby in and let it work."

"We may have to try a batch tonight. Evan will be out around three to start staining. Maybe Whit and I can whip up some dinner and ice cream while you two are staining. He promised to do the swing first so that y'all can hang it on the porch."

"We should be at a good stopping point around then. You can start trenching, so we'll have that done, and I'll run the wires through the conduit." She looked at Eli. "If Eli gets done tilling, she can be an extra set of hands when we start mounting the solar panels."

"I can do that. Just let me know when you get ready. I can go back to tilling later."

"I'd like to have one set of panels up today," Whit said. "We should be able to finish the install tomorrow and maybe by Wednesday we can begin generating solar power."

"That would give us Wednesday to tie up any loose ends on projects we've got started before the crew arrives." Eli speared another bite of salad. "You two did great with this salad. It hits the spot. Why don't we have the rest tonight with a pizza?"

"Are you going to make one?" Mitch asked.

"No, I thought Whit and I would start the ice cream and then run to town to that place you and Evan keep raving about. Will two larges with salad be enough?"

"I think so."

"Does that sound acceptable to you?" Eli grinned at Whit.

"You're making my mouth water already."

Eli stood. "Let's finish lunch and get back to work then."

"You two pull the trencher off the trailer, and I'll pick up in here and join you in a minute." Whit started clearing the table.

"You heard the boss, let's go," Eli called to Mitch.

†

After unloading the trencher, Mitch helped her unload the chicken wire and other supplies for the coops. He took the box of braces to the laundry room for the battery platform.

"Those should work nicely," Eli said while inspecting the platform. "You two work well together."

"Not bad. Whit tells me what to do, and I do it until I get it right."

"I bet she doesn't have to repeat herself too often."

When they walked out, Whit was walking across the yard. "What do you think of this?" She held out a stain sample for medium pecan.

"I like it," Eli said. "Not too dark or too light."

Whit looked at Mitch for his opinion.

"I like it, too."

"Great. Will you give Evan a call and see if they have it in stock? He can start a tab for any supplies he needs, and I'll pay it when I go into town."

"Sure thing, Whit."

"Hey," Eli called to him. "Ask him if he can stay for pizza."

"Will do," Mitch answered and walked a few feet away to make the call.

"Alright then, I'm off to the garden," Eli said.

"Hat and sunglasses," Whit reminded her.

"Thanks." Eli found that Whit had placed her cap and sunglasses on the kitchen counter. She pulled the hat over her head and donned her shades. "All set."

Cruz trotted along behind her. "Go get Molly, so y'all can play why we work." Eli heard an engine start and turned to see Whit giving Mitch instructions on operating the

180

trencher. *Damn, she's one smart cookie. She knows how to do everything.*

Eli bent down, primed the tiller, and pulled the cord to start the motor. She opened the gate to the garden and drove the machine inside, pulling the gate behind her. Cruz and Molly were racing toward her. They would make a mess of her garden. "You two, play outside," she called to Cruz.

Eli pulled the lever to activate the tiller, and the tines chewed into the soil. Instantly she could smell the richness of the earth as the machine inched forward, breaking open the packed dirt, allowing air, water, and nutrients to penetrate and nourish her plants. Eli concentrated on her work. When she reached the end of the row, she turned to inspect her performance. She was proud of how well the soil had turned, the darker soil glistening in the sunlight. Eli had longed for a large garden for years, and now that dream was coming true. She pulled a small towel from her pocket and wiped her face. "One down, many more to go." She tucked the towel in her pocket and spun the machine to the start of the next row.

†

Mitch was proficient with the trenching machine and wasted no time getting the lines dug for the conduit. After digging the lines to the cabin, he quickly broke the ground from the panels to the laundry building. The machine completed the bulk of the work, but keeping it moving in the correct direction and depth took some effort. His shirt was soaked when he finished.

When he turned the engine off, he looked up at Whit. "How'd I do?"

"I couldn't have done them near that perfect. Great job."

He smiled from her praise. "You ready for some Gatorade?"

"Grab three bottles, and let's go check on Eli. I'll finish stringing this last line while I wait for you."

"Yes, ma'am," he answered.

Whit was very proud of him. He had worked hard all day, and she knew once Evan got here, he would volunteer to help him stain. A glance at her watch revealed it was pushing three o'clock. They would check on Eli, and then if Evan hadn't arrived yet, they could lay the conduit in the trench. Filling the trenches would have to be done by hand, but that task could wait until the morning. She was pleased with what they had accomplished.

Mitch returned and handed her a bottle. "We did good today, didn't we?"

"We did. I thought after we checked on Eli, we could lay the conduit and break until Evan arrives."

"You don't want to get it covered today?"

"No, I think we need to wait until tomorrow in case we have to make adjustments. No need to cover it until we are positive it's ready." Not completely necessary, but Mitch had done enough for one day. "Let's go see how Eli is coming along."

Whit and Mitch reached the garden just as Eli reached the end of a row. Mitch held up a bottle of Gatorade, and she nodded and turned off the tiller.

"You've got it looking good, Aunt Eli."

Eli turned to look at her work. "It does look rich. Smells good, too. We've got so many blooms I lost count." She twisted the top off the bottle and took a drink. "That hits the spot." She wiped the sweat from her face. "How's your project coming?" she asked Mitch.

"I'm done trenching. We're going to lay the conduit and break until Evan gets here. You want me to take the swing out of the crate and get it ready to stain?"

"I thought maybe you could set up the sawhorses by the front steps. Whit and I can watch and play gopher if you need anything."

"That sounds good. I don't think it will take much time to stain the swing. We can load the buckets of stain and supplies in the Gator and drive it over to Whit's."

"Have you got some old shorts and a T-shirt you don't mind getting stain on?"

"I'm sure I can find something."

Cruz trotted over to the fence where Eli was leaning and looked up at her, with a tennis ball in her mouth. "We can play later. I've got a few more rows to till."

Mitch took the ball and tossed it toward the cabin. "Do you need anything?"

"Nope. I'm good. I shouldn't be too much longer. I'll see you at the cabin soon."

"Let's get this conduit in the ground then," Whit said.

Eli smiled and returned to her tiller. Whit heard the motor start, and she looked at Mitch walking beside her. "Your aunt is going to join us sooner than she thinks."

Mitch stopped and cocked his head. "Why?"

"What time is it?" Whit asked.

"A freckle shy of three," he answered.

Whit looked at her watch. "Five, four, three, two, one," she counted.

"Holy shit," they heard Eli yell.

Mitch broke out laughing and looked at Whit. "The sprinkler system is on a timer."

"Yes, it is set for six in the morning and three in the afternoon. I suspect your Aunt Eli will join us in just a minute."

Mitch tossed an arm around Whit's shoulders. "Well played, Whit. Well played." Mitch glanced over his shoulder to watch Eli perform an about-face with the tiller and rush to the nearest end of the row.

Whit dared not turn around for fear of Eli seeing the tears running down her face from laughing so hard. "We better get back to work," she told Mitch and hurried him along.

CHAPTER TWELVE

"That looks fantastic, guys," Eli said. She stepped back several feet and looked at the newly hung swing.

Evan grinned. "I'd give it overnight for that second coat to dry before you try it out."

Whit walked beside Eli. "That looks great. Are you two hungry? We've got the pizza warming in the oven?"

"I think we're both starved," Mitch answered. "It's hard to tell whose stomach has been growling the loudest. My salad is long gone."

Evan shrugged. "At least you had lunch. I worked through mine before I realized what time it was."

Eli motioned to them. "Go wash up in the laundry room, and we'll get the food on the table."

"Care to split that last slice?" Mitch asked Evan.

Evan shook his head. "Heaven's no. I can't eat another bite. That sure did hit the spot, though. Thanks, Eli."

"Too bad, you can't eat anymore. We have homemade ice cream for dessert." Eli stood and took the last pizza box to the counter.

"Aww, man, now you tell me?" Evan groaned loudly.

"I forgot about the ice cream."

Evan playfully punched Mitch in the arm. "Gee, thanks, buddy."

"Made with fresh strawberries from my patch, too," Whit said to entice them.

Evan grinned. "You sold me with strawberries."

Eli pulled the canister from inside the machine and placed it in the sink. "Will you do the honors, Ms. Brewer?" She smiled and handed Whit the scoop.

"Absolutely." She took the scoop from Eli and began filling bowls.

Evan took a large bite. "Aww, man, this is good."

Mitch dug into his bowl as well. "I think you need to practice more. At least every other day." He grinned at Eli.

"We used to have an ice cream machine, but it was one of the old ones you had to hand crank," Evan said.

Whit and Eli broke out laughing. "We talked about that earlier, having to crank for hours or sit on the lid to keep it sealed." Eli smiled. "It made you appreciate the sweet treat even more."

"I'd crank for hours for this," Evan admitted. "The strawberries are so sweet."

Mitch walked Evan out to his truck while Eli and Whit cleaned up from the meal.

"The ice cream was delicious," Whit said as she wrapped her arms around Eli's waist. "It makes me want a second dessert after a hot shower." She grinned up at Eli.

"Do I need to remind you I've already had a cold shower? I saw you nearly passing out from laughter, by the way." Eli frowned.

"Uh oh. I am so busted, but if you could have seen the look on your face. It was priceless." Whit smiled at her sweetly.

"I had forgotten all about the timer on the irrigation system. I admit, it works well, but damn that water was cold."

Whit leaned in for a quick kiss. "You only have a few rows left. You can finish them in the morning and then help us lift and install the panels."

"That works. I'm going to the barn to feed everyone and get the crew settled for the evening. Do you want to go ahead and shower?"

"No, I'll go help. Later, we can shower together."

"Fine with me."

They met Mitch in the yard. "We're going to feed the animals, and we'll be back in."

"If you don't mind or need me for anything else, I think I'm going to shower and hit the sack. I am so ready for my bed."

"You worked hard today," Eli reminded him. "Get a good rest, and I'll make pancakes in the morning."

"I'm so tired, I can't even think of eating," he teased.

"Dang, you must be tired." Whit chuckled.

"Love y'all. See you in the morning. Thanks for a great day."

"You too, Mitch. Love you most," Eli answered.

"No way, man."

"Goodnight, Mitch," Whit replied. She took Eli's hand, and they walked to the barn. "How are you feeling?"

Eli looked at her. "Me? I'm good. I didn't do all that manual labor like the two of you."

"After we feed the animals, would you walk with me?"

"I'll go anywhere with you." Eli bent down and kissed the tip of Whit's nose.

"It's not far."

Eli closed the door to Molly's stall and looked at Whit. "Where are we going?"

"You'll see in just a minute. I saw something last night that I'd like to share with you."

"I'm all yours," Eli said. She held out her hand. "Lead the way."

Whit led her to the bridge Evan and Mitch had built. She sat, dangling her feet over the edge, and waited for Eli to join her. "When I crossed over last night, I realized this was the perfect spot." She pointed across the water to the meadow in front of her cabin.

"Wow," Eli whispered. The meadow was filled with the glow of flashing fireflies. "Lightning bugs, my grandpa called them. They are beautiful."

"I thought you might like that. We also have a perfect view of both cabins from here. The boys couldn't have picked a better spot."

"You're right about that. Do you miss staying at your place?" Eli had wondered about that many times.

"Sometimes, I miss the familiar surroundings, but my heart is with you."

Eli leaned over and kissed her. "We can start spending some nights at your place."

"Maybe when Mark and Brad come up for a few weeks. We can turn your cabin over to them, and we can have some alone time at mine."

Eli cocked her head at Whit. "Do you mind Mitch staying with us? I know it doesn't allow for a lot of alone time."

"Absolutely, not. I've come to love Mitch dearly. I just thought if it were only the three of them, they could have some father-son bonding time."

"We can play that by ear. It might be less crowded if we did that. Three men in one house can be tight, especially with only two bathrooms."

Whit started laughing. "I hadn't thought about that. You do have the small one in the laundry building, too."

"That's true." A few minutes of comfortable silence fell between them until Eli took Whit's hand. "Have you gathered your head around to what happened at the cave?"

"I think Mitch had the most logical answer."

"Mitch? What did he say?"

"We've had time to chat while we were working. Mitch suggested the crystals were a gift for me from my father. They triggered a vision of the love he and my mother shared in that spot."

"Do you think he will come back for you?" Eli couldn't believe she had blurted that out, but it was on her mind.

Whit squeezed her hand. "I think if he wanted me, he would have come before now. I believe I was born to remain here on earth. He could have easily taken my mom and me when he was here, but he didn't."

"I guess that makes sense." Eli smiled at her lover. "I don't know what I'd do if I lost you."

"You don't need to worry about that. I'm here until you kick me to the curb. Or at least back across the creek."

Eli laughed. "No chance of that."

"That's comforting to hear. I don't want this whole Star Child thing to worry you. I don't plan on going anywhere."

"If it doesn't worry you, I won't let it bother me. I promise." Eli lifted Whit's hand to her mouth and kissed it.

"I don't know about you, but I'm in serious need of a shower."

"I am, too." Whit smiled and climbed to her feet. "Let's go."

"Wait." Eli stood and took Whit in her arms. "Thank you for sharing this with me. I think it will quickly become a favorite spot for us." She leaned down and kissed Whit deeply.

Whit moaned softly. "It just did," she grinned.

†

Their lovemaking left them spent and tangled in one another's arms.

"I love you," Eli whispered as her fingertips traced Whit's face.

Whit leaned into Eli's touch. "More," she replied with a smile.

"The big day is tomorrow. Do you foresee any problems with the conversion?"

"None at this point. We should have battery power up to speed by Wednesday. We'll keep the electricity on for a while until we're certain we can generate enough to run the entire house, but your bill will plummet."

"I'm not worried about the bill, but it's exciting to harness the power from Mother Nature. You never cease to amaze me with your skills and knowledge." Eli ran her fingers through Whit's hair. "I was watching you with Mitch today, and he is just as enthralled with you. He's learned so much in such a short time."

"He's an excellent student and a great partner in crime. We work together well."

"I noticed. Thank you."

"It's been a pleasure. I enjoy teaching someone so eager to learn."

"Goodnight, my love."

"Goodnight." Whit snuggled into Eli's body. "Wake me when you get up in the morning."

"I will." Eli kissed the top of her head.

Tomboy jumped up on the bed. Eli's hand found him and scratched under his chin until he curled up next to her.

✝

"I have to admit chocolate chip pancakes are awesome," Whit said. She drained her juice glass. "I'd eat them again."

"Good, they are one of my favorite breakfast meals and something I can cook." Mitch smiled at Eli.

"Now you tell me you can cook them?"

"Dad and I cook pancake breakfasts all the time at church. I've cooked thousands of pancakes."

"That's good. You can cook next time."

"That's a deal. I finished cutting the grass, so I'm ready to start on the solar system whenever you are," Mitch said to Whit.

"You can start filling in the trenches while Eli finishes her tilling. I'm going to put the leg braces on the battery bank platform, and hang the converter panel."

"I'll clean up here and join y'all as soon as I finish in the garden. I'm safe from the irrigation system this morning." Eli chuckled.

"Thanks for breakfast," Mitch said. He pulled on his cap and walked toward the door.

Eli called to him on his way out. "It's going to be warm today, so don't forget to drink."

"Yes, ma'am. Don't forget your hat and sunglasses."

"I'm on it." Eli chuckled.

"You two sound like an old married couple sometimes." Whit placed the empty glasses in the dishwasher.

"I reckon we do," Eli said and handed Whit the stack of plates. "How long until you think you'll finish the system?"

"Probably early afternoon if all goes as planned. We need to get the panels up to start harvesting the sun."

"Do we need to do that first?"

"Naw, finish your tilling. Then we'll get started. We've got plenty of sunlight today."

Eli leaned over and kissed Whit. "Consider me gone. Love you."

"Love you too." Whit closed the dishwasher and checked the refrigerator for Gatorade. "All stocked," she said and followed Eli out the door.

Cruz had already released Molly, and they were trotting beside Eli as she made her way to the garden. "What a sight," she said as she passed Mitch.

"Three peas in a pod." He laughed and continued shoveling dirt.

†

Eli started the tiller and allowed it a few minutes while she walked between the rows of corn. Water dripped onto her from the growing stalks, a reminder of the early morning watering. The corn stalks were nearly over her head, and she could see buds on the okra bushes. Her smile continued growing as she reached the tomato bushes and saw tiny tomatoes growing. The smell of the turned earth reminded her of the task at hand, so she returned to the tiller to tend the final rows.

†

Whit installed the leg braces and tested the strength of the platform. "This will do nicely." She unwrapped the battery packs and placed them on the platform and began connecting the units.

When she finished, she stepped into the bright sunlight. Mitch had made good progress in filling the trench, and the tiller motor was silent. Whit glanced toward the garden and saw Eli approaching.

"I guess I'd better get our tools together," she told Mitch.

Whit walked into the workshop to gather the tools they would need to install the panels. She picked up an extra battery in case they needed a fresh one and walked over to the first pole.

Eli and Mitch were unwrapping a solar panel. Eli looked up at her approach. "Do you want us to hold this in place while you secure the panel?"

"That will work nicely. You two are tall enough to steady the panels while I bolt them in. Let me just double-check my drill attachment to make sure I have the correct size."

"Let's get this in place," Eli told Mitch. They carried the first panel and slipped it in place. "I can hold this if you'll grab a ladder for Whit. She'll need it to be able to secure these."

"I knew I forgot something." Whit shrugged and waited for Mitch to set up the ladder for her. She tied a nail apron around her waist filled it with the washers and other hardware she'd need to secure the panels. Then she climbed the ladder. "All set."

Working together, they attached the three panels in the first section.

"That went well," Eli said as she steadied the ladder for Whit's descent. "If we lay the mounting platforms flat, I think Mitch and I can mount the rest of the panels if you want to start wiring them."

"We can give it a shot." Whit removed the nail apron and tied it around Eli's waist.

As Whit began the tedious work of connecting the panels to the battery, Eli and Mitch installed the rest. The sun was burning brightly overhead, which was great for the solar panels, but Eli could feel droplets of sweat dripping from her hair and sliding down her back.

"I think we can attest to having picked a great spot to garner the sunlight." Eli removed her hat and wiped her face.

"I'd have to agree with you," Mitch said. He wiped his forearm across his face. "I'm going to get some Gatorade."

"Thanks, we'll meet you on the porch." Eli looked at Whit, and her cheeks were flushed from the growing heat. "We all need to take a break from the sun."

"Just one second. Will you help me adjust this panel? Then we'll take a break," Whit promised. "Once everything is working and charged, the remote will make our adjustments, but we have to complete them manually."

"Not a problem. Just let me know what you need." Eli removed the nail apron and set it on the ground.

"I'll crank if you'll raise the top panel slowly. I don't think it will take much to adjust to maximum coverage." Whit started turning the handle as Eli lifted the top of the panel. "Just a few more turns. That's perfect."

Mitch handed them a bottle of Gatorade when they reached the front steps.

"Thanks, Mitch." Eli sat next to him. "Man, it's nice to take a break from the sun."

Whit sat on the other side of Mitch. "It is unusually warm today, but this will allow us to get a good idea of the energy we can generate."

Mitch grinned. "Was there any ice cream left last night?"

"There was a small bowl," Eli answered. "Finish it if you'd like. I'll put another batch on later with chocolate chips."

"Now we're talking." Mitch stood and walked inside for the container of ice cream and returned with three spoons. "For you, madame," he said and offered Whit a spoon. "Here you go, Aunt Eli."

"I see how you are." Eli laughed. "Whit gets the royal treatment, and I simply get a spoon."

"But I'm sharing," Mitch said in his defense. "If I were at home, there's no way I'd be sharing with Brad."

"Since you put it that way," Eli teased. She spooned out a bite of the frozen treat. "This is even better today." Whit licked her spoon in a way that made Eli's inside quiver. "I'm going to add some freezer containers to keep this in stock."

"I'll second that," Mitch said. "This is a perfect way to cool off on a hot day."

Eli took another bite and moaned. "Most definitely."

Whit didn't miss the moan, and Eli watched a different shade of red, grow on her face. *Paybacks.* Eli stifled a chuckle.

"Do you want me to finish filling the trench while you finish the wiring?" Mitch asked, oblivious to the intimate moment passing between the women sitting on either side of him.

Eli winked at Whit. "Yes, that would be great. Do either of you have any thoughts on supper?"

Mitch laughed. "I guess we worked through lunch."

"How much longer until we finish?" Eli asked Whit.

Whit wrinkled her nose. "Another hour or so."

"Let's finish and head into town. I think we deserve some red meat tonight," Eli suggested.

"Will you bring something back for me? I'd like to stay and help Evan with the stain project. I can fix a sandwich to hold me over."

Eli scowled. "I forgot about that. I can go to town to pick up steaks and cook them here."

"Not necessary. You two go out and have a great time. I promise I won't starve before you return."

Eli looked at Whit. "Okay, so you up for a date night?"

"Always." Whit smiled. "After a shower and some clean clothes."

"Yes, ma'am. I promise to clean up for you." Eli chuckled.

Mitch stood to take the bowl back inside. "Let's get back to it then."

"Yes, boss." Eli smiled at him.

†

Whit walked beside Eli. "That moan was delicious," she said and bumped into Eli's shoulder.

"Uh-huh. It was payback for that tongue action on your spoon."

"But the ice cream was so delectable. So savory," Whit stated.

"You are such a tease," Eli said as she slipped her arm across Whit's shoulders.

Whit smiled up at her. "Would you have me any other way?"

"I'll take you any way I can get you." Eli wiggled her eyebrows.

Whit shook her head and giggled. "I love you."

"Love you most," Eli answered.

When they reached the laundry building, Whit turned to Eli. "If I show you how to run the connections here, could you finish wiring the battery banks? I will connect the panels and then start wiring to the control box on the cabin."

"You would trust that I don't burn anything down?" Eli grinned.

"It's not all that difficult. Just tedious," Whit answered.

"Let's do it then." Eli watched as Whit demonstrated the process and then completed a circuit of her own.

"That's perfect," Whit praised. "As soon as I get the panels wired, we can see if we're generating yet. We probably won't have enough juice to try running the cabin today, but surely by tomorrow, we can test. I'd love to get you totally off the power grid."

Eli nodded. "That sounds exciting."

†

Whit left the building to begin plugging the panels into the wiring harness that would feed the battery banks. She then walked over to initiate the connections to the cabin.

She walked past Mitch. "You can stop about five feet from the cabin. Just in case we need to make some adjustments." Whit had already installed the power inverter to the home power grid through the AC fuse box. The standby generator wired to both sources would provide a backup during inclement weather, reduced sunlight, or other issues that would limit power to the cabin. Whit examined the fuses and plugged in the remaining connections. She turned to look at the panels gleaming in the sunlight. Fully functional, the system would generate fifteen thousand watts, more than enough current to run the cabin, barn, and all the outbuildings. With all the open fields between their two properties, Whit thought she and Eli might want to consider having a solar farm to sell power back to the electric company. *Hmm, I need to run that past Eli.*

Tires crunching on the gravel drive brought Whit's attention back to the present. "Dang, is it after three already?"

Mitch looked at his watch. "Nope, he's early today," he chuckled.

Evan parked his dad's truck beside Mitch. "Hey everybody," he said when he climbed out.

"When do you get your truck back?" Mitch asked.

"Thursday if the good weather holds so they can finish the painting. Dad loaned me the money to cover the insurance deductible. I can't wait to get her back. Dad's truck is nice and all, but she's not my baby," he chuckled.

Mitch grinned. "I understand that. It feels odd to drive Aunt Eli's and then climb back into mine."

"Hey, Evan," Eli said when she emerged from the laundry building. She looked for Whit. "I've got everything connected. I think," she added.

Whit turned to Mitch. "Will you go inside and turn the front porch lights on for me?"

He looked a bit confused. "Sure."

"It will be an easy way to test to see if we've got power generating," Whit explained.

"Ah, got ya," he said and trotted into the cabin.

"Okay, Eli, your turn. Flip the lever on the right-hand side of the battery banks." Whit walked back over to the power inverter and flipped a switch.

She met Eli, Evan, and Mitch, who had gathered together in the yard. They were intently staring at the front porch lights. "Give it a few minutes to begin converting the Direct Current energy from the solar panels to Alternating Current energy to power the cabin."

"How many watts can these bad boys generate?" Evan asked, nodding toward the panels.

"Fifteen thousand, way more than enough to run the house and keep the batteries charged for nighttime." Whit was about to continue her explanation when Mitch let out a whoop.

"There we go," he cried out. "It's alive."

"Oh, ye of little faith," she teased. "I think it's safe for you to fill in the rest of the trench."

"I'm all over it." Mitch and Evan walked back to the trench.

"Let's go see what we're generating," Whit suggested to Eli. They returned to the laundry room and looked at the control panel where the numbers were increasing slowly. "It will speed up the more extended time the system receives sunlight. The bulk of the power is running the house, but the batteries are also charging." She looked at Eli. "I hope you don't mind, but I downloaded a program on your laptop, which I connected to the remotes. It will make any necessary adjustments to maintain optimal sunlight absorption throughout the day."

"You are incredible." Eli pulled Whit into a hug. "What happens if we don't have sunlight for days and the batteries drain?"

"Then your standby generator kicks in. I don't think it will happen until maybe winter, but better to be prepared."

"Remarkable." Eli kissed her. "Are you ready to get ready to head to town? I plan on buying you the biggest steak they cook."

Whit chuckled. "A nice ribeye will suit me just fine. You might want to get the porterhouse for Mitch. He's worked hard physically to get the system up."

"That was a given. Should we see if Evan will join him for dinner? We should make it back before they run out of daylight."

"If we go now," Whit teased.

"Go start the shower, and I'll check in with the boys and join you in a few minutes."

"Hurry." Whit began walking toward the cabin.

†

"I am completely stuffed." Whit groaned as she climbed into Eli's truck. She took the large bag holding the boys' dinner and placed it in her lap.

Eli climbed into the driver's side. "That was a great meal. Thank you for joining me."

"I wouldn't miss it for the world." Whit smiled as they turned onto the highway.

"The ice cream should be ready when we get home. Maybe we can have some with Mitch and Evan while they eat dinner."

"I like the way you think, Ms. Fortner."

"Do you plan on working tonight?"

"Just for a little while. I promise I won't be gone long."

"No worries." Eli was about to say something else when the phone rang through the speaker system. "Carol," she chuckled. She pushed the button to answer the call. "Hey, Carol. How are you?"

"I'm doing great, thanks. I'm not pulling you away from dinner or anything, am I?"

"Nope. Whit and I are headed back out to the cabin. We just had a lovely steak dinner."

"Hey, Carol," Whit said.

"Hey, Whit. I'm looking forward to meeting you, and that's why I'm calling. May I come up for a visit? Next week is our last week of school for the year?"

"Sure. Mark and the rest of the family are coming up Thursday, but just for a long weekend. When were you thinking?"

"Two weeks, maybe, if that fits into your schedule."

Eli looked at Whit. She nodded. "That should work out well. It will be great to see you."

"I miss you terribly, but it sounds like you're having the time of your life."

"I am. Do you know what Whit and Mitch finished doing today?"

"No, tell me. Don't make me guess."

"They converted our power to a solar system today that runs everything down to my electric toothbrush." Eli chuckled.

"Oh, wow. That's very impressive. How is Mitch doing?"

"You won't believe how much he's grown physically and socially. He's blossomed up here, and we love having him as a partner."

"This all sounds too good to be true. I can't wait to get there."

"Come up sooner if your schedule works out. Mark will leave Monday going home, but after that, we'll have plenty of room."

"I'll let you know for sure what my plans are. I won't keep you, but I really can't wait to come up and see y'all. Love you, my friend."

"Love you, too. We'll talk soon. Goodnight, Carol."

"Goodnight, you two. Drive safe."

The sun was starting to set, and the glare was aiming right for Eli's brain as they drove west out of town. She reached up for her sunglasses and found Whit watching her. "What?"

"Isn't that the same Carol, the best friend who betrayed you?"

"It is, but I've long worked through that hurt. I should thank Carol, to be honest."

Whit's eyes grew wide. "For what?"

"Sara is an attractive woman who understands the art and power of seduction. Carol was lonely and fell for Sara's game when I wasn't there to give her the attention she craved."

"But still, Carol is your best friend. I don't get it."

"What she did ultimately was the greatest gift she could have ever given me. It started me moving in a positive direction that led me here, and to you. That's why I should thank her."

"That is so sweet." Whit reached over and took Eli's hand. "That's the most romantic thing someone has ever said to me. I'll have to thank her myself now."

"I think you'll like her. She has flaws like the rest of us, but Carol is a good person."

"She must be if you stand by her after that. You're more forgiving than I could be."

"Another one of my high-quality traits," Eli teased.

CHAPTER THIRTEEN

Eli stood, getting out of the swing for the fourth time in the last hour and began to pace.

"You're going to wear the stain off this swing, and a hole in the floorboards, if you don't stop pacing. Mark will get here when he gets here."

Eli spun around and looked at Whit. "I know. I'm just so excited for them to be here. Where is Mitch?"

"He's probably in the shower trying to scrub off the rest of the stain. He and Evan finished my cabin and decided to hold off on staining the lab until the crew heads back to Alabama." She grinned. "He looks good in medium pecan. I swear both of them were covered in stain when Evan left. He said he'd meet us at the diner later."

Eli spun on her heel when she heard tires crunching on the driveway gravel. Her shoulders slumped when she saw Mr. Henry's mail truck bumping along the drive.

"Good Lord. Why don't we go check out the garden or something before you crawl out of your skin?"

Eli chuckled. "I'm not that bad. Am I?"

Whit smiled. "Yes, you are. Let's go see what Mr. Henry has for us."

"Hey, Mr. Henry," Eli called when the truck came to a stop. "What brings you up the hill today?"

"I've got a package for Mitch," he said. He motioned in the back.

"Hang tight. I'll get it, Mr. Henry." Eli opened the back of the truck and smiled. She carried the box back to the side of the vehicle. "He's going to be so excited."

"What is it?" Whit asked.

"His fish he had mounted. Oh, my goodness, Mr. Henry, you've got to see this fish." Eli took out her phone and showed him the photograph of the monster trout Mitch had landed.

"Don't think I've ever seen one that big in these parts. A whopper for sure." He grinned. "Those trout you sent us sure were tasty. The missus keeps raving about that hushpuppy mix of yours."

"We're waiting on my brother and the rest of his family to get here. I'm sure the boys will be doing some fishing. Would you like Evan to bring you another mess of fish?"

"That would be delightful," Mr. Henry replied with a smile.

Eli smiled back at him. "I'll get Evan and Mitch to deliver them with more hushpuppy mix on Saturday. Is that good with you?"

"That'd be perfect, Ms. Fortner. I appreciate that. We love a good trout dinner, but my old bones just ain't cut out for fishing these days."

"We've got plenty of fishermen in this family. Just let us know when you want some fish. I never have to twist an arm to get anyone to fish."

"Appreciate that, and I'll let you know. We may become regulars," Mr. Henry chuckled.

"That's perfectly fine, too. Mitch will love it."

"Reckon I'd better be on my way iffin I'm gonna be home by dark," he said.

"Good to see you, Mr. Henry," Whit said.

"You, too, Doc Brewer. Y'all take care and have a good visit with the family."

They watched him turn around and waved as he drove down the drive. Eli turned to Whit. "Let me put this on the porch, and we can walk out to the garden."

Whit reached for her hand, and they walked to the garden. Cruz and Molly raced ahead of them and splashed into the creek.

"They are having a good time," Whit said as they laughed at the animals splashing in the water.

"I don't care how warm it is outside, that's still some cold water," Eli replied. She checked her watch to see if it was time for the irrigation system to come on. "We're good."

"It's already run for the afternoon." Whit opened the gate. "After you, ma'am."

They walked several rows, admiring the growth of the plants and bushes. Whit bent down to inspect some vegetables. "Everything is growing well, but it might not hurt to till in some compost next week."

"I can do that."

"I'll help you, too. I can haul it, and you can till it," Whit said. She looked at the tomato bushes. "Won't be long now.

You can have fried green tomatoes soon or wait for them to ripen."

"Do you have some tomatoes that are ready for picking? I've been thinking about some tomato sandwiches lately."

"I'm sure I probably do. I'll see if Laura wants to ride over to the garden with me while you and Mitch show Mark and Brad around."

Eli nodded. "That's a good plan." Her ears heard the approach of a vehicle, and she turned back to Whit. "That has to be them," she said.

Whit saw a silver Chevy truck approaching. "Silver truck?"

"Yes, that's them," Eli cried out. "Let's go." She reached for Whit's hand and nearly dragged her out of the garden.

"Go ahead. I'll close the gate and be right behind you." Whit grinned. "Go."

Cruz and Molly heard the excitement and joined Eli in the race back to the cabin. Cruz, of course, won.

Whit watched Brad bundle out of the truck and bend down to hug Cruz. "Hey, Aunt Eli." He stood and hugged her.

"Hey, Sis," Mark said when he stepped out of the truck. He looked over her shoulder. "Hey, Whit, did she leave you behind?"

"Lord, Mark, she's been pacing for hours." Whit chuckled. "She didn't think you were ever going to make it."

"He drove like a maniac," Laura said. She stretched and walked around the truck to hug them. "It's good to see you both."

"My goodness, you've been busy." Mark surveyed the property.

"As soon as your eldest emerges, we'll take you on tour. Are you hungry? Whit was going to ask Laura to help her pick some fresh tomatoes and see what other vegetables she has ready in her garden."

"That sounds like a good plan," Laura said. "After that ride I could use a nice walk to stretch my legs."

"Well, we don't have to walk far now. You don't even have to cross the old tree." Whit grinned.

"Really?" Mark asked.

"Brad, will you go get a Gator for Whit and your Mom?"

"Yes, ma'am."

"Then you can run back to get the other one."

Mitch walked out and grinned when he saw his parents. "Hey, Mom and Dad." He rushed over to hug them both.

"You look great, Mitch." Laura stepped back to take a good look. "Getting a tan and slimming down. It appears mountain life agrees with you."

"It's all the hard work he's been doing. We'll give you the tour as soon as Brad gets back with the second Gator." Eli looked at Mitch. "Before we forget, Mr. Henry delivered a package to you." She pointed at the box on the steps.

"Alright." Mitch rushed back to retrieve the box and used his pocketknife to cut the packing tape. He carefully opened the box and pulled out the contents. "Sweet!" He turned to show his dad the mounted fish.

"Oh, my goodness. It's even bigger in real life," Mark exclaimed. "I bet that was fun to catch. What are you planning to do with it?"

"It'll be on loan to Aunt Eli until we get a home built up here," Mitch told them. "Then, it's going over our fireplace."

"That's an awesome fish," Brad said. He pulled the Gator next to the first.

"Let me put this bad boy on the mantel for now. I'll be right back."

Eli looked at Mark. "That was a huge fish. I wish you could have seen him land it."

"Hopefully, there will be others," Mark said.

"Y'all have to catch up a mess this weekend. I promised Mr. Henry, our mailman, that Evan would bring them some to cook."

Brad smiled at Eli. "That shouldn't be a problem. I'm so ready to fish."

When Mitch returned, Eli looked at Whit. "You and Laura want to follow us, and then y'all can do some harvesting?"

"No, you can follow us," Whit teased. "Let's go, Laura."

The group piled into the Gators. Mitch drove and followed Whit to the bridge. "Oh, my goodness. Where did that bridge come from?" Mark asked.

Whit smiled at Mitch. "While I was away on business, Mitch and Evan made this for us. Isn't it fantastic?"

"What? Wait a minute. You built this, son?" Mark was amazed.

"Yes, sir. Evan and I did most of it. Aunt Eli added a few things like the solar lights for nighttime crossings."

"Okay," Laura said. "What did you do with my son, and where is my Mitch?"

"You're going to be amazed by what all Mitch has been able to accomplish." Eli smiled. "I am so proud of him."

Mark walked out onto the bridge and bounced up and down. "Not an inch of give. I'm very impressed, Mitch."

Mitch glowed from his Dad's praise. "It was Evan's design, but we built it together."

Mark patted his son's shoulder. "I look forward to meeting Evan. He seems like a fine young man."

"You're going to love him," Eli said. "He and Mitch make such a good team."

Mitch grinned. "He's going to meet us at the diner tonight, so you'll meet him."

Eli looked at Mark. "He'll also be around this weekend to fish and help out with some other projects."

"Sounds great."

Whit looked at Laura. "You ready to hit the garden?"

"Yes, ma'am. We'll see you later," she answered, and stepped back into the Gator.

†

Mitch looked at Eli. "Up the mountain first?"

"Yeah, I want to show Mark our new toy."

"I noticed that huge rack of firewood you have. That's pretty damned impressive."

Eli beamed. "That's one of them. We got a log splitter, and man, does it work well. I was able to split that pile in hours instead of days."

Mitch drove up the mountain until they reached the worksite. "We cut the poles for the bridge from here. I've also been cleaning up some of the downed trees, cutting it for firewood. We bought a chipper to turn the smaller limbs and brush into woodchips for use around the homestead."

"Damn, y'all have been busy." Mark grinned at Eli. "I can't wait to get up here this summer."

"We can't wait for you either. The garden should be in full swing by then, and there will be plenty to do." Eli bumped shoulders with him. "We're going to have some fun, too. Take the boys to Sliding Rock and some of our old haunts. Maybe to see the old home place in Transylvania County."

"I haven't been there in years. Brad was still in diapers. Broke my heart to see all those homes on our mountain. Man, we sure had some good times there."

"Yes, we did. Hopefully, we can create the same for future generations," Eli said.

"Speaking of which," Mark chuckled. "Are we going to meet Jessie?"

Eli smiled at the blush creeping up Mitch's neck.

"Yes, she'll be out Saturday for the butt you're cooking," Mitch replied.

"That's right. We have a Green Egg Grill that needs some breaking in. Jessie, Evan, and his girlfriend, Erin, will be joining us for the day." Eli looked at Brad. "Y'all can fish tomorrow, or you can fish Saturday."

"Or both," Mark said. "We can do a fish fry tomorrow night. If you want to invite Mr. Henry and his wife out, we can make a day of it."

"He would probably love that," Mitch said. "I'll give him a call tonight."

Eli nodded. "Fine with me. We can whip up some hush puppies, fresh veggies, and the pies from the diner. I'm getting hungry, just thinking about it."

Mark pointed out a few trees to Brad. "Those standing dead trees will make some mighty fine lumber one day."

Mark failed to see the look that passed between Eli and Mitch. Eli grinned and nodded to Mitch.

"Let's head back down then. We can show Dad his surprise, and you can show off the garden."

"Surprise?" Mark said. "I love surprises."

"You're going to love this one." Mitch smiled at Eli.

"Let's go, then." Mark rubbed his hands together with excitement like a little kid.

When Mitch pulled the Gator to a stop in front of the workshop, he trotted over to pull back the tarp revealing the sawmill.

"You've got to be freakin' kidding me? A chainsaw mill?" Mark looked between Mitch and Eli.

Eli could see the tears in her brother's eyes. "We thought we might have a use for this? Again, your son and Evan built this for you."

"That's cool, Dad," Brad said as they entered the mill.

"Aunt Eli cut a few of the standing dead trees for you to try it out, but that's going to have to wait until the morning." He pointed to six trees that were bucked and stacked behind the mill.

"What? Do I have to wait?" Mark cried out.

Mitch grinned at him. "Yes, can't have you getting all dirty before we go to the diner tonight."

"It has lights rigged up, and I bet you're pulling enough solar power to run them at night," Mark said.

"If you must, we can cut a few boards tonight when we get back from town," Mitch told him. "Man, does it cut sweet."

"You've already tried it out?" Brad asked.

"We needed Evan to train us on how it works. We might have cut a board or three," Eli teased. "We used some to build the battery platform for the solar power system. Which, by the way, was built almost entirely by Mitch and Whit."

Mark grabbed Mitch in a bear hug. "I am so proud of you, son. You've grown into a remarkable young man."

"Thanks, Dad."

Eli noticed it was Mitch's turn to have tears in his eyes. He had worked very hard to make Mark proud of his accomplishments.

"We have big plans for tomorrow. After milling some lumber, we will be making two portable chicken coops," Eli told Brad and Mark. "We've got all the supplies and just need the manpower and lumber."

Eli looked at the grin on Mark's face. "I hope you didn't think you were going to get to kick back and relax this trip."

"This is perfect," Mark said as he admired the sawmill. "I'm itching to get started."

"Let's walk down to the garden. Maybe Whit and Laura will be back. We can head to town then come back to make some lumber."

"Everything seems to grow so well here," Brad remarked. "Are those blueberry bushes?"

"Yes, we've got blueberries and blackberries planted here along with the fruit trees. I'm hoping we'll have fresh veggies here soon, so we can quit raiding Whit's garden."

"It looks like there will be plenty to can and freeze. I don't see how the three of y'all could eat all of this." Mark smiled at Eli. "Laura's never canned anything before, but she'd love to learn."

"Whit can educate her this summer then. She has got jars ready to go."

"I bet we could put in a root cellar, too?" Mark said. "Potatoes, Brussels sprouts, carrots, and even your canned jars would store well in one."

Eli nodded. "See, I hadn't even thought of that. There's another project for us to work on this summer." Eli stopped walking. "I just had a thought. Up near the building site for your cabin is a cave. I bet we could enclose the rear portion and use it. The temperature stays very cool back there."

"We can check it out tomorrow," Mark said. "Sounds very doable."

"Oh, heck yeah. I love caves," Brad said.

"Wait until you see what we found up top," Eli said. "It was a hideout for Cherokee warriors who made attacks on the soldiers who forced the clan to march on the Trail of Tears."

"You're kidding me."

"Nope, Mark, I'm not. Mr. Henry used to play out here with Whit's Grandpa as kids. He was the one to tell us about the story. One of the warriors was named Pisgah, and he believes that's where the name for Pisgah National Forrest may have originated."

"We found some cave art that seems to back the claim," Mitch added.

"Can we go now?" Brad asked.

Mitch shook his head. "Nope, but I'll take you up there tomorrow morning. That's if you can drag your butt out of bed early. We've got lots of work to do."

Eli was relieved Mitch omitted the part about the crystals and Whit's passing out. She wasn't sure Mark was ready for that revelation.

"I think I hear a Gator," Eli said. "Mitch, will you call Mr. Henry about tomorrow night and let Evan know we will be heading to town in fifteen minutes?"

"I'm all over it," he answered.

"Brad, will you run ahead and take the Gators back to the barn?"

"Yes, ma'am," he answered and took off at a jog.

"I wish I could get him to move that fast," Mark teased. "I'm impressed with the progress you've made, Sis."

"We have Mitch to thank for most of it. He's added the muscle power we needed."

"He doesn't seem at all like the immature young man I sent you. He's grown so much, and I don't mean physically."

"He's worked hard, and his confidence in himself has soared. He wanted to make you proud."

"He's completely done that. I couldn't be prouder."

Eli smiled. "Make sure you tell him that often this weekend. He needs to hear it from you."

Mark nodded. "Point taken."

"Are you ready to have your stomach filled with absolute goodness?"

"I thought you'd never ask." Mark grinned. "Let's go."

†

Eli and Mark marveled at the vegetables Whit and Laura had picked.

"I can't wait to sink my teeth in some of these," Mark said. "Just the smell of the tomatoes has my mouth-watering."

Laura smiled at Mark. "We picked some green ones, too, if you want some fried ones."

Mark looked at Eli. "You up for cooking a huge country breakfast in the morning?"

"Very ready. I even have country ham, if you'll make the red-eye gravy. Whit can bake some biscuits. Laura can fry us some green tomatoes, and we can make a mound of eggs and hash browns."

"Oh, heck yeah," Mitch said as he walked into the conversation.

"You two can go check out the cave while we old folk enjoy some coffee and start on breakfast." Eli grinned at Mitch. "Is that good for you?"

"I'll make sure he's up early," Mitch promised.

CHAPTER FOURTEEN

"I'm gonna die if I don't stop eating," Mark said after taking the last bite of pie.

"Move away from the table," Laura teased as she guarded her banana pudding.

"That was fantastic as usual, Ms. Judy," Eli said as the waitress started clearing the plates.

"I'm glad everyone enjoyed it. Some more than others," Judy added with a wink to Mark.

"That was some mighty fine vittles," Mark said. He started rubbing his swollen stomach.

"Come on, Jethro. We'd better get you up and moving before you collapse on us," Eli teased. She passed Judy a credit card. "Do you think you boys can get the old man to his truck?"

"I think so. Not sure we can lift Dad into it, though," Brad said.

"I would not recommend following too close behind once we get outside," Mark warned.

"Please make it outside first. I have to live here," Eli teased. "I can't be banned from the best eating spot this side of Asheville. Let me finish the bill and grab our pies, and we'll be all set. Mitch, you can drive him home if you want."

"I'm riding with Eli then," Laura said. "No way I'm riding in a truck with the three of y'all after that meal."

"You are more than welcome to join us. See you at the house, Mitch. Evan, what time will you be out? We had planned to cook a monster breakfast in the morning."

"I'll be out around eight if that's okay."

"That's perfect. I'll try to save you some breakfast." Whit smiled at him. "I can't vouch for the rest of this gang, but I'll keep a plate warm for you."

"Thanks, Whit," Evan smiled.

Mitch bumped fists with his friend. "Come ready to do some fishing. Mr. Henry and his wife are coming out for a fish fry tomorrow night."

"Awesome. I can't wait." He looked at Eli. "Is there anything I need to bring tomorrow?"

"Just a healthy appetite. Erin and Jessie if you want?"

Evan looked at Mitch. "Whatcha think?"

"Go for it. I know it's short notice, so the girls may have to come out after work." Mitch grinned. "It would be nice, though. Even if they might outfish us."

Evan chuckled. "There is that. I'm sure we can talk Mr. Henry into taking some filets home if we catch a bunch."

Mark cleared his throat. "We could freeze some to take back to 'Bama, too," he gently reminded them.

"Right," Evan grinned. "Okay, you want me to call the girls?"

"I'll call Jessie," Mitch said.

"I'll see you in the morning then. Thanks again for dinner."

"You're very welcome, Evan," Eli answered.

"I'll see y'all at the house," Mitch said. Brad and Mark rode with him.

Eli looked at Laura in the rearview mirror. "You've got your hands full with those three." Eli chuckled as she slipped into her seat belt.

"That is an understatement. I wouldn't trade any of them, though. Evan seems like an excellent addition."

"He's a great young man. I'm glad he came into our lives. He's a great friend to Mitch. Heck, all of us," Eli said. She put the truck in gear and pulled out behind Mitch.

†

Mark and the boys milled all six of the logs for the chicken coops. It was nearing ten when Eli looked at Laura. "Should I go round up the boys?"

"If you expect them up early in the morning," Laura teased.

"I'm not worried about Mitch. He pops right up these days, but those other two can be a challenge."

"Mark may not sleep tonight. He's been so excited to be here."

Whit smiled at Laura. "Open the bedroom window and he will be asleep in no time. The fresh air and sounds of the night will lull him to sleep."

"I'll be back then," Eli said.

When she walked out to the sawmill, Mark was finishing wiping the system down while the boys stacked the last of the boards.

"It's time to call it a night, boys. You can get back at it in the morning."

"This system is so sweet," Mark said. "We've cut more than enough boards for the chicken coops."

Eli chuckled. "You haven't seen the design Whit came up with yet. It's like the Taj Mahal of coops. Even has wheels for easy transporting."

"Oh, my," Mark said. "I hope I'm smart enough to figure out her design."

"No worries, Whit will be right there to help." Mitch grinned. "She likes to see her masterpieces come together."

"Yes, she does. It's time for us to hit the sack, so we get to it in the morning," Eli said. "Big plans for tomorrow, so you need to be rested."

"Yes, mama," Mark groaned. He turned off the light. "Let's go, boys."

†

Once everyone settled in for the night, Eli climbed the stairs for bed. Eli smiled as she walked by Brad, fast asleep with an arm draped over Cruz. They had played for a long time while Mark and Mitch milled wood and were both exhausted.

Dressed in a T-shirt and shorts, she crawled into bed beside Whit.

Whit turned and curled her body beside Eli. "That was a fun night. I don't think I've laughed so hard in my life."

"Mark and the boys are a laugh a minute," Eli said as she kissed Whit's head.

"You were right there with them. I've never seen that comical side of you before. I love it."

"Mark and I have always had a way of spinning off one another. We start to tell stories, embellishing them, and they just grow from there."

"I bet some of them were true, though. I could see the two of you getting into some of those shenanigans." Whit snuggled in closer.

"We were quite a pair of jokesters. I don't know how our parents survived raising us."

"I think you both turned out well. Laura seems to be surviving too. She just rolls her eyes and goes with the flow."

"Do not doubt that when any of them step out of line, she will be quick to put them back in place. She's very serious when it comes to their education and commitments. Laura nearly blew a gasket when Mitch stopped playing football after years of dragging him to practices and ballgames."

"Why did he quit?"

"He just fell out of love for the sport. When he explained that to Laura, she finally understood."

"Did you play sports in school?"

"Everything I could from volleyball in the fall to softball in the spring. I have sports to thank for all my creaky joints. It was fun, though, the same bunch of girls moving from one sport to the next."

"That sounds like fun. I never had any interest in sports growing up. I do like to hike, and I made it about halfway through the Appalachian Trail."

"Mitch and Brad want to do that. Maybe you can join them for a few sections."

"That's an idea. Would you go?"

"Probably not. I'm not all that big on sleeping on the ground and walking all day. I can keep y'all supplied and maybe meet up with you en route for a hot meal and warm shower."

"That could be fun. Maybe we can talk about it this summer."

Eli chuckled. "Just be prepared for them to hound you until you make plans. They can be like that at times."

"That sounds like someone else I know. Maybe we can complete a two-week section before the boys go back to school in the fall."

"Were you a Northbound or Southbound hiker?"

"Originally, Northbound, but it might be fun and a more temperate climate to start from the north."

"I could haul all of you and your gear to Katahdin. I've always wanted to visit that part of the country."

"Maine is beautiful, especially in the fall. The colors are beyond fantastic. Even more diverse than here."

"That is a must-see," Eli replied. "I didn't think anything could be more vibrant then the Carolinas in the fall."

"So many different species of trees are the most significant difference. It's like the creator tossed his whole array of colors in one place."

"Sounds dreamy," Eli said as she pulled the covers over them. "Sleep well. It's going to be a long day tomorrow."

"Yes, but so much fun. Love you, Eli."

"More," Eli replied and pulled her close.

†

Mark was already awake and making coffee when Eli and Whit descended the stairs. Eli looked over at the empty spot where Brad and Cruz had been sleeping.

"They've been gone for about a half hour. I know, I can't believe it myself," Mark chuckled. "I'm making Mama Bear some coffee, but I'll be right back."

"I'll start making some," Whit said as Mark passed.

"I've got the coffee if you want to start your biscuit dough."

"I need a coffee first," Whit answered.

"Okay, not a problem," Eli said as she started to brew.

"Do you want me to print out the design for the coops?"

"I've already done that. We can let Mark study them and ask any questions while we cook breakfast."

Whit smiled at Eli. "You're one step ahead of me."

"Do you know how hard that is to accomplish?" Eli teased.

"You can blame that on my grandpa. When he was teaching me to play chess, he always taught me to play four steps ahead."

"Smart man." Eli smiled as she handed Whit coffee.

Eli brewed three cups of coffee. Whit looked at her curiously. "Why three?"

"The third is for Mark to use in the redeye gravy."

"Ah, I see," Whit replied.

"Have you ever had redeye gravy?"

"Come to think of it, I don't think so."

"It's a bit on the salty side, but tasty. Mark cooks it well."

"What's that?" he asked as he returned.

"Your redeye gravy. Whit's never had it before."

"A redeye gravy virgin. I aim to convert you then," he teased.

"Come join us at the table. We can start breakfast in a bit."

Mark sat beside Whit. "I looked over your design this morning. It looks great. I love that you even added the dimensions and the quantity of each board needed. That will make the final cutting much easier."

"Do you have enough lumber, or do I need to bring a few more down?" Eli asked, then took a sip of coffee.

"Unless I mess up some cuts, we should have plenty. Measure twice, cut once," Mark grinned.

"That was certainly drilled into our heads early on," Eli chuckled.

"I guess when your dad is a master carpenter, you learn that quick."

"Your grandpa was a master carpenter?" Whit asked.

"Yes, he moved from Transylvania County in the twenties to help build the housing industry in Florida."

"That's beautiful countryside. Is that why you two love North Carolina so much?" Whit asked.

Eli nodded. "It's deep in our blood, and we lived for summer to come up and visit for a few weeks."

"That makes good sense. I'm glad you fell in love with the mountains."

Mark smirked at Eli. "We are, too. We might not ever have met you if we hadn't."

"Smooth, Baby Bro," Eli grinned at Mark.

"It's the truth." He smiled back at them.

"I'm going to start on my biscuit dough before it gets too deep in here to wade." Whit chuckled.

†

"This place is freaking awesome," Brad exclaimed as they walked deeper into the cave.

Mitch bent over and picked up several of the crystals on the floor of the cave and stuffed them into a drawstring bag.

"What are those?" Brad asked.

"We haven't identified them, yet. Whit has sent photographs to several of her science friends, but she hasn't heard back. Pretty cool, though, aren't they?"

"I've never seen anything like them." Brad rolled one over in his palm. "I know there's not a ray of sunlight back here, but I swear it feels warm."

"Yes, adds to their strangeness." Mitch reached for the crystal and dropped it in his bag."

"Do you think she'd let me have one?"

"Yes, but she may want to keep them until they get identified. I'm sure after that, she'll share."

"Cool, I'll ask her about it later. These cave art designs are amazing. He took his phone out and snapped several photos. "Mom will like these."

"Maybe it will tease her enough to come up here," Mitch grinned. Then he shook his head. "Naw, she ain't coming in here."

"Yeah, you remember how creeped out she got at the caverns, and they were well lit and much more open."

"Oh, I remember Dad complaining she was about to break his hand. He couldn't get her back out fast enough." Mitch chuckled. "I'm glad we didn't get her claustrophobia."

"Me too. Hey, can we stop off at the cave Dad wants to use as a root cellar?"

"Sure. Let's bolt," Mitch said. He placed a last handful of crystals in the sack.

†

"That's perfect timing," Mitch said as Evan pulled up in the yard.

"Grab another chair off the porch, and I'll get a plate." Eli walked into the kitchen.

"Good morning, everyone," Evan said as he stomped his boots at the front door, then walked in. "It smells good in here."

"Have a seat and dig in," Eli said as she handed him a plate.

"Don't mind if I do. My Eggo toaster waffle is long gone." He turned to Mitch. "Erin is going to pick Jessie up at noon to join us."

"That's excellent news. We might be ready to start fishing by then."

Evan looked at Eli. "Riley's ready to deliver hens whenever you are."

"After today, we should have the coops done. So, maybe Tuesday after the holiday?"

"I'll let him know. Oh, my gosh. Is that redeye gravy?"

"Yes, it is," Whit handed him the bowl. "I've never had it, but it's delicious, so send it my way when you get done."

"If there's any left," Evan winked at Whit.

There were two biscuits left and one slice of ham after everyone finished. "Let's see how long these last." Whit stuffed the bread with meat and sat them on the counter.

Mitch grinned at Evan. "Not long," he chuckled and handed one to Evan. "What?" He smiled at Whit. "I waited until everyone had their fill at the table. I can't see these go to waste. Right, Evan?"

Evan nodded and took a bite. "Too good to waste."

"At least I know the two of you will work it off. You better hurry. Your dad is already gathering tools."

"Hey," Whit called. "I'll be out as soon as we pick up here."

"Go," Laura said. "I'll help Eli and then will come out and watch the show."

Whit smiled. "See ya in a few then." She raced after Mitch.

Eli watched her walking with the boys, and felt the smile on her face.

"That looks good on you," Laura said.

"What?"

"That big smile every time you look at Whit. You two make an adorable couple, and we're so happy you found each other."

"Thanks. I do love her. She's been good for me. She makes me think and keeps me on my toes."

"Mitch thinks very highly of her, too. What do you think of Jessie?"

"She's a fine young lady. Her dad owns the John Deere dealership, and she works with him when she's not in school. She graduates next year, too." Eli grinned. "Big bonus that she loves to fish. A country girl who ain't scared to get her hands dirty as Mitch first described her."

"Right up his alley then."

"Yes, they hit it off well from the start. Mitch was hesitant to ask her out at first, but Evan and I encouraged him to go for it. He hasn't stopped smiling since."

"I look forward to meeting her. Mitch blushes every time her name comes up, so he must like her."

"They've just started dating, but I think they talk and text every day. That seems to be a staple of relationship-building today."

Laura nodded. "The kids today wouldn't know what to do without technology. I can remember party lines. You never knew who was listening to your conversation."

"Now we are aging ourselves. Don't let the boys hear you talking like that. They already think we're older than dirt."

"We are older than dirt," Laura teased.

"Maybe so, but I'm still kicking. Just not as high or often. I can keep up with Mitch. Most days, anyhow." Eli finished wiping down the counter. "Should we grab a chair and find a nice shady spot to watch the crew?"

"That sounds like an excellent plan to me. I know that we just finished a huge breakfast, but what do you have planned for lunch?"

"I know they will be ready to eat again in a few hours. I've got all kinds of deli meat for sandwiches. We can also do some tomato sandwiches. I've been craving those myself. Grab one of those." Eli nodded toward the folding camp chairs.

†

Whit allowed Mark to take the lead on building the coops.

"Once we get the boards cut for the frame, the boys can start hanging the wire. Then we can begin building the hen houses. I love your design, by the way."

"Thanks. I've had that idea in my head for a while. I just never had the motivation to build it."

"We can build as many as you want. I think after the first one is completed others will be easy." Mark handed Whit the tape measure. "You feel like helping me measure?"

"Absolutely. We should be able to get at least three two-by-fours from most of these boards for the frame. Should I get a chalk line?"

"Would probably be a good idea, until I've become more proficient in using the chainsaw mill. I'll bring my planer up on the next trip. That will be a huge help."

"Yes, it'll make finishing boards much cleaner. We will be okay for the coops. Do we want to leave live edges on for the hen house to give it a bit more of a rustic look?"

Mark grinned. "Yes, I think that would be great. Would allow us to waste less of the boards, too, if we cut them at the same time."

"I was thinking the same thing." Whit looked over at Laura and Eli, sitting under a shade tree, watching. "You know, I think it would be nice if we made a couple of those benches that convert into picnic tables. It appears they may get some good use."

Mark looked over and waved to the ladies. "We've probably got enough lumber to make at least one or two if we take down another tree or two. Do you think we've got the hardware?"

"If not, I know where to get some. If you've got things covered here, I'll find a plan and print it out. I bet I can find one on the Internet that will list the hardware and lumber dimensions we need."

"Not a problem. We've got enough cut for the boys to begin adding the chicken wire. If I need help, I'll get Eli to assist until you return."

"I won't be gone long."

†

Eli watched Whit walk back to the cabin. "I wonder what those two are plotting?"

227

"There's no telling. Mark alone can be devious." Laura laughed. "Add Whit to the mix, and lord only knows what they are scheming."

"I reckon we'll find out soon enough," Eli replied and stretched her legs out in front of her.

†

Whit turned on the laptop and began searching. She found plans for an eight-foot table-and-bench combo that she thought would be perfect. If they could make two, it would be excellent for the fish fry. She could divert Mark and the boys from the second coop to build the tables. The second coop would be a breeze, and they could construct it tomorrow. Wearing a huge grin, she printed off the design and then made a hardware list they would need. Eli and Laura could ride to town for the supplies while they finished the first coop.

Whit folded the plans and stuck them in her pocket. She picked up the hardware list and took it to Eli. "I need you two to run to the hardware store and pick up a few things we need."

"I thought we had everything?" Eli said.

"Nope, we need these," Whit handed her the list. "Do you mind going?"

"Nope, I'll run in and grab my keys. Be right back."

"Thanks," Whit said, and gave Eli a quick peck on the cheek before walking back to the mill.

†

As they were riding into town, Eli turned to Laura. "I know we had all the supplies we needed for the chicken coops, so those two are up to something."

"Without a doubt. I guess we'll see soon enough."

As they drove past the ice cream shop, Eli pointed it out. "Remind me to put some ice cream on to make when we get back. I promised Brad we'd have some strawberry ice cream tonight. We can pick berries when we get back."

Laura smiled. "I'll go get the berries if you start making the sandwiches. I'm sure they will be half-starved to death by the time we get back."

"You're right about that. The hard work stirs up an appetite."

"Mark is so excited to come up for a whole week next month," Laura said. "I wish I could come, but I'll at least spend a long weekend here. I've got a conference to attend in Asheville."

"That was perfect timing." Eli pulled into the lot at the hardware store. "Here we are."

Evan's dad beamed when Eli walked inside. "Good morning. Are y'all done with the coops already?"

"Nope, they are building the first one as we speak. My brother and Whit are up to something else." She turned to Laura. "This is my sister-in-law, Laura, mother of Mitch, Evan's co-conspirator." Eli chuckled.

"Pleased to meet you, ma'am. Mitch is a fine boy."

"Evan's incredible. If you ever put him up for adoption, I'll be first in line," Laura answered.

"They are so excited about the fish fry tonight. Evan was up at the crack of dawn this morning to get his fishing gear ready."

"Yes, those boys love to fish. We'll have plenty if you and your wife would like to join us."

"Thanks, but she's already hogtied me into dinner and a movie in Asheville tonight. I'd never confess to her, but I'd rather do the fish fry." He chuckled.

"There will be others, but do try to come out for a visit," Eli said.

"Will do. So, what are we looking for this morning?"

Eli handed him the list.

"Hmm, let me put this together for you. Feel free to browse if you want."

"Thanks," Eli turned to Laura. "Brad's got a birthday coming up soon. Any ideas you'd care to share?"

"He and Mark have been talking about pocketknives."

"A Sodbuster Junior?"

"Yeah, how'd you know?" Laura smiled.

"Dad gave us both Sodbusters as kids. Let's see what they have here. Hey, Mr. Merrill, do you carry Sodbusters?"

"Yes, Eli, at the very end of the front counter," he called from several rows over.

"Thanks," she replied. "Let's go check them out."

They walked over to the display case. "Oh, there it is right there." Eli pointed to a black knife.

"Wow, that's precisely what they've been looking to find. I can't believe it's been right here all along."

Mr. Merrill returned with a basket of hardware. "Which are you looking at?"

"The Sodbuster Junior," Eli said.

"One of the finest knives ever designed. A carbon steel blade that will carry an edge forever once it's sharpened. That's a great knife. For Mitch?"

"No, his younger brother, Brad, has a birthday coming up soon. Do you have a case to fit it?"

"Is the Pope Catholic?" Mr. Merrill teased.

"Why, yes, I do believe he is," Eli quipped back. "Add those to the order, please."

"Yes, ma'am." He took a boxed knife out and added a case in a box. "Sorry, I don't do gift wrapping," he grinned.

"No worries. I can come up with something at home." She grinned when he handed her a paper bag holding her hardware purchase. Eli chuckled. "You do provide gift wrapping after all." Eli pointed to the paper bag.

"Ha! Good point. I hope he enjoys the present. Thanks for your business. Have fun at the fish fry."

"Thanks, Mr. Merrill. Enjoy the movies."

"Right." He winked at Eli. "See you soon."

"You bet." Eli carried the bag out to the truck. "Is there anything you think we need?"

"I think you've got everything covered." Laura climbed into the truck.

"We have ice cream, a gift, and we can use a pie for a cake. Does that sound okay to you?"

"Perfect. Brad will be so surprised."

"Let's do this then." Eli grinned and headed for home.

CHAPTER FIFTEEN

When Laura and Eli returned with the hardware, Whit and the boys had attached the hen house to the chicken coop. Whit and Brad were working on installing the wheels to make it portable.

"Where's the rest of the crew?" Eli asked. Then she heard the sound of a chainsaw. "Cutting more trees?"

"Yes. Mark thought we needed two more," Whit answered with a grin.

Eli looked at the stack of boards they had already cut. "Well, okay. I'm going to start making sandwiches, and Laura will raid your strawberry patch so we can make ice cream."

"Now, we're talking," Brad said.

"I'm going to put the hardware on the workbench in the shop."

"You can just leave it here," Whit said.

"Nope, I need this bag," Eli grinned.

Whit cocked her head to the side. "Okay, if you say so."

Eli chuckled and took the hardware to the shop. She picked up a basket for Laura to use for the berries and returned to the cabin. "Do you want to take one of the Gators?"

"No, I think I'll stretch my legs a bit, but thanks for offering." She smiled when Eli placed the bag on the counter, next to the two small boxes. "I'll wrap those when I get back."

"Thanks, Sis. You know I don't wrap well."

"You could put it in a Ziploc bag, and Brad would still love it."

"I'm glad your boys are so easy to please."

"I'll see you in a while." Laura picked up the basket and walked out the door.

†

Eli opened a fresh loaf of bread and began the art of making sandwiches. Deli meats retrieved from the fridge and a basket of fresh tomatoes provided her palette. Mayo, cheese, and mustard also accompanied her future masterpieces. Eli took down two large platters to hold the sandwiches and began to slice tomatoes.

Cruz trotted inside and sat at the entrance to the kitchen. "All the activity outside, and you're sitting in here watching me?"

Cruz licked her lips. "Oh, I see how you are now," Eli chuckled. "You just love me for the food." She tossed Cruz a piece of cheese. "Good girl."

Movement on the back of the couch caught her eye. Tomboy had stood and was stretching, his green eyes blinking at Eli. "See what you've started?" She shook her head. "You guys will have to wait. There will be plenty of scraps left."

Eli went to work spreading mayo over ten pieces of bread and then placed the sliced tomatoes over them, cutting the sandwiches in half before placing them on the platter. Then she created the meat sandwiches, some with slices of cheese and tomato until she had both plates full. Eli retrieved paper plates and chips from the pantry. "Surely this should hold us over until dinner," she told Cruz, still sitting patiently.

Eli could hear the sawmill buzzing, so she knew the boys had returned with the trees. Eli stashed Brad's knife on a shelf. She prepared the ice cream maker, turned it on, then walked outside to check on the crew.

Mark looked up at her and smiled.

"Anyone out here hungry?"

"Does a bear shit in the woods?" Mark quipped.

"Come on then and grab some grub," Eli tossed back at him.

"Hey, check this out, Aunt Eli," Brad hollered as he picked up the front end of the chicken run and moved it quickly with one hand.

"Wow, that turned out great," she smiled back at him. "You all did a wonderful job."

"Hey, Sis, the boys are going to start fishing after we eat lunch. Can I keep Whit for a while?"

A smile passed between Mark and Whit. They were definitely up to something. "Yeah, Laura and I can watch the kids fish and then start on dinner preps." It was apparent they were excited about something, and Eli wasn't about to ruin that.

"Awesome," Mark said. "I hope you made some tomato sandwiches."

"I did, but there's plenty left if I need to make more. Come on, let's eat."

The boys stopped at the laundry room to wash up. Eli smiled at the smell of fresh-cut wood and the growing stack of sawdust forming in the sawmill. *Life is good. What the hell, life is great.*

✝

Erin and Jessie arrived just as lunch finished. After the introductions, Erin looked at Evan. "You boys ready for us to teach you how to fish?"

Jessie gave her a high five slap. "So right about that."

"You are on," Evan said. "How about we sweeten this up a bit? If you two catch more than us, we'll clean all the fish."

"You better get your knives ready then," Jessie said with a wink to Mitch.

"This is getting good," Eli told Laura. "Let's grab our tea, and we can watch from the deck."

"Someone has to keep score," Laura said. "You have a notepad, Eli?"

"I'm on it," Eli said, and walked into the cabin. Brad flew past her carrying his rod and a bucket. "Where are you going?"

"I'm claiming the bridge," he hollered back over his shoulder.

"Smart move. You can let the little one through," Eli called back and then laughed.

"Yes, ma'am. I'm on it!"

"Damn, that was a smart move," Mitch groaned.

"Language," Laura called to him.

"Sorry, ladies." He smiled back at his mom.

"That was a clever move. I can see we're going to have to keep an eye on Brad," Evan said. "He might outfish us all."

"Hey, don't forget you haven't touched the western creek yet," Eli reminded him.

"That's right. If we don't catch good here, we can go to the other side," Mitch told Evan. "This spot has never let us down, though."

"Tru dat, buddy. Let's show these girls how to fish." Evan picked up his rod and tackle box.

"This is getting better by the minute." Eli took a seat next to Laura. She could hear the buzzing of the sawmill, and her curiosity was growing. *I wonder what those two are doing?*

†

"This is almost too easy," Mark said as they assembled the top on the first folding table. "I bet we could make some of these and sell them at the Farmers' Market."

"I bet you wouldn't have to go that far. I'd bet Evan's dad would buy whatever you made to sell at his hardware store."

"That's a thought." Mark continued to use the drill to drive screws into the fresh wood.

Thirty minutes later, they assembled the first table. Mark folded it into the bench and then back out to a table. "That's near-perfect if I do say so myself."

"Fold it back into a bench. It'll be easier to carry. Let's go ahead and knock out the second, and we can get some young muscle to carry these for us," Whit suggested.

†

Back on the water, the battle of the sexes was neck and neck. The competition was fierce. Occasionally, Eli would hear a whoop from upstream, and she knew Brad had landed another. After such a noise, Eli told Laura, "I'm going to check on Brad."

"Okay," Laura replied after scoring another fish for the ladies.

Eli couldn't see Mark or Whit when she emerged from the house carrying two bottles of Gatorade. She started up the path and stepped onto the bridge just as Brad landed another fish. "How's Team Brad doing up here?"

"That's my fourth fish," Brad answered. His braces flashed in the sunshine as he gave her a huge smile.

"Is it safe to sit to the left of you?" she teased.

"Yeah, I'm a total right-hander when it comes to casting."

Eli waited until he took the fish off the hook to look into the bucket. "Those are nice-sized fish. You thirsty?" Eli offered him a Gatorade.

"Thanks, I left in such a rush I forgot something to drink. How are they catching down there?"

"It seems to be neck and neck. Everyone seems to be having a great time. How about you?"

"Heck yeah. I love it up here," Brad answered. He twisted the top on the bottle. Took a long drink and prepared to start his cast.

"I forgot to ask you about the cave trip this morning. Was that cool or what?"

"It was very cool. Mitch collected a bunch more of those crystals. I asked if he thought Whit might let me have one."

"Maybe after she can identify them," Eli answered.

"That's what Mitch said. It was weird, though."

"Weird how?"

"I know they hadn't seen any sunlight, but it felt warm in my hand."

"Whit told me that crystals have a way of emitting energy, which was the most likely explanation for the warm feeling. I asked her the same thing."

"That would make sense, I guess. Pulling energy from the earth or something like that?"

"I think that's probably as good of an explanation as any. Whit asked some scientist friends for help to identify what they are."

"We also stopped by the cave you talked about for a root cellar. It's got some natural indentations that would make some perfect shelves already."

"That's good information to know. Thanks, Brad."

Eli studied him in silence as he lengthened his cast and let the fly float softly onto the surface. Mark had done a fabulous job teaching the boys to fish. She eagerly watched as a big trout swam out of a pool heading for the fly. Eli held her breath until the trout struck, and Brad set the hook. "Great job," she cried out.

"Oh, that's my biggest one yet," Brad said as he reeled the line. "You must be my lucky charm."

"Well, let me take a seat, and we'll test out that theory."

Brad grinned and dropped the fish in the bucket. "One more, and I'm going to have to empty this one or get another bucket."

"I bet we can find another bucket somewhere."

Eli settled on the bridge, her feet dangling over the edge. The sun reflecting off the water was beautiful, but it sent pinpricks of pain to her eyes. She reached up to the top of her hat and put on her sunglasses. *That's much better.* The cool breeze blowing down the creek felt good against her bare skin. It was bright and sunny, but Brad had picked a great spot.

"Oh, yeah, Aunt Eli, you are my lucky charm," Brad said when he hooked another fish. "Look, it's a rainbow trout. My first one up here."

Brad lifted the fish, and it dangled in front of her. She could see the rainbow of colors that glistened in the sun.

"He's beautiful," she said.

"Prettier than the browns or natives," Brad said. "I wonder if they taste any different?"

"A little sweeter, maybe," Eli teased.

"Maybe. Once dressed, it'll be hard to tell."

"I'm sure no one will go hungry tonight. You guys are beasts when it comes to fishing. We'd better go hunt you a new bucket."

†

"There," Mark said as he drove in the final screw. "Let's check this one out and go get some help."

Mark and Whit folded and unfolded the new table/bench, and it worked according to plan. "When the boys finish the staining job, I'll get them to put a couple of coats on these."

"They are beautiful even though they are still raw wood." Mark stepped back to admire their work. "Great job, Whit." He gave her a fist bump.

"We make a good team," she said. "Let's go check on our fishermen and women."

†

Eli had sent Brad back up with an empty bucket after he showed his catches off to his brother.

"I'm going inside to start some of the dinner preps," she told Laura. "Keep counting. You need anything to drink?"

"I'd love a glass of your tea," Laura answered.

"I'll be right back then."

Eli took Laura a glass of tea and returned inside to make a batch of hushpuppy mix. She was just covering the bowl when Whit came inside.

"Can I steal you away for a few minutes? Mark and I have something we want to show you."

"Sure, sweetie. Just let me wash my hands."

When Eli joined Whit at the door, she saw Mitch, Evan, Mark, and Brad going inside the workshop. She smiled at Whit when she saw Mitch and Evan emerge carrying a bench. Then again, when Mark and Brad carried a second out. "Those are beautiful benches. So that was the project you all were scheming on this morning."

"Come, check them out." Whit grinned and took Eli's hand.

Mark was delivering instructions on where to set the benches up when they walked up. He looked around for Whit. "Are you ready?"

"I'll be right there." Whit walked to the opposite end from Mark and nodded. Together, they lifted the seat of the bench, and the group cheered as the picnic table came to life.

"Oh, my goodness. I have been drooling over those for some time," Eli said. "That is gorgeous."

Mark nodded, and Mitch and Evan unfolded the second.

"Now we never have to worry about where we're going to seat everyone when we have a cookout," Whit said.

Laura nodded. "These are perfect. Right timing, too, I think your guests have arrived.

Eli turned to see Mr. Henry and his wife, Flora, pulling in the drive. "I guess we better get started on some dinner."

Ms. Flora and Mr. Henry introduced themselves to everyone. "I brought some deviled eggs and potato salad," Ms. Flora said. "You know men; they never ask what they can bring."

Eli took the dishes from her. "That will go perfectly with dinner. Whit and Mitch were just showing off their new creation. They made benches that convert into picnic tables for us to use today."

"Come on over, and you can help us test them out," Mitch said.

"Anyone thirsty? I made a few pitchers of lemonade and tea," Eli said.

"Sounds great." Mark looked at Brad. "Come and help me bring them out. Then we'd better start cleaning fish."

"Oh, no," Erin said. "The boys lost the bet, so they have to clean the fish," she bragged.

Mitch hung his head, and then came up laughing. "They beat us by one fish. If you hadn't needed our muscle to carry the benches, I'm sure we would have both landed another fish."

"Yeah, right," Jessie said. "No worries. If we all pitch in, we can have them dressed in no time."

"I knew I liked you young ladies," Mark said. "That's good team spirit. Brad can help me set up the fish fryer, and we'll be good to go."

"What can we do?" Mr. Henry asked.

Mark smiled at him. "Hold down the table, and you can keep me company while I cook."

"Is there anything I can help with inside?" Ms. Flora asked.

"We could use someone to cut up strawberries to go in the ice cream," Whit answered.

"That's easy enough." She poured a glass of lemonade and walked inside with Whit and Eli.

Laura came in moments later. "The master of the fryer wants to know where the oil is? Mitch showed him where the fryer and propane are."

Whit opened the pantry and pulled out a large container of oil. "There's a second if he needs it."

"I'll probably be back then, thanks." Laura took the container from Whit.

Eli grinned at Whit. "Pull the other one out. She'll be back in just a few minutes."

Sure enough, just a few minutes later, Laura returned. "Thanks, Sis," she said when Eli handed her the second container.

Whit had Ms. Flora set up at the table slicing strawberries. "What do you need me to do?"

"You can unwrap those aluminum pans and line them with a few layers of paper towels. Mark can use them for the fish and hushpuppies."

Ms. Flora spoke up. "Speaking of your hushpuppies. They are delicious. Would you mind sharing your recipe?"

"I will print out a copy and send it with Mr. Henry this week," Eli replied. "It was our dad's recipe, so we have to give him credit."

"I bet he was a great cook," Ms. Flora said.

"There wasn't anything he couldn't cook, but he'd dirty up every pot and pan in the kitchen doing it," Eli chuckled. "A price well paid for such good food."

"I'd say you learned well."

"Mark, for sure, has Dad's cooking gene. I think mine is still processing."

"You haven't cooked anything I wouldn't eat, yet," Whit chimed in. "Don't let her fool ya, Ms. Flora, she's an excellent cook."

"Oh, hey, that reminds me. Mark is cooking Boston butts tomorrow if you and Mr. Henry don't have plans." Eli smiled and waited for her answer.

"Two nights in a row? If you're not careful, Henry might move in with you. We'd love to join you, but seriously what can we bring?"

"How about some of your great baked beans, Ms. Flora?" Whit suggested. "Eli, they are some of the best you'll ever put in your mouth."

"That's easy. What do you have planned for dessert?" Ms. Flora asked.

"Oh, oh, I know where you're going with this. You have to make some of your banana pudding. Oh, and make a small dish that I can hide away for my own," Whit teased.

"Dang, you've got my mouth watering already." Eli poured a large bag of cornmeal into a bowl and mixed in some additional seasonings. "It looks like the boys have delivered the first batch of filets to Mark." She looked at Whit. "If you grab a set of tongs and some slotted spoons, I'll carry the meal out so Mark can start cooking." Eli picked up the bowl. "Oh, and a roll of paper towels. You know he's messy."

Ms. Flora set the strawberries in the fridge. "Go ahead, and I'll bring the paper towels."

†

Everyone was sitting around, watching Mark cook. "Something's missing," Eli said.

243

"Where's Molly?" Mitch asked.

"That's what it is." Eli looked at Cruz. "Go get Molly."

They laughed as Cruz rushed across the yard into the barn. After several minutes elapsed, and Cruz hadn't returned, Eli looked at Mitch. Mitch stood up, and Cruz came to the door but didn't leave the barn.

"Something's wrong," Mitch said and took off at a full run.

Eli looked at Whit and then followed Mitch to the barn. When they arrived, Cruz was standing outside Molly's stall whining. Molly was curled up in a ball and not her usual bouncy self. Eli's heart raced with fear. She walked inside and knelt next to Molly.

"What's wrong, baby girl?" She stroked down Molly's body. She didn't feel feverish. She tried to stand Molly on her feet, but she wouldn't bear weight on her right front leg. "Did you hurt your leg?"

"Here, let me hold her," Mitch said and took Molly in his arms. "What's the matter, sweet girl?"

Eli ran her hand down Molly's leg. "Nothing feels broken, but I'm no vet." Eli looked at Whit, who had joined them. "Call Dr. Loren and see if she will come out."

"I'm on it." Whit ran back to the cabin for her phone.

"Carry her out to where we're sitting. Hopefully, Dr. Loren can come out."

Mitch carried her gently over to the table. "Aww, who is this precious creature?" Ms. Flora asked.

"This is Molly. Cruz's playmate. She's done something to her leg," Mitch said.

"May I hold her?"

Mitch lowered Molly into Ms. Flora's lap. Cruz sat down in front of her refusing to budge, watching every move Ms. Flora made as she softly stroked Molly's back.

"You're going to be okay, Molly," Ms. Flora assured her.

"Dr. Loren is on her way," Whit said as she joined them.

"Great. Molly doesn't appear in distress, but she won't bear weight on that leg." Eli looked more distressed than Molly, who had curled up in Ms. Flora's lap.

"Dr. Loren will have her fixed up in no time," Erin reassured Eli. "Try not to worry."

Whit looked at Erin and Jessie. "Will you girls help me set the table?"

"Sure, Doc Brewer," Jessie answered.

Whit stopped next to Eli. "I'm going to bring out two extras. I've asked Doc Loren and her wife, Macy, to join us if it's nothing serious."

"Great idea," Eli answered with a smile.

When Dr. Loren arrived, Mitch carried Molly back to the barn for an examination. He placed her gently on a fresh bed of straw. He and Eli waited patiently for Dr. Loren's diagnosis.

Dr. Loren palpated the length of Molly's leg and could not feel any abnormalities. "It doesn't appear she has any broken bones." She continued down to Molly's foot, and when she touched the foot, Molly cried out.

Cruz stepped over and licked Molly's head.

"It's okay, Cruz," Dr. Loren told her. "Mitch, will you hand me the flashlight from my bag?"

Mitch opened the bag and took out the light. "Do you need me to hold it?"

"Yes, that would be great. Molly has swelling and a tender spot on the back of her foot that I'd like to check out."

Mitch aimed the light. "That's perfect," Dr. Loren said. "Molly has a small abrasion that looks like it became infected. I'm going to give her a small injection for pain and some antibiotics and leave some antibiotic cream. Clean it twice a day with peroxide and then put some of the cream on it. I'd also recommend her resting for a couple of days, but she's going to be okay."

"Thanks, Doc," Mitch said when the vet gave Molly the injection.

"You're welcome. I'll drop by later in the week to check on Molly, but call me anytime you have any questions."

"Will do. I think we all have you on speed-dial now," Eli replied.

"That's perfectly fine." She closed her bag and handed it to Mitch. "Would you take this back to my truck, and then we can wash up and get ready to eat?"

"We should have it timed just right," Eli said. "I think they are bringing out the rest of the dishes now."

"Timing is everything," Dr. Loren said.

"Come on. We can wash up in the laundry room. It's closer than the cabin." Eli guided her into the small building.

Mark was cooking the last of the fish when they arrived. After Dr. Loren gave an update on Molly, Mr. Henry blessed the food, and the crowd began eating.

†

"That was one fine meal," Dr. Loren said. "If you don't mind, I'll check in on Molly before we head home."

"Not at all," Eli said.

When they walked inside the barn, Dr. Loren stopped. "She's got the best nursemaid on duty."

Eli returned her smile. "I wondered where she got off to. I should have guessed Cruz would be here."

"They are both sleeping, so I won't bother them," Dr. Loren whispered. She looked up at the loft at several pairs of green and yellow eyes looking down on them. "Everyone else doing well?"

"Other than getting spoiled to the core, yeah, everyone is fine." She smiled up at Cajun. "He keeps the clan in line."

"Cajun has always been the leader of the pack," Dr. Loren stated. "I'll drop back out Monday or Tuesday."

"That will be fine. We'll be here," Eli answered.

Whit and Macy were chatting by the truck when they emerged from the barn. Whit grinned up at Dr. Loren.

"Keep your bag packed. You two are joining us for BBQ tomorrow night."

"I won't complain. That's another night Macy doesn't have to eat my cooking."

"There's nothing wrong with your cooking, but a Boston butt is too good to pass on," Macy replied.

Dr. Loren smiled at Whit. "Is there anything we can bring?"

Whit shook her head. "Not that I can think of right now. I'll call you if we need anything, but I think we have it covered."

"Drive safe, and we'll see you tomorrow night." Eli waved as they pulled down the drive.

Mr. Henry and Ms. Flora were also heading home. "Thanks for a terrific night," he said. "I may not have to eat again until tomorrow night."

"Just come hungry then. I promise we'll fill you up again." Eli fished a piece of paper from her pocket and handed it to Ms. Flora. "Before I forget, the recipe you asked for."

"Thanks so much, Eli." Ms. Flora hugged her neck.

"That doesn't mean you can't come out for fish fries." Eli grinned.

"You can bet we'll be here," Mr. Henry said. "That was a fine meal."

"Be safe, and we'll see you tomorrow night." Whit closed the door behind him.

As they started to walk back toward the tables, Eli slipped an arm around Whit's shoulders. "I think it was a great day, don't you?"

Whit smiled up at her. "Fabulous, and we get to do it again tomorrow."

Eli saw Mitch pass some money to Evan, but didn't comment. *No telling what those two knuckleheads are up to now.*

"Hey, Aunt Eli," Mitch called out. "After we finish the second chicken coop tomorrow, we'd like to have a chance at redemption against the girls. We can send Mom and Dad home with some fish if that's okay with you?"

"That's perfect except for one thing," Eli answered. "I get to join Team Brad on the bridge, so we can show you all how fishing gets done."

Mitch laughed. "You are so on."

"Come on, let's take any leftovers back into the house," Whit said. "I think I'm ready for some coffee."

"Not much to take, but coffee does sound good." Mark picked up his empty pans.

"We'll see you gals tomorrow then," Eli said to Erin and Jessie. "Where's Brad?"

"In the barn, checking on Molly," Mitch answered.

"Let's go check on him," Eli told Mark.

Mark handed the pans to Laura. "See you in a few."

When they walked inside the barn, Mark lifted his finger to his lips. Eli looked into Molly's stall. Brad was sound asleep, sandwiched between Molly and Cruz. They backed out of the barn quietly.

"Should we wake him up?" Eli asked.

"Naw, he'll come in if he wakes up. I don't think there's any chance he'll get cold stuck between those two." Mark grinned.

"Thanks for a perfect day," Eli said as they walked back to the cabin.

"It did turn out pretty well, didn't it?"

"I don't know how it could have been any better. Thanks, Baby Bro."

"Thank you for making all of this possible."

CHAPTER SIXTEEN

Mark joined Eli out on the front steps early the next morning for coffee. "It looks like it will be another beautiful day." He sat down beside her.

"Yes, it does. We may get a late afternoon shower, but the rain usually doesn't last long."

He looked over at the garden, where the sprinklers were still running. "I see your irrigation system works well."

Eli grinned. "Every project Whit does works well."

"She is pretty amazing. I think the two of you make quite the pair."

"You wouldn't be biased or anything, would you?"

"Even if I was, it's still the truth." He sighed and took a drink. "I love this little community. The people are awesome."

"I couldn't have found a better spot. It's perfect for all of us."

The barn door opened, and Brad strolled out, Cruz right on his heels. "Good morning, Sunshine," Mark called to him. "How did you sleep?"

"Amazingly," he grinned. "Molly is already feeling better. I think she kicked me about ten times in her sleep."

"Do you want some breakfast or another hour of sleep?" Eli asked.

"Pancakes?"

"Chocolate chip, or I think there are a few strawberries left," Eli answered. "You need your energy today."

"What for?"

"Mitch and Evan have decided they want a second butt whooping, so they challenged the girls to another fishing competition. I told them Team Brad had a new member, and we wanted in on the challenge."

"You're going to fish with me?" He grinned widely. "Alright!"

"I claimed the bridge for us again, too," Eli told him.

"Good deal. I can hardly wait."

"We have to finish the second chicken coop first, but it won't take long," Mark told his youngest. He looked at Eli. "I'll get the fire started for the butts if you'll cook breakfast. I've already got them seasoned and chilling in the fridge."

"That sounds like a great plan. Pancakes, here we come." Eli stood as Mitch walked outside.

"Am I missing a party?" He asked, wiping his face.

"Nope, I'm going to start breakfast. Will you and Brad feed the animals and doctor Molly's foot?"

"I've already done that, but I didn't know what you fed her."

"Come along, dear brother, and I'll show you the routine."

"Are chocolate chip pancakes good for you?" Eli asked. "If not, your mom picked up some tofu yesterday."

"Pancakes are wonderful. Thanks, Aunt Eli."

"Tofu gets them every time," Mark chuckled. "I'll light the fire and come in to help."

"Sounds good, bro." Eli entered the kitchen and saw Whit at the coffee pot. "Me too," she said as she kissed the back of Whit's neck and placed her mug on the counter. "We're having bacon and pancakes this morning."

"Let me guess. Chocolate chip?" Whit chuckled.

"Yep, they seem to be Mitch's new favorite. Brad's too."

"Where are the boys?"

"Mitch and Brad are feeding the animals, and Mark is lighting the fire for the butts."

"What can I help with?" Whit asked.

"You can keep the cook company," Eli told her as she washed her hands. "Oh, and hand me some of that bacon from the fridge."

"I'd better pull out more butter to let it soften a bit," Whit said. She handed Eli two large packs of bacon.

"I'll get this going and start on the batter."

"I thought I heard voices," Laura said as she came down the hall.

"Good morning, sleepyhead. You're the last one awake," Eli teased.

"That bed is so comfortable, makes it hard to get out of it." She smiled as Whit handed her coffee. "Let me guess. Pancakes?"

"You know your boys well." Eli laughed.

"I did hear Brad and Mitch talking about them earlier," Laura admitted. "What can I help with?"

"You can set the table with fine china," Eli smirked.

"You got it, Sis." Laura opened the pantry and pulled out a stack of paper plates.

Eli poured the mix for the pancakes in a large bowl and started stirring it. When she began removing the cooked bacon from the grill, she poured large circles of batter and sprinkled them with chocolate chips.

Mark stepped back inside. "Damn, you gotta love the smell of bacon in the morning. What can I do, Sis?"

"Grab one of those large spatulas and get ready to flip," Eli told Mark. "I'll handle the bacon if you do the pancakes."

"Deal," Mark said and moved over beside her. "You know you've deprived me of my best pancake cooker, right?"

"Yeah, Mitch says y'all have cooked thousands of pancakes at church on Sunday mornings. I guess you'll just have to start breaking in Brad. I'm keeping Mitch."

"Hold on now, he's just on a temporary loan." Mark winked. "I get him back after the summer."

"Don't remind me how fast that will go. It's been fun having Mitch here, and he's been such a big help."

"I can't believe how he has grown working with you and Whit. He seems excited to do things. I usually have to threaten him with tofu to get him to move."

"He needed a chance to spread his wings and succeed. He's had a few things that didn't go as planned, but he's dealing with them. He's terrified of disappointing you."

Mark looked at Eli, and she could see his eyes watering. She threw her hip into him and bumped him. "He's not tough like you and I were. He's a sensitive kid who takes disapproval hard. You can't treat him like dad did us."

"I finally realize that," Mark said. "I appreciate you stepping in when I couldn't."

"Mitch is a great kid. I couldn't be prouder of him. Now stop before you make my eyes leak."

Laura groaned from her seat at the table. "Do I need to come and separate you two kids?"

Mark and Eli smiled at one another. "No, Mom," they said in unison then broke out laughing.

Cruz trotted in with Mitch and Brad right behind her.

"Get washed up. I'll have a big stack of pancakes ready when you get back."

"Yes, sir," Mitch answered. "You can take downstairs, and I'll go up to Aunt Eli's bathroom."

"What do you boys want to drink?" Laura called after them.

"Milk, please," Mitch answered.

"I'll take OJ," Brad replied.

"What about the rest of you?" Laura asked.

"OJ does sound good," Mark said.

"Milk for us, please," Whit answered. "We try to drink at least one glass per day."

"It helps my old rickety bones," Eli teased as she flipped some bacon.

"I love your old rickety bones," Whit reminded her.

"Who's got rickety bones?" Mitch asked as he came back down the steps.

"I do, but I'm still going to whoop you in catching fish today," Eli chuckled.

"In your dreams, old lady," Mitch tossed back.

"Hey, that's enough," Laura said.

"Sorry, Aunt Eli."

"I'm still young enough to keep you in line," she teased.

"That you are. Love you," Mitch answered.

"Most."

"Don't even get us started with that. I'd like to eat before noon," Mark said.

Eli took several pieces of bacon and crumbled them on a circle of batter. "Hey, hey, what do you think you're doing?" Mark asked.

"I want bacon in my cakes," she said. "I'm sweet enough already."

"That you are, Sis." He added a pancake on top of the bacon-filled one. "Go eat with the boys."

"Aye, aye, Captain." She saluted and took the plate to the table.

Mark heard a door slam and looked out the window to see Evan, Erin, and Jessie approaching. "How do kids always know the right time to show up?" Mark teased.

"Good morning. Y'all are just in time for breakfast," Whit said as they entered. "Who's hungry?"

"I smell bacon," Evan said and rubbed his hands together.

"We have pancakes, too," Eli reported between bites.

"So, who's up for pancakes?" Mark asked as he poured more batter on the grill.

"I could never turn down your cooking," Evan replied.

Mark looked at the girls, and they both nodded. "Whit, I need you," Mark said.

"What's up?" Whit asked.

"My partner is currently feeding her face. Will you mix me up some more batter?" Mark smiled at her.

"Certainly," Whit answered and whipped up another batch of batter.

Mark poured several circles on the grill. "Hotcakes, coming right up." He pulled six pancakes off the flat top. "Get them while they are hot."

Whit grabbed a piece of bacon and walked to the counter. "Who wants what to drink?"

"Milk's good for me," Evan said.

"Me too," Jessie replied.

"I'll take some OJ," Erin answered.

Whit brought the drinks to the table. "Who needs more coffee?"

"I'll take a cup," Eli replied.

"All good here," Laura said.

Mark grabbed a plate and filled it with pancakes and bacon. He joined the others around the table. "Does anybody need anything before I sit down?"

"I think we're all stuffed, Dad," Mitch said. "They were delicious too."

"If I keep eating out here, I'll need to start paying rent," Evan teased.

"We'll let you work it off in labor," Eli said with a wink.

"Did you?" Mitch said.

"Yes, I did," Evan said.

"Did I miss a few words in that conversation?" Whit asked.

"Evan made a store run for me this morning. We thought it would be nice to have some solar floodlights out by the picnic tables. We'll put them up this morning if that's okay with you, Aunt Eli?"

"That is a great idea. Go for it." She smiled at the two beaming young men. "You know, Whit and I can help your dad with the chicken coop if y'all want to start fishing."

"If we all pitch in, we can have it done in no time," Mitch said.

"As soon as your dad finishes breakfast, we can get started."

"We'll go hang the floodlights then," Mitch said.

"Thanks again for breakfast." Evan grinned, then downed his milk.

"We'll be out shortly," Whit called behind the kids.

"There are some perks to using paper plates," Eli said. "Easy cleanup, and they get added to the compost bin."

†

Mark checked the coals and put the butts on to start cooking. The smell of the cooking meat filled the air.

"That is so not fair," Mitch groaned.

"What?" Mark grinned.

"You've got the grill set up to blow that delicious smell right to where we'll be fishing."

"You noticed that, too, huh?" Evan replied.

"I want the smell to remind you of the great reward you'll get after filling my cooler with trout filets," Mark said. "Let's go wrap up that second coop, and y'all can get to fishing."

It didn't take the group long at all to finish, and both coops looked great near the garden plot.

"You guys get to fishing, and I'll tend to the meat."

"What do you need me to do inside?" Whit asked Eli.

Eli pulled down her fishing rod. "Brew a couple of gallons of tea and lemonade. With guests bringing dishes, I'm not sure we need much of anything else."

"How about some fresh corn to accompany the meat. I can also slice some tomatoes and onions. Maybe even a cucumber salad," Whit smiled.

"That sounds good. I'll help you with that while Eli catches fish," Laura offered.

Eli looked at Whit. "Mark will take over the kitchen for a bit later. I know he'll be whipping up a variety of sauces to go with the meat."

Whit grinned. "There's more than one sauce?"

"Dear Lord, don't let Mark hear you say that or you'll get an hour-long lecture. Just watch him, and he will put on a show." Laura grinned at Whit. "He does make some awesome sauces."

"Good luck fishing. We'll check on you when we go to the garden. Do you want us to bring you two something cold to drink?"

"Thanks, Whit. We'll probably be ready by then." Eli kissed her softly and walked off the porch. "Do you have our buckets?" she called to Brad.

Brad chuckled. "Yes, ma'am, we're all set to kick some butt."

"Let's get to it then. I feel like fishing." Eli caught up with Brad, and they walked to the bridge.

†

Eli flipped a bucket over and sat as she double-checked her fly. "So, how has life been treating you?"

Brad started his cast. "Pretty well. Since Mitch is up here, I've taken over the lawns he typically cuts during the summer. It's been hot as heck, but spending money is always nice."

"You have a steady girlfriend?"

"Shannon and I do the dinner and movie thing just about every week. I can't wait to get my license so we can go on a proper date and don't have to rely on a parent to drive us around." He frowned. "Dad can be a nuisance sometimes."

"He loves you dearly, and just wants to make sure you're having a good time." Eli smiled up at him. "Let's see if I remember how to do this." She began her cast and smiled when the fly floated down to the exact spot she wanted. "Just like riding a bike," she chuckled.

"Don't look now, but you're about to get a bite," Brad said with an excited tone.

"You are absolutely right," Eli said as she set the hook in the fish's mouth. She reeled a sizeable brown trout onto the bridge. "My first catch of the season."

"Good job, Aunt Eli." Brad gave her a high five. "My turn next."

†

Whit decided to take a Gator across to her garden. She and Laura loaded into the vehicle. They stopped on the bridge to deliver the water and check on the pair's fishing quota.

"Hey, who's keeping the score down there?" Brad asked.

"Your dad. It makes him take his boots and socks off so he can count," Laura teased.

"I am so telling him you said that," Brad warned.

"Go ahead. Mark knows I love him," Laura said with a wink to Eli.

"How many have they caught down there?" Eli asked.

"The boys have two. I couldn't tell you about the girls. They've moved over to the western creek. I've heard a few excited yells from over that direction," Whit replied.

"Too bad we're going to beat them all," Eli said as she hooked another fish.

"That's the spirit. We'll see you on the way back through," Whit told them.

As they settled back into fishing, Brad looked over at Eli. "I love this place. I hope we will be able to move here soon."

"You don't want to finish school in Alabama?" Eli asked, a bit surprised by his comment.

"Not really. Montgomery has changed so much, and not for the better. There are all kinds of crime, even in our protected little neighborhood. I think Mom breathes a sigh of relief every time she makes it home safely from downtown."

259

"I hope things will work out so that y'all can move up here sooner rather than later. The high school here apparently has outstanding academics and sports programs. I'll be sure to bring that into a conversation with your dad before y'all leave."

"Thanks, Aunt Eli. I would sleep in the hayloft if I had to." He grinned.

"There's no need for that. Although, I do appreciate you watching over Molly last night."

"She is so sweet," Brad smiled. "She's got a heck of a kick, though."

Eli chuckled. "I bet she does. I love to watch her and Cruz run and play together."

"They are so funny. I'm glad to see Cruz found a friend, too. Do you think Whit would take me up to the lab tonight?"

"I'm sure she would, but why don't you ask her? I think I hear them headed this way."

Brad looked over toward Whit's place. "You're right. It looks like they are loaded down, too."

"Why don't you offer to ride down and carry their baskets in for them. You could ask Whit then. I promise I won't catch all the fish while you're gone."

"I could do that."

"Grab an extra bucket too. I've gotten used to sitting on this one," Eli said.

Brad shook his head with a laugh. "You got it, Aunt Eli. Maybe we should build a bench for here. It seems to be a good fishing spot."

"That's not a bad idea. I bet we have enough leftover wood to build one. Maybe we could do it later?"

Brad's face lit up. "Yeah, we could do that."

"Okay, that's a plan. Put the Gator up for Whit, too, while you're down there. I bet you could find another bucket in the barn."

"I'll check in on Molly, too. Make sure she has fresh water."

"Thanks, Brad." She looked up when the Gator started up the bridge. "Whoa, looks like y'all made a haul. Brad's going to ride down and help you for a few minutes."

"We can always use young muscle," Whit replied. "Hop in."

Brad settled into the back seat, and Eli returned to her fishing. "Heck yeah," she hollered as she hooked another fish.

†

Brad carried the baskets of food into the cabin. He looked at Whit. "Could I ask a favor?"

"Sure, what can I do for you?"

"Aunt Eli and I want to build a small bench for the bridge. It's such a great fishing spot, but buckets aren't that comfortable for sitting. She thinks we have enough leftover wood to build one this afternoon. Would you see if you can find a design on the Internet and print it out?"

"I'd love to. That's a good idea." Whit smiled. "I'll have it ready for when you all finish fishing."

"Great, thanks, Whit." He shuffled his feet for a second. "Do you want me to take the Gator back to the barn?"

"That would be great. Thanks, Brad. Good luck with the fishing."

He smiled back at her. "I've got my good luck charm with me today."

"Go get 'em, tiger," Laura told him.

"Yes, ma'am." Brad jogged out of the cabin and climbed into the Gator. He drove over to the western creek to check on the girls' fish count. Brad pulled up and walked over to them.

"Wow, y'all are doing great," he said after taking a peek at their bucket.

"Not bad, but we're far from done," Erin said with a wink. "How are the boys doing?"

"I didn't check in with them, but I suppose I should. Good luck," Brad said and jogged back to the Gator.

†

When he walked back onto the bridge wearing a smile, Eli asked. "What's got you smiling so hard?"

"I checked on the girls, and they don't have near the fish we do."

"What about your brother and Evan?"

"I didn't check on them. It's been kind of quiet down there. I don't know if Mitch and Evan aren't catching much or are just being clever and lying low."

"It does make it hard to tell. Maybe the smell of your Dad's cooking is keeping them distracted. I'm so glad we are upwind of the grill."

"Me, too. The whiff I got when I was down there has my mouth watering."

"I have no idea what we are going to do for lunch," Eli said. "Any thoughts?"

"Fried chicken or burgers would be great," Brad answered.

"I'm going to stroll back to the cabin and see if I can convince Whit and your mom to make a food run. Like you, I could use something hot. I'll sneak a look at the boys' catch too."

"Good idea. How long are we supposed to fish anyhow?"

"I think once lunch gets here, we can call a halt to the competition." She reeled in her line. "I'll be back. You need anything?"

"A few more fish." He grinned back at her.

†

Eli walked into the cabin where Whit and Laura were shucking corn. "Brad and I would like to know if you two would make a food run into town?"

"No more sandwiches for lunch?" Whit asked.

"Nope, we need something hot. Like fried chicken or some burgers."

"We could get some of those burgers the boys are always raving about," Whit said. "I'll do a headcount and call in an order."

"You'd better plan for a couple of extras. Fishing is hard work," Eli grinned.

"Got it. We'll be back as soon as we can."

"Thanks, Whit. I'm going to check on Mark and get back to fishing. We're going to quit fishing when y'all get back."

"Thanks for the heads up."

†

Mark was sitting at the fire pit, watching the boys fish when Eli walked up.

"Hey, Sis," he said. "What's up?"

263

"Just checking in to see how everything is going? Whit and Laura are making a burger run to town. I thought we'd call off the competition when they return. How are the boys catching?"

"Not too bad. Mitch and Evan have caught a nice mess, but I think not having the girls in their sight has them worried."

"It's not the girls they should be worried about," Eli smirked. "I'd better get back to it. You need anything?"

"Nope, I'm perfect right here." Mark stretched his legs out in front of him and relaxed back into the chair.

Eli started back toward the bridge and Cruz trotted out of the barn. "Is everything okay with Molly?" She walked inside and found Molly curled up fast asleep. "Probably the best thing for her right now," she told Cruz. "Let's go."

Cruz rushed ahead of her onto the bridge and stuck her head in the bucket beside Brad. One of the fish smacked its tail against the bucket, and she started barking.

"It's okay. That fish won't get you," Brad told Cruz. "Come here," Brad called her to his side. He placed his hand on her head and scratched behind her ears.

"You'd better pay attention. I do believe you are getting a bite," Eli chuckled as she sat on the bucket. She glanced down into the second bucket. "It looks like I've got catching up to do."

"I think we're in good shape to win," Brad said. "Did you see how Evan and Mitch were doing?"

"Unless they have a bucket hidden somewhere, I think we've got them beat. The girls are the unknown factor," Eli shrugged. "Either way, win or lose, I've had a blast fishing with you."

"Me, too, Aunt Eli." Brad smiled and cast his line.

They were able to catch six more fish before Whit and Laura returned. "Let's take in our catch and get ready to eat. I'm hungry," Eli told Brad.

Between the three teams, thirty-two fish were landed, with Brad and Eli the winners by three fish. "It looks like you're going home with a cooler full of fish," Eli told Mark.

"I'm not complaining at all. That will be some delicious eating for a while. The best part is, I don't even have to clean the catch."

"Nope, we can have lunch and start dressing them and getting them ready for the freezer." Eli walked with Mark toward the picnic tables. "I need to go wash up. I'll be right there."

She walked into the laundry room where Mitch was washing his hands. "That was fun, wasn't it?" she asked.

"Yeah, but I hate getting my butt kicked two days in a row."

"It's all good. Your family has fish to take home, and we all had fun fishing." She shrugged. "Besides, you have the record for the biggest fish yet."

Mitch smiled at her. "Yeah, I do. Finish up so we can go grub. I'm starving."

"I never knew fishing was such hard work. I'm so ready for one of those burgers you rave about." She dried her hands. "Let's go."

Laura and Whit were placing burgers and fries on the table. Laura looked at Mitch. "Take a seat; they are all the same. You can add to or remove based on your tastes."

Eli bit into a burger. She wiped the juice running down her chin. "You weren't exaggerating when you raved how good these burgers are."

"They've been a local staple around here for years. Before these kids were even born," Whit replied. "They haven't changed a bit in all those years."

"It's impossible to improve upon perfection," Mitch said. "I could eat these every day."

"Even the seasoned fries are tasty," Laura said.

Mark nodded. "I have to admit they are pretty darn tasty."

"How are the butts coming along?" Eli asked.

"They've got another three or four hours before I take them out to rest. It will give me plenty of time to whip up some sauces."

"Are you doing some Alabama white sauce?" Brad asked.

"Yes, I'll do that, some Carolina mustard sauce and the red sauce from Florida."

"White barbeque sauce." Erin looked at Mark. "Do I want to know?"

Mark shrugged. "Probably not, but that leaves more for me."

"Trust me; you're going to love it," Mitch said.

"Can we watch?" Evan asked.

Mark was indeed in his element when he had an audience. "I charge admission," he said and shot a grin at Evan. "Of course, you can watch and learn from the master."

"I've been trying to get him to enter one of the BBQ cooking contests for years," Laura said.

Mark shrugged. "I cook for my friends and family. It's a passion for me, not a competition."

"As long as I get to continue to reap those rewards, I don't care if you enter contests or not." Eli smiled and took another bite of her burger.

†

Whit handed Brad a piece of paper after they finished eating. "This is pretty basic, and you should have enough wood to make it."

"Thanks, Whit." Brad hugged her neck and raced off to the workshop to start gathering boards.

"What was that all about?" Eli asked Whit.

"Brad asked me to find and print out a simple design for a bench. It appears his favorite aunt told him they could build one today." Whit's eyes sparkled as she teased Eli.

"Yes, I did. Can you handle the inside stuff while we create this masterpiece?"

"All we have left is to boil the corn to go on the grill. Everything else is sliced and ready to go. I'll take in the Mark sauce show while it boils."

"Be prepared to laugh. Mark's quite the showman when he has a captive audience."

Whit nodded. "Thanks for the warning."

"He may need an assistant during the show," Eli replied. "A go fer this and go fer that."

"Kinda like his big sister, huh?"

"What? Oh, yeah, kinda." She lightly punched Whit's shoulder. "I'll see you soon."

CHAPTER SEVENTEEN

"I'm not sure which sauce I liked the best," Dr. Loren said as she dipped a piece of meat in the Alabama white sauce. "They are all so tasty."

"You can take some of each home with you," Mark said. He smiled at her praise.

Mr. Henry shook his head. "I've got no doubt. I've had the Carolina mustard sauce all my life, but I think the Alabama white sauce has it beat."

"That's the luxury of pork. You can use so many different sauces to enhance the flavor." Mark popped a bite in his mouth.

"You can cook for me anytime, young man," Ms. Flora gave him a wink. "You're moving up next week, right?" she teased.

"Don't I wish," Mark answered. "I can't get up here soon enough."

"How long do you think it will be?" Macy asked.

Mark sighed. "Probably at least a year, maybe two."

"You can bet I'll lure him up here every chance I get," Eli said. "I think I've gained five pounds since he got here, though."

Mitch laughed. "Who are you kidding? You work it off as fast as you eat it."

Eli shook her head. "I dunno, Mitch, I don't remember these shorts being so tight."

"You probably just left them in the dryer too long," Brad said. "You look great, Aunt Eli."

"That's why I love these two so much." She grinned at Mark. "They always say the sweetest things."

"What? Don't look at me. They got that from her," Mark said, pointing to Laura.

"I'll take ownership of that." Laura smiled at her husband.

Dr. Loren turned to Mitch. "How's Molly today?"

"She's doing good. We've kept her in the stall all day, but she's up on it bearing weight." He nodded to Brad. "He slept out there with her and has been doctoring her foot."

"It sounds like you're doing a fine job then." She smiled at Brad. "Who won the fish-off I heard about today?"

"Team Brad!" he hollered. "Aunt Eli and I outfished them all."

"We're going to have a nice cooler of fish to take back with us," Mark added.

"That may hold us until we come back," Brad replied.

"When are you coming back?" Evan asked.

"Dad and I'll be here for a week next month. Mom's got a conference to attend, so she just gets a long weekend."

"Better than nothing," Laura said.

"Practice up, and maybe we'll have another fish-off." Brad teased Evan.

"Aww, Mitch and I were just taking it easy on y'all today." Evan grinned. "You won't be so lucky next time."

"Ha! I've got my lucky charm." Brad placed his arm around Eli's shoulder.

"Hey, I just realized we have light," Whit said. "The boys installed some solar floodlights this morning."

"They were so natural we didn't realize they came on," Eli bragged.

"I think that's our cue to head home, old man," Ms. Flora said.

"Hang on, and I'll fix you a to-go plate." Whit started piling food onto plates. "Sorry, none of your banana pudding survived. I'll wash your dishes and send them back with Mr. Henry this week."

"No rush," Ms. Flora said.

"The faster I send them back clean and empty, the faster they will be refilled." Whit chuckled.

"Just let me know when you're ready for more." She smiled at Whit.

"You can bet I will. What time is it?" Whit asked, and the others started laughing.

"I'll barter more pudding with another mess of those delicious trout," Ms. Flora said.

"You are so on, Ms. Flora. Next Friday?" Eli asked.

"That would be great." Mr. Henry rubbed his hands together.

"I'll see if I can convince Mitch to do some fishing next week," Eli said with a wink.

"Yeah, he needs the practice," Brad teased.

"I'll fish for you anytime, Ms. Flora, just give me a call. Aunt Eli never has to twist my arm." Mitch stood with her and picked up the plates. "Do you want me to carry these to the car for you?"

"You certainly can, young man. Thank you, thank you all for another lovely meal and a great weekend." She looked at Mr. Henry. "I think this has been the most fun we've had in a while."

Eli returned her smile. "You are welcome to come out and join us whenever you'd like. I can't always guarantee such good cooking, but I promise you won't go hungry."

"That means so much. Our kids are all grown and live so far away. It's nice to be around the energy of teenagers," Mr. Henry said.

"It is nice having young people around often," Eli agreed. "They work hard and play even harder."

"Here we go." Whit placed six small containers on the table. "Three containers of sauce for you and three for Doc and Macy."

"It looks like we both have lunch or dinner for tomorrow, Mr. Henry," Macy said.

"If it makes it past midnight," Ms. Flora gently poked Mr. Henry. "Someone has been getting up lately to raid the refrigerator, and I know it's not a bear."

Mr. Henry shrugged and grinned sheepishly. "What can I say? I need more food than sleep these days."

"There's nothing wrong with that. Nothing at all," Eli said. "I think we should all sleep in a bit tomorrow. It's been a fun but busy weekend."

"Good luck with that," Laura said. "If we manage to make it to seven, we're doing good."

"Speaking of which," Whit looked at Brad. "Would y'all mind if Brad and I take off for a little while?"

"Not at all. Have fun."

"Come on, Mr. Henry. Macy and I will follow you out to make sure you get home safely. Remember, the deer are moving right now, so we have to be careful."

"Don't I know it," Evan smirked. "Hey, Mitch. Do you want to ride with me to take the ladies home?"

Mitch looked to his Dad. Mark nodded. "Sure. Is there anything you need me to do before we go?"

Eli shook her head. "Nope, we've got this. It was great having you all here this weekend. We'll plan something again soon."

"Thanks, Eli. It was a lot of fun," Erin said. "This place is so amazing."

"We love it here, too," Eli replied.

"Let's go, Brad. We'll be back," Whit told them.

†

"This is so cool," Brad declared when Whit turned the telescope over to him.

"Mitch and I found a spot up by the cave that makes you feel like you can reach into the sky and pluck out a star. It's so beautiful. Maybe he will take you up tomorrow night."

"I can't believe tomorrow is our last day already. We just got here," he moaned.

"You'll be back, though." Whit sat down on the day bed. "Eli told me you and Mitch wanted to hike the AT. Is that still true?"

"Yes, but Dad said I have to wait until I'm sixteen, so I've got a year to go."

"Maybe we can do a section next summer then, when you're out of school. I'd like to go. I've done a few stages, but haven't finished the whole trail."

"That would be fun. Hey, maybe if Dad knew you were going with us, he'd let me go."

"We can talk about it when y'all come back up. You're still planning on staying for the summer, right?"

"Yes, ma'am, if that's all right."

"It's more than all right. There are lots of things to do, and some time just to explore the mountain is the perfect way to spend the day."

"Maybe Mitch and I could explore the section of trail that comes through here and spend a night or two on the trail to get some experience."

"That's not a bad idea. You could do some trail maintenance, too, if you see shelters that need repair or trees that are a danger to hikers. I think there are shelters roughly three miles in either direction on the trail." She thought for a second. "You could carry a pack, hike to the shelter, spend the night, and head back. It'll give you some idea for what being on the trail is like."

"I'll have to get a backpack and some supplies. Mitch, too." Brad wiggled with excitement.

"Why don't you let Mitch and I handle that from up here? We can get you both outfitted and ready for a short hike."

"That would be so awesome."

Whit charted the area she had been following. It was still enlarging, but not at the rate it was earlier. She was no closer to determining what it was, though.

She pulled her phone from her pocket to check her emails while Brad scoured the universe. She hoped she would find an email from one of her colleagues on the origin of the crystal. *Damn, nothing yet.* She tapped out a text to *Eli. Don't forget; we need to give Brad his gift.*

She saw the little bubbles appear on her phone, letting her know Eli was typing a response. *Setting up for it now. Let me know when you're on the way. Love you.*

More, Whit typed back. Give us five, and we'll be on our way.

†

Mark carried out the ice cream maker while Laura carried a tray of cupcakes she had secretly baked earlier. Mitch retrieved disposable bowls and spoons. Eli placed a small candle on top of one of the cakes. "Does anyone have a lighter or matches?"

"I've got one in the truck," Mark stated. "I'll be right back."

Mark made it back as the Gator crossed over the bridge. Mark lit the candle and turned with the cupcake in his hand as Brad approached.

The group sang *Happy Birthday* to him, and Brad blew out his candle.

"Thanks, y'all, but my birthday isn't for another week."

"We are quite well aware of that, but your brother and aunt wanted to celebrate with you." Laura ruffled his hair.

"It's not much, but we wanted to give you something," Eli said. She handed him the boxes wrapped in the paper sack. "You'll have to forgive the wrapping," Eli chuckled.

"You didn't have to get me anything, Aunt Eli. Just being here was enough." He began to open the paper, and when he saw the word Case written on the box, he let out a yell. "Please let this be a Sodbuster Junior."

Mark smiled at Eli. "We thought we'd just fill the box with rocks."

"Mark," Eli said. "Quit teasing him."

Brad opened the box, and his eyes were sparkling as he pulled out the knife. "My very first Sodbuster."

274

"The last you'll ever need if you take care of it," Mark said. "Keep going; there's more."

He opened the smaller box holding the case and slipped the knife into it. "It's a perfect fit. Will you help me hone it tomorrow?" he asked Mark.

"I sure will." Mark grinned.

"Thanks, Aunt Eli and Whit."

"I got you something, too," Mitch said to everyone's surprise. "You have to go to the workshop to get it. I didn't have wrapping paper, so it's still in the box."

Brad raced over to the workshop, and they heard a yell seconds later. When the door opened again, Brad came out sporting a hiking backpack, strapped across his shoulder. "This is awesome. Thanks."

"Happy birthday, Brad." Mitch smiled at his little brother. "I thought we could break it in this summer."

"So cool," Brad said as he turned to model the pack for the group. "All set for some hiking," he said to Whit.

"About that," Whit said. "When Brad comes up for the summer, would you be okay with Mitch and Brad taking an overnight trip to do some trail maintenance? There's a shelter about three miles north and south of ours. I haven't been there for some time. They could hike it, spend the night and come back the next day to resupply."

Mark looked at Laura. She nodded. "I think that would be some good trail experience," he answered.

"Great idea, Whit," Mitch said and gave her a high five.

Whit smiled and looked at Eli, then Mark. "I figured we could get them supplied up here, so you wouldn't have to haul anything from 'Bama. It will probably be cheaper here as well."

"Sounds like a plan to me," Eli responded. "I'm sure the three of you can come up with a shopping list tomorrow while we relax."

"Just remember, it's only an overnight trip, not a section hike, so don't overload your packs," Mark warned.

"Got it, Dad," Mitch said.

"Okay, let's eat this ice cream before it starts to melt," Laura said, and began scooping out bowls.

†

Eli heard the door close when Mitch came in later from taking the girls home. She and Whit snuggled in the bed.

"You can relax now," Whit teased. "Everyone is home and accounted for."

"Yes, they are. Thanks for another great day. I think everyone had fun and got fed well."

"Thank you. That was an excellent way to spend the weekend with family and friends."

"I can't believe how quickly time has passed. Only one more day and they have to go back." Eli ran her fingers through Whit's hair.

"They will be back soon. I'm looking forward to having Brad for most of the summer. He's a good kid, too."

"Much different from Mitch, but they get along reasonably well together. Brad is more of an explorer than a doer. He requires a bit more prompting than Mitch to get work done, but once you get him motivated, it's all good. That was a great idea about some short hikes."

"I thought it would be a great way for them to get experience on the trail, but still be close in case they needed us." Whit ran her fingers across Eli's stomach. "I was surprised, but pleased Laura gave her consent so easily."

"She can be overprotective, but I think Laura has realized her boys are growing up, and they need her trust to do what's right."

"They will be just fine," Whit said as she snuggled closer to Eli.

Eli reached down to find Tomboy lying next to her. "Yes, they will. I know you'll prepare them well for what to expect on the trail."

"Yes, ma'am, I will."

†

Eli was unable to sleep in, so she carefully climbed out of bed and dressed before going downstairs. The coffeepot was still warm, but there was nobody else in sight. She made a cup and walked outside. Eli was about to take a seat to enjoy her coffee when she heard Cruz barking from up the trail. *I wonder what that's all about?*

She stood and began walking up the path. The farther she walked, the louder the sound of Cruz's barking became. She smiled when she heard Mark's voice.

"You better hush. You're going to wake the house up and get us both in trouble." He threw the Frisbee, and Cruz took off across the field in pursuit.

When Cruz caught the Frisbee, she turned to rush back. When she saw Eli, Cruz ran past Mark, who turned to see his sister approaching. "I'm sorry if we woke you."

"You didn't. I find it hard to sleep late. The mornings are so beautiful here."

"That's for sure. I wanted to come up here to envision my future home nestled over by the creek." Mark smiled at Eli. "I can't wait to be up here for good."

They began to walk across the open field. "What visions do you have?" Eli asked.

"There, next to the cave we're going to use for a root cellar, I'd like to build a smokehouse." They kept walking. "Maybe a smaller workshop for projects. A springhouse, the cabin, of course, would go here, and a garage, there."

Eli smiled at him. "I like that plan. I can't wait to help you make it real."

"Not soon enough for me," Mark said. "I'm so tired of working for someone else. I like the company I work for, but that's all it is, work. I don't have the passion I used to have for it. Especially since I know this is waiting for me."

"Maybe it will be enough to keep you motivated to get here. Maybe we can start on a few projects this summer. The spring house, and smoker maybe?"

He nodded. "That would be fun. Maybe we can get a hog to try out in the smoker."

Eli guided their path to the creek. He noticed the orange markings. "What is this?"

"I'm going to have a bridge built this fall, to give us access higher on the mountain and for use once you're ready to get started building."

"That makes it pretty permanent," Mark smiled.

"We are going to do this," Eli said.

Cruz splashed into the creek, and Mark laughed. "She loves the water. You better dry off before we go home."

She stopped in the middle of the creek and shook.

"That's a good start," Eli said.

Marked laughed at the dog's antics. "Cruz is doing well here. It's obvious she loves her mama and her new family."

"She's settled in well. I'm so happy to have her back in my life."

"This place has done wonders for you. Laura says you look ten years younger. I have to admit, she's right."

"It's home, and everything I ever wanted is coming to fruition. I never realized how happy I could be. Until now."

"You're well past due for happiness. I'm glad I get to come here and share it with you."

"I wouldn't wish it any other way unless it was you never had to leave."

"One day, that wish will come true." Mark started to walk. "I think this trip has been good for Laura, too. She can see the possibilities that await us."

"Hopefully, something will work out where she can retire early or work remotely. We've got surprisingly great reception up here for phone and internet."

"That is a plus. I think even Brad is tired of Montgomery."

"That's what he told Whit and me yesterday. All the crime and violence are stressing him."

"Not at all like it is up here." Mark grinned.

Eli turned to Mark with a sigh. "What should we cook for breakfast? Surely someone has started to stir."

"The old standby SOS is easy and quick. The boys love it as much as you," Mark teased.

"Let me feed the animals and doctor Molly, and we can get started."

"I'll feed if you want to tend to her. I want to peek at the space in the barn we are going to use for drying lumber."

"We've got plenty of room left, or we could build a drying room."

Mark cocked his head. "That's not a bad idea." He turned to look at her. "You know, with the purchase of a trailer, I bet I could work a tree service part-time. We could use the hardwoods for lumber and sell the rest for firewood. That way we aren't diminishing our forest."

"That's a definite possibility. With the National Park on one border, we may also get permits to take down some of the standing dead trees." Eli chuckled. "The possibilities are endless as long as you're not afraid of hard work."

"The purchase of a splitter was ideal. Whatever we don't use, Brad or Mitch could split and stack for firewood. I like this more and more," Mark grinned.

"I think we've got enough butt left for lunch, but what do you want for dinner?" Mark asked.

"Mitch is undoubtedly your son. He's planning the next two meals before he eats the first."

"Brad hasn't gotten his fried chicken fix. What if Mitch and I drive to town for a bucket of chicken and some fixings?"

"I'd like that. It has been a while since we've had fried chicken."

"One step at a time. SOS, here we come."

Mitch and Brad were sitting on the front porch steps when Eli and Mark emerged from the barn. "Hold me up, Holy Ghost," Mark cried out.

"What?" Eli asked.

"Both of my sons are up before seven without having their lives threatened." He turned back to his sons. "Good morning, boys. You up for SOS this morning?"

"Heck, yes," Brad said.

"I'll even take toast duty," Mitch said.

Eli smiled at Mark. "He's gotten pretty killer on toast duty."

"You got the job, son. Let's go."

"We have fried chicken planned for tonight, too," Eli told Brad.

"Awesome. I love me some yard bird." He patted Eli's shoulder as they walked into the cabin.

Whit was standing in front of the coffee pot, waiting for her cup to brew. "Have a seat, and I'll bring it to you," Mitch offered.

"Thanks, Mitch." She looked at Eli. "Did he fall and hit his head or something? He's awful sweet this morning."

"Ha! It's a wonderful life in the mountains," Mitch crowed.

Eli frowned. "Now, I am worried." She lifted her hand to his forehead. "He's not feverish. His breath smells like toothpaste." She sniffed. "I don't smell any wacky weed on him."

Mark finally asked. "What is it you want, son?"

"Well, we were thinking," he nodded toward Brad. "He's out of school, so can he just stay up here instead of going home?"

"No." Mark reached for the container of flour.

Mitch looked at Eli, who just shrugged.

"If I let him stay, who do I have left to pick on? Your mom will kick my ass," Mark grinned.

"You can call ten times a day to pick on me. C'mon, Dad," Brad pleaded.

Mark turned around to look at Eli and Whit. "Would that be okay with you two?"

Eli shrugged again. "The more, the merrier. Besides, it's only a few weeks tacked on to Brad's sentence, um I mean vacation."

"Will you be sure to work him hard?" Mark snickered. "Good luck with that."

"You know I will. There's no slacking around here."

"If you can convince your mom, I'm okay with the idea. What about clothes?"

"We can take him to a thrift store," Eli teased.

"Ewww, never mind, I'm going home."

Eli laughed. "I'm just teasing. We can get him enough clothes to last for a while. We do have a fully functional laundry room too."

"Okay, you've convinced me. Mom is the one you need to start trying to convince. I'd start with coffee in bed," Mark recommended.

Brad rushed to make a cup of coffee to take to his mom. "Wish me luck," he said as he exited the kitchen.

The room was silent. "Well, I didn't hear any loud commotion. That's a good sign."

"Yes!" they heard Brad scream.

"Well, there's your answer. Good luck to ya, Sis."

"She said 'yes'," Brad said with excitement as he returned to the kitchen.

"We kind of figured that. Mr. Henry probably heard you in town," Mitch teased. Another round of toast popped up, and Mitch placed it on a cutting board to cut into bite-sized pieces. "Grab us some fine china from the pantry, and get everyone something to drink."

"I can see this is going to be fun already. My assistant has an assistant," Eli teased.

"May I go back with you, Mark?" Whit asked.

"What?" Eli said.

"It's no fair you have two assistants, and I have none." Whit pouted.

"Alright then, to keep it fair, you can have Brad for an assistant. Better?" Eli asked.

"Much. I've never had an assistant before." Whit grinned.

Eli put her hands on her hips. "What was I, sloppy seconds?"

Whit chuckled. "No, honey, you're the best partner ever."

"I knew you were brilliant, Whit," Mark said from the stove.

Laura emerged from the bedroom. "Do you two really know what you're getting into?"

"A whole lotta fun," Whit replied.

"Just as long as you know, you can send them BOTH home if they start acting out." No one in the room missed her emphasis on both.

"I know, but I seriously doubt that will be needed. Trust me; the boys will earn their keep." Eli smiled. "We have so much work ahead of us, they may be begging to come home."

"Be sure to send me proof-of-life pics," Laura teased.

"Will do," Whit said. "Enjoy the relaxing day today, boys. Tomorrow we go back to work."

CHAPTER EIGHTEEN

"You know what we need up here?" Mark asked Eli as they rocked on the porch.

"What's that, dear brother?"

"Some hammocks to hang between these trees. They would be perfect for a lazy afternoon like today." He smiled. "A gentle breeze is carrying the scent of the mountains. There are no bugs to eat you alive. I'd say it's damn near perfect."

"A good book to read or a long nap," Eli added.

"Yes, those would work well." He smiled at Eli. "I love dreaming with you."

"It's nice to know we can make some of them come true."

"Did I hear you tell Laura that Carol was coming up soon?"

"Yeah, you did. Carol will be up in a few weeks."

"I'm glad the two of you are talking. Despite what happened, Carol has been a good friend to you for a long time."

"Yes, she has. I can't just toss those years away so easily. We've had a lot of good times together, and I'm almost positive we'll have more."

The sound of boots on the porch floor turned their attention away from Carol. Mitch rounded the corner.

"Hey, Dad, Mom said to remind you that you promised to make a chicken run, and it's getting late."

Mark looked at his watch. "Can you believe it's almost five?"

"Time flies up here because, you know, we're always having fun," Eli teased. "Do you want me to go?"

"Nope, I have a driver just itching to go. Isn't that right, son?"

"Yes, sir, you are absolutely correct." Mitch grinned. "Any special requests?"

"Some of their hot wings if they have some," Eli requested. "Oh, and a gallon of milk. You guys wiped me out this morning. On second thought, make it two."

"Yes, ma'am. You need help, old man?"

"Naw, I can still make it out of a rocker. We'll be back if we don't end up in a ditch somewhere."

"Mitch, watch out for deer. Where there's one—" Eli started.

"I know, where there's one, there's two."

"I'm glad he listens to you. You're going to have to teach me that trick."

"Be safe, and hurry back." Eli waved as they pulled down the drive. When she looked back around, Whit had joined her. "Hey, baby. You snuck up on me."

"I was coming to check on you. You and Mark have been out here a while. Everything okay?"

"Things couldn't be more perfect, especially now that you're here. What are Brad and Laura doing?"

"Brad is looking at hiking gear on the Internet, and Laura is frosting a cake. I had a cake mix over at my place, and Mitch went to get it for me."

"I'm glad I told him to buy milk. Cake without a cold glass of milk is just wrong on so many levels." She reached for Whit and pulled her into her lap. "What have you been doing?"

"I doctored Molly and fed the animals. I think she'll be ready to cut loose tomorrow. She's feisty again."

"That's such a relief. It was nice having Loren and Macy come out, though. I like them."

"They are good people. There are a few other lesbian couples and some singles in town. Maybe we can throw another cookout when Carol comes up. Introduce her to some fine hillbilly ladies. She may never go home."

Eli hugged her close. "That wouldn't bother me one bit. I hope you like Carol. She's seen me through some hard times."

Whit leaned over and kissed her sweetly. "I'm sure I will. I like your taste in friends."

"How about something cold to drink? Let's grab something and take a look at what Brad has found. I'm sure you can advise him on what he needs for hiking."

Whit stood up and pulled Eli out of her rocker. "Let's go."

†

Mark looked over at his son as they rode to town. "I'm glad we got to spend this time together. I want you to know how proud of you I am. You are not the boy I knew from Montgomery. You've grown into a mature, hard-working young man."

"Eli and Whit have been a big help to me."

Mark nodded. "That's true, but the growth came from you. I'm impressed with all the projects you've helped to complete. I can't wait to return so I can work beside you again."

"That means a lot, Dad. I know I haven't been the easiest child to raise, but hey, you survived me, and now you have Brad to contend with."

"In some ways, Brad is more complicated than you ever dreamed of being. I hope the time he spends with you, Eli, and Whit this summer will help him. He's quite intelligent, but he has little ambition to use his talents."

"I'll do my best, Dad."

"I know you will, son. I hope you know that you can always talk to me if you need a fresh set of ears. Eli and Whit are great, but I don't know how they would do with a man-to-man talk."

"Oh, you don't have to worry about Aunt Eli, we've had several deep conversations about being a gentleman and how to treat others. You can bet she'll keep my ass in line."

"That's my sis. Don't ever hesitate to call me. I'll always be there for you."

"I know, Dad. I honestly didn't used to think that, but growing up has taught me how important you and Mom are to me."

Mark wiped at his eyes. "Damn, you make my eyes leak. I love you, Son."

"Most," Mitch replied with a grin.

"No way, man."

†

The rest of the evening passed all too quickly for Eli. She knew Mark would be back in a few weeks, but she still hated to see him go. They were cleaning up after dinner when she asked. "What time do you plan to roll out in the morning?"

"I'm in no rush to get back to Montgomery, but I know getting through Atlanta on a holiday weekend will be a bear." Mark sighed. "Can you just wiggle your nose or beam me up or something?"

Eli laughed. "I wish I could. You could live here all the time, and I could beam you to work and back."

"Doncha think he's scrambled up enough already without putting him through the transporter?" Brad asked.

"But it would be so cool to call you and say, 'Beam me up, Scotty.'" Mark laughed.

"So, how about biscuits and gravy before you go?" Mitch suggested.

"See what I'm talking about? He's already planning his next meal." Eli laughed and hugged Mitch.

"That's my man," Mark answered.

Eli was glad Mark referred to Mitch as a man. The young boy was rapidly disappearing. She smiled at them. "Biscuits and gravy it is."

†

"You know hiding up here isn't going to keep Mark from leaving. It's just going to prolong the time he's stuck in traffic in Atlanta," Whit said. "I know you're sad, but he'll be back."

"I know, I just wish he didn't feel like he had to go." Eli groaned as she stood up from the bed.

"One day he won't, but until then, we will cherish the time we have with them."

Eli pulled Whit into her arms for a kiss. "Thanks for coming into my life."

"Ditto, Babe. I needed you, and I didn't even know I did. One look at you and I was a goner. Still am. My heart races every time you look at me."

"Come on. All this mushy talk is going to make me cry."

"Let's go, Teddy Bear." Whit took her hand and led her to the stairs.

Mitch was carrying out the last of the suitcases.

"Damn, I wish y'all didn't have to go." She hugged Mark tight.

"One day we'll be here for good, and you may think, damn, won't he just go home."

"No way. I love you too much to ever think that." Eli felt her tears forming.

Mark hugged her tighter. "Just remember, I love you most."

"No way, man. Will you call to let us know you've made it home?"

"I am home, but I'll call you when we reach Montgomery. Make my sons work."

"You can bet they will," Whit stepped in to say. "Be careful."

"Bye, Dad," Brad hugged Mark, then ran around to hug his mom.

"I'll see you soon, son," Mark offered his hand to Mitch.

Mitch took his hand and pulled him in for a hug. "I'll never be too old to hug my dad." He walked over and kissed Laura's cheek. "Love you, Mom. Good luck being alone with him for a few weeks."

"I'll do my best not to harm him. I can always kick him out to come up here," Laura teased Mark.

"Hell, that's no punishment," Mark grinned and closed the door behind his wife.

"See you soon. Love y'all."

"Most," Mitch and Brad said.

Whit placed an arm around Eli's shoulders as they watched them drive away. When Mark's truck was no longer in sight, Whit looked at the boys. "Time to get to work."

"What's on the schedule for today?" Mitch asked.

Whit could sense Eli was still a bit choked up, so she smiled at Mitch. "We have three benches that need staining, two gardens that need tilling for starters. Take your pick."

"I don't mind staining," Brad volunteered.

"Wear some old clothing. We need to go to town today and buy some stuff for you, too," Eli said. "After we finish our projects, we can go to the store and the diner afterward." Eli looked at Mitch. "Is Evan coming out today?"

"Yeah, his dad closed the store for the holiday, so we're going to try to knock out the rest of Whit's lab." He grinned at Eli. "Speak of the devil."

They all looked to find Evan coming up the driveway.

"Perfect timing," Eli said. "I guess that leaves the tilling to us. It's time to add compost. Do you want to start in your garden or mine?"

"The tiller's already here, so let's work here first." She looked at Eli. "Yours is going to be smelly. We have all the fish waste in your compost pile."

"I'll have to till fast. Or do you want me to haul and you till?"

Whit shook her head. "You can till, but get your hat and sunglasses."

"I'll go grab them," Brad said and rushed back inside.

Eli looked at Mitch. "Will you get Brad set up to stain?"

"Yes, ma'am." He looked at Evan, who was walking up to the group. "Are you ready to knock out some stain?"

Evan smiled. "Good morning. I think we can finish it today."

"Dinner at the diner, if you do," Eli said.

"Heck yeah, let's go." Evan grinned.

"Brad's going to stain the tables and benches, so we've got to get him set up."

Evan nodded. "No problem. We've got about two gallons in one of the buckets. That should be plenty for those projects. Let's grab a Gator, and we can drive over for supplies."

"Hey," Eli called out. "Don't forget to grab something to drink. You've got to stay hydrated."

"Yes, ma'am. I'll grab the small cooler when we get back," Mitch answered.

Brad came running back with her hat and sunglasses. "That goes for us, too. We can't have anyone getting dehydrated."

"I'll grab us some Gatorade and meet you at the garden," Whit said.

Eli looked at Brad. "Mitch and Evan have gone to pick up stain and supplies for you. Why don't you grab the bench from the bridge and carry it over to the picnic tables? You can have a little bit of shade for a while."

"That's a great idea," Brad answered and started walking toward the bridge.

Eli walked to the garden and smiled when Cruz and Molly trotted along beside her. "I'm so glad you're feeling better," she said to Molly. "Y'all take it easy today."

†

Two hours later, Eli and Whit had finished turning her garden. When Eli drove the tiller out of the gate, Brad looked up toward her. Eli could see the heat in his cheeks, flushing his face. She turned to Whit and nodded toward Brad. "I think it's time we cooled down."

"Hey, Brad," Whit called out and motioned him over.

"Yes, ma'am. What do you need?" he asked after jogging over.

"It's time to cool off for a few minutes," Eli told him. "Come with us."

They walked to the western creek, and Eli bent down to pull her boots and socks off. "What are you two waiting on? Let's go."

Eli laughed and found a large rock in the middle of the creek and sat down. "Oh, my word, this feels heavenly," she called out.

Whit and Brad waded through the water to join her. Eli looked up at Whit. "You know I was thinking."

"Uh oh," Whit chuckled. "Dare we ask?"

"If we finish before Evan and Mitch, I say we drive up to the top of the trail and hit that pool to cool off."

"Heck yeah," Brad answered.

"That does sound refreshing. Great idea."

"It's not big enough to swim, but deep enough to submerge in and cool us off."

Whit looked at Eli. "Remind me to ask Evan about a swimming hole. I'm sure he'll know of one we can visit soon."

"Maybe we can pack a picnic and take a day off this weekend," Eli suggested.

"That sounds perfect," Whit smiled. "I'd like to start showing the guys around some since this will be their future home."

"Awesome," Brad answered. "I'm going to get back to it."

"Have you finished the bridge bench yet?" Whit asked.

"I started on it first. Two coats and it should be dry by now."

"I'll help you carry it to the bridge while Eli brings the tiller," Whit said.

"Done deal, or I can drive the tiller, and y'all can carry the bench."

"I like the way this man thinks," Eli said with a wink to Brad. "Let's go get our boots back on."

Whit walked with them and looked at Brad's boots. They were adequate for working, but would never survive the trail. "I think we need to get you a nice pair of Merrells to start breaking in before you hit the trail."

"Dad's got the Moab style, and he claims they are so comfortable," Brad said.

"Your dad has good taste," Eli grinned. She finished tying her bootlace.

Brad chuckled. "You can say that since you buy him a new pair every year for Christmas."

"I should buy stock in that company," Eli grinned.

"Yes, you should. We could all use a new pair." Whit pointed to Eli's worn boots.

"Point taken. It looks like we'll all be trying on new boots tonight." Eli picked up one end of the bench. "Let's roll."

†

"I don't think I need to compost yet. Everything's growing well. I'm going to grab the small tiller and turn the tight rows, while you do the big ones." Whit smiled up at Eli.

"That sounds good to me."

Brad arrived just as Eli was making her final turn. When she reached the end of the row and turned the tiller off, he grinned. "I'm all done and ready to get wet."

"Run up to the lab and see how close they are to finishing and let them know the plan. Tell Evan he can shower and wash his clothes in the laundry room."

"On it, Aunt Eli." Brad jogged off.

"Where's he going?" Whit asked.

"To check on Mitch and Evan and see if they want to join us for a dip."

"Let's store these tillers and get ready."

"If you put them in the barn, I'll grab us some towels," Whit replied.

"Deal." Eli began driving the tiller to the barn.

Brad came rushing back. "They've finished and are just working on cleaning up. Evan and Mitch will join us when done."

"Okay, we need to stop by the barn and put Molly in her stall. Cruz has been there before, but I don't want Molly that far from home."

"I'll go ahead and put her in. You can pick me up on the way by," Brad offered.

Eli walked to the Gator. "We'll see you in a few minutes. Whit went to grab some towels for us."

†

294

They parked the Gator at the top of the mountain and hiked the short distance to the trail.

"How did you find this?" Brad asked.

"Cruz and I were exploring one day, and we stumbled upon a nice lady from Florida who was hiking with her dog. They had stopped to cool off. It's a beautiful spring-fed pool."

"Sweet," Brad replied and jogged ahead with Cruz.

"Hey, don't get too far ahead, or you might miss it. Look for a path off to the left."

"Got it," Brad called back.

Whit looked toward her property. "I think I hear the other Gator."

"We'd better hurry then before they catch up with us," Eli teased.

When they turned onto the path, they heard Cruz barking as she and Brad splashed in the pool. "It sounds like they found it," Whit replied.

"I'd say so," Eli grinned. "How's the water?"

"Cold at first, but man, does it feel good."

Eli and Whit took off their boots and socks and emptied pockets before joining Brad. Eli was about to lay her phone down on the boulder when Mark called.

Eli hit the speaker. "Just wanted to let y'all know we made it."

"That's great. Can't wait for you to come back."

"I hear splashing. Are you in the creek?"

"No, not near deep enough, but there's a beautiful pool at the top of the mountain above Whit's property. We decided to take a dip to cool off after tilling and staining. Evan and Mitch are going to join us soon."

"That sounds good. It was brutal on the road."

"I'm glad you made it safely. I'll keep in touch on how things are going this week."

"Thanks. Love y'all."

"Most," Eli said and ended the call before Mark could reply. "Incoming, she hollered and ran into the pool." Cruz started to bark, and Eli splashed her with the cold water. "This is a bit chilly at first," Eli cried out.

"Once you go under, it gets a lot better." Whit brushed her wet hair back.

"Hey, hey, the gang's all here," Brad said when he saw Mitch and Evan come down the trail.

"This is pretty neat," Mitch said as he shed his boots, socks, and shirt.

"Oh, my eyes, my eyes," Brad teased. "Bro, it's time for you to start getting some sun on that chest. You almost blinded me."

"I know, but these stretch marks are embarrassing," Mitch replied.

"They just mean you grew fast." Evan tried to comfort him as he pulled his shirt off.

"That's not much help coming from ripped-abs and tanned-skin guy." Mitch grinned.

Evan shook his head. "Just look at how you've slimmed down over the last few weeks. You keep working this hard, and you'll have abs of steel."

Eli added her advice. "When we go shopping tonight, we can pick up some lotion. There are some specifically for stretch marks, that should help."

"Some sunscreen, too. The last thing you want is a sunburn," Whit tossed out.

"Hey, Evan, I've meant to ask you something earlier. Is there a nice lake or swimming hole around where we could spend the day and maybe have a picnic?"

"There are several I can take you to, not far from here. You know, I was thinking earlier, I have a younger sister,

Hayden, who just turned fourteen last month. Would you like to meet her, Brad?"

"I'm going to be here a while, so it would be nice to start meeting people my age." Brad smiled at Evan.

"There's one thing about it," Evan teased. "You two won't be kissing."

"Why's that?' Brad asked.

Evan chuckled. "She has braces too, and y'all might get tangled up."

"That could be majorly embarrassing," Brad replied. "Could you imagine sidestepping into an emergency room to get untangled?"

They all broke out laughing at his comment.

"What about this weekend?" Eli asked.

"It would have to be Sunday. I have to work for Dad Saturday."

"That would work. We can get a small portable grill and cook some hamburgers. Maybe get a watermelon to chill in the water." Eli looked around, and everyone was nodding.

"What about one of those small camp stoves? I could fry some tater tots. The boys could use it for their overnight trips," Whit suggested.

Eli chuckled. "I love it when a plan comes together."

†

After cooling off, they all went back to take showers and get ready to go to town. Whit pulled Mitch and Evan outside to the porch before they left and paid them for the staining job.

"This is way too much for that size of a job," Evan said.

"You've done extra projects around here too," Whit told them. "You've earned every penny of it."

"At least let us buy dinner tonight then," Mitch suggested.

"Great idea, Mitch," Evan agreed.

Whit nodded. "Only if you can beat your Aunt Eli to the check. You know she will insist on paying."

"I'll catch Judy when we go in and tell her Mitch and I are paying. That way, she knows to give one of us the check."

"Devious, but I like it," Mitch replied.

†

After dinner, they went boot and clothes shopping. Whit and Mitch picked out a small camp stove while Eli and Brad picked out work clothes and swim shorts.

When they got back home, they sat around the table and planned the rest of the week. Whit and Brad would focus on harvesting vegetables for canning and freezing from Whit's garden. Eli and Mitch would continue the cleanup of downed trees and remove the ones necessary to begin work on the western creek bridge. Saturday, they would go to town to shop for the picnic and get hamburger patties and veggies prepared. Mitch offered to fry bacon for the burgers.

"I'm getting hungry again just thinking about bacon cheeseburgers," Brad said.

"They will be epic," Mitch promised.

Eli smiled at her nephews. "Thanks for a great first day. We'd better get ready for bed, so we can get up and get busy in the morning."

"Hey, don't forget you'll need to fish Friday morning so that we can send them home with Mr. Henry," Whit reminded them.

"Not a problem," Brad said.

"Goodnight, guys," Eli said. "Love y'all."

"More," Mitch replied.

"For sure," Brad chimed in.

†

"I'm beyond tired," Eli said as she undressed. "We did have a great day though." She climbed into bed and pulled Whit into her arms. "Do you need to work this week?"

"I'll probably spend a few hours in the lab each night, but I won't be late. Would it be a problem if I take Brad up if he wants to go?"

"I think he'd jump at the chance to go up there with you."

"He does seem to enjoy it. I've got a smaller telescope we can mount on the railing for him to use."

"Yeah, he'd love that. I feel blessed that you enjoy being with my family."

"They are a great bunch, and I'm glad I get to be a part of your life."

"They all seem to enjoy being with you, too. My life couldn't be more perfect."

CHAPTER NINETEEN

Brad looked at the garden and then to Whit. "Where do we start?"

"We need to pick many things today. Why don't you start cutting the squash and cucumbers, and I'll tackle the peas?"

"Can we have a fresh vegetable dinner with some cornbread tonight?"

"I don't see why not. We probably need to add some protein in there. I've got some pork chops in the freezer. I'll go pull them out to thaw while you get started."

"Pork chops do sound good. Do you think you and I can cook together?"

"That's a great idea."

Brad smiled. "Mom says I need to expand my horizons in the kitchen."

"We can certainly do that, and maybe you and Mitch can cook a meal for them when they return."

"I'd like that," Brad said. "Aunt Eli said I could go up to the lab with you this week. Is that right?"

"Yes, I have a telescope we can mount to the railing, and you can explore all you want. I think there is supposed to be meteor showers this week."

"Awesome," Brad replied. "I'd better get to work." He picked up a basket and headed for the squash.

†

Mitch placed the chainsaw and a container of the gas mixture in the back of the Gator. "Where do you want to get started today?"

Eli pulled on her sunglasses. "Let's start up at the building site and remove the trees where the bridge will be constructed. I gave the contractor a call this morning, and they can start tomorrow if we're ready."

Mitch got out of the Gator.

"Where are you going?" Eli asked.

"We're going to need rubber boots to work at the creek."

Eli chuckled. "I'm glad you're thinking ahead this morning."

When Mitch returned, he placed two pairs of rubber boots in the back. "All set?"

"At least I remembered to pack a cooler," Eli replied.

"That's very important. Off we go."

Mitch stopped short of the creek, away from the trees they would be cutting.

"Are you ready to cut?" Eli asked.

Mitch's head snapped around. "You want me to cut?"

301

"Um, yeah, unless you have a problem with that."

"Not at all," Mitch replied. "I've been itching to use a chainsaw for weeks."

"Do you remember how I showed you how to notch a tree and back-cut it?"

"Yes, ma'am, I was paying attention. Planning my escape route, too, in case something goes wrong?"

Eli bumped shoulders with him. "You were listening. What else do you hear?"

Mitch concentrated, and all he could hear were birds singing and the gentle sigh of a breeze. "A slight breeze?"

"Yes, you always need to know which direction the wind is blowing before you start cutting."

"From west to east, so it should bring the trees this way," he gestured.

"Good job. There are four on this bank and two on the opposite we need to remove. Let's drop the first two, buck them up, and cut in eight-foot sections. This good hardwood will make mighty fine boards."

"You sound just like Dad, sometimes." Mitch shook his head.

"I'll drop you back at the barn for the tractor and start making a brush pile while waiting for you to arrive. I think we can use the bucket to take the logs down to the mill."

"You know it would be a good idea to get a small trailer to hook to the Gator. Something just the right size to haul logs."

Eli smiled at Mitch. "Sometimes, I think you are an absolute genius."

"Naw, just a bit of common sense."

"Let's drop all of the trees, get them bucked, and sectioned. By that time, it'll probably be close to lunch. We can check on Whit and Brad to see if they want to ride to town for lunch, and we can buy a trailer from Evan's dad."

"I could go for some pizza," Mitch said. "Let's get to it."

Eli monitored him as he prepared to cut his first tree. She was on standby to prevent any errors or danger, but Mitch did everything correctly. She nodded after they watched the tree fall precisely where they had it aimed. "Great job. Same thing with the next three."

Eli watched Mitch wipe the sweat from his brow. Then he smiled and nodded. "Yes, Ma'am."

The final tree crashed to the ground, and Mitch shut off the saw. He looked at Eli. "You did great. I'll get the small saw, and we can start bucking the limbs."

Mitch concentrated on cutting the larger limbs that Eli trimmed and kept the rounds to use for firewood. When they finished, there was a sizeable pile of limbs to shred and an ample stack to burn. Eli measured the logs into eight-foot sections, and Mitch made the cuts.

"Let's go see what Team Brad has accomplished."

They rode down the mountain and pulled into the yard just as Brad and Whit were carrying baskets inside. "Looks like someone else has been busy."

They followed them inside to see the baskets of vegetables they had harvested lining the counters.

"Wow," Eli exclaimed. "You guys have brought in a haul."

"We barely put a dent into the stuff ready to be harvested," Whit replied. "We thought we'd come down and unload so we can head back."

"Mitch came up with a brilliant idea to buy a small trailer to use in carrying logs and firewood down with the Gator. We thought you two might take a break and grab some pizza and a trailer."

Whit took a look at the baskets of vegetables. "Why don't you bring the pizza back, and Brad and I will start processing some of this?"

"We could do that," Eli answered.

Whit smiled. "It probably wouldn't hurt any of us to be out of the heat in the middle part of the day."

"Alright, then. The works on the pizzas?" Mitch asked.

Brad nodded. "Sounds great."

"We'll be back as quick as we can." Eli smiled at Whit. She was so in her element when she was working in her garden.

"Oh, by the way, Brad and I are cooking pork chops and fresh vegetables for dinner," Whit told them.

"Perfect," Mitch said. "Cornbread too?"

"Absolutely," Whit answered.

"Later, gators." Eli walked to the door.

Mitch caught up to her, and she handed him the keys. "I'll call ahead and see about the trailer and go ahead and order the pizza."

"Here, you can use my phone. I've already got the numbers stored in speed dial." Mitch laughed and handed her his phone.

†

Whit surveyed the baskets. "If you'll begin shucking the corn, I'll wash the other vegetables. We can have a slicing party and set some aside for dinner tonight."

"Will you dump one of your baskets in the sink so that I can use it for the corn husks?"

Whit dumped a basket of squash into the sink, then handed the basket to him. "You can dump those in the compost bin when the basket is full."

Evan's dad answered on the second ring. "Hello, Mr. Fortner. How can I help you today?"

"It's Eli," she answered. Eli explained her need for a trailer, and he assured her that he and Evan would have one ready when they arrived. Then she ordered the pizza to be prepared in an hour. "It shouldn't take us any longer than that, should it?" she asked.

"Nope, it should be perfect by the time we pick up the trailer."

Evan and a young woman were sitting out on a bench when Mitch pulled into the store. "I wonder if that's Hayden?" Mitch said.

"I'd bet on it. The girl and Evan favor," Eli replied.

Eli stepped out of the truck, and Evan looked up at her. "Hey, Eli, this is my sister, Hayden."

"Nice to meet you, Hayden."

"You too, ma'am." Hayden smiled, and Eli saw her braces.

Evan pointed to Mitch. "This big lug is Mitch. Don't worry, though, Brad is much cuter."

"Evan, don't be rude," Hayden chastised her brother.

"No worries, Evan's just a hater," Mitch teased. "Nice to meet you. You're much prettier than Evan."

Hayden smiled again. "Thanks, Mitch."

"What y'all gonna do with this trailer?" Evan asked.

"Use it to haul logs, firewood, and chippings most likely," Mitch answered. "Aunt Eli and I have been cutting trees to prepare for the bridge up to the building site."

"Hey, don't forget Riley is delivering your hens today. He's going to pick me up here, and we'll bring them out."

"I'm glad you said something. I had forgotten," Eli replied. "I'll go pay for the trailer if y'all want to hook her up."

"On it, Aunt Eli."

Hayden walked back inside with Eli. "Thanks for inviting me to the picnic Sunday. I'm looking forward to it." She smiled up at Eli.

"I'm glad Evan told us he had a sister. We're lucky to have you join us." Eli saw the smile grow brighter on Hayden's face. "Hey, does your Dad carry baskets for collecting eggs?"

"Yes, ma'am, how many would you like?"

"Just two I think," Eli smiled.

"I'll grab them and meet you at the counter."

"Thanks, Hayden," Eli replied and walked over to Mr. Merrill.

"Good afternoon, how are you?"

"Doing great, Mr. Merrill. The boys are hooking up the trailer, and Hayden's getting two egg baskets for me."

Mr. Merrill leaned forward. "Thanks for inviting her to the picnic. She's so excited."

"We are too. We've been working hard, so I think it's time for a break."

"Past time. Evan's been keeping me up to date on all the progress."

"He is such a fine young man. He's been a huge help to us in so many ways."

"My pride and joy. Here's my princess," he said when Hayden returned with the egg baskets. "Oh, that's right, you're getting hens today."

"Yes, I'm glad Evan reminded me. I'd forgotten Riley was coming out today."

"Could I ride out with them, Daddy?" Hayden asked.

"Okay, with you, Ms. Fortner?"

"That would be great. You can meet Brad." Eli grinned.

"Awesome. I'll see you later then."

"Thanks for getting the egg baskets for me."

"You're welcome," she answered and walked outside to watch Evan and Mitch.

Eli paid for her purchases and turned to leave.

"Thanks again for your business. I hope to see you again soon."

"Oh, you definitely will. Thanks, Mr. Merrill."

Eli walked outside. "Ready?" she asked Mitch.

"Waiting on you."

"See you two later," Eli smiled to Hayden.

"Huh?" Evan said. He looked at Hayden.

"Daddy said I could go with you and Riley to deliver the hens and meet Brad."

"Okay. You better go brush your hair then," Evan teased as he ruffled her hair.

"Bye for now," Eli said and climbed into the truck.

"She's a cutie," Mitch said.

"Is your brother prepared to meet her?" Eli grinned.

"No worries about him. He's super smooth when it comes to the fairer sex."

"A little stud muffin?" Eli teased.

"Yes, to go with your Love Muffin." Mitch chuckled.

Mitch pulled into the pizza place and parked. "I've got this," he said and left the truck. He returned moments later carrying two boxes. "I'm putting these in the back. They are steaming hot."

"Good, maybe they will be just right when we get home." Eli yawned.

"Are you tired?" Mitch asked.

"I could use a nap," Eli chuckled.

"Why don't you take one for a bit after we eat? I can help Whit and Brad until you get up."

"I may just do that." Eli fished through the console until she found a bottle of Tylenol.

"Are you still having headaches?" He frowned as she took the pills.

Eli placed her bottle back in the cupholder. "From time to time. Tylenol usually knocks it out, though."

Mitch started the truck. "So, when are you going to set up a doctor's appointment to get checked out?"

"I'm okay, Mitch. It's just headaches."

"Your concussion was weeks ago. You shouldn't be still having headaches. If they continue, will you promise me you'll go?" He held out his pinky finger.

Eli laughed at his gesture. She locked pink fingers with him. "I promise."

"You can't break a pinky promise."

"Mitch, I've never broken any promise to you."

"I know that. Now is not the time to start either."

Eli nodded. "Let's go home before the smell of that pizza drives us crazy."

†

Mitch knew that was Eli's way of changing the subject. He loved Eli almost as much as his parents, and couldn't stand the thought of her not being in his life. Mitch put the truck in gear and drove for home. The sun coming in through the windshield was brutal, so he reached over and pulled down the passenger side visor. A quick glimpse at Eli made his heart sink. Eli's head laid back on the headrest, and her eyes were closed. He could see the fine lines around her eyes, and he knew she was in pain. Mitch didn't know if

Whit knew about the headaches, but he would find a way to bring up the subject to her. Soon.

†

"That's your third trip to the compost bin," Whit said when Brad came rushing back inside.

"I didn't think we had that much corn," he shrugged. "What are we going to do with all of it?"

"Some we can parboil on the cob and freeze for short term use. The rest we can cut off the cob, and I could cook it to freeze for creamed corn or other uses."

"What kind of things do you can?"

Whit could see that he was genuinely interested. "Peas, beans, squash, tomatoes, just about anything we grow can be canned. Have you ever canned before?"

"No, ma'am. We never have this quantity of food at one time."

"When you all move up here, and we get three gardens growing, we will have enough food to feed an army." She smiled at Brad. "Do you want to learn how to can? I'd like to check the berries, too, so maybe we could make some jelly."

"You know, my grandma used to make the best jelly at Christmas. I used to watch her make it when I was little. It was apple cinnamon and the prettiest red for the holiday season. She made it with red hot candies and apple juice."

"Really? I bet we could find that recipe. Do you want to give it a try?"

"I'd like that. Those were some good times."

"Eli doesn't talk much about her parents. Did you know them well?"

"Grandma was fantastic."

Whit could see the frown grow on his face.

"She died of cancer when I was about eight, Grandpa from a stroke a few months after. Grandpa was heartbroken when she died. It was hard losing them both so close together."

"It sounds like you loved them both. I know it can be hard, especially when you're young. Hell, even when you're older. Loss of someone you love is never easy."

"No, I guess it's not."

"Well, I have plenty of jelly jars, so we will add apple juice and red hots to our shopping list. I bet that makes some awesome toast."

"It's hellish good on biscuits, too." Brad grinned.

"Damn, now you got my mouth watering." She pointed to the rinsed squash. "You up to doing some slicing? I'd like to sauté some of those tonight."

"Sure, just show me how thin you want them. Hey, do you have eggplants growing? Grandma used to make the best fried eggplant."

"I do. We can check when we go back later to see if we have some ready to cut. That does sound good. I haven't had that in ages."

Brad was sitting at the counter slicing squash when Mitch and Eli returned. "I think you can stop and wash up. Lunch has arrived."

"Great, I think your stomach was growling almost as loud as mine."

"Probably so." Whit placed a platter of sliced tomatoes and onions in the refrigerator for dinner. "We need to remember to keep a few tomatoes out for the burgers this weekend."

"Oh, I won't let you forget. Yours are the sweetest tomatoes I've ever eaten."

Whit hugged Brad tight. "I love you, kiddo. You make me feel great."

†

The door opened, and Mitch entered carrying the pizza. "Lunch is served. Grab some paper towels, Brad, and let's grub."

"Straight out of the box?" Whit asked.

"No need to dirty anything up. Straight out of the box is the best way."

"Alright, what are we drinking?"

"Tea for me, please," Eli said.

Whit looked at the boys. "Tea all around?"

"Works for me," Brad replied.

Mitch had a mouthful of pizza and nodded his head.

"You must be starving," Whit teased him.

"We all worked hard this morning. Oh, hey Brad, you've got a surprise coming this afternoon."

"What? What kind of surprise?"

"We met Hayden at the store, and she's going to come out with Riley and Evan to deliver the hens."

"Oh, heck, I forgot about that," Whit said.

"She's a cutie too," Mitch added.

"A mini-me of Evan, but she is cute," Eli agreed.

"Oh, wow," Brad said and took a bite of pizza.

"Well, we just got another use for some of these veggie trimmings. The hens will enjoy munching on them. No nightshade plants like eggplants, potatoes, or peppers."

Eli looked up at Whit. "That's good to know."

"Those peas we're going to shell for dinner. They will enjoy the hulls. Even green beans after cooking."

311

"I doubt there will be any of those left," Mitch said. "Will they still be considered free-range if they eat raw veggies?"

"Yes, they can be helpful to a garden too, keeping insects down, but we have to watch them from eating the young and tender plants. Their poop adds to the soil as a natural fertilizer, too."

"Brad, I nominate you to be the head chicken farmer," Mitch said.

"I can do that." Brad grinned.

"Riley is bringing everything we need to set up the coops, but we will need to keep a supply of clean straw or hay for the coops. Hens can be finicky where they lay their eggs." Whit smiled at Brad. "They can be aggressive when you collect their eggs, too, so wear gloves."

"I'm just glad we aren't getting a rooster. I know how aggressive those guys can be over their flock. I was chased by a rooster at the home place when I was little. Scared me to death." Eli laughed.

"I bet you guys have never eaten fresh eggs," Whit said. "I don't mean fresh from the grocery store. Straight out of the henhouse, eggs taste incredible. I can't wait for you to try them."

Eli looked at Whit. "It may take a week or so for them to settle and start laying, right?"

"Yes, so don't be disappointed if you check and you don't have them right away," Whit shared with the designated head chicken farmer.

"Got it." Brad grinned back at her.

Whit swallowed a bite. "This pizza tastes great."

"I told ya," Mitch winked and reached for another piece.

Eli glanced at the sink. "That's a lot of corn. What are you going to do with it?"

"We'll keep some out for dinner tonight. The rest we will get ready to freeze in some form or fashion. Brad and I are going to do some canning. Maybe tomorrow." Whit smiled at Brad.

"We're gonna make some of Grandma's apple cinnamon jelly, too," Brad announced.

"Really? Damn, I haven't had that in years." Eli looked at Whit. "Do I need to go back to the grocery store tonight?"

Whit shook her head. "Maybe not tonight, but soon."

"I could run you to the store after dinner," Mitch offered.

"We'll see how late it is," Whit promised. "This must be some excellent stuff to get all three of you excited."

"We knew it was Christmas when Mom started making the jelly," Eli said. "To be so simple, it is to die for. I don't know why some big company hasn't started producing it yet."

"It wouldn't be as special if it were mass-produced," Whit replied.

Eli nodded in agreement. "That's true. It's perfect for making memories."

"Memories we shall have," Brad announced.

When they were down to the last slice of pizza, Mitch asked, "Anyone want to split the last piece?"

"No, bro, I'm good."

"I can't eat any more either," Whit replied.

Mitch looked at Eli.

"Naw, you go ahead, you got heavy lifting to do this afternoon."

Whit looked at Eli. "Are y'all planning to bring some logs down today?"

"Hoping to, we have two more trees to take down on the far bank, and then we should be set for the bridge construction. The company will be here Thursday to start."

"One step closer to getting you guys up here." Whit smiled at Mitch. "Be careful and don't pull any muscles trying to be a he-man."

"I won't. We've already cut the trees into eight-foot sections. They shouldn't be too difficult to load."

Whit placed a hand on Mitch's arm. "Mark will be so tickled to have logs ready to turn into lumber."

Eli looked at Whit. "We've got a lot more of the smaller round sections that will make good firewood. We just need to come up with a way to store it until it seasons, then we can sell it this fall."

"You can use my racks," Whit suggested. "I have four large ones behind the cabin that you can use. They are empty right now. Being alone, I haven't burned much in my fireplace for years."

"We will correct that this year," Eli smiled. "I love a good fire in the fireplace."

"It's true. Aunt Eli's opened the doors just to be able to burn a fire."

"You don't have to tell all my secrets, Mitch." Eli punched him in the shoulder.

Whit winked at Mitch. "We'll talk more later."

"Less talking and more working. I'll drop these boxes in the compost bin, if you'll hook the trailer to the Gator," she told Mitch.

"Hey, I just thought of something. Isn't Aunt Carol coming up next week?" Mitch asked.

Eli nodded. "Yes, she'll be up Monday. Why?"

"What are we going to do about sleeping arrangements? Do you want me to sleep with Brad and give her my room?"

"Eww," Brad said. "No way. I'll sleep up in the lab."

"Actually," Whit said. "We thought you and Brad might enjoy staying at my place when your Dad returns. We will still do all the cooking, but you could have your man space while he is here."

Eli looked at Mitch. "How does that sound?"

"We could do some male bonding," he grinned.

"As long as that doesn't include farting in my cabin, that's fine," Whit teased.

"Aww, Whit, you take all the fun out of male bonding," Brad groaned.

Whit glared at Brad. "I'd expect it from Mitch and your dad, but I had high hopes for you."

Eli laughed. "He's got you so fooled. Brad's the worst of the bunch."

"Humph," Whit said and returned to the kitchen.

Eli looked at Mitch. "That's our cue to leave, and leave now. Good luck, Brad."

Brad didn't realize Whit was teasing, and Eli could see the color draining from his face. "Let's go," she half pushed Mitch out the door.

"How's your head?" Mitch asked when they were outside.

"Good, I think I may have been hungry. You ready to move some wood?"

"Yes, ma'am. I'll get us hitched."

"Good," Eli lowered her sunglasses and walked to the bin. Her head still ached, but it was mild compared to what it had been earlier.

When they returned to the building site, Eli suggested, "Let's drop those last two trees and drag them across to buck before we start loading."

"Not a problem," Mitch said and pulled on some rubber boots. He handed her a pair. "They aren't near as big, so they shouldn't be hard to bring across."

"Let's do it," Eli said and slipped into the boots.

†

"Let's put the cut-up veggies in the fridge and go see what else we can find for dinner," Whit said. She sliced the last carrot and tossed it in the container. "You can finish shelling those zipper peas when we get back."

"I bet it won't be much longer before the gang arrives with the hens," Brad said.

Whit looked up at the clock. "We'd better get moving then. Bring your knife."

"Ready to roll."

"I think some okra and eggplant should be enough with everything else we have. Don't let me forget the pork chops."

"Yes, Ma'am. Tonight, will be one heck of a dinner."

"We need to remember to take some pics and send them to your Dad."

"He's going to be so jealous. He loves home-cooked vegetables."

"Well, after tonight, you will know how to cook many of them, so you can cook when he gets here. How's that?"

"Sounds great. I think Dad will be impressed."

"I'm sure he would be."

They walked outside to the Gator. "I don't hear a chainsaw," Brad said.

"I saw them bring a load of logs down earlier," Whit replied. "Maybe they are making another load."

"If they aren't here when we get back, I'll go up and get them," Brad offered.

Whit nodded. "Let's go. You can cut some eggplant while I get the okra." Whit slipped on a long-sleeve shirt. "That okra tears me up."

"You want me to cut it?" Brad offered.

"Naw, I'm good with long sleeves. These are going to taste so good fried."

They looked at the eggplant. "Cut these eight. These are the perfect size for cooking."

"Have you ever cooked eggplant parmesan?" Brad asked.

"Can't say as I have. Do you want to cut a few more and we can give it a go?"

"Yeah, let's do it. We can both expand our cooking horizons," Brad joked.

"I'll look up recipes for that and the jelly while you start slicing. You know what size, so double that order," Whit told him.

Brad pulled up to Whit's cabin after they had finished. "I'll be right back. I just need to grab the pork chops."

When they crossed over the bridge, Mitch and Eli had just arrived with a load of logs. Whit turned to Brad. "Why don't you go help them, and I'll get us unloaded?"

"Yes, ma'am." He pulled to a stop next to Eli's cabin.

Whit carried their baskets inside and pulled off the long-sleeved shirt after placing the veggies on the counter. "That's much better," she said aloud.

Eli and the boys were stacking the last log when they heard a truck coming up the drive. "Here come our girls." Eli grinned.

Mitch jogged out and pointed toward the chicken coops. Riley nodded and pulled his truck in that direction. Whit stepped out onto the porch as the vehicle came to a stop, and three passengers emerged. Whit walked over to join the group.

"Hey, Riley. I haven't seen you in ages, and Hayden, when did grow so tall? The last time I saw you, you were about this big." Whit held out her arm just above her waist.

"That's been a while. Squirt shot up these last two years. If she keeps on, she's going to be taller than me." Evan smiled at his baby sister. "This is Eli's nephew, Brad."

"Nice to meet you." Brad smiled.

"You, too," Hayden said. "I'm looking forward to the picnic Sunday."

"Me, too, do you like to fish?" Brad asked.

"I do," Hayden said.

"Team Brad is the reigning champion of the fishing competitions we have. Maybe you can join me sometime."

"I'd like that," Hayden replied.

"Well, I hate to break up a blooming romance," Riley teased, "but we've got two dozen hens that need a new home."

"Good grief," Hayden said. "It's not like you three big boys need my help to carry them."

"That's right, Hayden," Eli said. She turned to Brad. "Didn't you save some pea hulls for these ladies?"

"I did," he answered.

"Why don't you and Hayden go back to the kitchen and get them," Eli suggested.

"Will do." He looked at Hayden. "You ready?"

"Sure," Hayden smiled back at him.

Whit stopped Hayden. "You know these guys are just teasing, right?"

"Yes, ma'am. It's Evan times three." She grinned. "No worries, I can handle them."

"I have no doubt," Whit replied.

"All right, you big thugs, let's get those hens home," Eli barked.

"Yes, ma'am," Riley said and handed one end of a crate to Evan. "You heard the lady, let's roll."

Eli looked at Mitch. "Come on, Mitch. I'll help you with the other crate."

"These are nice coops," Riley said as they opened a crate to release the hens.

"We built them this weekend," Whit answered.

"I love that they are portable too," Riley said. "They are used to foraging, but it will be nice to have a safe home for them at night."

"How will they do in my garden," Eli asked.

"They should be good. Just keep the hens away from the nightshade varieties."

Eli nodded. "We should be fine here for now, no nightshade plants."

"I'd give them free roam then, and entice them back to the coops before dark with some greens or organic scratch." Riley looked at Eli. "You know you won't have eggs right away. It may take a week or more for the ladies to settle into their new home."

Mitch nodded. "Whit has already told us, so we're not disappointed."

"This breed has fantastic layers and will give you big, beautiful eggs once they start laying. Get ready to have more eggs than you can eat." Riley smiled.

"You haven't seen how this crew eats," Evan teased.

"Still, that's a lot of eggs. You can always sell them at a farmers' market. Free-range eggs sell for almost six dollars a dozen. You may cut a deal with Melissa at the diner, to sell what you can't use."

"Lord knows we eat there often enough." Eli chuckled.

Brad and Hayden returned with two baskets of pea hulls. "I'd scatter them inside the runs and let them munch on those tonight. Don't worry if they don't eat right away. Keep those water troughs full of clean water. Laying hens drink often." Riley looked at Brad. "I hear you're going to be the head chicken farmer. Call me if you have any questions." He handed Brad and Eli a business card. "Please keep me in mind when you plan to expand or need to replace these ladies."

"Will do," Eli said and tucked his card in her pocket. She handed him cash to pay for the hens. "We appreciate you delivering them."

"Any time. Good luck," Riley said. "Are you two, ready to roll?"

"See you this weekend," Evan said.

"Bye, Hayden," Brad called to her.

She waved as they climbed into the truck and drove away.

Mitch bumped into him. "I told you she was cute."

"She's beautiful," Brad said in a dreamy sounding voice.

"Earth to Romeo," Whit teased. "Are we ready to start cooking dinner?"

"Yes, ma'am," he answered with a blush on his face.

"We've got one more load of logs to bring down, and then we'll be home for the evening. We can feed the cats and Molly before we come in for the night." She looked at Mitch. "Ready, Mitch?"

"Yes, ma'am," he answered, and they walked to the Gator.

"Let's go see what we can cook for dinner." Whit draped an arm around Brad's shoulders. "She is beautiful," she chuckled.

"Yeah, she is."

†

When Mitch and Eli returned, Whit and Brad had set the table. "We will be ready for dinner in a few minutes if y'all want to clean up."

320

"It smells great in here," Eli said as she peaked over Whit's shoulder.

"Yes, it does," Mitch agreed.

"Come back, and you can start carrying dishes to the table," Whit told them and shooed them from the kitchen.

"We've got to remember to take pics to send to Dad."

"That can be your job, while I finish the pork chops and fried okra," Whit told him.

"Did I hear fried okra?" Eli said as she climbed the stairs.

"Yes, ma'am, you did," Brad smiled up at her.

Brad began snapping photos on his phone and texting them to his Dad. Mere seconds after he sent the first batch of photos, his phone rang. "Hello, Dad," Brad said.

"I am so jealous," Mark said over the speaker. "Oh, my goodness, that looks delicious."

"Whit and I harvested everything but the pork chops, and she helped me cook this meal."

"You cooked?" Mark asked.

"He did the majority all by himself," Whit hollered. "I'm finishing the pork chops and fried okra, but Brad did everything else."

"Wow, son. I'm so proud of you," Mark replied. "Your mom will be too when I show her these pictures."

"I know how much you enjoy fresh vegetables, so I wanted to learn how to cook them, so I can cook dinner when you come back." Brad smiled at Whit.

"You've got my mouth watering. I can't wait to taste your cooking, son. Enjoy, and I'll be thinking of the good food you're eating when I'm suffering through your mom's tofu."

"Eww, love you, Dad, can't wait for you to come back."

"Love you most," Mark replied. "Hello, and goodnight to everyone."

"Goodnight, our love to Mom, too."

"If you pour some tea, we will be ready to eat," Whit said as she handed Mitch the two platters of food. "Grab those sliced onions and tomatoes, too, please."

†

"That was one fine meal," Eli said. "I bet Mark does wish he were here for it. Did I hear they had tofu?"

"You heard right." Mitch chuckled. "Some of it is okay, but nothing like all these fresh veggies. Anyone mind if I finish off that okra?"

"It's not great reheated, so knock yourself out," Eli said. "You two did an excellent job with supper."

"Brad did most of it," Whit smiled. "I coached."

"Damn fine job. Mitch and I can clean up if you two want to head up to the lab."

"Yeah, we can do that. I tried to clean as we finished a dish, so hopefully, it won't be too bad."

Eli stood. "Not many leftovers to store so that it won't take us long at all. I'm ready for a nice hot shower and some TV."

"I'm ready for a shower and bed," Mitch said. "We got a lot done today, though."

"Yes, we did. I thought that tomorrow we could get some metal plumbing pipes and make some racks to keep the logs off the ground."

"Hey, we can do that. Since the idea is in your head, why don't you go to town and pick up the materials we need, and I'll move the firewood to Whit's, and the brush piles over to the chipper."

"Brad and I can help him too. With three of us working together, it shouldn't take long." Whit kissed Eli. "Are you ready to roll, Brad?"

"Yes, ma'am. You want me to drive?"

"Heck, yeah," Whit answered. She turned back to Eli. "We won't be late."

"Goodnight then," Mitch hollered.

CHAPTER TWENTY

Whit studied the image on the screen intently. "Well, I'll be damned," she spoke aloud.

Brad, immersed in stargazing from the deck around the lab, heard her comment. "What's up, Whit?"

"Come here. You need to see this."

Brad returned to the lab and looked at the screen.

"Do you remember seeing the dark spot I have been watching for months?"

Brad nodded. "It looked bigger before, though."

"Yes," Whit said. "It has begun collapsing and shrinking in size. Do you see this faint ring of light?"

"I do. What is it?"

"It's a halo of light. What we are seeing is the beginning of a new black hole forming."

"Oh, wow, that's pretty rare, isn't it?" His voice filled with excitement.

"Yeah, it is. I've to get on the telephone, but I wanted you to see this."

"Okay, I'll be back outside if you need me."

Whit nodded and picked up her phone. She took a snapshot of the image on her screen and emailed it to several colleagues, and began making calls.

Whit was beyond excited as she received confirmation from several sources agreeing with her findings. "This is just amazing," she spoke out loud when she ended the last call.

Brad returned an hour later. "I hate to punk out on you, but I'm getting sleepy."

"Go ahead and store the telescope, I'll be done here in just a few minutes, and we'll go together."

"Yes, ma'am," he answered and started storing the equipment he had been using.

Whit took several more photos on her computer and documented measurements before shutting the system down.

"All set," she told Brad. He was sitting on the edge of the daybed, and she could see he was tired. "It's been a long day. Let's go crash."

"I won't argue with that." He grinned.

They returned the Gator to the barn, and Whit saw several pairs of green and yellow eyes peering at them from the hayloft. "Goodnight, guys," she whispered and closed the door behind her.

Brad shuffled into the cabin. "I'll see you in the morning," he said and walked down the hall.

"Goodnight, Brad." Whit poured a glass of water and climbed the stairs. The bathroom light was on, illuminating a small portion of the bedroom. Eli was curled up on her right side, snoring softly when Whit entered. She took a sip of the water and placed it on the nightstand. She undressed and climbed into the bed to snuggle Eli.

"Welcome home," Eli mumbled in her sleep and took Whit's hand and pulled her closer.

"Goodnight, sweetie," Whit whispered in return.

†

Eli woke the following morning and walked downstairs to brew a coffee. "Good morning," she said to Mitch, who was eating a bowl of cereal.

"Good morning, sunshine. How are you today?"

"Well rested and ready to get to work."

"Do you want a bowl of cereal?"

Eli shook her head and took a sip of coffee. "I think I'm going to have some peanut butter toast this morning."

"Come sit and enjoy your coffee, and I'll make us some," Mitch offered.

Mitch dropped four slices of bread into the toaster and poured some apple juice for Eli. That reminded him they needed to make a grocery list. He carried the juice to Eli and returned to the toaster.

"Don't forget we need to make a grocery list this morning. You can pick the supplies up after you hit the hardware store."

Eli took a sip of coffee. "I can do that." She reached for a notepad and pen. "Red hots, apple juice, fruit pectin, bread, hamburger, buns, tater tots. What else?"

"Milk, creamer, peanut butter," he chuckled. He scraped the bottom of the jar. "Oh, I need toilet paper and toothpaste too."

"I need to check laundry supplies."

Cruz trotted inside as Mitch brought the toast to the table. "Hang on, and I'll get your breakfast too."

Cruz let out a soft woof.

"Hush before you wake Brad and Whit." Mitch patted her head as he filled her bowl. "There ya go."

"Do I smell peanut butter toast?" Whit asked as she started down the stairs.

Mitch replied. "Yes, you do. You better eat my second slice, though, it appears we have run out of peanut butter."

"I'll find something else," Whit answered.

"No, I'm serious, take mine. I've already had a bowl of cereal." He pushed the slice of toast toward her. "Coffee?"

"Yes, please."

"We are making a shopping list," Eli said. "Any special requests?"

"Steaks. We need to celebrate," Whit smiled.

"That sounds great. What are we celebrating?" Eli asked as she added to the list.

"Last night, I finally discovered what that dark spot is that I've watched for months."

"Really?" Mitch and Eli spoke at the same time. "What is it?" Mitch asked.

"The birth of a new black hole," Whit said. "Last night, I could see the beginning of a halo of light forming around it. It's grown smaller, so it's beginning to come alive."

"Well, congratulations," Eli said. "I bet that's something that doesn't happen often and is very much celebration-worthy."

"I had it verified before we came home, so it's now official as BH-113." Whit chuckled.

"Will they name it after you?" Mitch asked.

"Eventually, after more study, it will be named the Brewer black hole."

"That is so neat. I'm proud of you, Whit," Eli told her and reached over to kiss her. "I've never met anyone that has found and has a black hole named for them."

"It's not something that happens often, and I was lucky to have stumbled across the area months ago." Whit took a bite of toast.

"That is cool, do you have photos I can share with Dad?"

"I'll send you some this morning." Whit smiled and looked at her phone. "There, I've sent them to both of you. Brad saw it first-hand."

Eli heard her phone buzz and picked it up. "Wow, that's beautiful."

"Is it dangerous?" Mitch asked.

"Not to earth. It may devour some long-dead space junk and a star or two, but it's many thousands of light-years from us."

"Steaks, baking potatoes. Do we need a head of lettuce for a salad?"

"Yes, yes, and yes." Whit laughed. "More bacon. Might as well get a couple of dozen eggs until our ladies start producing. I've got onion, but no mushrooms if you want them for steaks."

"That does sound good. More butter, too," Mitch added.

"Some peace and quiet," Brad groaned as he entered the room.

"Good morning to you, too, Grumpy," Mitch answered. "What will it take to improve your mood?"

"A bowl of cereal and glass of apple juice. Thanks, Mitch."

Eli reached over and ruffled his hair. "We're making a shopping list. Is there anything you need?"

"Toilet paper."

"I've got that already," Eli answered.

"Some manly smelling body wash and deodorant," Brad said.

"Got it. Something flowery and sweet," Eli teased.

"Oh, the ingredients for eggplant parmesan," Brad said.

"Brad and I are going to try out a recipe we found," Whit said.

Eli pushed the notepad and pen to Whit. "Add what you need, and I'll go check laundry supplies."

"I think we're due for a feed order today," Mitch mentioned. "Do I need to call and add some organic chicken scratch?"

"Yes, please," Eli said as she left the cabin.

Cruz trotted along beside her as she walked to the laundry room. Eli stopped in her tracks when she looked toward the garden and saw a sizeable buck grazing on the creek's tender grass. She pulled out her phone and snapped a picture. The click of the camera caught his attention, and he bolted to the woods for cover. Eli continued to the laundry room to inventory supplies.

"We need everything," Eli told Whit when she walked into the kitchen. "Hey, Mitch and Brad, look at what I saw." She pulled out her phone and showed them the buck.

"He's at least a ten-point, from what I can see," Mitch replied.

"A beauty for sure," Brad added.

Eli turned the phone for Whit to view.

"He is a big boy. He's been around here for some time by the looks of that rack. I wonder how many of the fawns we've seen are his?"

"Probably most if not all," Eli answered. She turned to Mitch. "Check the deer blocks and salt licks we put out. We may need to get more of those too. Oh, heck, just go ahead and add them to the order. If we don't need them now, we will soon."

"You got it," Mitch said. "I'll order them now."

Eli looked at Whit. "Are we all set on the grocery list?"

"I think so. I know you'll see a few things you'll probably add." Whit smiled.

Eli smirked back at her. "You know me so well. I'll hit the road in a minute." She turned to Brad. "Once I'm gone, go ahead and let the ladies out and open the garden gate. Just don't let Molly out unless there's someone around to supervise. I can't have her eating all my plants."

"Yes, ma'am," he answered.

Eli brushed her teeth and used the facilities before heading into town. "First stop, the hardware store," she spoke aloud.

†

"Whit and I are going to drive up and get started. Bring the other Gator up when you finish down here," Mitch told Brad.

"Alright, I'll see you in just a few," Brad said.

As they rode up the mountain, Mitch turned to Whit. "I don't want to alarm you or appear nosy, but are you aware Eli is still having headaches?"

Whit looked at him with an expression of surprise. "No, she hasn't mentioned anything recently. What's going on?"

"She has them a couple of times a week. Yesterday, when we were in town, she took some Tylenol. Eli hides pain well, but yesterday I could tell she was hurting. I'm worried about her."

"I will ask her about them tonight. I would expect an occasional headache as a remnant of the concussion, but not at that rate. I'll see if I can get her to go in for a checkup."

"Thanks, Whit. I'd die if anything happened to her."

"Thank you for letting me know. I know you've spent a lot of time with her lately. I promise I'll convince her to go."

Mitch grinned and held out his pinky finger. Whit locked her pinky with his. "Pinky swear," he said. "As good as gold."

They were busy loading the firewood onto the trailer when Brad pulled up. Cruz was sitting in the seat beside him. "I stopped off to check the deer blocks. It was a good thing you added them to the order. Those and the salt licks are almost gone."

"Thanks," Mitch said. "I had already forgotten about them. How were the hens?"

Brad looked at Whit. "They seemed pretty calm and headed right for the garden as soon as I let them out. I couldn't resist checking the coop. No eggs, though."

Whit smiled. "I'd have been surprised if you'd found one. Don't worry. They will start laying soon."

"I know," Brad smiled. "I just couldn't resist a peek."

"Come on, let's get this wood hauled," Mitch prompted. "We've got branches and brush to chip today as well."

"Yes, boss," Brad saluted and picked up a log to toss on the trailer. "Do you think Aunt Eli will let us come up and watch the bridge building tomorrow?"

Whit nodded. "I don't see why not as long as you stay clear of the workers."

"That would be cool," Mitch agreed.

"Hey, maybe you can bring up the boards leftover from the coops and place them in the cave. When Mark comes back, you can help him build a wall and door for the root cellar."

Mitch nodded. "That's easy. Especially now that we have the trailer."

"Okay, I think that's enough for the first load," Whit said.

At her cabin, they formed a chain and had the firewood stacked in record time. "One more load should do it, don't ya think, Mitch?"

"Yes, then we can haul the brush to the chipper."

†

Eli arrived at the hardware store and described to Evan and his dad her vision to store the logs off the ground.

"That should work well." Mr. Merrill smiled and turned to Evan. He gave him a list of pipes and connectors she would need to construct the racks. "Do you have a monkey wrench?"

"Plenty of all different sizes," she answered.

"You should be all set once Evan gets you loaded."

Eli paid for the purchase and met Evan at the truck. "If only grocery shopping were this easy," she grinned.

"I don't envy you that job at all, but I can help if you need it," he offered.

"Thanks, Evan. I've got this. See you soon."

"Bye for now. Call if you need anything," Evan said as she walked to the driver's door and climbed inside. He closed the tailgate and tapped to let her know he had finished.

The grocery trip wasn't as awful as she thought, and Whit was right, she did add a few more items. Kielbasa sausage to grill for an appetizer tonight, and a small cake with *Congratulations* written across the surface. She was very proud of Whit and wanted her to know just how much.

She lucked up when she returned, and the crew was at the cabin to help her unload groceries. She tossed Mitch the keys and asked him and Brad to unload the pipes. Inside, Whit had already begun putting the groceries away.

"Those are some beautiful steaks," she told Eli when she removed them from the bag.

"You can leave those out, and I'll get them started marinating. Leave the sausage in the fridge, please. I'm going to cook that as an appetizer."

"Sounds great. The boys and I were thinking about some tomato sandwiches and chips for lunch. Is that good with you?"

"Perfect," Eli said. She pulled Whit into her arms for a kiss. "I am so proud of you."

"Thanks," Whit replied. "I'm darn proud of me, too. My first big find."

"You want me to start slicing some tomatoes?"

"That would be great. I'm just about done putting the groceries away."

Mitch and Brad returned, and Mitch hung up her keys.

"Mitch, grab some paper plates and chips from the pantry. Brad, can you pour us something to drink?"

"You got it, Aunt Eli." Mitch and Brad went to work.

They danced around the kitchen, each doing their assigned jobs. *We're like bees in a hive,* Eli thought to herself.

Eli started slicing tomatoes. "How much did y'all get done?"

"All of it," Mitch smiled. "We didn't get the branches chipped yet, but everything is where it should be."

"Great job. Maybe I should go to town more often." Eli winked at Whit.

Whit smiled. "With all three of us pitching in, it went pretty quickly." Whit looked at Mitch and nodded.

"If we get the branches chipped and get the log racks in place, would you mind if Brad and I watched them build the bridge tomorrow?"

Eli placed the last of the slices on the plate. "I don't see why not. We all need some downtime. We've been working hard."

"Whit suggested we take the leftover boards up to the cave. That way, when Dad returns, we can work on that root cellar."

"Great idea. You can load the boards on the trailer today and take them up tomorrow."

Mitch grinned at Brad. "Or later today, if we have time. Maybe we can do that while you start grilling. It won't take us long."

Eli nodded. "Whichever works for y'all. Are you up to digging some holes for me with the auger?"

"Just point me to where you want them."

Eli began spreading mayo on slices of bread. "I don't think we'll need concrete for these. The weight of the logs will hold them steady."

"That's for sure," Brad replied. "Once we put those logs on there, it ain't going anywhere."

"I don't think so either," Whit added.

"Let's eat and get to it then," Eli grinned.

†

"Do you want Brad and me to chip up the branches?" Whit asked. "You and Mitch can concentrate on the log racks."

"Divide and conquer. I like it." Eli smiled.

"That way, you can start on dinner sooner. I am ready for one of your steaks," Whit admitted.

"Amen to that," Mitch said.

"Let's bust it then, and we can all have a relaxing day tomorrow." Eli placed the steaks in the fridge.

"You heard the lady, boys, let's move it," Whit instructed.

"Don't forget to wear gloves and safety glasses. You've got a phone with you, right?"

Brad patted his pocket. "Never leave home without it."

"Alright, let's do this." Eli looked at Mitch. "Can you bring the tractor and auger around while I get the other tools we'll need?"

Mitch grinned and pulled on his cap. "On my way."

"We'll see y'all later. Stay safe." Eli followed Mitch out the door.

Eli marked off the dimensions and used the spray paint to mark where she needed holes. When Mitch arrived with the tractor, he drilled the first four holes quickly.

"Let's see if this works." Eli had already connected a piece of pipe between the ones they would use for posts.

Mitch helped her guide them into the holes and checked to make sure they were level on all sides. "Looks pretty darn good if you ask me," he stated.

Eli nodded in agreement. "Let's cover these up and get them tamped, and we can do the other end."

When they completed the opposite end, Eli looked at Mitch. "It's now or never. Let's load some logs and see how they do."

Together they put six logs on the rack. Eli stepped back and smiled. "Looks like it might work."

"I do believe so, Aunt Eli." He climbed back into the tractor. "Ready to guide me?"

Eli nodded and gave him hand signals to drill the four remaining holes. Once they had the posts sunk, they added the remaining logs to both stacks.

"With room to spare." Mitch dusted off his gloves. "Are we going to add to them this week?"

"Possibly Friday, but let's see how things go tomorrow." She nodded toward the tractor. "You want to put her to bed?"

Mitch grinned and walked to the tractor while Eli headed toward the garden. The hens were busy pecking at the tilled earth and paid her no attention as she walked between the rows.

"You're going to get wet soon," she chuckled as she looked at her watch. Riley had left a small sample of scratch for them. Eli pulled the bag down from the top of the hen house and started calling to them while shaking the bag. Most of the hens rushed toward her while a few lagged in the garden.

"Don't say I didn't warn you."

The sprinklers started right on time, and the remaining hens ran out of the garden. Eli closed the gate and began to spread a light trail of scratch toward the coops. The hens followed her eager to peck at the fresh-cracked corn. Eli counted and was happy that all twenty-four had survived their first day on the farm.

"How do you recommend we sort them into the two coops?" Mitch asked as he walked up.

"I guess you'd better take some scratch and hope some of the hens follow you. Hopefully, their instinct or sense of smell will lead them to their home." Eli watched in amazement as the hens separated into two groups. "Well, I'll be damned." She tossed another handful of scratch into the run and closed the gate behind her.

"I reckon they are smarter than we give them credit for," Mitch said with a laugh. He closed the gate and smiled at Eli. "How'd they do in the garden?"

"Pretty well from the looks of it. The soil got a good turning in spots and fertilized at the same time." Eli took her cap off and scratched her head. She found it surprising most of the pea hulls had been eaten. "I guess we'd better rustle them some more garden scraps to eat. You up for helping me toss a salad?"

"Sure, I bet they'd love some carrot and cucumber peels. Maybe the outside layers of the lettuce and the core as well."

"Okay, you get to peeling, and I'll start chopping." The sound of the chipper broke the silence as they walked to the cabin. "I wonder how much more they have to do?"

"It shouldn't be much," Mitch replied. "Go check on them if you want, and I'll get started."

"Naw, they will finish when they finish." Eli grinned. "Let's wash up and get going."

Eli turned an oven on to begin preheating for the potatoes. Then she pulled them from the fridge and prepared them for baking while Mitch started peeling.

A few minutes later, Cruz came rushing in, and Eli looked out the kitchen window to see Whit pull the trailer to a stop at the sawmill. "It looks like they are going to load the boards tonight."

"Should I go offer to help them?" Mitch asked.

"No, let them handle it. Whit and Brad seem to enjoy working together."

Eli placed the potatoes in the oven. "Did we have corn on the cob left last night?"

"A few pieces, I think," Mitch replied. "Do you want me to check and pick some fresh?" He opened the fridge. "Three small cobs."

337

"Why don't we add that to the chicken basket and you go pick eight ears? We can boil them just a bit, and then I'll put them on the grill with some onions and mushrooms. Hey, while you're at Whit's, pick a couple of those red and yellow sweet peppers. They will add some color to the salad."

Mitch chuckled. "I guess I've never considered thinking of a salad as colorful before."

"I'll boil a few eggs, and we've got some shredded cheese."

"Getting better by the second," Mitch said, and dropped the cucumber peels in the basket. "I'll grab the corn and peppers before it starts to get dark. I'll finish the carrots when I return."

"I'll start the fire and get the salad started." A beeping sound caught her attention. Eli walked to the opposite side of the counter and saw that the ice cream maker had finished its cycle. "I guess we have cake and ice cream for dessert."

"Sounds like we've got all the bases covered. I'll be back shortly."

Eli walked onto the porch and started a fire in the grill. It would take thirty minutes or so for the coals to get right, so when she returned inside, she popped the cap off a cold beer and resumed making her salad. Eli poured fresh water over the boiled eggs to cool them down enough to slice while waiting on Mitch. Eli sliced several onions and the mushrooms she had bought and cradled them in a boat made of foil. She drizzled olive oil and some seasoning over them and sealed the top.

Mitch tromped in carrying a basket. "You get to shucking, and I'll slice these peppers."

"I think I heard Whit and Brad starting back when I stepped on the porch."

"Chicken man can take the basket of scraps out to the hens and feed the other animals while we cook dinner."

"I went ahead and peeled the carrots while you were gone."

"Thanks, I'm not all that good with a peeler," Mitch replied.

"I got your back," Eli winked.

"Do you want me to go ahead and put some water on to boil while I shuck these?" Mitch asked.

"That would be fine." Eli took the last drink of her beer and carried the peppers to the sink to rinse.

When Whit and Brad came home ten minutes later, a large salad was chilling, corn was on to boil, and the sausage was ready to go on the grill. Eli looked at Brad.

"You can take that basket to split between the hens. We bribed them with some scratch to get them home. Then if you'll feed Molly and the cats, dinner should be well on the way to being ready." She winked at Whit. "Whit, you can grab two beers and follow me out to the grill." She paused and looked at Mitch. "Boil that for ten minutes and then bring a tray with the corn and other veggies out. Yes, you can have a beer too."

"Thanks, Aunt Eli."

"Bring an O'Doul's for the chicken man," she added.

"You got it." Mitch grinned and continued shucking the corn.

"Let's go," Eli said to Whit.

Whit grabbed two beers and followed Eli onto the porch.

†

When the boys joined them, Eli walked inside for a paper plate and some toothpicks. She returned and pulled out a browned section of sausage, cut it into bite-sized pieces.

"Careful now, this is going to be still hot," she warned. "I didn't bring mustard out, but there's some in the fridge if anyone wants it."

"This will be perfect just by itself," Brad said. He picked up a slice and blew on it, hoping to cool it down.

Eli took out the other link of sausage and sliced it. She took a sip of her beer and placed the veggie-filled aluminum boat on the grill. Then she added the corn to give it a tasty grilled flavor. "Are we ready to put the steaks on?"

Mitch nodded as he waved his hand in front of his mouth. "I'll take that as a yes." Eli chuckled.

"It has been a while since we had those tomato sandwiches," Whit reminded her. "I think we've all worked up an appetite today."

"I hope so. Those steaks look like mini-roasts, but I couldn't pass them by."

"Steak and eggs in the morning if anything is left," Brad suggested.

"That very well may be a possibility," Eli said. "I'll be right back."

She placed a stick of butter in the microwave and melted it as she got tongs and a platter for the steaks. They were big, and she used both hands to deliver them safely to the grill. She placed the steaks on to cook and handed the dish she used for marinating to Mitch. "Rinse that for me and set it by the microwave," she instructed. She turned the corn and lowered the lid.

"That smell is heavenly," Brad said between bites.

Mitch returned and drained his beer. "Man, that was good."

"You and Brad can go inside and set the table when you're ready. It won't be long for these steaks to cook to perfection. Grab another cold one when you finish and bring them out, please."

"Yes, ma'am." Brad stood and followed Mitch into the cabin.

"Those are two hard-working boys," Whit said.

"They are enjoying themselves immensely," Eli said. "I'm kind of glad they want a chill day tomorrow to watch the bridge build. I could use a day off, too."

Whit chuckled. "It's not easy keeping up with two teen boys, is it?"

"Not in the least, but I'm having fun trying."

"What do you want to do to relax tomorrow?" Whit asked.

"Once we send the boys off after breakfast, why don't we sneak back upstairs for some adult relaxation?"

"That would be very nice," Whit replied.

"Do you think they will be able to finish the bridge in a day?" Eli asked.

"I would think so. Why?"

"The weatherman is calling for rain most of Friday. I doubt these guys want to work in the rain."

"That will give them extra incentive to finish tomorrow. The crew has probably assembled some of the sections already."

"Friday may turn into a jelly day," Whit said. "It may be a good day to try out that eggplant parmesan recipe too."

"That works for me." Eli stood and turned the steaks over. "Damn, these do smell good."

"You haven't let me down yet,"

"I'll try my best not to," Eli said and bent down to kiss her.

†

After dinner, Brad and Mitch volunteered to clean the kitchen. As predicted, there was enough steak left over for breakfast.

"You two just sit back and relax for a bit, and we can have cake and ice cream later," Mitch suggested.

"Oh, snap, I forgot we had cake and ice cream," Whit replied.

"It was messy as hell, but I bet Dad would love that corn. Where did you come up with that idea?"

"It's kind of like street corn. Boiled to soften, roasted on the grill, then bathed in melted butter and tossed with either Parmesan cheese or my favorite, like we had tonight, dry ranch dressing. You can use just about anything to shake onto it. From Cajun seasoning to just plain old salt and pepper."

"That was the bomb," Brad replied. "I think I could have made a meal of that."

"Well, keep it in mind when you cook Mark his veggie meal," Whit told him.

He grinned and nodded to Whit. "That's going on the top of my menu."

"You want to go out on the porch and kick back in the swing for a bit?" Eli asked. "The boys can join us when they finish in here."

"Do you mind if I take a shower first?" Mitch asked. "I'm beginning to offend myself."

"By all means then, please do. You also, Brad, we can't be assaulted by man funk."

"Alright, Aunt Eli." He chuckled. "That's the price you pay for all this hard labor."

Eli ruffled his hair. "You both did a great job today with so many things. What time do you want to head out to watch them build? I imagine they will start early."

"Maybe around seven," Mitch said. "Unless you two want to sleep in for a while. Brad and I can fix breakfast on our own, you know."

"I do not doubt that it would be an epic breakfast," Eli raved, "but we'll probably be up anyway."

"We might lay back down after you guys head out," Whit told them.

"Alrighty then. You want me to bring you some coffee out before I shower?"

Whit looked at Eli. "Thanks, Mitch, but we can wait until we have cake and ice cream."

CHAPTER TWENTY-ONE

Whit lay in Eli's arms, breathless from their lovemaking. "Maybe we should send the boys out more often," she teased. "Wow, that was intense."

Eli smiled at her. "It was fantastic. Well overdue. It's been nice cuddling and snuggling with you this morning."

"You know, I've gotten so used to others in the cabin that it almost seems surreal to be so quiet."

"It wasn't quiet just a few minutes ago," Eli teased. "It's a good thing the boys are up on the mountain."

Whit propped up on her elbow. "We didn't discuss lunch with them today. What should we do?"

Eli broke out laughing. "You're beginning to sound like Mitch."

"Should we call and see what they have planned?"

"You can call while I go shower and get dressed. Thank you for this morning." Eli leaned down and kissed Whit.

"The pleasure was all mine," Whit chuckled and reached for her phone.

"Not all of it," Eli hollered as she entered the bathroom.

Just as she picked up her phone, Whit's email pinged. She opened the email from a geologist friend at the Smithsonian Institute. "Hey, Eli, you in the shower yet?"

"No, babe, what's up?"

"I just got an email from John at the Smithsonian about the crystals. The closest thing he can find is a blue celestite, but he doesn't believe that determination is correct. He's asking I send a sample to him for testing."

"Well, you have plenty, so send him one." Eli started the shower. "We can take it to town when we grab some lunch. I'd bet the boys want more of that fried chicken or at least something hot."

"You're probably right. I'll email John for an address and call Mitch."

"Hey, ask Mitch to see how many workers are up there and if they'd like lunch," Eli called from the shower.

Whit called Mitch, and he agreed that fried chicken was a great idea. He also said four men were building the bridge, and they would love some chicken.

"Okay, tell them I will bring them lunch as well."

†

"Fried chicken is a popular vote." Whit slid past Eli into the shower as Eli was drying off. "I have a suggestion. Why don't you fix a cooler full of drinks and spend some time with Cruz while I run to town? We've been so busy lately I think Cruz is feeling a bit neglected."

Eli looked at the doorway where Cruz lay watching her. "Do you need some special time, baby girl?"

Cruz lifted her head and wiggled her stump of a tail. "I'll take that as a yes." Eli laughed. "You sure you don't mind?"

"Not at all," Whit answered.

"Deal then, but put lunch on my card, please," Eli requested.

"Okay, I can do that. Is there anything special you want?"

"Some chicken livers if they have them today," Eli said.

"Yuck, but okay," Whit teased.

"They are good for you." Eli grinned.

"No, thank you. I'll get my source for iron through greens."

†

Whit placed several of the crystals in a small pouch and headed to town. Her first stop was at a friend's local jewelry store. Whit wanted to have one of the crystals made into a necklace for Eli, mainly if they emitted healing energy. She, like Mitch, was worried about Eli having continued headaches from her concussion.

Julia, Whit's friend, looked at the crystals closely. "I've never seen anything quite like this," she said. "You don't know what they are?"

"No, I've got a scientist friend trying to identify them for me. Without a physical specimen to examine the closest match, blue celestite isn't an exact match. So, I'm sending him a sample today."

Julia picked out the smallest of the three crystals. "I think this one would work best. Can you give me a half hour?"

"I need to run to the post office and stop off for a large chicken order so that half hour won't be a problem. I'll even bring you lunch." Whit gave her an excited smile.

"That isn't necessary, but it's much appreciated. I forgot my sandwich this morning." Julia shrugged.

"Consider it done then. I'll be back as soon as I can. Thanks for doing this right away."

"No problem. Hey, let me know what the crystals are when you find out. I'd be interested in buying several from you."

"Will do. Thanks, Julia."

†

Whit drove to the post office and purchased a small box to send the crystal to John. The postmaster, Ed, smiled at her when she brought the package to him for payment.

"Mr. Henry keeps raving about all the good food he's eating at the Brewer Place. What's a guy got to do to get an invite to one of these shindigs?"

"I'll be sure to keep you in mind for the next fish fry," Whit promised as she handed him cash for the purchase.

"Mr. Henry swears that Boston butt with Alabama white sauce is the best thing he's ever put in his mouth. At his age, that's quite a compliment."

Whit chuckled. "That was Eli's brother Mark's creation. He is quite the wizard on the grill. I hope he and his family will be moving up here in the next few years."

"I hope so, too," Ed replied. "Just keep me in mind."

"I will, Ed. Have a great day."

Whit was lucky to beat the lunch rush and returned to the jewelry store loaded down with chicken. She took the box into Julia, who wore a huge grin.

"I like how this turned out." She held up a length of brown leather with the crystal wrapped in a platinum cage.

"That is beautiful," Whit said as she admired the necklace.

Julia smiled at her praise. "You can shorten the length to whatever is comfortable."

"This is perfect. Thank you, Julia. How much do I owe you?"

"Nothing, consider it a welcome gift for Eli. You need to bring her in so I can meet her."

"I will." Whit's mind began to churn. "She has a single friend coming up from Florida in a few days. Would you care to meet us at the diner one night?"

"Single, huh? You wouldn't be matchmaking, would you Whit?"

"Not me," Whit said and took the package from Julia. "Enjoy your chicken, and I'll talk to you next week."

"Thanks, Whit," Julia replied and started laughing.

†

Whit left the package in the truck and began carrying food over to the Gator. Eli and Cruz were playing Frisbee when she pulled up, and they walked over to her.

"You were absolutely right about Cruz. She's nearly worn my arm out, throwing the Frisbee for her. I think it did us both good to spend some time together. Even old grumpy Oscar came by for scratches."

"I see you have the cooler loaded. Are we ready to head up?"

"Yes, ma'am, I tossed in some paper towels and plates as well."

"They loaded me up at the restaurant, but we can never have too many," Whit replied.

"Did they have livers?"

"Yes, darling. I got you a large order with ranch dressing and ketchup. I didn't know which one you used."

Eli's nose wrinkled up. "No ketchup on livers for me. I'm ranch all the way. Thank you!"

"Let's go feed some hungry men."

†

Eli was amazed by the amount of work completed on the bridge. The supervisor told her they hoped to finish by lunchtime tomorrow at the latest.

"That's incredible," Eli replied.

"Thanks for lunch. That saved us a good hour from having to drive to get something to eat. We're still shooting to get it built today, but I'm not one hundred percent sure we'll make it."

"Tomorrow is excellent. We aren't ready to start building yet, but I wanted to get the bridge in place first."

"These guys are awesome," Mitch raved.

"Have you been staying out of their way?"

"Yes, Aunt Eli. We've been sitting on the bank watching them. They worked together so well. Even Mr. No Attention Span has watched them," he teased Brad.

"They are pretty incredible. I would have fallen at least five times by now," Brad grinned.

349

"I'd bet after falling the first time, you wouldn't make the same mistake again," Whit told him.

Mitch looked at Eli's plate. "Are those livers?"

"Yes, they are. Would you like some?"

"I've never tried them. Dad gave me gizzards once, and I thought I was going to die."

"I won't kill you. Try this." Eli dipped a liver into the ranch dressing and passed it to him.

She watched his face closely as he bit into her offering. At first, he frowned, but as he began to chew, his eyes grew wide.

"Those are good," Mitch said. "I'll trade you a wing for some more." He dangled a wing in front of Eli.

Eli chuckled. "Keep your wing. Whit got way too many for me to eat, so the rest are yours."

"Seriously?"

"Yes, Mitch." Eli handed him the box. "Except for that one." She took another liver from the container. "Another convert. You sure you don't want to try, Whit?"

"Uhm, no thanks. I'd hate to deprive Mitch of even a bite."

Mitch grinned. "Aww, c'mon, Whit. Where's your sense of adventure?"

"Tucked away where it's safe," she answered. "I'll stick to my wings, thank you."

"That's a good thing. It looks like we have leftover chicken for dinner."

"Nothing wrong with that," Mitch said. "We'll see you back home when the crew leaves."

†

The crew completed the construction, and it was just after nightfall when the boys walked inside. Whit and Eli were watching the weather channel.

"Good thing they finished today. It looks like it's going to be a rainy day tomorrow," Mitch said.

"Jelly, canning and eggplant parmesan day," Whit smiled and told Brad. "We'll have to make a run to my house for the jars."

"You guys ready for some chicken?" Eli asked.

"I'm sad I ate all the livers now," Mitch said. "Those were tasty."

"We can get some more next time." Eli stood and stretched. "Let's eat, and we can relax the rest of tonight."

"What are we going to do tomorrow?" Mitch asked.

Eli looked at him. "We've got some lumber left. We could build some drying racks for your Dad in the barn. I don't think we'll melt between here and there."

"I won't melt at all." Mitch grinned.

†

Eli woke to the gentle tapping of the rain on the roof. She looked beside her and found an empty bed. As she walked downstairs, she could see the front door open, and she looked outside to find Whit sipping coffee in a rocking chair. "Good morning, sweetheart."

"Good morning," Whit looked up at her sweetly. "Did you sleep well?"

"Like a rock. I'm going to fix a cup. Do you need a refill?"

"Not yet. I'm enjoying this beautiful crisp morning."

"I'll be back then. Save me a seat."

351

When Eli returned, Whit handed her a small box.

"What's this?"

"Open it, and you'll see. I had something made for you. Oh, I think I found a date for Carol next week."

"A date? What do you mean?"

"Well, it just so happens that a friend of mine who is a jeweler is single and wants to meet you. I just so happened to mention Carol coming to town next week and suggested we go to the diner together."

"I see," Eli grinned. "Playing matchmaker?" She opened the box and pulled out the crystal. "I thought you were sending one to John."

"I did, but I also asked Julia to make this for you."

"It's beautiful. Wow, the crystal pops in that setting. Silver?"

"Platinum," Whit answered. "I thought she did a good job."

"It's fantastic." Eli placed the leather around her neck, and the crystal rested just above her cleavage.

"It can be shortened if you want." Whit reached over and touched her arm.

"No, I think it's perfect. When the crystal touched her skin, it glowed for several seconds. "Look," Eli said.

Whit removed her hand, and the crystal faded. "What the heck?"

Eli looked at her. "Touch me again."

Whit placed her hand on Eli's, and the crystal began to glow. When she removed it, the glow disappeared.

"Our love connection," Whit chuckled.

"Don't laugh, I think you may be on to something."

"You think?"

"It only glowed for you before. Not for Mitch or me. You gave it to me, and when you touch me, it shines. Touch me again."

Whit covered her hand with her own, and the crystal began to pulse. "I don't know what to think about that."

"Me either, but thank you for such a beautiful gift."

"I have an ulterior motive as well. I suspect the crystal has some healing energy as well."

Eli frowned. "Do you think I need healing?"

"I had to learn from Mitch that you are still having headaches. He's worried about you, too."

"They aren't that bad." Eli looked at Whit.

"Well then, wear this and see if it helps, but I want you to promise me that you'll be honest with me and go get checked out if they persist." She frowned at Eli. "Don't be mad with Mitch for talking to me about it. He adores you and doesn't want anything to happen to you, either."

"I won't," Eli said.

Whit held out her pinky and smiled. "You can't break a pinky promise."

Eli laughed and hooked her pinky with Whit's. They both grinned when the crystal pulsed against Eli's skin. "I think we've entered the Twilight Zone."

Mitch walked out the door, wiping sleep from his eyes. "What did I miss that's so funny?"

"Watch this." Eli showed him the crystal. Then she reached over and touched Whit. The shine from the necklace steadily grew.

"What the hell?" He cocked his head. "It is pretty. Is that from the cave?"

"Yes, Whit had it made for me. She thinks it will help with my headaches."

"I hope so," Mitch said. He hung his head waiting for Eli to chastise him for telling Whit.

"What's for breakfast?" Eli asked him instead.

His head whipped up. "I can make pancakes?"

"With bacon?" Eli asked.

"With anything you want." Mitch smiled. "You two need more coffee?"

"Yes, please," Eli held out their empty mugs.

Whit watched him leave. "You handled that nicely. Thank you."

Eli smiled. "I love bacon, and I love that kid."

†

Mitch and Eli spent most of the day between the barn and workshop while Whit and Brad toiled in the kitchen. After a lunch of sandwiches, Eli and Mitch decided to supervise the activity in the kitchen. They sat at the counter and watched as Whit talked Brad through making the jelly.

When Brad portioned the beautiful red solution into the jars, Whit remarked, "That is a beautiful color."

"Just wait until you taste it," Brad said.

"Biscuits tomorrow?" Whit asked.

Eli grinned. "Oh, heck yeah. A big breakfast for a Saturday morning."

"What are the plans for tomorrow?" Mitch asked as he toyed with a pen.

"I think I'd like to work on cutting a few of the downed trees. I think you and Brad should fish and take some to Mr. Henry."

Mitch looked at Brad. "You up for that?"

"I'm always up for fishing."

"That reminds me. When I was at the post office, Ed, the Postmaster, asked about all our shindigs and what he had to do to get an invite. Mr. Henry is raving about Mark's Boston butt and the fish fries."

Eli chuckled. "Don't tell Mark that. He's got a big enough head already."

"Ain't that the truth," Brad said. He jumped when the popping sound of a lid sealing and caught him off guard.

Everyone got a good laugh over that.

"I think I'll get everything ready for the picnic unless you need me?" Whit asked Eli.

"I always need you, but I don't plan on anything strenuous. After you get everything together, you can check in with me. I just feel like I need some time on the mountain."

Whit smiled. "I understand that completely."

†

The picnic turned into a perfect day. Eli fell asleep, floating in an inner tube, so Evan and Whit decided to cook the burgers.

"It's such a beautiful day," she sighed when they put the burgers on the grill.

The smell of cooking food reached Eli, and she woke to find everyone watching her and paddled to the shore.

She joined the group cooking. "I fell asleep, didn't I?" she asked nobody in particular.

"Yes, it's so peaceful out here that you drifted off even with all the kids' noise," Whit said.

Eli stretched. "This is an excellent spot, Evan. We need to come here frequently this summer."

"I don't think anybody will argue with that." Whit smiled at her.

†

Carol arrived early on Monday. She told Eli that she drove to Atlanta to spend the night so she could make the most of her time visiting.

"You know there's no rush to leave. Mark will be up in a few days, and he and the boys will take over Whit's house for some male bonding time," Eli told Carol. "You can stay as long as you like."

"I don't mind if you put me to work," Carol replied. "You know I can cook, too, and I haven't canned in years since Mom passed, but I can relearn."

"Brad and Whit would love to have another set of hands in the kitchen." Eli hugged Carol again. "I'm just glad you're here."

"Me, too. I thought this day would never arrive. So, take me around and show me the place."

Eli smiled at Whit. "We're going on a tour. We'll be back in time for lunch. Can we have some tomato sandwiches?"

"Of course you can. Is that good with you, Carol?" Whit asked.

Carol returned her smile. "I'll never pass up a homegrown tomato sandwich."

"Let's roll then," Eli said.

They passed Brad and Mitch coming out of the barn on a Gator.

"Aunt Carol," Mitch cried out and left the Gator to hug her. "I haven't seen you in a long time. How are you?"

Brad stepped out of the Gator and hugged Carol.

"I'm great, but my goodness at how the two of y'all have grown up. It's only been a couple of years."

Eli chuckled. "You blink, and these two grow an inch. They've been a blessing to have up here this summer."

Carol hugged Brad. "I bet, and they look like they may be having just a bit of fun, too. Where are you two going?"

Mitch pointed to the baskets in the rear of the Gator. "Over to Whit's garden to pick some veggies. She and Brad have been canning and cooking like crazy."

"Sounds like fun." She looked at Brad. "Would you mind if I help you and Whit?"

"The more, the merrier." Brad smiled back at her.

"I'm going to take Carol on tour. Tomato sandwiches for lunch so pick some extras."

"Yes, ma'am. We'll see you for lunch. C'mon Brad, daylight's a-wasting."

They walked into the barn to retrieve the other Gator.

"My goodness." Carol stopped walking when they swung the door open. The loft and perches filled with black cats were all watching them." She looked at Eli. "Did you corner the market on black cats?"

"Thirteen in total counting Oscar, who was Whit's original cat. Black cats are so hard to adopt, so I took them all. I got a call from my vet; we may have a few more arriving soon. They are hilarious to watch and keep the bugs and mice population low."

Cruz came running into the barn. "Hey, pretty girl," Carol said and petted her head.

"Watch this. Cruz go get Molly."

Cruz trotted through the barn to Molly's stall. She pulled the rope to open the door, and Molly came bouncing out. Molly rushed over to Eli and went to a sliding stop.

"Molly was also rescued from the Humane Society and has been a terrific playmate for Cruz."

"I can see why. Molly is a bundle of energy, just like Cruz. What a cutie." Carol knelt to rub Molly's head.

"She's the only one who can wear Cruz out." Eli chuckled. "Come on, and I'll show you around. You two, go play."

Cruz and Molly raced out of the barn.

"They are adorable together."

"It's great fun to watch them play. Even that can wear you out, though."

Eli backed the Gator out, and they started toward the garden. As she rolled past the outbuildings, she explained each one.

"Has it been a hardship with having a laundry separate from the house?"

"Not at all, however, Mitch says we need a TV out there."

"I can't get over how much both of them have grown," Carol stated.

"Mitch will graduate next year and make a beeline back here. I think he still wants to go to mechanic school here. Who knows? That can change in a year."

Eli drove forward. "Here we have our solar garden. Whit and Mitch installed it a few weeks back, and my power bill dropped to zero immediately."

"They did it?" Carol's eyebrow shot upward.

"Yes, Whit was a child genius and graduated with a doctorate from MIT before she was twenty. There's very little she can't figure out. Mitch has learned so much from her, and Brad is coming right along. He made eggplant parmesan for the first time the other night. It was delicious."

Eli moved over to the chicken coops. The hens were busily pecking at the ground. "These ladies are our newest addition. We got our first eggs yesterday."

"Incredible," Carol answered.

When they reached the verdant garden plot, Eli smiled. "This is our new garden. I did most of the work on it, with some help from Evan, a nice young man who planted the fruit trees and berries."

"How do you water all of that?" Carol asked.

Eli drove past the garden to the western creek and pointed out the pump. "Whit and I put in an irrigation system. It waters the garden twice a day."

"So, you have two creeks on the property?"

"Yes, and several springs. The water tastes so terrific. Wait until you try it for yourself."

Eli drove back beyond the barn to the path leading up the mountain. She watched as Carol took in all the sights and scents of the forest.

"Everything smells so fresh," Carol sighed.

The next stop was one of the fields they would cut for hay soon. "We have nut trees planted here that also have an irrigation system. We will end up cutting this field for hay in a few weeks."

"I can't believe you have managed to do all this work so quickly. It's impressive."

"Whit and the boys have been a big help. Wait until you see the bridge Mitch and Evan built to cross onto Whit's property. We had to drive around or cross over a downed log to get there before."

"Bet that was fun. Anyone take an unplanned dip?"

"Thankfully, no, but the boys came up with a wonderful solution."

They continued up the trail until they reached the building site for Mark's home. Eli pointed out the cave they would use as a root cellar and then drove to the place where she would have a cabin built.

Carol looked at the creek. "That's not the bridge they built, is it?"

Eli chuckled. "No, but it's just as impressive. I had a company build that last week, so when they start work on

Mark's cabin, they can drive up here and not have to come through my side of the property."

"When do you think he'll be ready to build?"

"Yesterday if it were only up to Mark. But maybe a year or two before they can leave 'Bama."

"That must be driving Mark crazy." Carol laughed.

"It does. Mark is so excited to be here. I can't wait for that day to come as well."

Eli stopped at the spring closest to the future cabin site. "Grab one of those bottles."

They stepped out of the Gator and filled their bottles with the flowing water. Carol lifted the bottle to her lips. "Wow, that is so cold and refreshing."

"Isn't it, though?" Eli grinned. "We haven't made it to the top yet."

"There's more?"

Eli nodded and turned back onto the trail. She pulled to a halt at the end. "If you walk a short distance, you will come to the edge of the property, and the Appalachian Trail runs above the property."

"Oh, Eli, this place is just perfect for you. I can see what makes you so happy. You have a wonderful home, and a woman who dearly loves you." Carol smiled. "I can see from your expression how much Whit means to you."

"She means the world to me. I think fate had a hand in getting me up here."

"I certainly can't disagree."

Eli started down the mountain and she drove across the bridge to Whit's property. The boys were loading baskets of fresh veggies into the Gator.

"That's quite a haul," Carol said to them.

"I know, and this isn't even all of what is ready to be picked," Mitch said as he adjusted a basket.

Carol looked back at Eli. "What's going to happen when your garden starts producing?"

"We will have veggies galore. I'm not sure we will be able to can or freeze all of them."

"We may need to see if Melissa at the diner will buy some of them," Mitch suggested.

"I'd bet they would. That way, they could serve fresh veggies on the menu." Eli smiled. "We have a diner date this week anyhow."

"We do?" Brad asked.

"Nope, sorry, ladies only," she grinned. "Don't cry. I'm just teasing. Whit has set up a blind date for Carol."

Carol's head whipped around. "She did what?"

"She's set you up with a date with one of her single friends."

"And you were going to tell me this when?" Carol asked.

"Well, you just got here, but now you know," Eli grinned. "I haven't met her either, so relax."

"She could be an ax murderer or something like that," Mitch teased.

"Mitch!" Eli cried out while struggling to keep from laughing at the look on Carol's face. "Whit wouldn't have a friend like that."

"Whit likes everybody," Brad said to add insult to injury.

"You are not helping either. I think Julia will be a perfectly fine dinner companion. It's in a public space, so I'm pretty sure you'll be safe."

"Well, now that we have that resolved, can we go eat?" Mitch asked.

"I'm going to run Carol up to the lab. We'll meet you at home."

Mitch nodded, and they drove toward the bridge.

"Lab? Is she like a mad scientist or something?" Carol asked.

"Whit does all kinds of things, writes college textbooks, does work for the government, but her true love, besides me, is astrophysics." Eli pointed to the tree with the lab built around it. "She's got a mighty powerful telescope and all types of electronic gadgets up there. Last week she identified a new black hole formation."

"Holy cow," Carol said. "She's that smart and still fell for you?"

"That makes her even more brilliant," Eli chuckled. "At one time, her grandparents owned the whole side of the mountain, but sold off two hundred acres years ago."

"You were so lucky to have such an adorable, smart, and kind neighbor."

"Pretty decent cook, too," Eli added. "Let's go get some sandwiches."

†

Wednesday night they had their dinner date. The boys invited Evan, Erin, Jessie, and Hayden to join them. They decided to sit at a table away from the "old folks" as Mitch called them.

Eli thought that Julia was attractive. She and Carol seemed to hit it off pretty well. So well that Julia asked Carol out for a movie date the following night, and Carol accepted.

Whit shot a wink to Eli. On the ride home, Whit turned to Carol. "Not bad for an ax murderer, huh?"

Carol smacked the back of Eli's headrest. "Dammit, Eli, did you have to tell Whit about that?"

"I didn't. Mitch did, and they had another good laugh at your expense."

"Hmph," Carol said and remained quiet on the ride home.

Whit smiled at Carol. "We're going to have some coffee on the porch, would you care to join us?"

"Sounds lovely," Carol replied.

"Y'all grab a rocker or the swing, and I'll bring coffee out."

"Thanks, sweetie," Eli replied.

Carol took a rocker, so Eli claimed the swing. "Were you serious when you said I could stay as long as I liked?"

"Yes, I was. You are welcome here for however long you want."

"I like it here," Carol said.

"Does that have anything to do with tonight's company?"

"I've got to admit, that was the best blind date ever." Carol smiled as she began to rock.

Eli's phone chimed with a text message. It was Mitch. *Dad said to answer your text.*

What text? Oh, the one about him coming up tomorrow? I didn't see it until just now.

Yeah, that one.

I'll answer him now. Be safe, and don't be out late.

Love you.

Love y'all too.

"Everything okay?" Whit asked as she delivered coffee and sat in the swing beside Eli.

"Yeah, I put my phone on vibrate and missed a text from Mark. He wants to come up tomorrow."

"By all means, tell him to come on now." Whit grinned.

"No, better not. He might just do it."

See you tomorrow, Eli answered.

K, love ya.

Most.

"I wouldn't be surprised if we wake up to find him cooking breakfast," Eli chuckled.

Whit took a sip and nodded. "I wouldn't put it past him."

"We have got to buy more Boston butts. Those were delicious."

"Don't forget, you have to invite Ed and now Julia," Whit teased.

"Who is Ed?"

Whit laughed softly. "The local postmaster. I've always thought he had a little sugar in his britches. Anyhow, Mr. Henry, our mailman, and his wife, Ms. Flora, have joined us for fish fries and Mark's butts. He's been raving to John about them."

Eli nodded. "Maybe we can do butts this weekend, and fish next weekend. That way, Mark can take more fish home."

"That sounds like an excellent plan. The kids can have another fishing competition. I think you'll get booted from Team Brad, though, honey."

"Yeah, Hayden likes to fish, but that's okay. I'm glad she and Brad are having fun."

"Me, too," Whit replied. "They text all day long."

"Really?" Eli chuckled. "I guess that's today's mode of flirting."

"I still prefer the old-fashioned way," Carol said.

"I did notice you and Julia locked eyes several times tonight," Eli said as she leaned into Whit.

"Uh huh, I did, too," Whit agreed.

"She has such lovely eyes," Carol said with a soft sigh.

Eli looked at Whit. "Brad may not be the only one crushing in this house."

"Good grief, we're both too old for crushes, but maybe a teensy bit of mutual attraction exists."

Eli finished her coffee and stretched. "I think I'm going to call it a night, ladies. I need my beauty sleep before hurricane Mark arrives."

"I'm so looking forward to seeing him again." Carol stood and glanced over Eli's head. "The fireflies are dancing."

Whit smiled. "Aren't they beautiful? We are blessed with them almost every night."

CHAPTER TWENTY-TWO

Time always seemed to fly when Mark was visiting. They had spent days working on the root cellar and building a smokehouse.

"I know I'm nowhere close to starting to smoke meats, but the wood will be seasoned and ready to begin smoking as soon as I can get here."

Eli smiled at Mark's excitement. "What are you planning to smoke?"

"You know, I've been hearing a great deal about the wild hog explosion and how they are destroying crops and fields. There have been dozens of ads from ranchers and farmers promising bounties for any hog harvested." He smiled at Mitch. "They breed like rabbits, and their appetites are voracious."

"So, you are thinking wild hog?" Mitch asked.

"I think we could give it a try. The bounty would at least pay for our gas and some ammunition. I've never had wild hog meat, but we could make sausage and bacon if nothing else. We can try some of the meat on the grill to see if it's worth the time to process."

"Can Brad and I go hunting with you?" Mitch asked.

"I was hoping you would. We'd have to purchase a sausage grinder and casings, but I think the expense would be minimal."

"It would be worth it to have sausage we've made to eat," Eli replied. "Pick out the equipment you need, and I'll order it."

"You don't have to pay for everything," Mark replied. "I'll go ahead and order, and we can do some experimenting before we come up for Christmas."

"Good deal," Eli answered.

†

Mark was indeed in his element when he was feeding a mass of people. Whit noticed the smile on his face as he brought out the second tray of pulled pork. She leaned over to Eli. "He loves cooking for people, doesn't he?"

Eli grinned back at her. "He's happy when he knows he's filled everyone up with his cooking. He'll tell you it's 'My labor of love,' if you ask him. Dad was like that. He'd cook for seventy-five to a hundred or more when he did cookouts for his customers, so I guess Mark inherited that love from Dad."

Whit swallowed the bite she had taken. "He has some mad skills on the grill."

Eli nodded and smiled to her brother. "Yes, he does."

"Do you still hope to go over the plans for the cabin while he's here this week?"

"Yes, I've made a few tweaks and want to know what he thinks. I'd love to surprise them with keys to their new home at Christmas if I could. I know it won't get used often, but it will be ready as soon as they can move."

Whit smiled at her lover. "That would be a great Christmas present for them. Do you want me to start configuring a solar system?"

"Only if you can do it on the down-low. There's no way Mitch and Brad can keep that secret." Eli chuckled. "No way."

†

When Laura joined them Friday evening, she was impressed by her husband and sons' work. The boys were excited to have another fishing competition, and the usual guests would arrive midafternoon on Saturday for another sumptuous feast.

Whit and the boys had also picked fresh veggies to send home with their guests. They had spent the week freezing and canning and were well on the way to filling the root cellar. Eli's garden had just begun producing, so there was no lack of fresh vegetables on the property. Mitch had negotiated a deal with Melissa to provide fresh vegetables and trout in exchange for meal credits at the diner. Eli was proud of him for coming up with the idea and making the arrangements.

Carol and Julia were developing a sweet friendship, and Eli could see how it could develop into something more for them. She elbowed Whit and motioned for her to watch them as they chatted at the fish fry.

"More than just a crush," Whit whispered.

"It's so much fun cooking for this crowd," Mark said as they cleaned up after the guests had departed.

Whit and the kids had gone up to the lab to do some stargazing, so Mark, Laura, Carol, and Julia helped with the cleanup.

"Anyone up for a cup of coffee or a cold beer?" Eli asked.

"I'll join you in a beer," Mark replied. "I think we've earned it today."

Carol looked at Julia. "Thanks, but I need to head back into town. Thank you for everything. It was a wonderful day."

"You're very welcome to join us anytime," Eli told her.

"I'm going to walk Julia out." Carol looked at Laura. "Is there any of that wine left?"

Laura smiled. "About a half of the bottle. I'll pour us a glass."

"Thanks."

†

Mark waited until they were out of earshot to whisper to Eli. "Those two seem to be hitting it off pretty well."

"Yes, they do. I think Carol may extend her visit a while longer," Eli chuckled.

"There's nothing wrong with that," Laura added. "I wish we could stay longer. It's so peaceful here."

"One day, we'll never have to leave," Mark promised.

"I still can't get over the change in both boys up here," Laura smiled. "Even Brad is motivated to get up and do stuff before ten o'clock in the morning."

"They've been a tremendous help to both Whit and I. Brad is becoming quite proficient in the kitchen." Eli walked to the fridge took out two beers and a bottle of wine. "Should we sit on the deck?"

Laura pulled down two wine glasses and filled them. "One more bottle down," she chuckled. "The deck is perfect."

†

The moon had risen, and the shine from it made the treetops glow. Thousands of fireflies filled the meadow between the two cabins, and a gentle breeze had begun to blow. The scent of the mountain filled the air, and a chorus of crickets broke the silence. Eli noticed that Mark had closed his eyes.

"A penny for your thoughts?" she asked.

Mark opened his eyes and looked at Eli. "I was just thinking of how perfect this moment is. We couldn't ask for a better night to enjoy out here."

Eli nodded. "One day soon, it will be an everyday reality, but I promise you, every day is just as special as this one."

"I'm ready for that one day soon to be here." Mark smiled and then closed his eyes to listen to the chorus.

RECIPES

This story contains a few new recipes I haven't written about before that I would like to share with the readers. These are two of my favorites. Enjoy!

Alabama White BBQ Sauce Recipe
(Great for pork and chicken)
:

Ingredients:
- 2 cups mayonnaise
- 1 cup apple cider vinegar
- 2 tablespoons lemon juice
- 1/4 teaspoon to 1 tablespoon black pepper (coarsely ground, to taste)
- 1 teaspoon salt

- 1/2 teaspoon cayenne pepper
- Optional: 1 clove garlic (minced)
- Optional: 1 tablespoon spicy brown mustard
- Optional: 1 teaspoon sugar
- Optional: 2 teaspoons horseradish
- A splash of Worcestershire sauce (aka wash your sister sauce)
- A splash of dill pickle juice

Steps to make it.

1. Gather the ingredients.
2. In a medium bowl, whisk together mayonnaise, cider vinegar, and lemon juice until creamy and smooth. If you do not want the sauce quite as tart, use half the amount of apple cider vinegar.
3. Stir in black pepper, salt, cayenne pepper, and optional garlic, mustard, sugar, and horseradish. Cover and refrigerate for at least 30 minutes before using.
4. Brush lightly over chicken, turkey, or pork during the last few minutes of grilling. Since this sauce also is great as a dipping sauce to serve at the table, set some aside before you start grilling the meat.
5. The unused sauce can be stored in an airtight container in the refrigerator for 3 to 4 days.

Apple Cinnamon Jelly

Ingredients:
    4 cups apple juice, fresh or store bought
    1/2 cup hot cinnamon candies, such as Red Hots
    One 1 3/4-ounce package powdered fruit pectin
    4 1/2 cups sugar

Special equipment:
An 8-quart stockpot, canning tongs, six 8-ounce mason jars with lids and screw-on rings, a wide-mouth canning funnel, a magnetic lid holder.

Directions.

1. Fill a large stockpot with cold water, enough to cover your jars by 4 inches. Bring the water to a simmer and place the jars and the center lids in the water. Keep the water on a low simmer until ready to jar the jelly.
2. In a large saucepan, combine the apple juice, cinnamon candies, and fruit pectin. Bring to a full boil over high heat, stirring constantly until the jelly begins to thicken, about 5 minutes. Stir in the sugar and bring back to a boil for 2 minutes. Remove from the heat and skim off any foam.
3. Remove the jars from the simmering water using the canning tongs and dry them off using a clean towel. Using a wide-mouth funnel, ladle the jelly into each jar, leaving 1/4 inch of space at the top. Wipe the rim of the jar with a clean, wet cloth to remove any residue or stickiness. Remove the center lid from the water using the magnetic lid

holder and place the lid on top of the jar. Put the screw bands on the jars, tighten. Repeat with the remaining jars.

4. Place the jars back into the large stockpot and fill with cold water. Bring the water to a boil and cook for 15 to 20 minutes. Remove the jars from the water and let cool completely to room temperature, 2 to 3 hours. You will hear a pop from the lid letting you know that each jar has been sealed.

5. Serve on a muffin or toast. (I prefer biscuits)

The Star Child

CAST IRON FARM SERIES SNEAK PEEK BOOK 3

AVAILABLE MARCH 2021
CHAPTER ONE

As the summer rolled along, Whit helped Mitch and Brad plan their first overnight adventure on the Appalachian Trail. She had purchased them both a set of waterproof trail maps for their packs, which would allow them to study the southbound trek they would begin in a few weeks.

Eli scowled as she watched the weather forecast for Thursday when the boys were scheduled to head south. "It looks like some rain will be moving in tomorrow," she growled while pacing the living room floor.

"That will be an excellent experience for them. Mitch and Brad have rain gear, and we will have the potential of trekking through lousy weather when we hike for two weeks." Whit smiled at her lover. "They will be just fine. Besides, I put a GPS tracker on both of their phones. The boys are just going three miles."

Eli still frowned. "I know, but I will worry the entire time they are gone."

Whit smiled and ran her fingers down Eli's face. "I'd be worried about you if you weren't."

Carol chuckled from across the room. "You two are so adorable."

Eli whipped her head around to look at Carol. "What?"

"You, my dear, are worse than an expectant father. Relax with the knowledge that you and Whit have trained them well to handle any situation."

"We could give them an hour's head start and then I could follow them," Eli suggested.

"No," both Whit and Carol responded.

Whit shook her head. "If you did that, the boys would lose the confidence you have instilled in them. Let them live."

Eli chuckled. "I guess I am a tad overprotective."

"More than just a tad," Carol replied. "They need to show you how well they can do on their own. Their hero can't always guide them, so trust them to do the right things. If they don't make a good decision, they will choose another avenue until it is the right one."

Eli grumbled. "I know."

Carol smiled. "Your dad didn't keep your training wheels on your bicycle until you were ten. He was always there to dust you off and kiss your booboos, but he allowed you to fail and learn."

Eli flopped down on the couch beside Whit with a heavy sigh. "I know y'all are right, but it's so hard to let them grow."

"Everything will be fine," Whit told her. She covered Eli's hand with hers.

Eli could feel the crystal necklace pulsing against her skin.

Mitch and Brad came in from feeding the animals. Mitch looked at the worried expression on Eli's face.

"Is there something wrong, Aunt Eli? You look like you've lost your best friend, but I see them both sitting with you," he teased.

"No, I'm fine. It just hit me that you two are going out on the trail alone tomorrow."

"Everything is going to be fine. If it rains, we get wet. We'll both probably need a good shower anyhow," Mitch said.

Eli smiled as his comment. "Probably so. I'll worry until I see you two come back safely."

Brad looked at Whit. "Should we get her a valium or something?"

Eli picked up a pillow and tossed it at him. "No, silly, it just means I love your two goofy asses."

"We know that. Trust me. Whit has drilled us on every possible thing we need to know to hike three miles down and three miles back." Mitch looked at Brad.

"At least three times over," Brad added. "We'll be gone after breakfast tomorrow and back before supper on Friday."

"I guess we need to plan a big meal for Friday then," Carol said to lighten the spirit.

"How about bacon cheeseburgers and tater tots? Lots of them too." Brad grinned.

"That's easy enough. I'll make some ice cream, too," Eli said, finally smiling again.

Whit added, "We can make a huge breakfast in the morning and send you boys off with some biscuits to snack on tomorrow."

"Are your packs all set?" Eli asked.

"Yes, ma'am. We want Whit to double-check us tonight, though," Mitch replied.

"That's a good plan. Carol and I are going to start on dinner. Why don't y'all check the packs now?"

"Yes, ma'am," Mitch said and offered a hand to Whit to get her off the couch.

†

"What are we cooking?" Carol asked.

"I thought we could grill chicken on the flat top to go with leftover veggies, and I want to try Hasselback potatoes. I saw a recipe for them on the Internet, and they look awesome."

"Okay, just tell me what you need me to do." Carol waited for instruction.

"Wash eight of those baking potatoes for me and dry them for starters." Eli grinned at her friend. "I'm so glad you've decided to stay up here longer. It's been fun having you here."

Carol moved next to Eli at the sink. "Do you think Whit would consider renting her cabin to me?"

Eli stopped washing the chicken. "Are you thinking of moving here?"

Carol nodded. "I have been giving it some thought. I'm fully vested in my retirement and thought I might check into openings at the local schools."

"That's fantastic news. What about you and Julia?" Eli grinned.

"Maybe we could move in together if we can find someplace suitable. Julia only has a tiny apartment. I don't think it would work, and we both love it out here."

Eli shrugged. "Why don't you ask her about it after the boys leave tomorrow? She hasn't talked about the cabin much. It's been in her family for a long time."

†

Eli guided Carol through the first phase of prepping the potatoes. "You know me; I've got to put my spin on the recipe. We're going to use butter and dry ranch dressing for the basting sauce instead of the herbs. Baste them good and bake them for another forty-five minutes, basting every fifteen."

"That even sounds delicious," Carol said. "When do you want me to fan the slices open?"

Eli smiled at her friend. "You can go ahead and do it now to get the sauce deep inside."

"Wow, something smells wonderful in here," Mitch said as they entered the cabin.

"Your aunt is trying out a new recipe for baked potatoes," Carol informed him.

Eli grinned at Mitch. "Hey, Mitch, can you whip up some of the white BBQ sauce for this chicken?"

"I'd love to, Aunt Eli."

"Are your packs all set?" Eli asked Brad.

Brad nodded. "Yes, ma'am. All we need to add is our water bottles and last-minute items."

"What do you need help with?" Whit asked.

"Brad can set the table. It's too early to heat leftovers just yet, but you can get them ready. Thanks for double-checking the packs."

"My pleasure," Whit answered and started pulling dishes from the fridge.

†

"Damn, that's some good sauce," Carol said as she spread the white sauce over the chicken breast and poured some on her plate to use as a dip. "The potatoes turned out pretty good, too."

"I could eat them every day," Mitch said as he put another bite in his mouth. "I like the ranch and sea salt on them. Crunchy on the outside and soft on the inside."

"What are you guys taking for food?" Carol asked.

"We've got jerky and trail mix and some MREs as well as a small stove."

Carol cocked her head at Mitch. "What the heck is an MRE?"

"Meals ready to eat," Brad piped in. "It's the same type of meal our soldiers eat while on deployment if they are away from camp. High in protein and calories, but easy to prepare with minimal effort."

"Easy to pack, too," Mitch added.

"Are you using the hammock tents?" Eli asked.

"Only if the shelter isn't in good shape. Otherwise, we'll use our sleeping bags in the shelter," Mitch replied.

"First-aid kit?" Eli asked.

Whit grinned. "In both packs. Even a snake bite kit."

Mitch shot a wink to Whit. "I'm beginning to think you don't want us to go, Aunt Eli."

Eli's head raised as she stopped cutting her food. "I want you to go, but I damn sure want you to have everything you might need."

"The X-box and TV are too big for our packs," Brad nonchalantly answered.

Eli broke out laughing. "I get it. You haven't even turned on an X-box since you've been here."

"Do we even have one?" Mitch asked.

"I thought you brought yours up here?" Brad said.

"Nope, no time to waste on games," Mitch grinned. "Seriously, though, Aunt Eli, if we pack anything else, we might need to take a Gator."

"That kind of defeats the purpose of hiking." Eli smiled.

"My point exactly." Mitch reached over and put his hand on her arm. "Will it help if we call every hour?"

Eli made a motion to answer, but Whit interrupted her. "Absolutely not, you two are on an adventure, so you need to enjoy it. Your Aunt Eli will just have to get her panties out of a wad until you get back. Call if you need anything, or if you send pictures."

"Get my panties out of a wad. Really Whit?" Eli grumbled.

"Yes. Now, let's finish this great meal in peace."

Carol chuckled and took another bite of chicken. "Damn, this is good."

†

Eli pulled the bed linens over their bodies. She took Whit's hand and placed it between her bare legs. "See, my panties aren't in a wad," she laughed.

"Well, no, ma'am, they aren't." Whit took Eli's invitation and stroked her lover into a glorious orgasm.

"Remind me to have you check my panties again tomorrow." Eli chuckled.

"With pleasure," Whit replied and kissed Eli deeply. "Let's get some sleep, so we'll be fresh in the morning to see the hikers off."

†

When Eli woke the next morning, she found Whit was already downstairs. She listened and heard the soft humming noises Whit made when she was making biscuits. Eli grinned and, after relieving her bladder, dressed and went downstairs.

"Good morning, sunshine," she said and kissed Whit's cheek. "You need a refill?" Eli asked as she walked to the coffee pot.

"Not yet, sweetie."

Eli started her coffee. "Are we the only ones awake?"

"Nope, Mitch is in the barn feeding the animals, and Brad is in the shower."

"They must be excited. Is Mitch checking for eggs?" Eli asked.

Whit pointed to a basket at the end of the counter. "Brad collected eight and fed the ladies before hitting the shower."

"I guess I need to pull out some meat to go with those eggs and your biscuits." Eli opened the refrigerator. "Ham, bacon, or sausage?"

"Do the ham and sausage. We can keep the bacon for the burgers tomorrow night."

Eli removed the packages from the fridge. "Did the boys pack toilet paper?"

Whit started laughing. "I got them some nature friendly, it can be covered up, and they won't have to pack it out."

"Eww, just the thought," Eli groaned.

"I can see why you've never considered hiking as a pastime." Whit teased.

"I'll admit, I enjoy my creature comforts too much, but pooping in the woods is not my idea of a good time."

"Gross," Carol said as she walked in on the conversation. She wiped the hair from her face. "I'd have to agree with you on that one, Eli. Sorry, Whit."

"No need to be sorry. Hiking is not an easy lifestyle. I hope it will teach the boys how much they have to appreciate what they take for granted when we start the AT." Whit continued cutting biscuits. "I think every teen should go for a few weeks of hiking for that reason."

"That is a good idea," Eli agreed. "I'll be much more comfortable when you join them for their trip, though."

"I do not doubt that Mitch and Brad would be okay, but I'm looking forward to it. I'll be missing you, but I'll have a trip to remember with the boys."

"You're starting to make me jealous," Eli teased.

"You can always choose to come with us," Whit reminded her.

Eli grinned. "I'd bitch and moan the whole way. I'd rather support your adventure from a comfortable bed."

"I understand that. I don't think these old bones could do it either," Carol said. "What can I help with?"

Eli pointed to the basket of eggs. "You can whip those up and put some of the shredded cheddar cheese in them. I'll scramble them once I get the meat cooking. Have a cup first, though."

"I think I'll climb the stairs and use your potty. I think from the singing coming from the bathroom, Brad is taking a long shower, and I need to seriously pee."

"Yeah, he can be a bit of a diva in the shower." Eli chuckled. "I'll start your coffee."

"Thanks," Carol replied and headed for the stairs.

Eli started brewing a cup and returned to cooking the meat on the flat top. "I know you won't make it far on this trip, but maybe when you get closer to home, I could join you for a section of the hike. I know it may be a summer or two from now."

"I think that would be fun. Maybe after Mitch graduates next year, we can hike longer than two weeks. It may be more difficult once he starts technical school or whatever he decides on doing."

Eli turned to Whit. "That's true. Maybe even on spring break if the weather is good."

Whit picked up a large pan of biscuits. "Will you open the oven for me?"

Eli opened the oven door and closed it once the pan of biscuits was safely inside. "That's enough for the boys, so what are we going to eat?"

"Oh, you were hungry?" Whit teased. "That's a double batch. Even Mitch can't eat all those."

"What can't I eat?" Mitch asked as he stepped inside.

"The three dozen biscuits Whit just put in the oven," Eli chuckled.

"Nope, but I'll be sure to fill a Ziploc full of them," Mitch replied.

"I've no doubt any of them will go to waste." Eli looked at Mitch. "Scrambled eggs with cheese good for you?"

"Sounds wonderful, Aunt Eli."

"Thanks for feeding the animals this morning," Eli said as she flipped some sausage patties.

"No problem. Is there anything you need me to do before we leave?"

Eli turned to look at Whit. "I can't think of anything. Can you?"

"No, I think we're in good shape, but thanks for asking." Whit looked at Mitch. "I know you have a small camp stove, so have you considered breaking down a fly rod to take with you? A little bit of oil and some meal, and you could fry fresh fish? I know there's a small creek along your trail south."

"That wouldn't be a problem. It's a great idea. We can save the MREs for another trip."

Whit held up her hand. "I'd still take them, just in case, but if you can catch fresh fish, that would be so much better."

Carol returned and began getting the eggs ready to scramble.

"What can I do?" Mitch asked.

Whit gave him a chore. "Go ahead and set the table and pull glasses down for juice."

Brad wandered into the kitchen.

"Hey, beautiful," Mitch teased. "I don't think you need to pack your hair product for this trip. Grab a hat to cover that head."

"Nothing like brotherly love first thing in the morning." Brad chuckled. "We may meet girls on the trail."

"Should I text Hayden what you just said?" Eli warned.

"No, ma'am. I just don't want to scare anyone. Looking at Mitch first thing in the morning will be scary enough. Are there Bigfoots in North Carolina?"

"There have been many reports of sightings on the AT," Whit told them.

"Just be careful they don't confuse you two for juvenile Sasquatches," Eli teased. "I can't imagine how I'd explain that to your mom."

"They'd bring us back quickly when they see how much we eat," Mitch chuckled as he placed plates on the table. "Speaking of which, we're taking our fly rods, to see if we can have fresh fish tonight."

"Cool idea," Brad said.

Mitch pointed at Whit. "It was all her idea."

"I should have known," Brad stated.

Eli just shook her head as she continued cooking. After the meats cooked, she poured the eggs on the grill. "You two can go ahead and pour drinks," she said as she handed Carol platters of cooked meat. "Eggs and biscuits will be up shortly."

"Mind if I grab some apple cinnamon jelly?" Brad asked.

"That's what we made it for, silly," Whit said and ruffled his hair.

Carol rubbed her hands together. "Yummy. I loved that stuff when your mom made it at Christmas."

"Brad and Whit made a nice batch and hopefully will make more as the jars empty," Eli said. "It is a tasty treat."

Whit pulled out the biscuits and placed them on a platter. Then she took the bowl of scrambled eggs from Eli, put a spoon in them, and carried them to the table. "Here we are," she said.

Eli carried their coffee to the table. "Dig in." She grinned and watched Mitch fill three biscuits with ham and sausage and place them on a napkin. When he looked up to see her watching, she smiled. "Making sure you have a stash to take with you?"

"Yes, ma'am. Is that okay?"

"Perfect, Mitch. If we don't have enough, we can cook some more," Eli told him. "I'm pretty sure no one will leave the table hungry."

Eli passed the jelly to Brad. "You've got your maps, and you know where to pick up the trail, right?"

Brad nodded. "Yes, ma'am, we just need to fill up our water bottles and grab our fly rods, and we'll be good to go."

Mitch's phone rang, and he laughed. "It's Dad." He answered the phone and put him on speaker.

"Today is the big day. Are you two all set?" Mark asked.

"Yes, sir. Aunt Eli and Whit have quadruple checked our packs."

"Great. I just wanted to tell you both to have fun. Have you left yet?"

"No, sir, we're finishing up a monster breakfast, so say hi to everybody."

"Hey, everyone," Mark said with a giggle. "I'm very excited for you, boys. I wish I were there to go with you."

"We'll call and tell you all about it when we get home tomorrow night."

"Alright, son. You two have fun and take pics if you can. Love y'all."

"Most," Mitch answered. "Talk to you soon."

"Bye, son."

Mitch looked at Brad. "Do you want to bet on Mom calling as soon as we hit the trail?"

Brad grinned and looked at his watch. "That would be about right."

"Keep those phones handy," Whit teased. "I promise to hide Eli's today so you'll have some peace."

"Hey, now, I'm sitting right here and hear every word you're saying. I promise I won't bug the boys...too bad."

Mitch walked to the pantry and pulled out two Ziploc bags, handing one to Brad. "No time like the present," he told Brad.

"I've already filled your water bottles. They are in the freezer," Whit said. "They didn't have time to freeze so you can drink off the bat if needed." She pulled out a small bottle of oil and a bag of corn meal and handed them to Mitch.

They packed the biscuits and water, and supplies in their backpacks. Mitch looked at Brad. "Let's grab our rods, and we can get going."

Eli felt her eyes fill with tears as the boys shouldered their packs. She pushed them back with her hands and followed them out to the porch. "Be careful, have fun, and we'll see you sometime tomorrow. Call if you need anything."

"Will do. Love you, Aunt Eli." Mitch said as he hugged her. "Don't let your eyes leak," he whispered into her ear.

She nodded and hugged Brad. "See you soon."

Carol and Whit joined her on the porch. They waved and watched as the boys disappeared up the trail to the top of the mountain.

"Damn, I should have gotten a picture," Whit said.

"Next time, I won't let you forget," Eli promised.

"It's a damn good thing I've got your backs." Carol smiled as her phone pinged when she sent them a picture.

"Thanks," Eli said.

They walked inside and cleaned up the kitchen. Whit looked at Eli. "Why don't we drive around a bit and show Carol more of the area since she's interested in making this home?"

Eli knew it was Whit's way of keeping her busy so she didn't worry about the boys. She smiled at her lover. "Sounds good. Maybe we can hijack Julia for dinner at the steakhouse tonight?"

"Sounding better by the minute," Whit responded.

"I'd never pass up a good dinner with great friends," Carol added. "I'll give her a call."

ABOUT THE AUTHOR

Ali Spooner lives in beautiful northwest Florida with her long-term partner and several fur babies. Ali's writing began as a hobby, and with the assistance of the Affinity Rainbow Publishing team has advanced her love of storytelling to a new level.

Ali's characters are primarily everyday people, from cowgirls to psychics. Ali also has created a few supernatural characters in her paranormal series. Several of her twenty-plus books have been Amazon-rated number one choices and always include a happily ever after. Ali's hobbies include photography, reading, travel, college sports, and spending time with family and friends.

OTHER AFFINITY BOOKS

<u>My Dear Vet</u> by JM Dragon

Ava Lawrence a research veterinarian is thrown in the deep end when her uncle asks her to cover his country practice while he has a vacation of a lifetime. How could she refuse? His team shouldn't be any different than the crew at her parents' practice, oh, was she so wrong. What she now has to work with is a sassy nurse, an obnoxious receptionist, and an animal whisperer, or so it seems. Ava finds herself embroiled in taking care of animals in the area and local issues outside her experience, making her question her sanity. Add chickens, cats, dogs, a donkey named Theo, along with various other animals. This turns out to be Ava's unexpected adventure with far reaching romantic benefits.

<u>One Shot at Love</u> by Annette Mori

Blair returns to her hometown after the death of her sister. Always an activist she vows to use her voice to advocate for better gun control. She meets Maribel, an irresistible, sexy woman who proves to be an enigma to Blair. Maribel can't help approaching the weeping woman and learning the origin of Blair's grief, Maribel thinks she is the last person who should form a friendship with Blair. Ultimately, the allure is too much for Maribel, but how long can she keep her secret and continue to nurture their burgeoning feelings for one another. A committed left-wing social activist could never fall for the poster child of the NRA. Unless taking that one shot at love matters more than anything else.

The Mountain Whispers by Ali Spooner
Arriving home and discovering the betrayal by her best friend and lover, Eli Fortner leaves to run off her anger and hurt. A chance stop at a convenience store and the purchase of lottery tickets sends Eli's life into a whirlwind of change. Able to now pursue her dreams, Eli heads off to see what else fate has in store for her.

Whit Brewer, Eli's neighbor, is everything Eli never knew she needed and wanted. But can she let go of the betrayal long enough to let Whit in? Thirteen black cats, a baby goat, and Cruz, her furry best friend, join Eli on her adventure, new life, and the possibility of real love.

Charlie by Erin O'Reilly
At fourteen, Hannah Garvin met 'the one,' Charlene Gaines, and her life was never the same. They were inseparable and spent every moment they could together. One day, Charlie left without a word and again, Hannah's life took a dramatic change. Hannah vowed to never fall in love again. When she meets Mick, a new arrival to the small Texas panhandle town near her family's farm, her heart remembers what being in love was like, and yearns for more. Will Hannah let the memory of Charlie go so she can start a new life with Mick? Or will her heart betray her and hold on to her love for Charlie?

Misha's Promise by Renee MacKenzie
Misha Wyatt has settled into a peaceful existence as a healer in Karst, New America. When an airplane crashes in the meadow outside of Karst, Misha hurries to help the pilot. Misha is not expecting the pilot to be alive...or so beautiful. Will her uncontrollable desire to keep the pilot safe be her downfall? Can *they* survive their journey? The last book in the Karst series brings our characters to their physical and emotional limits. Don't miss the culmination of this exciting series!

Heart Strings Attached by Ali Spooner & Annette Mori
Socialite Remy has her world shaken. Bartender Chancy has her orderly life turned around. A mutually beneficial business agreement between Remy and Chancy turns into undeniable attraction. Will the two ignore culture norms to explore their intense desire for each other?

The Panty Thief by Annette Mori
Someone is stealing panties, but who? And why? Joey Hartford is a fourth-year medical student who insists she doesn't have time for a relationship. A new tenant in her apartment building is proving too tempting to ignore. Sabrina is in her final year of her doctoral program and focused on completing her dissertation. Meeting Joey is dangerous for so many reasons. Add a suicidal ex-girlfriend who suddenly reappears in Sabrina's life and Joey's jealous friend-with-benefits, and things get complicated quickly.

Country Living by Jen Silver
Peri Sanderson achieves her dream of moving from London to a cottage in the English countryside with her wife, Karla. Peri sees their future as pastoral while chatting with

the locals in a quaint village pub. Sexy urbanite, Karla, has other ideas. Secrets are everywhere. Peri quickly senses something not quite right among her rural neighbours and also with Karla. Temptation, betrayal, and intrigue combine to change the lives of both women beyond anything they could have imagined.

Before the Light by Samantha Hicks

One year after her long-time partner Meredith's abduction and their subsequent break-up, Kathleen Bowden-Scott's life is spiralling out of control. She meets Bethany Jones and despite an instant attraction Kathleen shies away. In this fast-paced, romantic suspense, lies are exposed and hearts unite as Kathleen and Beth fight for their future.

Wanted for Christmas by JM Dragon

Belle Farrow knew what she wanted for Christmas–work. She had little to offer but a minor degree in cookery and household management. Certainly not enough for a decent chef or housekeeper position. Then she saw an advert in the local newspaper. Wanted: Housekeeper/cook/nanny for the period of Christmas until the New Year. This is Christmas. Perhaps Santa reads the ad column too and pushes a little spirit of the season to that request.

Affinity
Rainbow Publications

eBooks, Print, Free eBooks

Visit our website for more publications available online.

www.affinityrainbowpublications.com

Published by Affinity Rainbow Publications
A Division of Affinity eBook Press NZ LTD
Canterbury, New Zealand

Registered Company 2517228

www.ingramcontent.com/pod-product-compliance
Lightning Source LLC
Chambersburg PA
CBHW051441260626
47162CB00001B/192